The Fred Parker Show

The Fred Parker Show, Volume 1

Vincent Glen

Published by Magic Rainbow, 2023.

THE FRED PARKER SHOW

First edition. June 1, 2023.

Copyright © 2023 Vincent Glen.

ISBN: 978-1735311098

Written by Vincent Glen.

SHOWTIME

A sold-out crowd of four thousand packed the theater inside the luxurious Magic Rainbow Hotel & Casino on the Las Vegas Strip. Opening night for the new musical comedy show, *The Fred Parker Show,* was about to commence as technicians and staff personnel inside the theater busied themselves putting last minute touches together before the show began.

On the main stage of the Magic Rainbow Hotel & Casino Theater, a dazzling, gold curtain, standing forty feet high and thirty feet wide, had the name *The Fred Parker Show* emblazed on the curtain. An eager kind of fervor seemed to pulsate around the packed theater as the crowd waited for this new musical comedy show to start. *The Fred Parker Show* had been promoted and advertised for weeks, and now, the moment had finally arrived when showtime neared.

Suddenly the house lights inside the packed theater dimmed as a bright spotlight began to shine directly on the dazzling, gold curtain on the main stage. The emcee, master of ceremonies, came over the theater's sound system and spoke to the audience.

"Welcome, everyone, to the grand, opulent Magic Rainbow Hotel & Casino on the fabulous Las Vegas Strip," the emcee said in a rich baritone voice. "Tonight, we welcome you to *The Fred Parker Show.* And without further ado, let's welcome the star of the show to the stage. Everyone, let's give a warm welcome to Mr. Fred Parker."

The audience of four thousand applauded as the forty-piece Magic Rainbow Hotel & Casino Orchestra, located right below the stage in the orchestra pit, played a lively, upbeat intro number. Suddenly a husky brown and white St. Bernard dog, escorted by two beautiful showgirls on each side of him, came out from the gleaming, gold curtain as he approached a microphone stand that stood three feet high. When the musical intro number ended, the big St. Bernard dog sat his backside on the stage floor in front of the three-foot microphone stand and gazed out into the audience.

"Hello, everyone. I'm Fred Parker," the husky St. Bernard dog said into the microphone as the two beautiful showgirls, dressed in glittering gold G-string bottoms, rhinestone-encrusted bras, and huge feathery headdresses, stood beside him and smiled. "I see by all the strange looks I'm getting that you weren't expecting a talking St. Bernard dog to come out here. Well, folks, I have a few friendly words for all of you—YOU'RE NOT HALLUCINATING!"

Laughter suddenly broke out around the packed audience.

"That's right, folks," the big St. Bernard dog said in a boastful voice as he continued. "I've got the gift of gab and it ain't nothing you can do about it."

The laughter continued.

"Now, I want to welcome everyone here tonight to the grand opening of *The Fred Parker Show*. I know all of you want to know what *The Fred Parker Show* is all about, but first let me introduce these two wonderful, beautiful showgirls who you see standing next to me. To my right is the exquisite, lovely Cassie, and standing to my left, is the stunning, gorgeous Lonnie. Everyone, give a warm welcome to these two lovely showgirls."

A round of applause thundered around the packed theatre.

"Cassie, why don't you say hello to the wonderful audience."

"Hello," the sultry voice of the beautiful showgirl said into her microphone headset as she beamed a million-dollar smile.

"And Lonnie, give the audience a greeting also."

"*H-e-l-l-o*," she said in an even sultrier voice as she also flashed a million-dollar smile.

"You know, folks, they say a dog always likes to bury his bone, and by looking at these two lovely beauties standing next to me, I sure know where I'd love to bury *my* bone."

"Now Freddy," Cassie suddenly said in a guarded voice. "Let's be a good dog tonight on the first night of your show."

"Oh, I'm *certainly* going to be a good dog tonight. Because as soon as we get back into our hotel suite later on tonight, we're going to do some doggy stuffy that we ain't never—"

"Freddy!"

"What?"

"The audience."

"They can come watch if they want to."

The audience roared with laughter.

"Oh, sorry, you meant that you want me to focus on the show."

"Yes, Freddy," Lonnie said with a nod as she laughed. "The show, remember?"

"Yeah, you're right," Fred said in a sheepish voice. "Well, folks, believe it or not, but I've been in the entertainment business for a good number of years now. Me and the rest of the cast members of *The Fred Parker Show*, who happen to be highly trained talking show animals also, have performed all around the world. We do everything. We're performers, singers, actors, stand-up comedians, musicians, artists, you name it, we do it. And now that I finally have my own musical comedy show here at the beautiful Magic Rainbow Hotel & Casino right here in fabulous Las Vegas, me and my fellow co-hosts of the show can't wait to show everyone what we can do."

The audience suddenly applauded.

"That's wonderful, Freddy," Cassie said with a beaming smile when the applause ended. "You've worked so hard all of these years honing your skills in the entertainment business and now it's finally paid off. Now you've hit the big time."

"That's true, Cassie. But it certainly wasn't an easy road to the top. I can tell you some wild stories of some of the crazy jobs I've had to do along the way to the top that you just won't believe."

"What kind of jobs, Freddy?"

"Take this one time when I was working as an all-night guard dog for this bakery that made all sorts of wedding and birthday cakes. Well, one night when I was on the job, this four-hundred-pound lady, who was on a diet, suddenly approached me outside the bakery and demanded that I hand over to her all the cakes that we had in the place. I said, 'Madam, these are birthday and wedding cakes. I can't just hand over all the cakes that we have in here to you."

"What did she say?"

"She looked at me and said, 'I've already been married and divorced six times, have twenty-three kids, and have had more birthdays than I want to remember.' I said, 'Madam, what the hell does that have to do with anything?"

"What did she say then?"

"She looked at me and said, 'Nothing. But if you don't move out of the way and let me enter that bakery so I can satisfy my sweet tooth craving, I'm going to have a big ass hot dog instead.' So, I quickly moved out of the way and let that big, fat mama have her way!"

The audience roared with laughter as the stage spotlight circled out into the audience, then it settled back once again on Fred and the showgirls at center stage.

"You know, Lonnie, speaking of jobs that I've had, did you know before I made it big in show business, that one day I was a substitute teacher for these kids at this elementary school?"

"*You,* a St. Bernard dog, was a substitute teacher for some elementary school kids?" Lonnie said with a hearty chuckle. "I don't believe it, Freddy."

"Oh, it's true, Lonnie."

"Well, I guess stranger things have happened in the world," Lonnie said with a cackle. "So, tell me Freddy, how did your day go as substitute teacher for those elementary school kids?"

"Terrible."

"It was?"

"Yep."

"What happened?"

"Oh, Lonnie, they made my day a living hell."

"What did they do?"

"First they tied my legs together and swung me around and around by my tail, then they spray painted my fur coat all kind of psychedelic colors, then they glued all of these little girly ribbons to my head, and worse, they even set fire to my nose."

"Oh, Freddy, that was terrible."

"Yeah, it was," Fred said in a drab voice. "I was finally able to get a break from all those bratty kids and relax a little when they went outside for recess."

"I bet you were happy to get a break from all those kids when they went to recess."

"Oh, yeah, you bet I was." Fred acknowledged. "But you know what, I got all of them back when they returned from recess to eat their afternoon snack that was waiting for them."

"You did?"

"Yep."

"What did they have to eat for their afternoon snack?"

"Chocolate pie."

"Freddy, how was them eating chocolate pie getting back at them?"

"Let's just say I added a little something *extra* to their chocolate pie!"

The crowd exploded with laughter as the Magic Rainbow Hotel & Casino Theater suddenly scrawled a message across its big stage video screen monitor to the audience that said: THE FRED PARKER SHOW IS BEING SPONSORED BY THE #1 DOG POOPER SCOOOPER ON THE MARKET.

"You know, Cassie," Fred said after the message had scrawled across the screen, "speaking of jobs that I've had, rich people will hire you to do some of the craziest stuff just to get their kicks."

"What do you mean, Freddy?"

"Well, one time this rich family hired me to be a watchdog for their house. The only thing they wanted me to do was chase the mailman every day so they could watch me bite him. It was like some big-time sport to them."

"Really?"

"Yep. At first I was real good at it, that is until the mailman got too fast for me and my efficient rating began to drop."

"It did?"

"Yeah. It got so bad, the mailman started teasing me telling me how slow I was. He even started calling me all kind of cruel, vindictive names. It really hurt my feelings. So finally, the family ended up firing me and told me when I left that they were going to hire an upgrade."

"Oh, that's terrible, Freddy."

"Yeah, it was. But I got the last laugh, though."

"You did?"

"Yep. When the family hired this cheetah from Africa, I bought a courtside seat at that house to come watch that cheetah tear that mailman's ass up every day. And I loved it!"

A gala of laughter thundered around the theater.

"You know, Lonnie," Fred said when the laughter subsided, "I went to Washington to the White House on a tour one time, and I couldn't believe how well trained some of those Marine sentries who stand guard at the White House door are."

"What do you mean by that, Freddy?"

"I walked up to one of the sentry guards standing guard outside the White House and I asked him a question, and he wouldn't answer me."

"Well, Freddy, those sentry guards at the White House are all trained not to speak to the public. They're there to do a very important job and they're not allowed to be disturbed."

"Boy, you're telling me." Fred chuckled. "At first I thought he wouldn't say anything to me because I was a dog, but I soon found out he wouldn't speak to anybody."

"That's right," Lonnie said with a smile. "They're trained professionals at the art of sentry. You won't get them to say anything."

"Not only would that sentry guard not say anything to me, but he wouldn't smile, laugh, frown, or even gesture. He just stood perfectly still and wouldn't move a muscle."

"That's what they're trained to do."

"Well, after a while, I got a little angry when he wouldn't answer me, so I started saying all kind of stuff to see if I could get him riled."

"What did you say to him?"

"I told him he had a big jumbo head like Jack of *Jack In The Box*, that his father wore a pink tutu to work every day, and that his mother played backup linebacker for the Pittsburgh Steelers."

"Did that get him riled?"

"No," Fred said as he shamefully lowered his head. "He just remained perfectly still and wouldn't say a word."

"See there," Lonnie said with a chuckle. "I told you those sentries are trained professionals at their craft to not interact with the public no matter what."

"Well, he eventually did speak to me."

"Oh . . . he did?"

"Yeah."

"What did he say to you?"

"*YOU CREEP!*"

"Freddy," Lonnie said as she suddenly glared down at him. "Did you say something nasty about his family to make him say that to you?"

"No. I peed on his leg!"

The theater audience roared with laughter.

"You know, Cassie, I used that video social networking service TikTok that everyone is raving about for the first time a couple of days ago."

"What a minute," Cassie suddenly said as she giggled. "You mean *you*, a St. Bernard dog, used TikTok?"

"I sure did."

"What did you do on TikTok?"

"I recorded this video prank of me landing on Mars in this flying saucer."

"Did anyone see it?"

"Oh, I've been getting a ton of feedback from that video. Millions of people saw the video and thought it was just downright hilarious."

"They did?"

"Absolutely. Some people even commented on TikTok that the video was done so well and so professionally, that it *actually* did look like I had landed on Mars in some flying saucer," Fred said with a hearty chuckle. "Can you believe that?"

"Wow, that's really amazing, Freddy."

"Yeah, it is. But you know, Cassie, a really strange thing happened to me the other night in response to that hilarious video."

"What happened, Freddy?"

"Last night these little green Martian government men suddenly showed up at my door. They angrily informed me that they viewed my video and realized that I hadn't paid their highway toll when I landed on their planet. So they quickly arrested me, put me on their flying saucer, and hauled me all the way to Mars so I could pay the toll!"

The audience rocked with laughter as the Magic Rainbow Hotel & Casino Orchestra played a few notes to the theme song to *Star Trek* then they stopped.

"You know, Lonnie," Fred said as he continued his monologue, "I found out that King Kong ain't nothing but a spoiled, pampered brat that'll throw one hell of a tantrum if he doesn't get his way."

"What do you mean by that, Freddy?" Lonnie chuckled.

"Well, the other night they were having this big monster award show that they have annually in New York where all the citizens of New York would vote for their favorite monster of the year and King Kong was one of the nominees. He was going up against all of these other famous monster nominees like Godzilla, Hellboy, Freddy Krueger, Frankenstein, The Mummy, Candyman, and plenty of others."

"Did King Kong win the award?"

"No, he lost to Godzilla."

"Did King Kong get upset when he didn't win?"

"Was he *upset*?" Freddy said with a hearty chuckle. "You should've seen the hellish tantrum he threw when he found out that the citizens of New York didn't vote for him."

"What did King Kong do?"

"He got so freaking mad with the people of the Big Apple that he stormed out of the award show, climbed up to the top of the Empire State Building, pulled down his pants, and mooned all of New York!"

The audience roared with laughter as the Michelin Man and the Kool-Aid Man suddenly came onto the stage for a heavyweight boxing title fight. When the Michelin Man punched the Kool-Aid Man in the gut with one punch and Kool-Aid spilled all over the stage, the Michelin Man was crowned heavyweight champ.

After the custodians came onto the stage and quickly mopped up all of the Kool-Aid from the floor, Fred finally said, "You know, Cassie, I play a lot of video games."

"Freddy," Cassie said with a hearty chuckle, "you mean to tell me that you, a St. Bernard dog, play a lot of video games?"

"I sure do."

"But you have no hands. How do you play?"

"I make good use of my paws."

"Oh, sorry." Cassie chuckled. "So, what are some of your favorite video games that you like to play?"

"*Call of Duty, Mortal Kombat, Minecraft* and a bunch of other games, too."

"I see."

"You know, Cassie, I'm thinking about putting out my own video game that I've spent years creating so everybody can play it."

"You have your own video game, Freddy?"

"Oh, yeah."

"What's it called?"

"Schemers."

"How do you play it?"

"Well, the object of the game is that you try to beat and scheme your opponent by using all sorts of deceiving underhanded tricks and tactics."

"Sounds like a really devious game to play, Freddy." Cassie snickered. "So, how do you get this video game of yours?"

"Oh, you just send me $19.95 in the mail plus your email address and I'll send you a website address. They'll be a code on the website where you can download the game online."

"Okay, what's the website address?"

"www.youjustgotsuckered.com"

"Freddy," Cassie said as she suddenly glared down at him. "That's just being totally dishonest."

"No. That's how you play my game Schemers!"

The audience erupted with laughter.

"Freddy," Cassie said as she let out long, aggravated sigh when the laughter finally died away. "You're so bad and naughty, I just don't know what I'm going to do with you."

"Oh, I know what you can do for me," Fred suddenly said in a promiscuous voice as he began to wag his tail. "You can take me on up to your private suite here at the Magic Rainbow Hotel & Casino, lie me on your big, spacious waterbed and—"

"Freddy." She began to chuckle. "Please don't go there."

"Alright," he said as he slowly gazed up at her. "Maybe later then?"

"*Freddy!*"

The theater audience busted out laughing.

"Oh, I guess you want me to change the subject, huh?"

"Yes, Freddy, please do."

"Alright . . . alright," Fred said with a sigh as the audience laughed. "You know, Lonnie, I'm studying to be a chef. Did you know that?"

"A St. Bernard dog who's going to become a chef." Lonnie chuckled. "I think I'd rather believe the world is flat than believe something like that."

"Oh, but I am. I'm *really* studying to become a chef."

"Well, I can't wait to see you in that big, white chef hat." She giggled. "That'll be to die for to see that."

"I can't wait either."

"So, Freddy, what's going to be your favorite dish to cook for your customers when you finally become this big, famous chef?"

"Whatever left over food scraps I can find from the garbage can."

"*From the garbage can?*"

"What's wrong with that?"

"Freddy," Lonnie said in a horrified expression. "I thought you were learning to be a chef so you can fix something like Roast Duck, Beef Wellington, or Baked Alaska."

"Not where I'm going to be a chef at."

"Well, where are you going to be a chef at?"

"At the city dog pound."

"Oh, I see," Lonnie said as she began to chuckle. "You're going to be a chef for *those* kind of customers."

"Yeah."

"Well, I'm sure your customers down at the dog pound are going to love your divine gourmet cooking, Freddy."

"I'm sure they will, too. And I can't wait to get cooking, either."

"Raring to go, huh?"

"You bet I am. And that's not all. I got Gunter from the movie *Sing*, Pumbaa from the movie *The Lion King*, and the pig *Babe*, from that big box office Universal Pictures movie, coming along with me also to the dog pound."

"Wow, those are some really famous celebrity pigs in show business coming along with you."

"You bet they are."

"Oh, I see," Lonnie said as she flashed a grand smile. "So, I guess Gunter, Pumbaa, and *Babe* are going to be chefs down at the dog pound to help you cook, too, huh?"

"Heck no."

"I don't understand, Freddy."

"Look, those homeless mongrels and mutts down at the dog pound can eat whatever slop from the garbage can that I cook for them, but when I go on my lunch break, you can bet I'm going to be eating high on the hog!"

The audience roared with laughter as a monkey dressed in a white tuxedo and a black top hat suddenly ran onto the stage and held up a sign to the audience that said: DON'T WORRY THEY'LL BE PLENTY OF LEFTOVERS, SO PIGS IN A BLANKET, HOT RIBS, AND HAM SANDWICHES WILL BE SOLD AT THE INTERMISSION OF THE SHOW. After flashing the sign to the audience, the monkey ran off the stage.

"Folks, I want to once again welcome you all to *The Fred Parker Show*," Fred said to the audience. "*The Fred Parker Show* consist of a series of three theatrical plays that'll be presented right on this stage as a musical comedy show. The show is based on the lives of myself, a wise, caring Scandinavian St. Bernard dog; Joe, a wild, cigar-smoking orangutan from the jungles of Sumatra; Chipper, a scarlet macaw parrot from the Amazon Rainforest who has a gifted magical eye; and Elvyra, a very rare, talented Mexican Siamese cat."

"Wow, now that's certainly a motley mix of characters!" Cassie said with a laugh.

"The show is all about this fifteen-year-old boy who runs away to Mexico, and after saving a guy's life, he's given possession of these four very talented performing show animals that have the miraculous ability to speak. The kid tries to make it big in show business with his talking show animals on the entertainment circuit down in Mexico, but he soon finds out that the road to success is long and hard.

"Finally, destitute and with no place to go, this homeless fifteen-year-old boy and his talking performing show animals wind up in Las Vegas looking for work at this old, rundown hotel casino named the Lucky Jackpot Hotel as we hope to become the hotel's main entertainment attraction," Fred said as he continued. "It's our very last shot at trying to make it in show business, or else we'll wind up as hapless vagabonds living on the street."

"Sounds very intriguing," Cassie suddenly said.

"You bet it is, Cassie. This new musical comedy show, that's about to be presented, has been the talk going all around Las Vegas for weeks. In fact, we've got all kind of celebrities here in attendance tonight that wouldn't dream of missing this fabulous show."

"What celebrities do we have here tonight in attendance, Freddy?"

"*The Pink Panther* is here with us tonight."

"Really?"

"Oh, yeah," Fred said in an upbeat voice. "The Pink Panther told me backstage that if he missed the opening night of *The Fred Parker Show*, he'd be so angry, he'd paint himself blue all over, head to a comedy club and wouldn't go home until the comedian on stage tickled him pink!"

Laughter roared around the theater.

"Jack Harlow is here tonight, too."

"He is?" Cassie said with a wonderous smile.

"Oh, yeah. Jack Harlow told me backstage that if he missed the opening night of *The Fred Parker Show*, he'd be so angry, he'd give up the rap game and take a job going door to door as a singing telegram artist dressed in a bunny suit."

The audience thundered with laughter.

"Harry Styles is here tonight."

"Really?" Lonnie said with a huge smile.

"Oh, yeah. Harry Styles told me backstage that if he missed the opening night of *The Fred Parker Show*, he'd be so angry, he'd take all of his Grammy Awards he's won over the years and have them melted down into a gold bowling ball so he can take with him bowling when he and his former bandmates, One Direction, have their weekly bowling night."

The audience boomed with laughter.

"Stephen Curry, of the Golden State Warriors, is here."

"He is?"

"Oh, yeah. Steph Curry told me backstage that if he missed the opening night of *The Fred Parker Show*, he'd be so angry, he'd personally put in a petition for the NBA to eliminate the three-point shot."

A raucous of laughter erupted.

"Rihanna is here with us tonight."

"Is she really?" Cassie said with a splendid smile.

"Oh, yeah. Rihanna told me backstage that—"

Fred suddenly stopped in mid-sentence as he began to take notice of a man and a woman being escorted to their seats down near the front of the stage by an usher with a flashlight.

"Oh, look what we have here, folks," Fred said in a sarcastic tone. "We have some latecomers. People, the show starts at 8 p.m. on the dot, not whenever the hell you feel like showing up."

The audience suddenly laughed.

"What happened?" Fred called out to the latecomers. "Were two lying in bed and tried to get in a quickie, but ended up going longer than you expected?"

Laughter roared around the packed theater.

"Now, Freddy," Cassie said in a wary voice. "Let's be nice."

"Okay . . . okay," Fred mumbled in an apologetic tone. "I was just trying to say—"

A dwarf suddenly sauntered onto the stage interrupting Fred's monologue. The dwarf looked like a muscled bound biker wearing black boots, blue jeans, and a white T-shirt with his sleeves rolled up to his shoulders. A tattoo of a gorgeous naked woman gleamed from both of his rippling biceps as the dwarf headed straight over to Fred.

"Hey, Big Chief, me and the boys just got back with those twenty cases of beer and we need you to cough up for your share of the money," the dwarf said. "You said you were paying for seventeen of the cases."

"Oh, hell no, Lou," Fred quickly replied. "I said I was putting up for only ten cases of beer. You, Eddie, Sammy, Mike, and Frank better not try to pull that bull over on me."

"Well, hey, if we don't get the money for all seventeen cases, then me and the rest of the boys are going to keep all the cases."

"You drunk scumbags try to keep my cases of beer and I'll bite a new hole in your scrawny tail."

The dwarf suddenly threw a middle finger up at Fred and walked off the stage as the audience laughed.

"Same to you, you little dipshit!" Fred yelled toward the departing dwarf.

The audience could hardly control their laughter.

"Folks, that was Lou of the Wonder Gang," Fred said when the laughter died away. "The Wonder Gang is an entertainment troupe outfit of five dwarfs who performed on the road with us for years before we made it big. They can do anything, folks. They're comedians, acrobats, jugglers, they can sing, act, dance, and they're some of the best musicians around. I asked them to come join the show and you're going to love them. The only thing is when they're around you, it's best to keep your women and booze locked up, because those little dipshits are some of the horniest, beer guzzling winos around."

The audience laughed.

"You know, Lonnie, I coach a basketball team with nothing but dwarfs and we haven't lost a game yet," Fred said.

"You mean your team is undefeated?" Lonnie replied.

"Yep. In fact, we're so good, we just beat a team that had all seven footers by a score of 118-0."

"Really, Freddy?"

"Absolutely."

"How was your squad able to beat a team with all seven footers?"

"Well, right before the game started, I just told my team to go out there and kick the other team in the balls!"

The audience suddenly roared with laughter.

"Folks, are y'all ready to get *The Fred Parker Show* underway?"

"Yeah!" the crowd yelled.

"I said are y'all *ready* to get *The Fred Parker Show* underway?" Fred shouted louder.

"*YEAH*!"

"THEN, FOLKS, LET'S GO!"

Fred, and his two lovely showgirl escorts, turned and headed off the stage as the crowd cheered.

ACT I

The Fred Parker Show's massive, dazzling gold curtain opened on the main stage. Sitting at the head of a table in a modest style parlor with black sunglasses on and wearing an awful looking multicolored suit was Abner Redder. He was the obnoxious, fifty-eight-year-old owner of the Lucky Jackpot Hotel, a rundown hotel casino located on the outskirts of Las Vegas where bums, drifters, and tramps often traversed.

Abner, who was blind and big as a house, ran the Lucky Jackpot Hotel like a ruthless tyrant. His word was law and his decisions were never to be questioned. His wife, the fifty-six-year-old slim figured Tutty Redder who was her husband's menial assistant and secretary, stood beside Abner at the head of the table in the parlor as she smoked on a cigarette. She was busy scanning over a list of candidates who were to be interviewed for the position of assistant hotel manager that her husband was currently conducting interviews for.

Also sitting at the table in the parlor was Abner's eighty-year-old mother, Mama Lulu. She lived with Abner and Tutty inside the owner's suite on the grounds of the Lucky Jackpot Hotel. Mama Lulu, who was sweet at heart but was as slow and dumb as an elephant running backwards, suffered from a deranged, psychosis state which required her to be looked after and cared for by Abner and Tutty.

The meeting inside the owner's suite of the Lucky Jackpot Hotel was about to boil over. It was ten o'clock at night and the meeting had been going on for several long hours. Abner was constantly snapping and berating Tutty as he impatiently wanted more information on the potential applicants for the assistant hotel manager's position, and Tutty was about ready to smash a vase down on her husband's head because he'd now gotten on her last nerve.

The situation inside the parlor was as strained and tense as it could get. On top of that Mama Lulu, who was constantly butting in and meddling into the business meeting with her ridiculous, idiotic suggestions on how to spruce up the hotel, simply made matters worse. Tutty and Abner both seemed like they were about ready to put a straitjacket around the eighty-year-old dunce and send her straight to bed.

"Abner, you've interviewed the last ten applicants who've walked through that door and none of them have seemed to impress you," Tutty said angrily. "I'm not about to stand here all night and relay to you every little tidbit of information on each applicant if you're not going to hire any of them."

"Woman, you just keep reading the information that you have on that fact sheet of each applicant like I told you," Abner yelled back. "We're going to keep at this if it takes all night."

"I don't think so, mister," Tutty said as she glanced at the cuckoo clock on the wall in the parlor that looked just like a post office. "It's already past ten o'clock," she said in a hot, fiery tone. "Ain't no more applicants coming in here for an interview tonight. Plus, I'm tired and I'm ready to go to bed."

"Oh," Abner suddenly said with a hefty chuckle, "can't wait for big papa to come to bed and start working the nightshift. Get my drift?"

"Mister," she said as she glared at Abner, "tonight you'll definitely be working the nightshift all alone. *You get my drift*?"

"Tutty, I need to find the right person for this assistant hotel manager's job even if it takes all night," Abner bellowed out as he returned to the subject at hand. "They'll be more applicants coming in the morning to interview for the job, so we're going to keep at it. You know, it takes a very special, highly trained person to handle the demands of running this grand, luxurious hotel."

"*This grand luxurious hotel?*" she said with a chuckle. "Mister, you've been blind for far too long. This place is one of the worst dumps in all of Las Vegas and it's all because of your doing, you fat slob."

"What in the world you mean by that, woman?"

"Abner, when you hit the lottery for eight hundred million dollars twelve years ago and that oil company paid us five hundred million dollars when oil was discovered on our land, we had it made. We should've just moved to Hawaii or some nice island in the Caribbean and just lived our lives out in heavenly peace," Tutty said angrily. "But no, you got this wild, harebrained of an idea to buy some land on the outskirts of Las Vegas, build this big, stupid hotel casino and try to run it yourself."

"And that's just what I did, woman." Abner boasted proudly. "I built a fabulous hotel casino and I'm proud of it."

"Baby, this ain't the MGM Grand," she said with a scowl. "This is more like the Las Vegas Landfill Junkyard Hotel."

"Woman, I'm not going to sit here and let you insult my great life achievement!" Abner yelled. "This has been a very profitable enterprise."

"A profitable enterprise?" Tutty yelled back as fire literally smoldered in her eyes. "We've got five hundred rooms in this cruddy hotel and we can barely keep a hundred of them filled at any time. Guests are constantly complaining of the lack of amenities we offer at this hotel, we have a high staff turnover rate, we get no conventions to come here, our entertainment is one of the worst in all of Las Vegas, and we're steadily losing money because of some of the dumb, idiotic decisions that you've implemented over the years."

"Name me one of them."

"How about the time you tried to book the magician David Copperfield to perform at the hotel, but your cheap butt found out how much it would take to get him, so instead, you ended up booking that no talent bum magician who claimed he could do anything with fire. He ended up burning down the entire stage in the main showroom and we had at least ten people to sue us in court for third degree burns."

"I didn't know that he was a convicted arsonist. I thought—"

"Or what about the time you booked those darling, sweet nuns to perform that silly dance routine skit at the hotel," Tutty said in a sarcastic voice as she interrupted him. "Well, those innocent, sweet nuns who you hired ended up robbing our casino vault for six million dollars and we ain't seen a dollar of that money since."

"I thought they were real nuns!" Abner blasted. "How did I know they had just escaped from that women's prison?"

"And what about that time you let all of those dozens of hookers roam the hotel, soliciting those businessmen that were staying here a couple of years ago?"

"That was to keep all those businessmen happy so they'd stay longer."

"Well, none of them ended up paying their hotel bill because the police ended up raiding the place and arresting everybody!" Tutty yelled. "That was a real smart move, Mister CEO!"

"Hey, I didn't know the police—"

"Listen, Abner," Tutty said in a pointed voice. "Twelve years ago you let two shyster con artists developers build you this rat trap hotel for seven hundred million dollars. They sold you that line that this was a five hundred room state of the art hotel casino that could rival any hotel in Las Vegas, and you bought it like a country blind sucker who'd just set foot in the big city.

"I tried to warn you before you bought this shamble of a place, but you just wouldn't listen," she said shaking her head. "Now we only have a few hundred thousand dollars left out of all those millions that we started out with. I say we try to sell this dump, get what we can for it, and let's move back to Texas where we came from and start over."

"Are you crazy, woman?" Abner yelled. "This hotel is my illustrious life's work. I'm Abner Redder, President and CEO of the Lucky Jackpot Hotel," he said with great pride as he raised his fist and shook it into the air, "and I'm going to keep on running this grand, luxurious hotel like the great executive that I am for years to come."

"Like the great executive that you are?" Tutty cackled as she shook her head. "Abner, before you went blind, before you won the lottery, and before oil was discovered on our farm, you were nothing but a tree logger who worked for that lumber yard ever since you dropped out of high school when you were only sixteen-years-old. All you knew your whole life was menial labor. You didn't know a thing about the business of running a Las Vegas hotel casino, and you *still* don't for that matter."

"Woman—"

"Abner, let's just sell this place, get what we can for it, and leave," Tutty said in a scolding voice. "The sooner we cut our losses and get out of this rat trap, the better off we'll be."

"Never!" Abner said heatedly. "This hotel is my great life's achievement and I'm never leaving it. Do you understand—*NEVER*!"

Tutty let out a long, slow sigh as she shook her head and glared at her husband. They'd been married for forty years, and at times Abner could make her so mad, that she could sometimes feel the fire literally burning her skin. At the moment, Tutty was so riled and upset, that she wanted to buy her blind, two-ton of a husband a no return ticket on a long cruise; possibly on the Titanic.

"Alright Abner, so this hotel is your *great life's achievement* and you want to stick it out," she said with repulse as she glared at Abner. "But if you're determined to keep this rat trap of a hotel, then you're definitely going to have to make some improvements around here. And I'm specifically referring to our entertainment department."

"What about our entertainment department?"

"Take our hotel house band for one thing."

"What about them?"

"Nobody wants to hear that old, tired music they be playing for the guests at night." Tutty complained. "Gus, Aarron, and the rest of those guys have been playing that same old routine every night for the past ten years. They bore the guests and put everybody to sleep. Gus and the rest of those guys have gotten so old, they almost need to be put into a nursing home. About the only thing we've got going good around here is the casino and our showgirls—"

"I can be a showgirl," Mama Lulu, Abner's eighty-year-old mother, suddenly said with a broad smile as she sat at the table in the parlor. Tonight she wore an old, frumpy dress and looked as if she'd just escaped from some nursing home. "I'm nimble, beautiful, and have elegant grace," she said like a young school girl. "I can be a showgirl and help out."

"Mama, nobody wants to see no four-foot-eight, eighty-year-old woman dancing around in a glittery G-string bottom, rhinestone encrusted bra, and some huge feathery headdress!" Abner said with malice. "I've already got a comedy routine at night. I sure don't need no eighty-year-old woman with a mental case dancing around in her diapers!"

"You watch what you say to me," Mama Lulu said as she pointed a crooked, wrinkled finger over at Abner. "You've promised to make me a showgirl for the longest, and mister, I want to be one."

"I ain't never made you no promise to be a showgirl!" Abner bellowed out.

"Yes, you did!"

"Only in your warped, confused mind could you ever believe that I said I was going to make you a showgirl," Abner said with intensity. "What I *should* do is send you out to some funny farm and let you strut around in the open field in some glittery outfit. Maybe the cows and the pigs on that funny farm will get a kick out of seeing you perform."

"You watch what you say to me, you fat lard," Mama Lulu said as she suddenly balled up her fist and shook it at Abner. "I can be a showgirl and dance for the people. You just won't let me."

"Mama—"

"I can be a big box office attraction and save this hotel."

"Mama—"

"I can oil up my legs just like all those other showgirls and smile and prance around just like they do."

"That ought to drive all the men wild," Abner said with a hearty chuckle.

"Why you—"

"Mama Lulu," Tutty suddenly said in a calm voice as Mama Lulu began to get riled. "Don't you think you're a little too old to be dancing around with the showgirls at night? I mean all of our showgirls are young, flexible, and beautiful. The medication you take at night for your psychosis barely keeps you awake at night sometimes."

"You shut up, you tramp!" Mama Lulu snapped as she balled up her fist and shook it at Tutty. "It's because of your old whorish ways that you trapped my boy into marrying you in the first place. You just wanted a pipeline to get into this family."

"And now that pipe don't work no more," Tutty mumbled.

"I'm a beautiful, refined queen just like Madam Cureall," Mama Lulu said with a smile. "And just like the beautiful Madam Cureall, the world needs to see my beauty and elegance. So that's why you need to make me a showgirl," she said in a determined voice as she suddenly glared back at Abner. "Just like Madam Cureall, the entire world needs to see the superwoman that's in me."

"Oh, my goodness. See this is all your fault, Tutty!" Abner said in a frustrated voice as he suddenly slammed the table with his fist. "You should've never bought those stupid Madam Cureall coloring books for Mama. Ever since you bought those stupid coloring books for her, she's been going around here thinking that she's some superhero."

"Look, Abner, when I took Mama Lulu to her psychiatrist appointment to see Dr. Leachman a couple of months ago and we stopped at the drugstore to get her prescription filled, Mama Lulu has had a fixation on those Madam Cureall coloring books since the first time she saw them on the bookrack when we passed down that children's magazine aisle," Tutty said in a hesitant voice. "She's just been hooked on them ever since and she won't let them go."

"You shouldn't have bought the first coloring book in the first place!" Abner yelled. "Now you've made her crazy, loony psychosis even worse. Now she's wandering around here every day, believing that she's some beautiful superhero."

"I am beautiful." Mama Lulu crooned as she suddenly smiled. "Just as beautiful as Madam Cureall."

"See what you've started!" Abner said in a hot voice. "Why just the other day, you told me she was wandering around here with her bed sheet tied around her neck like some cape pretending to be that superhero woman. And because of reading that stupid coloring book, now she wants to be a showgirl of all things. If you ask me, she's just as loony as she can be."

"Yeah," Tutty said as she glared at Abner. "The apple certainly don't fall too far from the tree, does it?"

"What?"

"Look, Abner, I'm sorry," Tutty finally said in an apologetic voice. "But you should've seen her face the first time she saw those coloring books. Her face just lit up like a child at Christmas. She'd been down and depressed for so long, and Dr. Leachman told me to try to find her something to try to get her spirits up. So . . . well . . ." she said as she tried to find the right words to say. "Well . . . I bought the coloring books and I'm sorry, Abner. I'll take the blame for it."

"Yeah, those stupid coloring books and all of those crazy cuckoo clocks of hers are about all we can take around here."

"What did you say about Benny?" Mama Lulu suddenly said in an enraged voice.

"Oh, please, Abner." Tutty quickly tried to intervene. "Please don't get her started up about Benny."

"You say one word about Benny and I'm going to smack that fat head of yours all the way back to Texas," Mama Lulu said in a riled voice. "You better not say one—"

"Mama, you've had that crazy cuckoo clock in your room for so long, talking to it all through the night and caring for it like a baby for so many years, that the stupid thing has literally become human now!"

"Please, Abner—"

"I'm sorry, Tutty. But she's got that crazy cuckoo clock of hers all over this house," Abner said in a furious voice. "She's got one in her bedroom, one here in the parlor, one in my office, one in the dining room, and *even* one in our bedroom. I've had it with that stupid clock, and the first thing come morning, I'm having it taken out of every room and thrown in the dumpster."

"You better not lay a hand on Benny!" Mama Lulu suddenly rose from the table as she began to whack at the back of Abner's head repeatedly. "Don't you lay a finger on Benny!"

"Stop it, mama, stop it!" Abner yelled as Mama Lulu continued to whack the living daylights out of him. "STOP IT, I SAID! STOP IT!"

Tutty finally got control of the hysterical eighty-year-old woman as she escorted her to her bedroom. The entire time as she helped Mama Lulu get into her pajamas and slip into bed for the night, the anguish call for the welfare of Benny, kept crying out from her lips.

Fifteen minutes later, Tutty finally came back into the parlor after getting Mama Lulu off to bed. Tutty saw that Abner had now taken off his jacket, his tie, and had unbuttoned the top button of his shirt as he began to relax. He'd even gone over to the bar and had poured himself a glass of his favorite drink, a glass of rum.

"Look, Abner," Tutty said as she approached him sitting at the table as she slowly folded her arms. "I know you like to run this hotel your own way and you like to walk around here feeling like the *big, mighty important* king around here in all. But you can't sit there and ignore the fact that business has been steadily going downhill for months."

"Tutty, I'm the CEO and owner of the Lucky Jackpot Hotel and I don't need no advice from my menial, nagging secretary." Abner barked out in an angry tone as he took a sip from his glass. "I built this hotel and I know how to run it."

"Well, I keep the books around here, mister, and I'm telling you we're deep in the red," Tutty said as she quickly countered. "Our room occupancy rate has hit rock bottom, the cost of keeping a good staff employed at the hotel is escalating, and our reserved funds in the bank are *definitely* running low. Hiring some assistant hotel manager ain't going to solve the problem around here. What you need to do, if you want to keep this hell hole of a hotel, is to come up with something that's going to draw more people here and that's going to keep them entertained. Abner, you've got to try something new and inventive."

"Like what?"

"I don't know," Tutty said as she let out a long sigh. "Maybe . . . maybe try getting some animal acts or something like that to entertain the guests."

"Animal acts!" Abner said. He suddenly began to shudder and shake uncontrollably as if he were about to have a complete nervous breakdown. "You know I can't stand no animals or children to be around me at no time! You know that!" he said like an angry bear. "NO ANIMALS OR CHILDREN ARE PERMITTED AT THIS HOTEL! IS THAT UNDERSTOOD?"

"Alright, Abner, just calm down," Tutty said with concern. "Please, don't bust a blood vessel and have a stroke." When Abner finally began to calm down and was once again breathing normally, Tutty looked at him and said, "You just remember what I said, Abner. This hotel of yours is in deep red," she said as she glared at him. "I'm tired. I'm going to bed now."

When Tutty turned and headed for the bedroom, Abner suddenly grabbed his glass of rum and white cane as he rose from the table and lumbered over in her direction.

"Hey, speaking of red," Abner said as he put his arm around Tutty and nestled up against her as she stood in the doorway of their bedroom. "You remember that red, sexy negligee that you used to wear to bed back when we used to live in Texas?"

"You mean the one I used to wear that turned you on before you went blind?" Tutty said in an alluring voice as the Magic Rainbow Hotel & Casino Orchestra suddenly began to play a soft, soothing melody that made the mood so romantic.

"Yeah, that's the one. Do you still have it?"

"I most certainly do."

"And you used to look good in it, too." Abner chuckled as he slowly caressed her body. "Why don't you refresh my mind of how good you used to look in it?"

"You mean when I used to slip into that tight, red negligee that made my body look so desirable?" Tutty said in an alluring voice. "And do you remember when we used to turn on that red nightlight?"

"Oh, yeah!"

"And remember we used to burn that sweet-smelling cherry incense that made our entire bedroom smell like our very own luscious, paradise suite?"

"Ah, Tutty, you make it all sound so *good and fruity*," Abner said with a huge smile as he continued to caress her body. "Say, Tutty . . . ."

"Yeah, big cutie?"

"Why don't you let me come on to bed now so I can do my duty?"

"You know what, big cutie?" she said with a smile as she caressed his chest.

"What's that, Tutty?"

"You still ain't getting none of this."

Tutty suddenly slammed the door, leaving Abner standing all alone outside their bedroom door as the soft music from the Magic Rainbow Hotel & Casino Orchestra slowly faded away.

Tango Parker, and his array of highly trained show animals, suddenly arrived on the grounds of the Lucky Jackpot Hotel. It was late at night and the fifteen-year-old Tango, who looked like a homeless vagabond as he carried all of his worldly possessions in a lone duffle bag over his shoulder, stopped to take in the sight of the shabby, rundown hotel before him.

Tired, hungry, and having only two measly dollars in his pocket, Tango stared up at the leaning hotel marquee sign at the entrance of the hotel that had half of its lights blown out. He and his motley crew of animals looked like members of some traveling circus that just escaped or were thrown off of the circus truck they had traveled on.

There was a buffoonish-looking orangutan dressed in a brown, faded suit with a red and white polka dotted tie on. There was a big, husky St. Bernard dog, a scarlet macaw parrot, and a beautiful, Mexican Siamese cat with a bell attached around her neck. They and their scruffy looking owner had traveled miles, hitchhiking and traversing over dangerous roads to reach their destination, and now they'd finally arrived.

"Don't tell me that this is the dump that we traveled all of this way for?" the buffoonish looking orangutan said as he puffed on a fat cigar.

"Yeah, this is the place," Tango said as he slid the duffle bag down to the ground to give his tired, aching shoulder a break. "Two weeks ago I got a letter from Zimmy who used to be on the entertainment circuit with us. He works here now. In the letter that he wrote, he said that the owner of this place was hiring."

"This place—you got to be kidding me!" the angry orangutan said. "Man, we've performed in dives *way* better than this dump in some of the worse places down in South America, Mexico, and Africa put together."

"You got any better suggestions of where we should go, you stupid ape?" the big, husky St. Bernard dog said with hostility.

"I'm going to have to agree with the ape on this one, Tango," the scarlet macaw parrot suddenly said in a sleepy voice. "We've performed at cheap carnivals and lousy fairs that were better than this place. I know Dr. Glittermoon certainly wouldn't approve of me abiding in such a place as this. He'd say it's not good for my philosophical mind."

"Hey, Chipper, when is your next appointment to see Dr. Fruitcake?" the Siamese cat said with a giggle.

"His name is *Dr. Glittermoon*, you silly, stupid cat. And I can't go see him unless I've had plenty of kerweekee," the scarlet macaw parrot said in a hoarse voice. "By the way, Tango, when am I going to get my next batch of kerweekee? You know it's almost been two weeks since I last had some, and a highly advanced, enlightened parrot as myself needs some every day. My voice is already going hoarse and starting to give out because I ain't had none in a while."

"Can't fly straight without it, can you?" the Siamese cat said with a hearty giggle. "How many times does the world turn when you've had your daily dose?" She giggled. "Twenty?"

"Listen, guys, the reason why we're here is because we're flat broke, we have no place to stay, and we have no other gigs on the horizon," Tango said to his animals. "This may be our last hope of getting any kind of work and performing before we end up on the street."

"This is just wonderful," the angry orangutan said as he glared at the rundown hotel. "I'm a highly trained performer that should be working in only the best places and best hotels that Las Vegas has to offer, but instead, I'm forced to come beg for work in a dump like this."

"Ain't we got an overinflated opinion of ourselves," the big St. Bernard dog said to the orangutan in a condescending voice. "Looks like to me that this hotel here could be the perfect place for you to brush up on your skills."

"Brush up on my skills?" The orangutan suddenly gave the big St. Bernard dog an enraged look. "Tell me what magician you know who can do this."

The orangutan in the faded brown suit suddenly pounded his chest twice with his fist and snapped his finger. Poof! A cloud of purple smoke mushroomed in the air as a muzzle suddenly appeared wired and locked over the big St. Bernard dog's mouth.

"That ought to keep the big mutt's mouth shut," the orangutan said with a hearty laugh as he puffed on his cigar and flashed his pearly white smile.

"Look at Fred." The Siamese cat suddenly giggled. "For once he has nothing to say."

"Alright, Joe, take it off right now," Tango said as he gave the orangutan a perturbed look.

The orangutan pounded his chest twice with his fist again, snapped his finger, and poof, the muzzle suddenly went away.

"You ain't got to show off, ape," the scarlet macaw parrot said in a lazy voice. "We've all got our talents."

"Yeah, you, me, and Elvyra have talent," the orangutan said as he glared over at the big St. Bernard dog, "but that stupid mutt over there is the one holding us all back."

"What are you talking about, you crazy ape?" the big St. Bernard dog said with a growl.

"Me, Elvyra, and Chipper are the only ones the people want to see when we perform," the orangutan said with spite. "We were the Mystical Three long before you even joined the group. You were only a guard dog for our very first owner, Ivan 'The Butcher' Malakhov, when we first started performing."

"So, what if I was only a guard dog?"

"When Ivan 'The Butcher' Malakhov had that African witchdoctor hypnotist to put a spell on us that gave us the ability to speak way back all those years ago, he just brought you along out of sympathy and told the hypnotist to give you the ability to speak, too," the orangutan said in a cocky voice as he continued. "But 'The Butcher' never intended for you to start performing with us, because you had no talent."

"I got more talent than you'll ever know, you hairy ape."

"Sure you do, dog." He gave a condescending chuckle as he puffed on his cigar. "And furthermore, you didn't start performing with us until Tango, over here, made you part of the group two years ago. Now we're the Magnificent Four and we've been going downhill ever since. And it's all because of your no talent mutt self!"

"You know, I wish that witchdoctor hypnotist hadn't given us the ability to speak at all," the big St. Bernard dog said with a growl. "At least then, I wouldn't have to listen to your stupid, loud mouth."

"Ah, stuff it, you no talent mutt."

"Alright, guys, that's enough," Tango said as he quickly tried to squash the argument. "Now, we need to get this gig at this hotel because there's simply nowhere else for us to go."

"You know, Tango, ever since we've come into your possession two years ago, we've steadily been going downhill," the orangutan said as he eyed Tango. "The other owners that we've been under the control of in the past had us at least performing in better places than this dump."

"Come on, Joe, don't start that," the scarlet macaw parrot said in a lazy voice. "We're going to hit the big time one day."

"Yeah, Joe, lighten up," the Siamese cat said. "Anyway, I like Tango," she said with a sultry purr. "He's been the nicest, sweetest owner that we've ever had."

"Oh, we all know why *you* like him, Elvyra," the orangutan said in a snide tone.

"Look, you stupid, moron ape," the big St. Bernard dog said as he once again glared at the orangutan. "Tango has been the best owner that we've ever had. He's good, decent, and he truly cares for all of us. He's certainly way better than some of those other crooked, shyster owners that we've been under the control of in the past, especially the ones who only cared about getting rich off of us."

"Dog, you just like him because he's made you his favorite dumb pet—*man's best friend*," he said in a condescending tone. "Tango can't take us to the big time. He's nothing but a stupid kid himself, and a runaway at that. As long as we stay up under him, we're going to keep on performing in dives like this—especially if he thinks you got the talent and skill to perform with us on stage. I mean look at where we're at," he said as he pointed up at the leaning marquee sign with half the lights blown out. "We've hit rock bottom!"

"Well, the reason we've hit rock bottom is because of all the crazy, lunatic shenanigans you keep pulling off everywhere we go!" the big St. Bernard dog yelled at the orangutan. "You've gotten us fired or thrown out of virtually every place that we've worked at. If they ask me, they ought to haul you away to the nearest insane asylum."

"Ah, go fetch a ball, you no talent guard dog."

"Why don't you go back to the jungle and climb a tree, you stupid ape."

"Alright, that's enough. Just can it you two!" Tango suddenly said like a crack of a whip. "Joe," he said in a subdued voice as he looked at the orangutan, "we're going to hit the big time. Just be patient. It's only a matter of time."

"Promises . . . *promises*."

"I wonder what Dr. Glittermoon would think of all of this constant fighting and bickering," the scarlet macaw parrot said as he let a deep sigh slowly escape from his beak. "I just wish I had my kerweekee."

"So you can go watch the world turn, huh?" the Siamese cat said with a giggle.

"Alright, everybody, listen closely," Tango said as he slowly cast his eyes around at all of the animals. "When we go in there, I don't want none of you to—"

"Tango, I wish you would take this stupid bell off from around my neck," the Siamese cat suddenly said as she interrupted him. "I'd much rather wear one of my beautiful silk scarves, preferably the green one. No, the royal blue one. No, the peach one. No, the red one," she said with a giggle. "The red one makes my green eyes stand out and makes me look *so* divine."

"Still stuck on your looks like some two dollar whore, huh?" the scarlet macaw parrot said in a sleepy voice.

The Siamese cat began to emit a cloud of green smoke from her feline body that matched the color of her emerald eyes. Within seconds, she suddenly transformed from a Siamese cat into a beautiful six-foot Mexican woman like the werecat that she was.

"You better watch your mouth, sweet thing," the stunning, Mexican beauty said in an alluring voice to the scarlet macaw parrot. "If you don't, this senorita might just have herself some parrot stew for dinner tonight."

The green smoke once again began to seep from her body as she transformed back into the Siamese cat. Tango was already rummaging through his duffle bag searching through his belongings for the red silk scarf that Elvyra craved and wanted.

"Oh, here it is," Tango said as he took the bell from around Elvyra's neck and tied the red silk scarf there in its place. "There, satisfied?"

"How do I look?" she said like a prima donna.

"You look divine, Elvyra," the big St. Bernard dog said.

"I don't know why you even tied that bell around my neck anyway, Tango. You know I hate that thing."

"Because when we were in that drive-in market before we arrived here, you wandered off in the direction of that trucker who went to go get a six pack of beer. I didn't know if you were coming right back or not. You've run off before, Elvyra."

"Hey, he was kind of cute," she said with a giggle. "I thought he was nice, too."

"Let me guess," the scarlet macaw parrot said in a lazy voice. "You were going to give him a discount in the bathroom, right?"

"That parrot stew is sounding better by the minute, Chipper," the Siamese cat said as she glared at the parrot.

"Alright, as I was saying," Tango repeated himself as he eyed all the animals. "When we go in there, I don't want none of you to say a single—"

"Oh, Tango, *please* tell me you didn't forget to bring my precious teddy bear," Elvyra said in a panic as she interrupted him again. "You know how I love to rub up against Teddy's nice furry body at night."

"Elvyra, you love to rub up against any guy at night that has a good stiff—"

Tango quickly gave the scarlet macaw parrot a hard, critical gaze as the parrot immediately closed his beak.

"Yes, Elvyra," Tango finally said with a heavy sigh, "I've brought your teddy bear along."

"Good!"

"Now, as I was saying," Tango said as he continued. "When we go in there, I don't want no one to say a single word. I'll do all of the talking. Understood?"

"I still don't know why we've got to come here and beg for work at this stupid dump!" the orangutan said in a heated voice as he continued to puff on his cigar.

"Because Tango says so!" the big St. Bernard dog said angrily. "And put that cigar out!"

"Dog, if you think I'm listening to you, then you're dumber than you—"

"Put it out, Joe," Tango quickly said.

The orangutan began to sulk as he took one last draw from his cigar, then dropped it on the ground.

"Alright." Tango looked around once more at all the animals. "Is everything understood? No one—and I mean no one—says a single word. Got it?"

"I just wish I had my kerweekee," Chipper said with a deep sigh. "All of this is just twisting my mind all around."

"All of that kerweekee you've been smoking has already warped your mind," the Siamese cat said with a hearty giggle as everyone suddenly laughed.

Lying in bed for the past hour unable to go to sleep, Tutty finally rose out of bed and slipped on her nightgown. She left out of the bedroom and headed for the kitchen to fix some cocoa so it could maybe help her to drift off to sleep.

As she began to walk through the parlor, Tutty suddenly saw that Mama Lulu had gotten out of bed. She was now down on her knees literally begging Abner not to get rid of her precious cuckoo clocks while Abner, looking as content as he could be, sat on the couch in the parlor drinking rum and bobbing his head to some late night music on the radio.

Tutty couldn't help but to snicker at the sight of the two as she headed into the kitchen. She knew that Mama Lulu would do almost anything to save her precious Benny if she thought that she was about to lose him. The fact that Abner, the jackass that he was, continually sipped from his glass of rum while he ignored her constant begging and pleading, made it even more hilarious. If Mama Lulu would only realize that the fat moron had threatened many times to do away with her precious Benny and he never did, then she could go on back to bed and rest her mind of the whole situation. But no, she had to beg and plead the fat hippo down on her knees like he was the almighty Godfather.

"Go on and kiss the Godfather's ring, you loony nut," Tutty mumbled to herself as she snickered.

When Tutty entered the kitchen, she pulled out a pot, poured some cocoa and milk into the pot, placed the pot on the stove and turned on the eye. While she waited for her cocoa to heat up, she lit up a cigarette and began to contemplate over the affairs of the hotel.

Tutty couldn't help but to remember the day that Abner won the lottery for eight hundred million dollars twelve years ago. The astonishing thing was the very next day after winning the lottery, oil was discovered on their farm back in Texas and an oil company paid them an additional five hundred million dollars for the right to drill on their land.

Against the strong advice of several financial advisors and accountants warning Abner not to invest his new windfall of money into such a risky business adventure, he ignored these warnings and immediately plucked down eight hundred million dollars of his new wealth to build a hotel casino on the outskirts of Las Vegas. Abner had no business acumen on how to run a hotel casino after spending so many years as a tree logger for a lumber yard, but he still went ahead and plunged head first into the business enterprise anyway.

What made the situation even worse was the day that Abner, Tutty, and Mama Lulu were set to leave for Las Vegas. Abner decided, at the very last second, to make a pit stop by his former workplace so he could curse out his old boss and gloat over his newfound wealth. However, that fateful decision ended up backfiring in the worst possible way; a tree log accidently fell off one of the trucks in the lumber yard hitting Abner dead on top of his head, rendering him permanently blind.

Since that ominous, ill-fated day, Abner's luck continued to spiral downward faster than a casket buried at sea. Bad business decisions, shyster con men continually ripping him off, and Abner constantly loaning money to his family members who wanted to promote their stupid, harebrained ideas began to quickly erode what was left of his wealth. Within ten years, with the Lucky Jackpot Hotel steadily losing money along with other negating factors pulling against him, Abner's once great wealth had virtually disappeared.

Tutty slowly puffed on her cigarette, silently pondering over all of their past misfortune as she finally turned off the eye on the stove when the cocoa had gotten good and piping hot. She was about to pour herself a cup of hot cocoa when she suddenly heard a knock at the kitchen door.

Noticing by the clock on the kitchen wall that it was eleven thirty at night, Tutty quickly grabbed her 9mm Beretta pistol out of the kitchen cabinet drawer. No one ever came to their side kitchen door at night, other than drunks, drifters, or vagabonds looking for spare change. The Las Vegas night always brought out the freaks and the misfits, which was why Tutty always kept a loaded gun around just in case it was needed.

With the loaded gun firmly in her hand, Tutty slowly went to the kitchen door. She switched on the outside light and peered through the peephole of the door. Noticing a scraggily, homeless looking kid with some animals, Tutty figured it was some drifter who'd come to beg for money. The kid outside the door looked harmless, but Tutty kept her gun cocked and ready just in case.

Tutty slowly opened the kitchen door as she stood face to face with the intruder that had come knocking at her door. In the distance, she could see the leaning hotel marquee sign with half of its lights blown out as it flickered the *Lucky Jackpot Hotel* into the night. Tutty, with the 9mm Beretta pistol at her side, slowly puffed on her cigarette as she looked over the scraggily, scrawny kid and his array of animals.

"Can I help you?"

"Yes, I'm Tango Parker," he said nervously. "I received a letter from Zimmy Castillo a couple weeks ago informing me that the owner of this hotel was looking to hire some entertainment acts for the hotel, and I was hoping to get some work here."

"It's kind of late to be looking for work. Don't you think?"

"Yes ma'am. But we've come a long way."

"How old are you, kid?"

"Fifteen."

"And you say Zimmy wrote you about getting a job here?"

"Yes, ma'am."

"Well Zimmy works in our custodial department. He was probably telling you about getting a job in that department."

"I didn't get that impression from the letter, ma'am," he said hesitantly. "It just said that the owner of the hotel would consider hiring me."

Tutty began to scan over the array of animals that stood beside him as she slowly smoked on her cigarette. "These your animals?"

"Yes, ma'am."

"You put on some kind of animal show or something?"

"Yes, ma'am. These animals are highly trained and they can do just about anything."

"Like what?"

"They can do juggling acts, hula hoop acts, magic tricks, and they can even do comedy routines. We've been working mostly down in Mexico for the last couple of months at assorted fairs and carnivals entertaining crowds. These animals are the best around, ma'am, and I'm sure the guests at your hotel would really enjoy the act that they put on."

Tutty puffed on her cigarette as she continued to glance over the animals. She couldn't help but get a kick out of how the cat was adorned with a red silk scarf around her neck and how the orangutan was dressed in a faded brown suit with a red and white polka dotted tie on.

"Well, I can certainly say one thing," she said with a slight chuckle. "They're certainly cute. But here's the thing, kid. What did you say your name was again?"

"Tango Parker."

"Here's the thing. My husband, who owns the hotel, cares absolutely nothing for animal acts of any kind. In fact, he terribly hates all animals with a deep passion. And the only job he's currently hiring for is for the position of assistant hotel manager."

"He's not hiring any animal acts?"

"I'm afraid not. My husband hates animals so much, he would have a nervous breakdown fit if he knew an animal was even near him," Tutty said as she stared at the boy as he slowly began to hang his head in utter dejection. "Listen, kid, why don't I give you a few dollars and you can be on your way. Maybe you can get you something to eat. You look like you haven't had a decent meal in a long—"

"Hey, lady, we didn't come here for no hand out!" The orangutan suddenly lashed out. "You're looking at three of the most talented entertainers in the entire world!"

"Shut up, you stupid ape," the big St. Bernard dog quickly whispered to the orangutan.

"They're four of us, Joe, remember." The Siamese cat suddenly giggled. "Don't forget about Fred."

"Lady, you wouldn't happen to have any kerweekee around here, would you?" the scarlet macaw parrot said in a lazy voice. "I can't go on like this."

"Can't wait to see Dr. Fruitcake, can you?" Elvyra giggled.

Tutty suddenly started coughing and gagging on the smoke of her cigarette as she looked wide eyed at the animals before her in total disbelief. Her heart fluttered like mad as she struggled to get a single word out.

"You mean to tell me you have *talking*—"

"Yeah." Tango nodded. "It's a long story, ma'am."

"Oh, my goodness," Tutty said in an almost delirious voice. "Come in! Come in!"

When Tango and his crew entered the kitchen, Tutty closed the door and quickly put the gun back into the cabinet drawer. She was so out of sorts, she was almost shaking as she stared at Tango and his crew.

"I'm Tutty Redder," she finally said in a somewhat stuttering voice. "Do you have proof of ownership of these animals?"

Tango dug into his faded blue jeans pocket and pulled out the ownership paper and showed it to Tutty. She glanced at the ownership paper thoroughly, then gave it back to Tango.

"What . . . what are their names?"

"I'm Joe, madam, the world's greatest entertainer," the orangutan quickly said with a pompous air as he beamed a brilliant smile.

"I'm Elvyra." The cat giggled. "Want me to sing you a song?"

"The name is Chipper, lady," the scarlet macaw parrot said in an unenthused voice.

"And I'm Fred."

"This is unbelievable," Tutty said with a look of utter shock. "I can't believe it. This is the answer to all of our prayers. Oh, I've got to tell this to my husband!" she said in an elated voice. "Y'all, follow me. My husband is blind, so I'll explain everything to him."

Tango and his array of animals followed Tutty as she took them into the parlor. Abner was still sitting on the couch in the parlor enjoying his music, while Mama Lulu continued to beg and plead with Abner not to throw out her precious cuckoo clocks. Tutty, not wasting a single second, quickly rushed over to the radio and turned off the music.

"What happen to the radio?" Abner bellowed out.

"I turned it off," Tutty quickly answered. "Abner, there's some—"

"Why you turn the radio off for, woman?" Abner shouted. "You won't give me no loving, at least you can do is let me listen to some music."

"Abner, I've got something important to tell you."

"Tutty, please don't let Abner harm poor Benny," Mama Lulu said in a pitiful, childlike voice as she approached Tutty. "I need Benny and he needs me."

"Mama Lulu, he ain't going to do nothing to those stupid cuckoo clocks of yours," Tutty said in a riled voice. "Now I got to tell Abner something important—"

"Make him promise me he won't harm Benny." Mama Lulu continued in a persistent voice.

"Mama Lulu—"

"Please, Tutty, you got to make him promise me."

"Mama Lulu, will you—"

"You're just a mean old daughter-in-law." Mama Lulu began to rage. "You want Benny gone just the same as he does."

"Mama Lulu, will you listen—"

"You just siding with him, you lying whore."

"Mama Lulu—"

"Well, I've had it with your lying butt and I've had it with him, too," Mama Lulu said in a riled voice as she suddenly raised her fist in the air. "I ain't going to let neither one of you harm my precious Benny!"

"Mama Lulu, ain't nobody—"

Mama Lulu suddenly began to whack the living daylights out of the back of Abner's head again. She beat and pounded with both of her fists with such force, that she was almost like an eighty-year-old, four-foot-eight boxer who'd come out of retirement to reclaim her long lost title.

"Mama, will you stop it!" Abner cried out as Mama Lulu kept whacking him, knocking off his black shades in the process. "STOP IT, MAMA, STOP IT!"

Tutty finally grabbed and restrained the pesky little fighter and shoved her down into an armchair next to the couch.

"Will you sit your nutty tail down and stay in that seat!" Tutty said with fire as she pointed a long, firm finger at her.

When Mama Lulu finally obliged, Abner slipped his black shades back on.

"When's her next appointment to see Dr. Leachman?" Abner said in a riled voice. "She's getting just as nutty and screwy as a dodo bird."

"Never mind her, Abner," Tutty quickly said. "I'm trying to tell you there's—"

"What you trying to tell me, woman? You changed your mind or something?" Abner suddenly said with a hefty smile. "You ready for big daddy to come to bed now?"

"Abner, I'm trying to tell you there's someone here who has—"

"What, there's someone here?"

"Yes! And he has talking—"

"What, someone has come for an interview for the assistant hotel manager's job this late?"

"No, Abner," Tutty said in a frustrated voice. "Will you listen to me—"

"Well, I'm finished conducting interviews for the night, Tutty," Abner said with authority. "Tell the gentleman to come back tomorrow. I'll interview him in the morning."

"Abner, he's not here for—"

"Woman, you won't give me no loving. You won't let me listen to my music in peace, and now you're pestering me to do some late night interview to some Johnny come lately."

"Abner, will you just listen to me—"

"Alright, Tutty, alright!" Abner finally said in frustration. "Since you're pestering me so much, I guess I'll do the interview now."

"Abner, you can't—"

"Now, woman, don't come pestering me on how to conduct the interview," he yelled. "I've been doing these interviews all day and I know what I'm looking for in an applicant. Remember, you are only my secretary and you do as I say. I run this hotel, woman!" he suddenly bellowed out at the top of his lungs. "AND I'LL CONDUCT THE INTERVIEW HOWEVER I PLEASE. YOU JUST TAKE NOTES! THAT'S YOUR ROLE, WOMAN. YOU TAKE NOTES AND I DO THE INTERVIEWS! UNDERSTOOD?"

Tutty sighed as she finally threw up her hands in frustration. She looked at Tango and motioned for him and his crew to have a seat on the sofa across from Abner. They, along with the parrot who flew and landed on the armrest of the sofa, did as they were told as they had a seat and waited for the head man in charge to speak.

"Now, let me introduce myself. I'm Abner Redder, president and owner of this fine hotel," Abner said in an arrogant, haughty voice. "Who am I speaking to?"

"Tango Parker," he said somewhat nervously.

"You sound a little nervous," Abner said with a chuckle. "I guess that's understandable, applying for such a prestigious job at such a grand, beautiful place as the Lucky Jackpot Hotel."

Tutty couldn't help but to smirk.

"Abner, why is there an ape dressed in a suit, a dog, a cat, and a bird in here?" Mama Lulu suddenly said with a frown as she stared over at Tango and his array of animals as they lounged on the couch.

"Mama, there ain't no apes, dogs, cats, or nor birds in here," Abner said in a hostile voice.

"There is, too!"

"Mama—"

"You get these mangy looking critters out of here right now!" Mama Lulu protested as she glared over at Tango and his animals. "I won't stand to be in the same room with these filthy animals."

"Tutty, what in the world is she talking about?"

"I don't know, Abner," Tutty said as she stifled a giggle. "You know how Mama Lulu gets sometimes."

"Don't I ever," Abner said as he shook his head. "Sir, you'll have to excuse my mother over here. She's not all right in the head."

Joe, the orangutan, sitting the closes to Mama Lulu as she sat in her armchair, suddenly beamed his big white smile at her.

"Don't you smile at me, you mangy ape!"

"Mama, stop it!" Abner said with reproach. "Sir, we'll try to conduct this interview without any more interruptions from my mother. Now," he said as he leaned back on the couch, "what other hotels have you been a manager of?"

Tango looked nervously at Tutty. She quickly mouthed silently to Tango what she wanted him to say.

"Well, I've previously been a manager at a hotel in Los Angeles and was recently a manager at a hotel in Carson City, Nevada," he said as he read Tutty's lips. "I've had ten years experience in hotel managerial positions."

"You sound a little young, Mr. Parker. How old are you?"

He once again looked over at Tutty and read her lips. "I'm thirty-six-years old, sir."

"I see." Abner nodded. "Tutty, how does Mr. Parker's résumé look?"

"Excellent." Tutty snickered silently. "The best one I've seen thus far."

"Tell me, Mr. Parker, what made you want to apply for the assistant hotel manager's position here at the Lucky Jackpot Hotel?"

"Because a dump like this hotel needs an experienced manager to run it," Tango said as he read Tutty's lips.

"Pardon me?" Abner quickly said in a grizzled voice.

Tutty slapped her hand over her mouth as she held back a laugh. She couldn't help but to throw that one out.

"What I meant to say is that I would very much like to be a part of a fine upstanding hotel establishment as the one you've built here, sir." Tango quickly corrected himself when he once again read Tutty's mouth. "If I get the chance, I'll show you, sir, what a fine managerial associate that I am."

"I see." Abner nodded. "Tell me, what would you do to help improve the Lucky Jackpot Hotel?"

Take a bulldozer and run this dilapidated heap straight into the ground, Tutty thought.

"Well, sir, I would find ways to maybe spruce up the entertainment sector of the hotel," Tango said as he kept a close eye on Tutty's lips. "I would give the guests a form of unique entertainment that they'd never stop talking about."

"Abner, this mangy ape over here keeps smiling at me!" Mama Lulu said with a huff.

"Mama, will you sit in that chair and be quiet!" Abner yelled. "There ain't no apes, monkeys, cows, or whatever you think that's in this room. I wish something could keep that stupid mouth of yours shut!"

Joe flashed his brilliant, bodacious smile even wider at Mama Lulu as he pounded his chest twice with his fist and snapped his finger. Poof! A cloud of purple smoke mushroomed in the air as two hospital orderlies suddenly appeared as they put a straitjacket around Mama Lulu and gagged her mouth. Within seconds, the orderlies disappeared into thin air, leaving Mama Lulu restrained and gagged.

Tutty's mouth flew open in total shock. She could hardly believe what she saw. Not only could this orangutan in the faded brown suit and polka dotted tie speak and talk, but he could perform magic that was simply out of this world!

"Now Mr. Parker, if hired as assistant manager here at the Lucky Jackpot Hotel, what kind of salary would you expect?"

Tango quickly looked over at Tutty for guidance, but Tutty was too busy mesmerized by the comical scene of Mama Lulu squirming and struggling in that straitjacket as her mouth was gagged shut.

"Well, I'm waiting, Mr. Parker," Abner said impatiently.

"Around fifty thousand, sir," Tango said when Tutty finally mouthed the words to him.

"That's a little steep, Mr. Parker," Abner said with a gruff. "I generally pay my assistant hotel managers around thirty thousand a year."

"You ain't never had an assistant hotel manager before, Abner," Tutty spoke up as she kept her eyes focused on the comical scene of Mama Lulu continuing to squirm in the straitjacket with her mouth gagged. "The boy . . . I mean Mr. Parker is a very experienced hotel manager. His résumé is impeccable. If you don't give him the salary that he deserves, then we're going to lose him. There's plenty of competition from other hotels around here in Las Vegas, you know."

As Tutty and Abner began to get into a squabble over salary, Joe suddenly pulled out a cigar from his faded brown suit and lit up. He continued flashing his huge, bodacious smile at Mama Lulu while he smoked as she continued to squirm and struggle in the straitjacket.

"Put that cigar out, you stupid moron, and take that straitjacket off of her," Fred whispered over to Joe while Tutty and Abner continued arguing, but Joe wasn't paying any attention to him. "Take it off!" he suddenly shouted to Joe.

"What was that?" Abner said as he broke from the argument with Tutty. "I heard another voice. Is someone else in here?"

Tango seemed at a loss of words, so Tutty quickly intervened.

"Yes, they're four other people who are part of Mr. Parker's agency that are here also," Tutty quickly said.

"His agency?"

"Yes, the Parker Incorporated Agency. Mr. Parker here has his own staffing service."

"I'm not paying no four salaries," Abner said angrily. "Mr. Parker, you can consider this interview over. Goodnight."

"Well, you wouldn't have to pay four salaries if you hired Mr. Parker," Tutty quickly said. "The other four salaries are paid through an outside source that the government pays. So, you'll actually be getting the work of five hotel managerial workers for the salary of only one. Isn't that right, Mr. Parker?"

Tango seemed totally confused. Tutty quickly smiled and nodded for him to go along with the clever ruse.

"Yes," he finally answered. "Yes, that's correct, Mr. Redder."

"I see," Abner said as he seemed to ponder over the situation. "Well, before I make a decision, I'd like you to introduce your staff to me, Mr. Parker."

"Well . . ." Tango said nervously as he looked at his animals. "This is—"

"Beasley Upchurch," Joe quickly said in a snooty English accent as he cast a witty smile over at Abner. "I'm a former butler who worked at the famous Buckingham Palace over in England before coming over to America and joining Mr. Parker's agency. I can't wait to become a part of this fine, luxurious hotel that you have here."

"And I'm Romeno Mendez," Elvyra said in a sensuous, flirtatious voice. "I can't wait to work next to you, Mr. Redder, as your personal secretary. You can certainly count on me for *anything* that you need."

"Is that a fact?" Abner said with a chuckle as he began to blush. "Well, you sound like a very efficient secretary, Ms. Mendez."

"Oh, I am, Mr. Redder," she said again in a flirtatious voice. "I'll make you one happy boss. And please, call me Romeno."

"I will," he said with a blush.

"And I'm Blue Hendrix," Chipper said in a raspy voice. "I was a former concert promoter before I joined Mr. Parker's agency. I know all about the music business and I can help with the entertainment department here at the hotel."

"I see," Abner said with a nod. "And who is the fourth person of your agency, Mr. Parker?"

"I'm Bob," Fred said.

"Just Bob?"

"You got it."

"And what was your background before you joined Mr. Parker's agency?"

"I was a former dog catcher."

"A dog catcher," Abner said with a chuckle as he shook his head. "How did you go from being a former dog catcher into the hotel industry?"

"Got tired of chasing all those dogs, sir," Fred said as Tutty snickered.

"Well, Mr. Parker, based on your résumé and what I've heard here tonight, I think I can take you and your staff on here at the Lucky Jackpot Hotel, provided that I don't have to pay your staff and we come to a better mutual understanding of what your salary will be," Abner said as he pondered. "Let's say thirty-five-thousand a year. How does that sound?"

Tango quickly looked over at Tutty as she finally nodded. "Yes sir," he said with a giant smile. "I'll take it!"

"Good."

"Abner, we have some employee residential rooms available here at the hotel," Tutty said as she looked at Tango and his crew. "Since you insist on low balling Mr. Parker on his salary, we can at least give him and his staff free accommodations here at the hotel."

"Well, I guess that won't be a problem," Abner said. "I guess you'll be needing five rooms for you and your staff, Mr. Parker. Correct?"

"Don't forget about the Wonder Gang coming tomorrow," Fred quickly whispered to Tango.

"Well, actually sir, we could use another additional room if you have one to spare."

"Why another room?"

"I have a few more junior assistances that assist me in my agency," Tango said nervously. "It'll all be for the benefit of providing the hotel the best service that we can provide, and once again, you won't have to pay any additional salaries."

"Well, I don't think that'll be a problem."

"Thank you, sir."

"Well, Mr. Parker, I want to welcome you and your staff to the Lucky Jackpot Hotel."

Mama Lulu continued to squirm and struggle in the straitjacket she was locked in as Joe, still beaming his bodacious smile, finally pounded his chest twice with his fist and snapped his finger. The straitjacket and the contraption that had her mouth gagged suddenly disappeared.

"ABNER, I'M GOING TO KILL THIS MANGY APE!" Mama Lulu hollered out when her mouth was finally freed.

Tutty couldn't help but to bust out laughing.

Tango and his motley crew of animals were in one of the hotel's employee residential rooms trying to get adjusted to their new environment. The room was somewhat small with only a single bed, a small closet for clothes, a lone dresser, and a nightstand with a lamp and a phone. The room was pretty plain and bare, but it was a pleasure palace compared to where they'd been. Over the last several days as they traveled and hitchhiked to get to the Lucky Jackpot Hotel, nothing but filthy restrooms of gas stations and truck stops had been their lodging place. They'd been homeless the last several weeks, but now they had accommodations; and in the end, that was all that really mattered.

Fred stayed near Tango as Tango sat on the lone bed in the room talking on the phone, while Joe, Chipper, and Elvyra acted a plum fool on the other side of the room as they carried on with their wild shenanigans. Fred didn't ever like to partake in the wild, silly shenanigans that Joe, Chipper, and Elvyra often engaged in. He always liked to stay near Tango—his master—like the good, faithful dog that he was.

When Tango hung up the phone, Fred glanced at his owner and saw the concern on his face. He was more than anxious to find out what troubled him.

"Who was that on the phone?"

"That was Mrs. Tutty," Tango said as he rubbed his forehead. "She's sending over a suit of clothes for me to wear tomorrow. It's like some managerial suit that I'm supposed to wear."

"You kind of worried that you want be able to pull it off, aren't you?"

"Wouldn't you be?" Tango laughed nervously. "I mean I'm fifteen-years-old and the last school grade that I completed was the seventh grade before I ran away to become an animal trainer. I'm not quite qualified to be an assistant hotel manager of some Las Vegas hotel. This is just crazy."

"Well, by the look of this hotel from the outside and after talking to the genius who owns it, I'd say the bar is set *pretty* low," Fred said with a chuckle.

"Come on, Fred," Tango said in a serious tone. "We're performers, not some managerial associates of some Parker Incorporated Agency. We entertain people. We don't run and manage hotels, or even know how to."

"I think that Tutty will have your back, Tango," Fred said in a supportive voice. "She'll be the one who'll probably take care of things. After all, she was the one who actually told her husband that we were managerial workers for your employment agency. I think that was the only way that she could convince that lamebrain husband of hers to keep us around."

"Yeah, I suppose you're right."

"Just hang in there," Fred said in an encouraging tone. "Look at it this way. This hotel just might actually be the place to take us to where we've been trying to go."

"Well, we certainly don't have anywhere else to go," Tango said in a dejected voice. "It's either this place or we hit the street."

"Are you going to give us all rooms?"

Tango suddenly glanced over at Joe, Chipper, and Elvyra as they carried on with their wild antics. He shook his head as he watched Joe, the wildest of them all, as he climbed the walls and hung upside down from the ceiling light fixture as he shrieked out his wild jungle call.

"Not right off," he said with a sigh. "Maybe in a few days I will. First, we need to wait until the Wonder Gang gets here tomorrow. They can be a big help with Chipper and Elvyra. I know Chipper is going to need his kerweekee soon and Elvyra is a prima donna who has all kind of needs, and I'm probably going to be too busy around here the next few days trying to pretend to be the assistant hotel manager of this place to tend to Chipper and Elvyra's every day needs. And Joe," he said with a deep, long sigh, "I think he's going to be a problem."

"Yeah," Fred said with a snarl as he watched Joe hanging from the ceiling light fixture. "You can bet that stupid ape moron is *definitely* going to be a big problem."

"That's why I'm going to need you to be my eyes and ears around here, old buddy," Tango said. "I'm going to need you to look after the gang when I'm not around and make sure everyone is behaving themselves."

"You got it."

"And that goes for the Wonder Gang, too. You know how wild and crazy they can get sometimes," he said in a leery voice. "We simply can't get fired because of something that one of us ends up doing that'll make Redder throw us out on the street."

"You know you can always count on me, Tango."

"I know I can, old buddy," Tango said as he gave Fred an affectionate rub on the head.

When there was a sudden knock at the door, Tango got up from the bed as he went over to the door and opened it. Zimmy Castillo, the seventeen-year-old employee of the Lucky Jackpot Hotel who worked in the custodial department, came into the room as he and Tango greeted each other like old, good friends.

Zimmy had worked on the entertainment circuit with Tango and his crew over a year ago when they were down in Mexico entertaining crowds at various carnivals and fairs. He was the emcee of many of their functions, and before he worked with Tango and his crew, he'd been in several circus outfits performing as a trapeze act, unicyclist, acrobat, and even as a flame thrower. Zimmy, like Tango, had run away at a young age to be a part of the entertainment business, which drew him close to Tango since they both had a lot in common. Zimmy and Tango, who were both experienced animal handlers, knew the ends and outs of the entertainment business well. They were virtually like brothers.

"Long time no see, old pal," Tango said with a giant smile as he and Zimmy gave each other high fives. Fred was right by their side, wanting to be near his two favorite people. He liked Zimmy almost as much as he did Tango. "How have you been, my man?"

"Apparently not as good as you," Zimmy said with a hearty laugh.

"What do you mean by that?"

"Man, word has spread all around this hotel that Abner Redder just hired you to be the new assistant hotel manager," he said as he giggled. "Please tell me it's not true."

"Oh, it's definitely true," Tango said with a sigh as he shook his head. "And furthermore, he thinks my crew over here that's acting a plum fool is part of some managerial employee agency that I run. It's called the Parker Incorporated Agency to be exact."

"You mean old man Redder has no idea whatsoever that you have performing animals that have the special ability to talk?"

"Not a clue, Zimmy," Tango said as he shook his head. "Actually, it was Mrs. Redder that cooked up this crazy hoax. I just went along with it."

"Yeah, the reason why she probably cooked up that hoax is because Abner Redder hates all animals. He wouldn't care one bit that they have this incredible, special gift. He still wouldn't allow any animal acts to be anywhere even near this hotel. You see, the owner of this hotel has this irrational phobia for all animals."

"Well, why did you write me to tell me that this hotel was hiring then?"

"I only wrote you to tell you that there was an opening in the custodial department here at this hotel, just in case you ever got tired of being out on the road. I know how those gigs can all of a sudden start drying up out there on the entertainment circuit."

"Yeah," Tango said with a nod. "I guess you would know about that better than anybody would."

"Oh, absolutely. I know the world of show business can be pretty rough sometimes," Zimmy said in a compassionate voice. "When I wrote you, I didn't really mean to imply that the hotel was looking to hire some entertainment acts, not that this dump couldn't use some better entertainment."

"What kind of entertainment does this hotel have?"

"Just some tired, old men playing a jazz ensemble in the bar and lounge area at night while twelve showgirls do their nightly dance routine on stage," Zimmy said as he shook his head in disgust. "We don't even use the main showroom anymore. Believe me. This place could *definitely* use some better form of entertainment."

"You mean like some great entertainment from a talented animal group called the Magnificent Four," Tango said as he broke into a smile.

"Dude," Zimmy said as he smiled back, "that's exactly what I mean."

"You think we'll ever get the opportunity to perform at this hotel?"

"I guess if Tutty can ever convince Redder of what he really has under his roof, or if she can somehow keep fooling him, then maybe so," he said with a slight trace of optimism.

"I hope she can."

"But don't count on it, man. Old man Redder can be pretty stubborn when he wants to be. He likes to let everyone around here know that he's the big boss and that he runs this hotel the way he wants to, which is the very reason why this dump has been steadily going downhill."

A loud crash on the other side of the room suddenly caught Tango, Zimmy, and Fred's attention. Joe had fallen from the ceiling light fixture, crashed into the dresser and had knocked it over.

The orangutan was now going berserk. He quickly rose from the floor, jumping all around the room hooping and yelping like a patient in a lunatic asylum who needed to be restrained. While Joe went ballistic, Chipper whistled *The Star-Spangled Banner* as Elvyra laughed her head off.

"I see things are pretty normal around here." Zimmy laughed.

"Yep, they are," Tango said with a sigh as he watched Joe jumping all around the room like an insane maniac. "It's pretty normal."

Zimmy suddenly got a call on his cell phone as he answered it. After having a brief conversation, he hung up as he put his cell phone back into his pocket.

"Hey, I got to head back now," Zimmy said as he looked at Tango. "Some drunk just vomited in the casino and I got to go clean it up."

"That sounds very exciting," Tango said with a chuckle.

"Yeah, we get all kind of drunks and misfits who wander in here all the time who cause all kind of disturbances," Zimmy said as he shook his head. "Hey, why don't you come with me and I can show you around a little bit. I'll introduce you to some of the staff. Plus, you've got to meet Chloe and Maria."

"Who are Chloe and Maria?"

"They work part time here at the hotel, mostly at night. They work in the concierge department. They're some pretty cool chicks and nice looking, too."

"Sure, why not."

"Great. Let's go."

As Tango and Zimmy were about to head out the door, Tango suddenly stopped as he turned around and looked over at Joe, Elvyra, and Chipper. Fred had followed Tango to the door and Tango slowly bent down on his knee next to Fred.

"Hey, boy, I want you to keep an eye on things in here for me while I'm gone," Tango said to Fred. "And don't let anybody leave out of this room. Got it?"

"You can count on me, Tango."

"Good boy," Tango said as he gave Fred a gentle pat on the head.

When Tango and Zimmy left out of the room, Fred slowly turned around and looked at the crew. Joe was still acting a plum fool, going berserk as he jumped all around the room, hooping and yelping like the jungle ape that he was.

"Alright, listen everybody," Fred said as he tried to get order in the room. "Hey, you crazy stupid ape, knock it off!"

Joe finally stopped all of his hooping, yelping, and jumping around the room as Elvyra and Chipper also began to pay attention.

"Now Tango left me in charge while he's away, and we're going to keep some order around here," Fred said in a firm voice. "So, let's hold it down in here—"

"Ah, go somewhere and dig for a bone you no fun hound," Joe exclaimed.

"I'm not a hound you stupid ape. I'm a St. Bernard!"

"Fred always likes to play the big boss whenever Tango is not around," Elvyra said with a giggle.

"Yeah, Fred," Chipper said in a hoarse voice. "Lighten up a little."

"And I bet you can't wait to light up, can you Chipper?" Elvyra said with a hearty giggle. "How long has it been since you last seen Dr. Fruitcake?"

"It's *Dr. Glittermoon*, you stupid, silly cat."

"Hey, let's roam around and see what this dump is all about," Joe said to everybody. "Let's see what we came all this way for."

"No!" Fred said as he guarded the door. "Tango says no one is to leave this room tonight."

"Listen to the big guard dog over here, everybody," Joe said with a smile. "That's all he ever was when Ivan "The Butcher" Malakhov owned us, remember? Fred was nothing but a big old stupid guard dog. He had no talent, and he still has no talent. Malakhov knew that from the very beginning. Me, Elvyra, and Chipper were the Mystical Three, performing every night on stage before Tango finally came along, felt sorry for the big mutt and decided to make him part of the group."

"Oh, leave Freddy alone, Joe," Elvyra said in a sympathetic voice. "He tries really hard."

"Oh, yeah, Fred's got a whole lot of talent," Joe said facetiously. "If you call a big mutt going round and round on stage trying to sniff his butt talent. Then yeah, he's got *plenty* of talent."

"Why you stupid, hairy ape—"

"Hey, y'all remember that time when we were in Paris, France a couple of years back and we were on the same bill with Igor and the Mummy?" Joe said as he suddenly cut Fred off from attacking him. "Remember that act they used to do when the mummy would hypnotize Igor, the scientist, and make him do all those silly, ridiculous things at his command? Man, I swear, that was the best act ever."

"I thought Fat Man and Little Piper at that gig in Scotland had the best act," Chipper said in a lazy voice.

"You mean that stupid duo of magicians who were each a hundred-years-old," Joe said as he pulled out a cigar from his faded brown suit and lit up. "Please, give me a break. Those two old bums could never hang with me. I'd teach both of them a quick lesson, drop them off at a nursing home, and put those two old geezers straight to bed."

"They were way better than you, you dumb ape," Fred said with a snarl.

Joe suddenly pounded his chest twice with his fist and snapped his finger. Poof! A cloud of purple smoke mushroomed in the air as a miniature propeller plane suddenly appeared with a long banner behind it that said—YOU CAN'T TURN A NO TALENT STUPID DOG INTO A STAR!

The propeller plane, with the long banner hooked behind it, buzzed and flew around Fred's head repeatedly. Fred, seething with anger, finally swatted the miniature propeller plane out of the air as it crashed and exploded.

"Hey, do y'all remember that gig we had down in Puerto Rico that time when Alvin the Leach performed on the same bill with us?" Joe asked.

"Sure do," Chipper said. "He was that pickpocket magician who could rob everybody in the audience of all of their money and valuables while standing on stage."

"That's right," Joe said as he puffed on his cigar and brandished a big smile. "Now that was one fine magician."

"I remember him." Elvyra purred as her black and white fur suddenly began to change multiple shades of color as if she were blushing. "I liked him. He was *really* nice."

"What man haven't you liked, Elvyra?" Chipper said with a chuckle. "You know when it comes to men, Elvyra, you've been just like a big cruise ship. Over the years, you've invited so many men from all around the world to come cruise on your ship that they've started to call you the International Harlot Cruise Line."

"I'm getting really hungry for that parrot stew once again!" Elvyra said to Chipper in a tart voice as she swished her tail.

"Hey, do y'all remember that time when we performed down in Brazil?" Joe said with a wide smile.

"Now you're talking about my native homeland, Joe," Chipper said with reverence as his left eye suddenly began to beam out like a red sun setting over the sea. "Man, there's no place in the world that's better than the Amazon Rainforest," he said with deep fondness in his voice. "It's where the weather is always warm, the music is right, and the kerweekee is plentiful."

"Wish you there right now, don't you?" Elvyra giggled. "I bet you could smoke up all the kerweekee that the rainforest has right about now. Couldn't you?"

"Shut up, you international slut." Chipper grumbled. "Go make a port-a-call somewhere."

"Hey, we've performed virtually all over the world, but we've never performed here in Las Vegas before," Joe said with fondness. "Wouldn't it be great if we were to get a big time gig in one of these grand, fabulous hotels here in Vegas instead of this dump that we're in now."

"Yeah, I guess it would," Chipper said.

"Sure, why not," Elvyra said with a giggle.

"I mean just picture it," Joe said as he puffed on his cigar. "We'd ride up in a limousine to one of these grand, luxurious hotels and a bellboy would be right there to serve us and wait on us hand and foot."

Joe quickly did his magical ritual again and poof! After the purple smoke had faded, Fred was suddenly garbed in a brown and white bellboy uniform with a cap on his head that said BELLBOY.

"Look at Fred." Elvyra giggled. "Don't Freddy look cute."

"There ain't a St. Bernard dog that looks better." Chipper added.

"Bellboy, go get our luggage!" Joe shouted with a hearty laugh as he puffed on his cigar. "And hop to it!"

Fred, all dressed up in his bellboy uniform, looked at Joe, Elvyra, and Chipper as they laughed their heads off. Knowing he was the butt of the joke, Fred began to slowly shake his head. "I guess that's what you get from being around a stupid, moron ape," he said as he let out a long, agonizing sigh.

Two malicious looking bank robbers had everyone inside the Third Union National Bank lying face down on the floor as they robbed the place. The bank customers lying on the floor watched the gun wielding robbers in terror as the robbers demanded the bank teller behind the counter to fill up their bag with all the cash. The bank teller behind the counter had already secretly pushed the button for help as she continued to fill up the bank robbers' money bag. She, and probably everyone else who was being held up, could only hope that help would come quickly.

Suddenly, like the strong gust of a hurricane, a beautiful, dashing woman wearing a long white flowing cape, black tights, and had Madam Cureall going across her armored shield, came storming through the bank doors. The robbers immediately became petrified at the sight of this magnificent superhero. Madam Cureall was known far and wide for helping the defenseless and putting down crime wherever crime popped up its evil head. She was feared and loathed by evildoers, and on the flip side, loved and cherished by millions around the world who supported justice and the sanctity of life.

"Look, it's Madam Cureall!" one of the bank robbers said with a terrified shriek. "What do we do?"

"Shoot her!"

The two bank robbers started firing their guns at Madam Cureall as she immediately caught the bullets in her hand as if the hot flying bullets were merely flies. Seeing that their futile efforts had failed against Madam Cureall's awesome super powers, the bank robbers tried to make a quick getaway. Madam Cureall, however, quickly shot a huge net out of her armored shield at the fleeing bank robbers as the net ensnarled the robbers, thwarting their getaway.

The people in the bank, who'd feared for their lives only moments ago, immediately erupted with cheers of celebration when the bank robbers were captured. A chant of 'The great Madam Cureall, we love you! We love you!' suddenly kept reverberating over and over among the jubilant crowd in the bank.

Mama Lulu slowly began to wake up from her dream as she suddenly realized that she was back in the comfort of her cozy bedroom. Her bedroom definitely had the look of an eighty-year-old woman who didn't want to let go of the past. Antiques were everywhere. Two old wooden dressers were propped up against two of the walls, a decrepit looking nightstand stood next to her bed, and decades old porcelain figures and little trinkets of all varieties literally cluttered the shelves of her bedroom. But what stood out in the midst of all the antique junk that she had stored in her bedroom, was the massive cuckoo clock that hung on the wall near her bed.

The cuckoo clock on her wall, which was a foot wide and two feet in height, was an automation clock of an old farmhouse that contained a barn, silo, and the farmhouse itself that had a chimney. An old mechanical farmer, wearing old dingy overalls and a big floppy straw hat who Mama Lulu precisely named Benny, would always come out of the farmhouse on a mechanical track carrying a pitch fork in his hand when the clock struck on the hour.

The automation cuckoo clock had now been in Mama Lulu's possession for over fifty years and it was her pride and joy. Over the years, Mama Lulu had sweet talked, flattered, and cajoled the mechanical farmer with the pitch fork so much, that the mechanical farmer had literally become a species of the human race. He could talk, communicate, and associate with anyone, which Mama Lulu loved to death. Although Benny was now part of the human race, he was never one to be kind.

Always coming out of the farmhouse with a perpetual scowl on his face, he often got into heated spats with Mama Lulu and he was *always* demeaning her.

Mama Lulu, although she loved her precious Benny with a powerful love that no one could match, often kept a baseball bat beside her bed just in case Benny got out of line, which he often did. The sight of the old, shambled farmhouse was clear evidence of just that. It had more dents, knocks, and bangs in it from where Mama Lulu had often taken her baseball bat and whacked the living daylights out of the farmhouse when Benny had gotten out of line.

When Mama Lulu had finally awakened from her nighttime slumber, she turned on her lamp on the nightstand next to her bed as she immediately opened the nightstand drawer. She rummaged through the drawer and pulled out all of the mounds of coloring books that she had stored in the drawer. When she found the coloring book *The Great Adventures of Madam Cureall,* she immediately smiled as she quickly began to flip through it.

The coloring book, which was one of literally dozens that Tutty had bought for her over the last couple of months, was filled with pages of adventure that the super heroine, Madam Cureall, had been engaged in. Mama Lulu's smile began to spread even further when she realized that she'd not only just dreamt the same action sequences as the coloring book portrayed, but she, herself, had become the glorious superhero Madam Cureall in her dream.

It was the fifth straight night that Mama Lulu had dreamt that she was the great Madam Cureall, and Mama Lulu couldn't be any happier than she was at the present moment. The pages inside the coloring book may have looked like some first grader had colored the pages because they were so messy and colored all outside the lines, but at the moment, Mama Lulu could've cared less how she'd colored her coloring book. The only thing that mattered was that she had become the great Madam Cureall, and absolutely nothing could top that.

After scanning through a couple pages of *The Great Adventures of Madam Cureall*, Mama Lulu put aside the coloring book as she looked at the farmhouse cuckoo clock on the wall near her nightstand. It was 2:59 a.m. and Mama Lulu was ready for some nighttime company. As three o'clock neared, her bright smile began to blaze even brighter, as if she were a little girl waiting for her father to come home from work with a sack full of candy. She was in her pajamas between the sheets of her bed with her gray hair sticking all over her head, counting down the seconds to three o'clock.

"Benny," Mama Lulu called toward the farmhouse cuckoo clock with a giant smile when 3 a.m. finally struck. "It's time to come out. It's three o'clock." She waited a couple of seconds for her pride and joy to come out. "Benny, where are you?" she called once again. "I've got something to tell you."

Suddenly Benny, the three inch high mechanical farmer dressed in old, dingy overalls and wearing a big floppy straw hat, came out of the farmhouse on a mechanical track holding a pitch fork. He had a nasty, surly scowl, as he always did, but tonight the scowl seemed even more menacing.

"Woman, what in the world do you want?" he said in a bad-tempered voice. "Do you know what time it is?"

"It's three o'clock, Benny," she said in a soothing voice as she continued to smile. "You know what that means?"

"It means that you're a loony wacko nut, woman, if you thought that I was going to come out here at the top of the hour," he said as he glared at Mama Lulu. "I was sleeping good until you woke me up. I've got to get up early in the morning and tend to this farm. I ain't got time to talk to you."

"Benny, I just had another marvelous dream," Mama Lulu said as her smile brightened even wider. "This time I dreamed that I stopped a bunch of mean old bank robbers from robbing a bank. I stopped the bank robbers cold in their tracks and all the people in the bank loved me for it. They shouted and cheered their love and appreciation for my great deed. Wasn't that wonderful of them?"

"You woke me up to tell me about some stupid Madam Cureall coloring books again?" Benny said with spite. "Woman, you got more than a screw loose, you missing all of the nuts, bolts, and washers, too. At least all the kings men thought they could put Humpty Dumpty back together, but I don't think even Radio Shack got enough bolts, nuts, and washers to even attempt to try to put you back together."

"You watch what you say to me, Benny," Mama Lulu said as she suddenly pointed a firm finger at him. "I've raised you to be a good, wholesome farmer and I won't tolerate no mean back talk. I've been a good mother to you, Benny."

"If you were my mother, I'd sue the state to become an orphan."

"Why you—"

"Benny, who in the world are you out here talking to this late at night?" a woman said as she suddenly raised the bedroom window to the farmhouse and stuck her head out.

"Who else, but the greatest loony tune of them all."

"Oh, it's you, Mama Lulu," the woman said with a smile. "How have you been, girl?"

"Edna, I just had me the most incredible dream," Mama Lulu said with a bright smile. "I dreamed that I stopped some mean old bank robbers from robbing a bank, and when I did, all of the people in the bank cheered and praised me."

"Oh, that's so wonderful, girl," the woman said with a giant smile. "You must be having those Madam Cureall dreams again."

"Edna, don't be edging her on!" Benny snapped. "She's already loony enough as it is now!"

"Benny, now you be kind to dear, sweet Mama Lulu," she said in a caring voice. "She just needs somebody to listen to her. Mama Lulu is as sweet as they come. If she said she stopped a bunch of bank robbers and the people all praised her, then you be happy for her great achievement."

"Thank you, Edna," Mama Lulu said with a smile.

"Her great achievement." Benny let out a sarcastic huff. "As dumb as that woman is, if she could learn to tie her shoes, that would be a great achievement for her."

"Benny, you stop talking mean about Mama Lulu or I'm not letting you back into this house!" she said angrily. "And first thing come morning, I want you to fix the roof of this farmhouse. It's a shame how you've let this farmhouse go to shambles all this time. Just look at how that roof looks. It's all beat up, torn to pieces, and falling down."

"Woman, don't start nagging me about that roof again!" Benny yelled. "Every time I fix it, this loony woman out here just starts beating at it all over again."

"Well, it's because of your ornery mouth that she does," she said in a scolding voice. "Now first thing come morning, you get started fixing on that roof, and I don't want to hear another word about it!"

The woman slammed the bedroom window down as Benny let out a long sigh.

"I got a nagging wife and a stupid dumbbell for a neighbor," Benny said as he glared at Mama Lulu. "Listen, I got a lot of work to do around this farm in the morning. Can I go back into the house and go to sleep, or is there something else you wanted to tell me."

"There is something else."

"What is it?"

"Well, there was this old mangy ape, this bird, cat, and a dog that came here tonight and they were actually talking. But it was that old, mean mangy ape that I couldn't stand," Mama Lulu said in a heated voice as her pleasant disposition turned to anger. "Somehow, that old mangy ape did this magic stuff and made these big men all of a sudden appear. Those big men strapped this white jacket around me where I couldn't even move and they stuffed this cloth thing into my mouth where I couldn't say a word. And I swear," Mama Lulu said as she suddenly balled up her fist, "I'm going to get that old, mangy ape if it's the last thing that I do!"

"Sounds like you were in a straitjacket and your mouth was gagged."

"It was," Mama Lulu said in a riled voice. "And I swear I'm going to get that old mangy ape for what he did to me."

"Well, you tell that old mangy ape to come talk to me."

"What for?"

"Because the next time I want him to put you on a boat, sail you out to sea, and torpedo the stupid thing."

Benny suddenly went back into the farmhouse as Mama Lulu became even more riled. She slowly climbed out of bed, grabbed the baseball bat lying next to the nightstand, and went to swinging at the old farmhouse like an eighty-year-old Babe Ruth.

"You come back out here this instant Benny and apologize!" Mama Lulu yelled as she banged the living daylights out of the farmhouse. "You hear me?"

"Benny, what did you say to her this time?" Edna yelled from inside the farmhouse.

"I didn't say nothing to that old nitwit!"

"You always running your mouth causing her to get mad!"

"Ah, she's just loony as a dumb bat is all!"

"You go back out there and apologize! She's going to tear this house down!"

"I ain't going back out there, woman!"

"WELL, WE AIN'T GOING TO GET NO SLEEP AROUND HERE UNTIL YOU DO!"

Benny and Edna's argument inside the farmhouse continued to escalate as Mama Lulu kept right on swinging and hitting homeruns.

A little after 3 a. m. that night as the crew was fast asleep on the floor, Tango finally came back into the dark room. He immediately stripped from his clothes down to his underwear and climbed into bed. As soon as his head hit the pillow, he quickly drifted off to sleep.

Fred, lying on the floor next to Tango's bed, watched his master as he slept peacefully under the sheets of his bed. As Tango slept, Fred couldn't help but remember the first day that Tango acquired ownership of him, Joe, Elvyra, and Chipper.

Their previous owner at the time, a shoddy, unscrupulous handler named Sanchez Rodriguez, was afraid that the animals' original owner, a notorious Russian mobster named Ivan "The Butcher" Malakhov, was beginning to get close to finding the whereabouts of his stolen animals. Rodriguez was afraid that he was about to be eliminated by Malakhov's henchmen, as a few of the unfortunate previous owners before him were. Fearing for his life and ailing sick, Rodriguez practically gave Tango the animals when they happened to be in the same hospital clinic down in Mexico when Tango gave him blood to stay alive; a rare blood type that only Tango possessed at the time.

Tango, barely thirteen-years-old at the time and a runaway, was a good-natured kid that Fred took a liking to right away. He knew that Tango was going to be the best owner that they'd ever had, and he certainly wasn't wrong. Compared to all the other crooked, deceitful owners that they'd come into contact with over the time of them being in show business, Tango had been virtually a saint, which drew Fred even closer to the good natured kid.

But Fred, having a strong affinity and a close knit bond with their lovable owner, also feared for Tango's well-being and safety. He knew that Malakhov and his henchmen were still out there somewhere, and he knew that if he and the rest of the crew ever started to become successful, he had a strong feeling that Malakhov and his henchmen would someday come after them. It was a thought that often made Fred shudder and tremble at night, because he knew one day, those dark shadows could very well come lurking.

As Fred pondered over those things in the darkness of the room, Elvyra suddenly awoke from her slumber as she rose from the floor. Fred watched the black and white Siamese cat as she jumped onto Tango's bed and began to rub and nestle up against him as he slept. Elvyra always had a frisky nature about her whenever it came to men; men were her mice and she loved to devour them in the most scrumptious way.

"Tango, wake up," Elvyra whispered into his ear as she giggled. "It's time to play with the kitty."

"Cut it out, Elvyra," Tango said with his eyes closed as he tried to continue his sleep. But Elvyra wasn't about to leave him alone.

"Come on, sweet cutie." Elvyra crawled over his chest and whispered into his other ear in a sexy voice. "It's been way too long and you know you still want it."

"Cut it out, Elvyra," he grumbled a little louder as he buried his face in his pillow. "Go back to sleep."

"You look all up tight and stressed out. Let kitty give you a special massage," she said flirtatiously as she began to slowly weave and sway her body down Tango's chest. "Does that tickle?" she giggled.

"Elvyra, no."

"Don't say no," she said as her feline body began to glow in the dark, changing colors like a neon motel sign flickering in the night. The motel sign even flashed the words—*Vacancy For Two*. "Come on," she purred as she weaved her way back up to his ear. "Kitty is so hot and horny tonight. Come on, let's do it."

When Tango began to snore slightly, Elvyra finally gave up her quest. The frisky Siamese cat all of a sudden began to emit a cloud of green smoke from her body that matched the color of her emerald green eyes. She suddenly transformed from a Siamese cat into a beautiful six-foot Mexican bombshell of a woman like the werecat that she was.

Standing beside Tango's bedside wearing nothing but a black see through negligee, she slowly placed her hands on her hips as she stared down at Tango as he slept.

"Tango, you know you're mine," she said as she began to play with her long, beautiful black hair. "And, sweetie, I just want you to know that I'm never *ever* letting you go."

A musical theatrical song began.

Elvyra turned on the main stage and faced the audience as she began to dance and sing a song for her deep love for Tango as the Magic Rainbow Hotel & Casino Orchestra played a romantic number. A line of showgirls, dressed in glittering gold G-string bottoms, rhinestone-encrusted bras, and huge feathery headdresses, suddenly formed a line behind Elvyra on the main stage as they began to dance and sing along with her.

"My love for Tango started one late evening night on a beach down in Cancun, Mexico," Elvyra sung as the orchestra played a romantic melody. "We made love on the beach all alone as the moon casted its love down on us."

"*Oh, how sweet*," the showgirls sung in unison.

"I may have had a few other lovers since Tango and I first christened our love, but there's never been another who's touched my heart the way he has."

"*Your heart always speaks the truth*."

"The truth of the matter is I've been foolish, letting others corral my love with a little sweet flattery or a pretty face," she sung. "But I know now that my real love lies right here, and I'll never stray again from my true love."

"*Is this really sincere?*"

"It's truly sincere." Elvyra suddenly turned and gazed down at Tango fondly as he slept. "You're mine forever, my sweet cutie," she crooned to him as the violins of the orchestra swoon and fluttered softly. "Is that clear, my dear?"

The musical theatrical song came to a smooth ending as the audience inside the Magic Rainbow Hotel & Casino Theater applauded as the showgirls faded away. When the scene on the main stage returned to normal, Elvyra began to emit a green fog once again as she turned back into the black and white Siamese cat. She climbed back onto the bed and nestled up against Tango as he slept.

"Sleep tight, my sweet thing," she whispered into his ear as she giggled. "I'll see you in the morning."

Elvyra jumped down from the bed as she went back to her spot on the floor, curled up, and went back to sleep.

Fred had watched the whole affair from his position on the floor. For a long time he, along with Chipper and Joe, knew that Elvyra and Tango had intertwined love many times in the past. However, lately Tango had been dismissing Elvyra whenever she would try to seduce him and Fred knew the reason for that.

Tango, when he first took ownership of them, had fallen deeply in love with Elvyra and he simply couldn't do without her. But Elvyra, the free spirit that she was, often latched onto other men like a vivacious cat lusting after fish, and soon it wasn't long before Tango's heart was broken.

Over time, to prevent any further sorrow to his lovesick heart, Tango simply removed any physical relationship that he had with Elvyra. Instead, he decided to just keep their relationship merely platonic, or in the very least, strictly a business relationship. But Fred knew that for Tango, trying to keep Elvyra's lustful attempts at bay was like trying to keep a bull from charging at a red cape. Elvyra was the type of girl that liked to have her cake and eat it too.

Fred knew that Tango was a good, decent owner, and as much as he cared for him dearly, he didn't want to see him get his heart broken anymore by Elvyra's attempts at love. But there was another reason why Fred wanted Elvyra to stay away from Tango. Fred, himself, had eyes for the mysterious cat named Elvyra.

Tango was nervous as he stood outside Abner and Tutty's residential suite as he got ready to ring their doorbell. He was dressed in a nice gold blazer jacket that had the *Lucky Jackpot Hotel* emblem on the jacket, a starched white shirt, nice black slacks, polished black shoes, and a black tie on. The whole clothing arrangement had been sent over last night by Tutty for him to wear on his first day on the job as assistant hotel manager, and Tango had never looked so dapper in his entire life. He was totally out of his comfort zone and he knew it. Used to wearing nothing but scrubby jeans, sneakers, and a T-shirt, he now looked like a business professional ready to take on the corporate business world. There was only one problem though; he knew absolutely nothing about being an assistant hotel manager.

Seeing that it was getting close to 7:45 a.m. on his watch, Tango took a deep breath and rang Abner and Tutty's doorbell. He didn't want to be late for his first assistant hotel manager's meeting with the big boss. There was a lot to discuss and he had a feeling that Abner Redder would probably hit the ceiling if he were even the slightest bit late.

After ringing the doorbell for a second time, Tutty finally opened the door. She casually smoked on a cigarette as she stood in the doorway, glancing over him from head to toe as if he were a male fashion model getting ready to stroll down a runway. She slowly puffed on her cigarette, checking every aspect of him when all of a sudden she nodded.

"You look nice," she finally said with a smile. "Come on in."

Tutty ushered the nervous new hotel assistant manager into the parlor. Only Mama Lulu was sitting in the parlor when they entered. She sat in her favorite armchair and immediately became hostile when she saw Tango.

"Where is that mangy ape of yours?" Mama Lulu blurted out as she suddenly balled up her fist. "I'm going to skin his hairy hide. Where is he at, boy?"

"Mama Lulu, now you just sit over there and be quiet until it's time for your psychiatrist appointment," Tutty said to Mama Lulu. "Me and this young gentleman have some very important things that we need to discuss."

"You tell that mangy ape of yours that I'm going to—"

"Mama Lulu, zip it!" Tutty said in a firm voice as she pointed a finger at her.

When Mama Lulu clammed up, Tutty turned her focus back to their new assistant hotel manager.

"Mrs. Redder, I'm a little nervous about this whole thing," Tango said in a somewhat shaky voice. "I didn't want to be late for the meeting, so I hurried on over here as soon as I got dressed."

"Call me Tutty, and you're not late," she said as she fixed the knot in his tie, making sure that it looked just right. "Your meeting with my husband is at eight o'clock. I wanted you to come early so we can get a few things out of the way."

"Like what?"

"First of all, you need to sign an agreement with the Lucky Jackpot Hotel stating that you are indeed the sole owner of these performing animals and you're giving us the exclusive rights to use them in an entertainment capacity," Tutty said as she handed Tango a contract on a clipboard. "The contract is for a year."

Tango slowly looked over the contract, and for a second, he was a little hesitant to sign it. Even though Tango had signed papers from the animals' previous owner that showed that he had ownership of the animals, he was still a little apprehensive whenever he had to sign a contract, knowing the tangled history with the original owner, Ivan "The Butcher" Malakhov.

"Is there a problem?" Tutty said in a skeptical voice.

"No," Tango finally said as he scribbled his name on the contract and gave the clipboard back to her. "No problem."

"Alright, there are a few things you need to know," she said as she stared Tango straight in the eyes. "Never—*ever*—mention that you have animals on the premises of this hotel in the presence of my husband. He doesn't like children and he has this crazy irrational fear of animals of all kind. He'll literary start breathing heavily, shouting, and become extremely angry and have an explosive attack if he knew that any animals were on the facility of this hotel. A couple years ago we had an animal act to perform at the hotel for a single day, and my husband almost had a heart attack he became so angry."

"Why does he hate animals so much?"

"One time when he was a little kid, a dog bit him and gave him rabies and he never got over that," she said. "Same thing happened another time when he was a kid and he went to the zoo. A monkey got loose from his cage, chased him all around the zoo, bit him on the butt, and he got rabies once again. Ever since those two incidents, he's had this crazy irrational fear of animals."

"Well, why does he hate kids?"

"Some years back when he was a young tree logger working in the woods, this group of kids would come to the woods every day to tease him and throw rocks at him," Tutty said with a chuckle. "Ever since then, he couldn't stand children."

"Tutty, I'm a little nervous about all of this," Tango once again said in a shaken voice. "I mean, what do I supposed to do as an assistant hotel manager?"

"Don't worry, young man, I'll have your back," she said in a supportive voice. "I know you're very young, inexperienced, and you didn't intend to come to this hotel to accept some managerial position, but right now let's not rock the boat. I've just got to find a way to tell my husband of this incredible discovery that's under our roof at this hotel without him having a heart attack. If these animals are as good as they seem to be, this could virtually mean millions and millions of dollars for this hotel."

"But what am I supposed to do in the mean time being the hotel assistant manager—"

"You just be yourself," Tutty said as she tried to ease his fears. "I'll guide you along on the requirements that a hotel assistant manager must implement. To be quite frank with you, you certainly can't do any worse than what my incompetent husband has been doing all of these years running this hotel into the ground with all of his bumbling decisions," she said with a crack. "You just remember to smile and be courteous to all the guests. And if you're ever in doubt of what to do or need something answered, then you come to me. Understand?"

Tango slowly nodded.

"Now, I've already informed the entire hotel staff about the animals and I told them to never mention that we have these talking animals whenever my husband is around," Tutty quickly said. "Now my husband likes to roam around the hotel from time to time, so just be on the lookout for him. He may be blind, but Abner has the sense of a seeing eye dog. So he certainly knows his way around this hotel."

"Well, what do I supposed to do with my animals until you're able to tell your husband about them?" Tango said in an unsure voice. "They're performing animals, you know. They're not used to being locked up in a room for some long period of time."

"Yeah, I know," Tutty said with a long sigh. "Okay, just find them something to do around the hotel. Maybe by having the animals out and about around the hotel, we can get them ingratiated with all the hotel guests and they'll want to see these incredible animals perform. Maybe that'll build up some kind of demand for them."

"Well, how are you going to keep it from your husband then?" Tango replied. "Surely some of the guests will let it be known to your husband about the animals."

"You just let me worry about that," Tutty said in an assured voice as she gave him a wink. "But right now, it's eight o'clock and it's time to go see the big boss for your first meeting as the new hotel assistant manager," she said with a smile. "So, come on."

Tutty escorted Tango into Abner's private office. Abner, with his black sunglasses on, big as a sumo wrestler, and wearing one of his favorite multi-colored suits, sat behind his desk in his office listening to a recorded tape of the hotel's projected inventory cost figures that Tutty had recorded for him. Tutty was his sole secretary, and with him being blind, Abner often relied on Tutty to keep him abreast with the hotel cost figures, the profit and loss margin, and other important hotel items that he needed to know.

"Abner," Tutty said as she approached his desk, "Mr. Parker is here for his eight o'clock meeting."

"Oh, Mr. Parker," Abner said as he turned off the recorded tape. "Well, have a seat, Mr. Parker. We have a lot of things to discuss."

Tango had a seat in a chair in front of Abner's desk. The nervousness he felt quivering through his body suddenly took over him and he immediately began to bite his nails. Tutty quickly put a comforting hand on Tango's shoulder as he sat in the chair.

"Abner, I've already discussed a lot of the important matters about the hotel to Mr. Parker—"

"Tutty, you may be excused now." Abner interrupted her as he leaned back in his chair. "I want to have a private consultation with my new assistant hotel manager."

"I may be *excused*," she said as she glared at Abner. "Now hold on—"

"Woman, I'm the president of this hotel, not you." He snapped like an angry bear. "You seem to forget that you're my secretary, and I don't need no advice from my secretary."

"Mister, you need all the advice you can—"

"Woman, if I need some shorthand or dictation done, I'll call you," Abner bellowed out. "But for now, please leave the office!"

Tutty gave Abner a look that could kill a vicious wolf if they were in a stare off. She slowly looked down at Tango as he sat in the chair and mouthed the words "*just be calm*" then she turned and headed out of the office.

"Women," Abner said with a chuckle when the door closed. "They never know when to leave you alone, and they always think they can do something better than a man."

Abner's office phone suddenly began to ring on his desk. When he answered the phone, Tango took the time to scan and survey the surroundings of the office.

The room looked like a normal office with a filing cabinet, computer, and other assorted stuff that made an office complete, but what struck Tango's curiosity was the unique looking cuckoo clock on the wall behind Abner's desk. It was a nice size cuckoo clock that resembled a fire station. The fire station even had a pole for the fireman to come down from.

"Sorry for that interruption, Mr. Parker," Abner said when he hung up. "But there's always something going on around this hotel that needs my attention."

Tango, still somewhat nervous, wanted to start the conversation off on a light note between him and his new boss, so he focused on the unique looking cuckoo clock that resembled a fire station on the wall behind Abner's desk.

"Mr. Redder, that's a very unique looking cuckoo clock that you have there on the wall behind you," Tango said as he gave Abner a smile. "You don't find many cuckoo clocks that look like that. It looks very valuable. I know you probably love that clock to death."

"I hate it!" Abner said with a snarl.

"Sir?"

"My mother gave me that stupid cuckoo clock years ago and I've hated it ever since," he said with a grumble. "She has four other clocks like that all around this house. She has a thing for those stupid cuckoo clocks. That's the only reason why I even put up with them. This one here is a fire station, and I can't stand that stupid mechanical fireman that comes out of it. My mother calls him Benny."

"Oh, I didn't know," Tango said with a whimper, wishing now he hadn't said anything about the cuckoo clock. "Sorry, sir."

"Well, let's get down to business," Abner said with authority. "Mr. Parker, as you may have noticed, the Lucky Jackpot Hotel is much different then all of these other fancy high rise hotel casinos that you see around here in Las Vegas. I had this grand, luxurious hotel built from the ground up to suit my sophisticated tastes."

"You built a dump, you fat hippo!" the three inch mechanical fireman shouted as he suddenly came out of the fire station, then quickly dashed back inside.

"What?" Abner said in confusion. "Oh, that must've been that stupid fireman. Don't pay him no mind, Mr. Parker. He's nothing but a little pest," he said with an angry huff. "Now, where was I?"

"You were telling me how you had this grand, luxurious hotel built, sir," Tango said with a trace of nervousness.

"Yes, that's right," Abner said as he regained his train of thought. "Well, never mind that. Mr. Parker, I want to get right to the point of why I hired you. I expect—*no I demand*—that you bring in some conventions to the Lucky Jackpot Hotel within the next few weeks. We haven't had any conventions to come through here in over a year and business has been down because of that. So that's your project, Mr. Parker," he said as his voice rose. "Start working on how you'll bring some conventions to the Lucky Jackpot Hotel. I expect a thorough report from you on my desk by the end of this week."

"Pardon me, sir," Tango said sheepishly, "but how do you think I should go about doing that?"

"You have your own managerial staff don't you? You said you run the Parker Incorporated Agency, correct?"

"Oh, that," Tango said nervously as he suddenly felt his stomach turn three flips. "Yes, sir. That's correct."

"Well, get your staff to help you. That Beasley fellow, Mr. Blue Hendrix, and that Ms. Romeno Mendez sounded like some very competent managerial associates of yours. On the other hand, that other fellow who said he was once a former dog catcher. What was his name again?"

"Oh, you mean Bob."

"Yeah, he was the only one on your staff who didn't sound too bright to me," Abner said with a hearty chuckle. "I don't know how in the world he was able to get into the hotel managerial industry."

"Well, Bob is very resourceful and smart," Tango said nervously. "You just have to get to know him."

"By the way, Mr. Parker, my work load around here keeps increasing every day and I could certainly use another secretary around here besides my nagging wife," Abner said. "Do you mind if Ms. Romeno Mendez come and work for me from time to time?"

"Well, no," Tango said hesitantly. "Not at all."

"Good," Abner said as he suddenly broke into a smile. "By the way, Mr. Parker, that Ms. Mendez sounded mighty good last night. Is she hot?"

"Oh, yes. She's pretty hot, sir."

"I mean is she *hot hot*?"

"Yes, sir, she's really hot."

"I mean is she—*SIZZLING HOT?*" he yelled with a lustful smile.

Siren! Siren! Siren!

Red flashing lights suddenly lit up from the fire station cuckoo clock on the wall behind Abner's desk as a wailing siren began to shriek out. Benny, the three inch high mechanical fireman dressed in a red, shiny fireman suit, quickly came down the fire pole carrying a fire hose.

"What's hot?" Benny shouted. "Where's the fire?"

Benny suddenly sprayed a blast of water from his fire hose down on Abner's head.

"Fat man on fire!" Benny yelled as he kept spraying. "Fat man on fire!"

When Benny finally turned the spigot off and dashed back into the fire station, Abner was drenching wet and madder than a pack of bees. The fire station siren had suddenly gone silent as Abner sat in his chair, huffing and puffing like a mad rhino.

"THAT STUPID CUCKOO CLOCK!" he yelled.

"What in the world is going on in here?" Tutty suddenly barged into Abner's office. "Oh, I see Benny must've sprayed you," she said with a snicker when she glanced at Abner who was dripping wet. "Do you need your lowly trusted secretary to get you a towel, sir?"

"Just get out of here and close the door!"

Tutty went out laughing as Abner tried to dry his face.

"Now, where were we?" he said with a gruff tone.

"You wanted to know about Elvy—" Tango said as he quickly caught himself. "I mean you wanted to know about Ms. Mendez, sir. You wanted to know if she was ho—"

"DON'T SAY THE WORD!"

"Sorry, sir."

"Let's just continue on with our meeting," Abner said as he continued drying his face. "Mr. Parker, the most important thing here at this hotel is that our guests receive the best service. I want happy guests here at the Lucky Jackpot Hotel. That will come up under your department to see that all guests are happy here at this hotel at all times. You'll have an office near the front lobby of the hotel that's not far from the casino, the bar and lounge area, and our restaurant. You are to take care of any complaints or issues that any of our guests may call to your office with and see to it that they are resolved to the satisfaction of our guests. Understood?"

"Yes, sir."

"Now, another reason why I hired you, Mr. Parker, is that here at the Lucky Jackpot Hotel, we need an overhaul with our entertainment department. When I heard that one of your managerial associates was once a former concert promoter, I knew that your team could probably put together some ideas to help improve the entertainment around here. So, what kind of suggestions do you have?"

"Well, sir, you could maybe try putting on a course of plays during a particular week that have the same theme related with it," Tango said hesitantly. "Then the following week, you could have a whole new set of plays that have a totally different set of related themes."

"Sounds interesting. What else?"

"You could maybe have the showgirls put on a musical several nights a week."

"I already have the showgirls performing in a skit every night. What else do you have?"

"Well," Tango said as he pondered, "once I remember seeing this act where this monkey was giving this dog a bath and the audience—"

"What did you say?" Abner said harshly. "I don't want no animal acts around here. Do you hear me?" he yelled as he started breathing heavily.

"Oh, sorry, sir." Tango quickly apologized. "I didn't mean to—"

"YOU BRING ANY ANIMAL ACTS TO THIS HOTEL AND YOU'RE FIRED!"

"Yes, sir," Tango said with a cringe.

"Even hearing about some animals literally burns me up!"

Siren! Siren! Siren!

Flashing lights once again lit up the fire station cuckoo clock as a wailing siren began to shriek out. Benny quickly came down the fire pole once again carrying a fire hose.

"Something burning?" Benny said in a panicked voice as he immediately began to spray Abner's head full blast with his fire hose. "Don't worry folks. The fire will be put out in just a second." Benny began to ramble on as if he were talking to a group of people who'd suddenly gathered on the street as they watched a building on fire. "Benny's Fire Department will always make sure that the public is safe and that all fires are put out, folks. It's just fat man blowing off steam and he needs cooling off, people. Everything will be taken care of, folks."

When Benny turned off the spigot to the fire hose, he quickly dashed back into the fire station as the siren went silent. Abner was once again soaking wet and madder than hell.

"THAT STUPID CUCKOO CLOCK!" he bellowed out like an angry elephant.

Tango tried to be of some assistance to his soaking wet boss as he pulled out a handkerchief from his pocket.

"Sir, I have a handkerchief if you need—"

"I don't need no handkerchief!" he shouted as he wiped the water raining down his face with his hand. "You just make sure those guests out there are happy. Now get out there and make my hotel the best in all of Las Vegas. I'm not paying you to sit around here and twiddle your thumbs!" he yelled as he suddenly smashed his desk with his fist. "GET TO WORK—AND I MEAN PRONTO!"

"Yes, sir!" Tango quickly said.

He jumped up out of his chair and flew out of Abner's office faster than a crook running from the law.

Tutty arrived with Mama Lulu at Dr. Leachman's office for Mama Lulu's weekly ten o'clock appointment to see her psychiatrist. For over a year now, Tutty had brought Mama Lulu to see a psychiatrist for her ongoing psychosis problem.

Mama Lulu's psychosis problem started years ago but it became worse when Tutty first began to buy Mama Lulu those Madam Cureall coloring books from the grocery store. At the time, Mama Lulu had been so down and depressed that when she first saw the Madam Cureall coloring books in the grocery store aisle and her face lit up like a child at Christmas time, Tutty couldn't help but to buy them for her. However, when Mama Lulu started becoming attached to the characters in the coloring books, she began to develop an irrational obsession for all things related to Madam Cureall.

The examples were plenty. One morning Tutty came into Mama Lulu's bedroom and found Mama Lulu's bed sheet tied around her neck as Mama Lulu imitated the white cape that the superhero, Madam Cureall, wore in her coloring books. Another time Tutty came into Mama Lulu's bedroom and discovered a lampshade on her head as Mama Lulu imitated the gold crown that the beautiful queen, Madam Cureall, wore in another version of one of her coloring books. And another time Tutty found Mama Lulu one day with her nylon stocking over her head as she imitated Madam Cureall as an undercover secret agent. Mama Lulu's psychosis was an ongoing problem and her weekly visits were always interesting.

Dr. Leachman gave Tutty and Mama Lulu a big, courteous smile when they finally entered his office and had a seat. He was always kind and polite to Mama Lulu during her weekly visits to his office as he tried to help remedy her problem.

"Well, Mama Lulu, how are we on this lovely morning?" Dr. Leachman said with a smile as he had a seat behind his desk.

"I swear I'm going to get him!" Mama Lulu immediately began to rave as she suddenly balled up her fist and waved it in the air.

"Oh, aren't we all in a rage this morning," Dr. Leachman said with a smile. "And just who are you going to get, Mama Lulu?"

"That old mangy ape!" Mama Lulu said with a grouch. "I'm going to skin his hairy hide!"

"It's not like Mama Lulu to come to our session in such a hostile mood," Dr. Leachman said to Tutty with concern. "Is this ape some new character in the Madam Cureall coloring books?"

"No, you see doctor, this fifteen-year-old kid who has these trained performing show animals has come to the Lucky Jackpot Hotel looking for work, and one of the animals happens to be this performing ape that Mama Lulu doesn't like very much," Tutty said. "Let's just say that he's rubbed Mama Lulu the wrong way."

"Performing show animals," Dr. Leachman said in a confused voice. "But I thought that your husband doesn't care for any animals."

"He doesn't," Tutty said as she chuckled. "But he thinks that these particular performing show animals are managerial associates of this fifteen-year-old kid's managerial agency."

"I don't quite understand," Dr. Leachman said in confusion. "I know your husband is blind, but how can he confuse some trained performing show animals for managerial associates?"

"Because you see, doctor," she said with a wide smile, "these particular performing show animals are very special and unique. These particular animals have the incredible gift to speak and communicate."

Dr. Leachman was almost tongue tied as his giant smile widened even further. "You got to be kidding me. This is incredible."

"Absolutely, doctor," Tutty said with a chuckle. "This could be the big boon for our hotel that we've been looking for, this amazing gift landing right in our lap. I just have to find a way to tell my husband of what we have without him having some kind of seizure or a heart attack, considering how he tremendously loathes and hates all animals."

"Yes, I see," Dr. Leachman said with an intrigued smile. "But how has this ape upset Mama Lulu so much? Sweet, dear Mama Lulu is always raving about the adventures of Madam Cureall or Benny from her cuckoo clock. What could he have done that made sweet Mama Lulu so upset?"

"He tied me up and I'm going to get him!" Mama Lulu yelled as she waved her fist in the air. "You just watch me. I'm going to get him!"

"Doctor, this kid has a St. Bernard dog, a Siamese cat, a parrot, and an orangutan," Tutty explained. "But the orangutan happens to be this magician and he put Mama Lulu into a straitjacket and gagged her mouth the other night, and Mama Lulu has been all wired up ever since. It was literally quite amazing to see, doctor."

"You don't say," Dr. Leachman said as he watched Mama Lulu becoming more aggressive and mumbling to herself as she continued to rant about getting the ape. "Well, I can prescribe a certain type of sedative for Mama Lulu to keep her mind at ease so she won't worry so much about this ape. I'll prescribe a low dosage for her."

"That'll really be appreciated, Dr. Leachman."

Dr. Leachman pulled out his medical pad and began to write a prescription.

"I'm going to get him!" Mama Lulu suddenly yelled once again as she shook her fist. "I'M GOING TO GET HIM!"

"On second thought, I better double that dosage."

It was 2 p.m. and Fred had been steadily guarding the door in Tango's room all day preventing Joe, Elvyra, and Chipper from leaving. Tango had told Fred when he left to start his first day at work to not let any of the gang leave the room until he came back, and Fred was endearing to his master's request to the letter.

Tango's request, however, was causing great animosity inside the room. All of the animosity and hostility were directed toward the big, brown and white St. Bernard dog who wouldn't let his peers leave the room. No matter what they said or try to do to trick the big St. Bernard, he wouldn't fall for it. Even the deep crush that Fred had for the vivacious Siamese werecat wasn't working in Elvyra's favor; Fred had been given orders and he simply wasn't about to let anyone leave.

"You big, dumb floppy eared dog!" Joe yelled as Fred stood in front of the door, preventing anyone from leaving. "Let us out!"

"Yeah, Fred, we want to see what this place is all about," Chipper said in a languished voice. "We've been stuck in this room since last night and we want to get out of here. A refined scarlet macaw parrot like myself not only needs his kerweekee, but I need to be free to fly about."

"Come on, Freddy, let us out," Elvyra said in a seductive voice as she began to rub up against Fred, swishing her tail in his face. "A girl like me needs to be free so she can roam about."

"Look, for the hundredth time, Tango told me not to let anybody out until he gets back and that's what I'm going to do," Fred said in a stern voice. "And that's final."

"That kid ain't got what it takes to take us to the top," Joe said as he fumed. "Why you keep brown nosing after that stupid kid?"

"Because he's my owner and he's *your* owner, you stupid ape," Fred said heatedly. "And he's a good owner at that."

"You and that runaway kid can kiss my—"

"You better watch what you say, you tree climbing ape!"

Joe suddenly pounded his chest twice with his fist and he started to snap his finger when Fred quickly jumped in his face.

"Try it, and I'll bite you until I have at least a quart of that red jungle juice," Fred said as he began growling and showing the whites of his teeth.

"Elvyra, you better come over here and get your *boyfriend* before I put this dog's lights out," Joe said with fire in his eyes.

When Fred and Joe were about to annihilate each other, the door suddenly opened as Tango walked in. Immediately, Tango was besieged by a bunch of angry prisoners who wanted to get out of their cell.

"Hey, we want to get out of here!"

"This ain't right keeping us locked up in here!"

"Yeah, Tango, we're going to take you to court and sue you for neglect!"

"Make this crazy guard dog let us out!"

"Alright, everybody, just calm down," Tango said to the gang. "We need to talk about a few things."

"The only thing we need to talk about is getting out of here!" Joe yelled.

"You're going to get out of here, but first we've got some important stuff to discuss," Tango said as he eyed everybody. "Now I talked to Tutty this morning and she wants me to somewhat ingratiate you guys with the hotel guests so they can become accustomed to you."

"Are we going to start performing here or what?" Joe asked in a hostile voice.

"No, we're not going to start out performing."

"Then why did we come all the way here for?"

"Listen, Mr. Redder doesn't know that we're a performing animal group. He fiercely hates all animals and if he knew that there were animals at this hotel, he'd throw us out on the street faster than you'd know," Tango said as he began to explain. "Now his wife is going to try to tell him about us so we can maybe start performing here, but until she's able to convince him of our situation, we're going to have to start out in a general working capacity here."

"What does that mean?"

"It means we're going to start out as regular staff workers here at this hotel."

"Regular staff workers?"

"Yep, that's right," Tango said with a nod. "Now I've already worked it out with Tutty. Joe, starting tomorrow, you're going to start out working as one of the hotel bellboys."

"*A bellboy!*" Joe yelled.

"Look who's a bellboy now," Fred said with a hearty chuckle. "Instead of putting me into a bellboy uniform, I think you might want to snap your own self into a spiffy looking uniform."

"I ain't no bellboy," Joe shouted. "I'm a world fabulous magician and entertainer. Can a bellboy do this?"

Joe suddenly pounded his chest twice with his fist and snapped his finger. Poof! A cloud of purple smoke mushroomed in the air as the room suddenly disappeared and in its place was nothing but empty desert.

"Can a bellboy do that?"

"Very nice," Tango said in an unenthused voice. "Now take us back."

Joe once again did his magical ritual and poof the desert went away.

"Now, Chipper, you're going to have a booth in the front lobby of the hotel where you'll entertain all the guests that come by with your singing, storytelling, and comedy," Tango said as he continued. "Elvyra, you're going to be a hotel announcer that'll give out different information about the hotel over the hotel intercom system to all the guests every hour or so. And Fred, you're going to be working as a hotel greeter. You'll wander around the hotel greeting all the guests, making them feel welcome and comfortable. You'll be working with the hotel concierge staff."

"Hey, why does Chipper get a booth to entertain the guests?" Joe questioned Tango in a fiery voice. "And why does that no talent mutt get to be a hotel greeter?"

"Because I have style and grace," Fred said with a chuckle. "You just get ready to haul that luggage tomorrow *bellboy.*"

"Man, I've had it with this group!" Joe exploded. "I'm heading out on my own."

"You wouldn't last two minutes on your own, you stupid ape," Fred said with a snarl.

"It's because of your no talent mutt self why we've ended up in this stupid dump of a hotel!"

"You're the one that's got us fired everywhere we've been and the reason why we've ended up here!"

All the squabbling and arguing continued to heat up to a feverish pitch, when all of a sudden, a knock at the door halted the bickering. Tango went over and opened the door as five dwarfs suddenly entered the room.

The five dwarfs who entered the room looked like a raunchy, hardcore motorcycle gang that had traveled a long way to get to the Lucky Jackpot Hotel. They were all dressed alike; all had long hair, and all of them had salacious looking tattoos engraved on their forearms. Wearing blue jeans, work boots, and white short sleeve T-shirts with the sleeves rolled up to their armpits as they showed off their rippling biceps, they looked mean, hard, and ready to fight anyone at the drop of a dime. They were Lou, Eddie, Sammy, Mike, and Frank, the five performing members of the entertainment troupe outfit, the Wonder Gang.

"I didn't think you bums were ever going to get here," Fred said to the Wonder Gang. "What took you so long?"

"We had to stop and get Chipper's kerweekee, Big Chief," Lou answered. "We got forty pounds of it."

"Oh, sweet yummy mummy!" Chipper said with a hearty whistle.

"Look out." Elvyra suddenly giggled. "Here comes Dr. Glittermoon."

"What's with the jacket and tie, man?" Lou said with a grin as he glanced at Tango's spiffy attire.

"Yeah, man, you look like you're the manager of the hotel or something," Eddie said with a chuckle.

"I am the manager of this hotel," Tango replied.

"*You're what*?" they all said in startled voices.

Before Tango could explain to the Wonder Gang about his new job title, a cell phone he'd been given suddenly rang as he quickly answered it.

"I got to get back down to the office," Tango said when he hung up. "I have a meeting to go to."

"You have an office?"

"You have a meeting to get to?"

"What's all this?" the questions kept coming from the Wonder Gang.

"They'll explain it to you," Tango said as he quickly opened the door. "I have to go."

"Hey, tell this crazy guard dog to let us out!" Joe demanded.

"Yeah, we want to get out of here." Chipper added.

"Tango, sweetie, it's time to let us flee the coop," Elvyra said with a giggle.

Tango looked over the animals for a second as he stood in the doorway, then he slowly nodded. "Alright, Fred, you can let them out," he said with a sigh. "But don't none of you get into any trouble—especially you Joe."

They rushed out of the room faster than a tornado. Joe was the only one who lingered in the doorway for a second as he looked back at Fred.

"Bye, you dumb mutt of a warden." Joe laughed at Fred as he quickly rushed out of the room.

When Tango, Elvyra, Chipper, and Joe had departed, Lou and the rest of the members of the Wonder Gang slowly looked over at Fred with puzzled stares.

"What's going on around here, Big Chief?" Lou finally said.

"Alright, fellows, here's the deal."

Fred began to explain to the newcomers all about the crazy situation at the Lucky Jackpot Hotel.

Early the next morning, Abner held a conference meeting with his entire hotel staff in the main conference hall to introduce his new hotel assistant manager and his four member staff of the Parker Incorporated Agency. The Lucky Jackpot Hotel had a staff of nearly seventy workers. Front desk clerks, restaurant staff, casino workers, showgirls, housekeeping staff, concierges, bellhops, and other essential hotel staff were standing in a long horizontal line as Abner conducted the meeting.

Abner, with his black sunglasses on and aided by his white cane, walked back and forth in front of his hotel staff like a five star general surveying his glorious troops as he lectured them. He had on the most outrageous, colorful suit that he'd ever worn. His ridiculous, loud colorful suit made him look just like a three hundred pound peacock blimp, and it was all thanks to Tutty.

Tutty had picked out his wardrobe today, as she did on most occasions because of his blindness, and today she'd made sure he had on the most ridiculous outfit in his closet that she could find. Upset by the loud, contentious argument they had when they first woke up this morning, Tutty inflicted a little payback on her precious husband and she loved it. It was one of the little things in her arsenal that she often used whenever Abner had gotten on her last nerve.

Standing at the forefront directly across from the hotel staff as the conference meeting took place was Tutty. Standing right next to her was Tango, then Fred, Chipper, Joe, Elvyra, and the new arrivals, the Wonder Gang, who were all dressed in black leather jackets today. They, along with the rest of Tango's staff, drew a lot of attention from the rest of the Lucky Jackpot Hotel staff members as Abner ranted on and on with his lecture. It seemed as if they couldn't help but to stare in wonderment at their new fellow employees.

"Who are the little Harley Davidson Hell Riders down there at the end of the line," Tutty whispered to Tango as Abner continued to conduct the conference meeting.

"They're the Wonder Gang," Tango whispered back to her with a chuckle. "They arrived here yesterday. They're entertainers who were on the road with us down in Mexico. They've got one of the employee rooms that your husband has given us. They'll be helping out around here."

"Are they part of your entertainment act?"

"Somewhat."

"They look wild and raunchy."

"They can be," Tango said with a snicker. "But all in all, they're some pretty cool guys."

"Well, don't mention to Abner anything about them being here," Tutty whispered back. "That's one part of the Parker Incorporated Agency that he doesn't have to know about."

"Okay."

"And once again, don't ever mention anything about the animals being here around Abner," Tutty whispered. "Just in case one of the animals does something wrong or causes some kind of a stir around the hotel, I can tell Abner that it was one of the workers from a temporary agency that sends over workers to us from time to time."

"Alright, but how long do you want me to keep the animals in a working capacity around the hotel," Tango whispered nervously. "They're entertainers, not hotel workers. I don't know if this is really going to work, Tutty."

"Just give me a little time to try to break it to my husband about the animals," she whispered to him. "I think it'll work."

"But I don't get it," Tango whispered back. "Want word get around to your husband about the animals being here anyway? Surely one of the hotel guests will spill the beans about the animals."

"Will you let me worry about that," Tutty whispered. "I just don't want none of the hotel staff around here to mention anything about the animals to him. If one of the guests happens to mention something to Abner about the animals, I'll handle that. Besides," she said with a snicker as she shook her head. "Abner ain't too bright anyway."

"Alright, but—"

"Be quiet." Tutty quickly hushed Tango. "I think Abner is getting ready to introduce to everyone his new hotel assistant manager and the rest of the Parker Incorporated Agency."

"Now, everyone, I'd like you to meet the new man that I've hired to be my hotel assistant manager around here," Abner said to his hotel staff. "He's a very bright, astute gentleman that also has his own managerial staff to help out. Everyone, meet Mr. Tango Parker."

The entire hotel staff suddenly applauded.

"As I said, Mr. Parker has his own managerial staff named the Parker Incorporated Agency," Abner said as he continued. "His four member staff will be working right along with Mr. Parker under my supervision to help make the Lucky Jackpot Hotel one of the best in all of Las Vegas. Now let me introduce his four member staff to you," he said with great pomp. "Everyone, meet Mr. Beasley Upchurch, Ms. Romeno Mendez, Mr. Blue Hendrix, and Bob."

The entire hotel staff once again applauded as a few chuckles could be heard.

"Now, I expect each department of this hotel to work closely with Mr. Parker and his staff to help produce the success that I expect we should achieve," Abner said as he continued. "We at the Lucky Jackpot Hotel are a team that . . ."

As Abner ranted on with his lecture, Joe suddenly pounded his chest twice with his fist and snapped his finger. Poof! A cloud of purple smoke mushroomed in the air as a foot long blimp suddenly hovered over Abner's head with a message scrawled across the blimp that said ABNER'S BIG BUTT IS BIGGER THAN A RHINO!

The entire hotel staff began to laugh.

"What's going on?" Abner said as he stopped his lecturing. "Did somebody say something funny?"

As Abner disregarded the interruption and continued on with his lecture, Chipper soon got in on the charade. He suddenly cocked opened his beak and made a sound of a loud, blaring trumpet.

"What was that?" Abner said as he quickly jerked his head around as the entire hotel staff laughed. "Where in the world did that trumpet sound come from?"

When no one said anything, Abner continued on with his speech. But no sooner as he continued lecturing his hotel staff, Chipper once again cocked opened his beak and made a sound of an organ playing the musical notes of *Here Comes The Bride*. Joe immediately did his magical ritual once again. When the purple smoke had cleared, a gorilla suddenly appeared standing next to Abner dressed in a white wedding gown and holding a bridal bouquet. The entire hotel staff suddenly boomed with laughter.

"What in the world is going on?" Abner said angrily. "Somebody answer me."

Joe quickly snapped his finger and poof, the gorilla suddenly went away.

With an angry huff when the laughter died away, Abner continued on with his lecture. But as soon as Abner continued his lecturing, Chipper once again cocked opened his beak and began singing.

"I think I want to sing in the rain," Chipper began to sing in a beautiful falsetto voice. "Just hum along in the rain. What a super duper feeling it is to get soaked in the rain."

"Who in the world is that singing about some rain?" Abner said with a sneer as he suddenly stopped lecturing once again.

Joe quickly did his magical ritual again as a dark cloud suddenly formed over Abner's head. A rumble of thunder and a bolt of lightning flickered through the cloud as a heavy rain shower came cascading down from the cloud onto Abner's head.

"What is this?" Abner shouted angrily as he got drenched while the entire hotel staff roared with laughter.

Joe quickly snapped his finger and poof, the dark cloud over Abner's head disappeared as the laughter began to die away.

Abner was now like an angry, drenching wet bull, and the angry bull was ready to charge at anyone who even cracked a single giggle.

"If I get anymore foolishness from any one of you," Abner said to his hotel staff in a steamed voice, "I'm docking the whole entire hotel staff a week's pay!"

When total silence reigned over the conference hall, Abner finally continued on with his lecturing. But neither Chipper nor Joe was about to quit their antics. Between the two of them, they conjured up enough musical mischief and hilarious magic while Abner lectured his hotel staff until Fred finally whispered angrily, "Will you two morons stop it!"

By midday, the hotel was functioning on all levels with people coming and going throughout the lobby of the hotel. Fred was being the kind, gracious host that Tango had asked him to be. He stood at the entrance of the hotel as he greeted all the guests who ventured through the doors of the hotel. Two beautiful Las Vegas style showgirls, dressed in glittering gold G-string bottoms, rhinestone-encrusted bras, and huge feathery headdresses, also stood at the entrance of the hotel as they greeted all the guests.

Wearing a special gold colored dog vest around his body that said Welcome to the Lucky Jackpot Hotel, Fred drew a lot of attention and curious smiles from the guests as they entered the hotel. But what really seemed to shock the socks off the guests as they entered the hotel was the sound of a fully grown talking dog.

When a taxi cab suddenly pulled in front of the hotel awning of the Lucky Jackpot Hotel and two ladies got out of the cab, Fred could immediately tell that these ladies had definitely been partying and were drunk. However, Fred was a consummate professional and he was ready to show the new arriving guests the same amount of courtesy that he'd shown to all of the guests that had arrived at the hotel.

"Hello, ladies, and welcome to the Lucky Jackpot Hotel," Fred said in a cheerful voice for the hundredth time when the two ladies suddenly approached the hotel doors. "I hope your stay here at the Lucky Jackpot Hotel is a pleasant one, ladies."

"Why Betty Jean, I can't believe my ears," the lady said with a hefty smile as she stared down at Fred in amazement. "They have a talking dog at this hotel. Did you hear that dog just talk?"

"I certainly did, Mildred," the other lady said with a laugh.

"I hope to be of service to you ladies in anyway if I can," Fred said courteously.

"Oh, honey, you sure can," the lady said in a sensuous voice as she knelt and gave Fred a hearty rub on his head as Fred smelled the foul booze on her breath. "You know, sweetie, me and my dog back home in Texas usually get it on three nights a week. But I sure would like to see what a big, husky dog like you can do."

"Yeah, Mildred, maybe we'll both see what all he can do with that tongue of his besides talk," her friend said with a slur.

"And besides, you know what they say, Betty Jean," the other lady said. "What happens in Vegas stays in Vegas."

The two ladies suddenly had a hearty, loud laugh as they ventured on into the hotel.

"Oh brother," Fred said with a sigh. "I wonder how much liquor she has to give that mutt of hers back in Texas every night before he'll hump that old witch," he said in a cheerless voice.

"You know, Freddy, you meet all kind of people here at the Lucky Jackpot Hotel," one of the showgirls standing on one side of the entrance said with a smile.

"Absolutely, Freddy," the other showgirl standing on the other side of the entrance said with a smile. "No matter what, just keep smiling. Or in your case, just keep wagging that beautiful tail."

"Cassie and Lonnie," Fred said with a chuckle, "I'll certainly remember that."

Fred left his post as he ventured on into the hotel. The hotel lobby, though certainly not packed, had a considerable amount of folk coming and going. On the right there was the front desk, the casino, the bar and lounge area, a restaurant, the convention hall, a gift shop, and Tango's office. On the left side of the lobby were two showrooms for shows and entertainment; a small showroom and a large showroom. There was also a dance club and a small movie theater.

Immediately, Fred noticed that despite the rundown look that the Lucky Jackpot Hotel presented on the outside, on the inside, the hotel wasn't really that bad at all. Maybe a remodeling job to help improve the facade of the outside would be what the hotel needed to help bring in more guests. But Fred had a distinct feeling that the obnoxious owner of the Lucky Jackpot Hotel probably wouldn't spare a single dollar to help improve the hotel even if his life depended on it.

Fred finally wandered over to a table where about a dozen or so guests were huddled around. The table was an entertainment center and Chipper was the main attraction. Two showgirls stood behind the table and assisted Chipper. A big sign behind the table had the name Chipper's Entertainment Booth printed on it, and it was an attraction that Tango had set up to entertain the guests. Fred watched the proceedings at the table and he noticed that Chipper was in rare form as he interacted with the guests.

"Step right up to the table folks, and let Chipper entertain you," he said in a spry voice to all the people who surrounded the table.

"Wow, this parrot can really talk," one of the guests said with a wondrous smile.

"What can you do?" another guest asked.

"The question, madam, is what do you want me to do?"

"Sing us a song."

"I'm so musical I'm just like a jukebox," Chipper began to sing. "Reggae, rock, hip-hop, or country it makes no difference to me. I'll have you dancing—"

"*Yeah!*" the showgirls behind him began dancing and singing backup.

"And singing—"

"*Yeah!*"

"Just throw your money in the air and I'll give you an encore."

When the song came to an erupt stop, the group huddled around the table began to applaud and cheer. A few of the guests even began to toss a couple of coins to Chipper as he caught them into his mouth as if they were yummy gummy bears to eat.

"Hey, tell us a joke," a lady said.

"Folks, did you know that Lurch has left his job working as a butler for the *Addams Family* and has taken on another job."

"What job did he take?"

"He works for the New York Stock Exchange now."

"What does he do there?"

"Every opening and closing bell, he comes out and says—YOU RANG!"

The group huddled around the table enjoyed a hearty laugh.

Tango suddenly came out of his new office dressed in his spiffy gold jacket that had the *Lucky Jackpot Hotel* emblem on it as he strolled over to Chipper's entertainment center where the crowd was huddled around. He stood by Fred as he watched Chipper entertain the folk.

"So, how's Chipper doing?" Tango asked.

"He's got them eating out of the palm of his beak," Fred said with a chuckle.

"And how are you holding up on your end?"

"No sweat," Fred said as he gazed up at Tango. "I've met a few weirdos, but all in all, I kind of like meeting and greeting the people who enter the hotel."

"Good," Tango said. "Just keep doing what you're doing. In fact, roam around a little, specifically in the casino and the bar and lounge area and make the guests feel welcome."

"No problem."

"Right now I'm a little busy trying to get Elvyra's department ready," Tango said as he watched the people around the table suddenly applaud when Chipper and his showgirl assistants concluded a song as they began another one. "I got the Wonder Gang helping me to get the intercom system ready for Elvyra to make her hourly announcements."

"Have you seen the big boss wandering around yet?"

"No, but keep an eye out for him," Tango said in a wary voice. "We certainly don't need him getting suspicious of anything."

"I got you."

"And speaking of keeping an eye out, where's Joe? I'm already starting to get calls of complaints to my office about him harassing some of the guests."

"I just saw that moron smack a lady on the ass a couple of minutes ago as he was taking her bags up to her room," Fred said in an agitated voice. "That stupid ape ain't no bellhop, Tango. He's going to be nothing but trouble. You just watch and see."

Joe, with a bellhop uniform on and a hat that said the Lucky Jackpot Hotel, was helping a well-dressed gentleman with his bags up to his room. The gentleman seemed to be thoroughly enjoying Joe's company and Joe was steadily pouring on the charm like a seasoned concierge.

"Wow, I'm totally amazed that this hotel actually has a talking orangutan," the gentleman said with a wide smile as they got off the elevator on the second floor as Joe carried his bags. "Have they programmed you to talk in some kind of way or something?"

"Why, not at all, sir," Joe said in a courteous voice as he gushed a huge smile at the gentleman. "Me and my other animal friends that work at this elegant hotel have been given the ability to speak by a very fine witch doctor by the name of Zwalheele Bhoulee some years ago."

"This is totally incredible!"

"Ah, but wait to you see us perform, my good gentleman," Joe said as he continued flaunting his beaming smile.

"Perform?"

"We're entertainers, my good gent," he said as he beamed his smile even wider. "And we're the best there is."

"Wow, I've got to call my wife back in Minnesota and tell her all about this," the man said with a smile. "She's not going to believe this."

When they reached his hotel room, the gentleman opened the door with his key and went in. Joe followed the man into the room with his bags. When the gentleman was about to tip Joe, he suddenly got a call on his cell phone.

While the man turned his back to Joe and was busy talking on his cell phone, Joe suddenly pulled out a pack of firecrackers from his bellhop uniform and attached the pack of firecrackers to the back of the gentleman's belt. He lit the long fuse attached to the firecrackers as the fuse quickly began to sizzle.

"Well, you've certainly been a big help," the gentleman said when he got off the phone and turned around. "Here, let me give you a tip," he said as he gave Joe a five dollar bill.

"I thank you, sir," Joe said with a dazzling smile as he tipped his hat. "And I wish you a good stay here at the Lucky Jackpot Hotel."

When Joe left out of the man's room, he closed the door as he hesitated by the hotel door for a couple of seconds, beaming a huge smile as he waited and listened. Within seconds, a succession of thunderous, loud bangs erupted like the sound of automatic gunfire as a shriek of horror came from the man's room. With a look of sheer glee, Joe suddenly went running down the hallway, hooping, hollering, and laughing like a wild ape that had gone mad.

Throughout the day, Joe began to pull a series of wild pranks and stunts on the hotel guests in his role as a bellhop. He set fire to a lady's hair, conjured up his magic and made a hornet of bees sting an elderly man, threw a pie in a lady's face, spray painted blue paint on a woman's brand new wedding gown, smacked a lady on the behind while taking her bags up to her room, and gave a Catholic priest a free night pass to go to a raunchy Las Vegas strip club. The calls of complaints flooded into Tango's office every half hour and it seemed that Joe was just getting started.

By late that afternoon, Joe escorted a heavy set lady wearing a pink wig along with her little girl with their luggage up to their room. The lady had a lot of expensive luggage and she was complaining the entire time as they rode on the elevator. During all of her grumbling and complaining, Joe simply flashed his brilliant smile at her and the little girl as he stood there on the elevator holding the baggage cart full of their luggage.

"What kind of crazy hotel is this that hires an orangutan as a member of one of its staff?" the woman asked rhetorically as she glared at Joe.

"Only the best hotel, madam," Joe said as he continued beaming his dynamite smile.

"He can talk, mommy!" the little girl said with a huge smile. "The orangutan can talk!"

"Indeed I can, my little princess."

"I like you," she said with a giggle. "You're funny."

"And how old are you, my sweet little princess?"

"I'm six."

"Why here's a yummy treat for you, my little princess," Joe said as he performed his magic and produced a two foot giant lollipop. He held it out for her to take as she stared wide-eyed at the lollipop, but her mother quickly snatched it away before she could take it.

"Don't you *dare* hand my daughter anything," she said with a vicious scowl. "I don't know where you've come from, but you're certainly not going to poison my daughter?"

"I wouldn't dream of doing such a thing, madam," Joe said as he continued smiling.

"Now I had ten pieces of luggage when I checked into this hotel," she said tartly. "Did you get all of them?"

"Yes, madam."

"Well, you better had."

"I even got this one piece of item that fell out of one of your suitcases, madam," he said with a giant smile as he held up one of her large panties.

"Hand me that!" the lady yelled as she snatched her panties.

When the elevator doors opened on the third floor, the angry woman took her daughter's hand and quickly strolled down the hallway to her room as she continued fussing and complaining.

While Joe followed the hefty woman down the hallway with the baggage cart full of her luggage, he suddenly pounded his chest twice with his fist and snapped his finger. Poof! A cloud of purple smoke mushroomed in the air as a miniature helicopter with a banner hooked on behind it that said THIS WOMAN IS A FAT RHINOCEROS began flying behind her head.

When Joe arrived with the baggage cart at the woman's hotel room number as she began to open the door, the little girl suddenly spotted the miniature helicopter flying above the woman's head.

"Mommy look!" the little girl said in awe. "It's a helicopter, look!"

The woman looked up. "Why you—"

Joe suddenly snatched the woman's pink wig off her head and ran down the hall.

"You come back here, you beast!" the woman yelled. "Come back here!"

Joe twirled the woman's pink wig with glee as he suddenly turned around and threw up his middle finger at her. He then started climbing the walls of the hallway, yelping and shrieking like a wild jungle ape as he went running down the hall.

When Joe finally arrived back down in the lobby and he went outside to the front of the hotel, a brand-new shiny Mercedes Benz suddenly pulled up near the hotel awning as a man got out to check into the hotel. As the man began to have a conversation with two other bellhops, Joe, seeing that the engine to the Mercedes was still running, quickly hopped into the Mercedes, skidding out of the parking lot like a bat out of hell and took off.

Fred had been mingling around the hotel engaging with the guests for hours. He'd gotten plenty of compliments, patted and rubbed on the head several times, and even gotten a couple rude remarks from some guests, but all in all, the first day as a hotel greeter was going pretty well. The shock of hearing a talking dog was what all the guests raved about, and Fred didn't mind all the weird questions, stares, and being fondled all over like he was some prized pet possession. He was there to make the guests feel comfortable and welcomed, and he would endure just about anything if it would help the Lucky Jackpot Hotel prosper.

After socializing with some of the guests in the casino, Fred finally ventured over to the two empty showrooms. The smaller showroom had a stage and a seating capacity that looked like it held around two-hundred fifty people, but when Fred ventured over to the big, main showroom, he saw that it had a bigger stage and a seating capacity that probably held around five hundred people.

As Fred stood in the middle of the empty main showroom, he began to wonder would he and the rest of the Magnificent Four ever get to perform there. Standing there all alone suddenly made him contemplate his own position within the group. Despite always getting into heated squabbles with Joe and not liking all of the wild antics that he often pulled that got Tango and the rest of the group into trouble wherever they went, he had to admit that Joe was right when it came to him not being up to par with the rest of the group.

Fred knew he wasn't as talented as his worthy peers and it bothered him deeply. He desperately wanted to dispel the notion that he was just a guard dog that had no talent, and was only added to the group because of the kindness that Tango showed him once he took possession of them. He didn't have the formal training that Joe, Chipper, and Elvyra had in the beginning.

In fact, Fred was never intended to be in show business. He was just Ivan "The Butcher" Malakhov's guard dog that was only given the ability to talk because "The Butcher" had added Fred along with the others when he found the African witch doctor, Zwalheele Bhoulee, to perform his incredible magic on the animals. Fred was simply a throw in that wasn't meant for the world of show business.

The longer Fred pondered over his situation, the more determined he became. He *was* an entertainer, and he was going to show the others that he was as good as they were no matter what it took.

When Fred suddenly heard Elvyra's voice come over the hotel intercom system as he stood there in the empty big showroom, it shattered his train of thought.

"Hello everyone and welcome to the Lucky Jackpot Hotel," Elvyra said in a sultry, sophisticated voice over the intercom. "I want to invite everyone to our fabulous casino so you can try your luck at the slot machines, or the roulette wheel, the blackjack table, or try your luck at the crap table and win a fortune. When you hit that big jackpot, just take me along when you leave and I'll help you spend all of that dough," Elvyra said with a giggle.

"If you're hungry, come on down to our lovely restaurant which is right next to our bar and lounge area, or come and relax in our wonderful swimming pool located on the east side of our fabulous hotel. Don't have a swimsuit, don't worry. Just come on by and take a skinny-dip. We *certainly* won't mind," she said with a chuckle.

"Also, stop by our gift shop located next to our restaurant and pick up a few trinkets or knickknacks to take home with you when you leave. But please don't hurry to leave," she said as she continued her announcement. "Here at the Lucky Jackpot Hotel, there's always something more to see or do. So what's the hurry? You just might find that special someone that you've always been searching for—*meow*," she said with a lustful cat purr. "Well, everyone, until next time—tah-tah!"

When Elvyra concluded her announcement over the hotel intercom, Fred's heart was pounding like mad. Her sultry voice had always made him weak, but to hear her alluring voice over the hotel intercom almost made him shiver to the bone. He wanted Elvyra badly, but he knew he'd probably never get her. He knew that a big St. Bernard dog and a beautiful Siamese werecat together, probably weren't on cupid's list.

Tango suddenly wandered into the main showroom. His face looked worried and scared.

"Oh, there you are," Tango said as he approached Fred. "I've been looking all around for you."

"What's wrong, Tango?" Fred said with concern. "You don't look so good."

"Have you heard what Joe did?"

"What's that crazy ape done now?"

"He hopped into a Mercedes and just took off when one of the guests pulled up and got out of the car to check into the hotel," he said in a flabbergasted voice. "And he's been gone for over an hour now."

"I didn't know that stupid ape could even drive a car."

"Well, undoubtedly he can," Tango said with a sigh. "What's worse is Mr. Redder has heard about it and he's angry as can be. Even Tutty has been all over my back about it. And the owner of the Mercedes has threatened to sue the hotel if he doesn't get his car back in good working order."

"Oh, Tango, this is terrible."

"You're telling me. Redder just might kick us out on the street by tonight if we don't get that car back."

"What are we going to do?"

"I don't know," Tango said with a frown. "But we got to find that car and quick."

Tango suddenly turned and headed out of the main showroom. Fred could only shake his head in despair. He looked around the empty main showroom once more and wondered seriously would they *indeed* get the chance to even perform there now.

Fred headed out of the main showroom, crossed the lobby and entered the bar and lounge area. The place was partially filled with people sitting at tables and at the bar. There was a small stage near the bar that had a glimmering, gold curtain pulled together.

With the place not that crowded, Fred decided to jump into an empty seat at the bar. The bartender, who was six-feet-six inches and weighed nearly three-hundred pounds, suddenly came over to where Fred sat at the bar. The bartender had a big, wondrous smile as he looked at Fred.

"Well, I believe you're the first St. Bernard dog that's ever hopped into a seat at this bar," he said with a laugh. "I'm Big Curly. What will it be? Beer, wine, or whiskey in a bowl?" he chuckled.

"Very funny, Big Curly," Fred said as he chuckled along. "But you know staff members aren't supposed to drink on the job."

"You know, you four new employees have got this entire hotel and all of the staff members around here buzzing with all sorts of gossip," he said as he continued smiling. "Who'd ever thought there'd actually be some talking animals working at the Lucky Jackpot Hotel. And to think that Mr. Redder can't stand being around animals at all." He busted out laughing. "This is unbelievable!"

"Yeah, a riot, isn't it?"

"You're telling me. And he hired that kid, Tango, to be the assistant manager of this hotel," he said shaking his head and chuckling. "I know Mr. Redder is blind and all, but what kind of number did you guys pull on the old douche bag to make him do a thing like that?"

"Well, we had a lot of help from Mrs. Tutty for starters," Fred said with a chuckle. "But all in all, we just did what we had to do to prevent from being homeless. We're entertainers, you know."

"Yeah, everyone around here has heard about that. What do you guys do?"

"We do everything. We're comedians, we act, we sing, and we're even musicians. We're called the Magnificent Four and we've performed virtually all around the world," Fred said as he was suddenly reminded that he had a way to go before he was up to par with the others. "We can't wait to perform here."

"Good luck convincing Mr. Redder in letting you perform," Big Curly said with a chuckle. "Tell me, how in the world did you four attain the ability to talk in the first place?"

"Ah, the million dollar question everyone wants to know," Fred said with his own chuckle. "Well, we attained the ability to speak thanks to this African witch doctor hypnotist by the name of Zwalheele Bhoulee."

"He must have some unbelievable power."

"You can certainly say that." Fred nodded as he looked around at the partially filled bar and lounge area. "Tell me, Big Curly, what's it like working here? I mean, I like what I'm doing here on my first day in all, but maybe you can give me a little more insight."

"Well, business has been a little down lately, thanks a lot to Mr. Redder's own screwball decisions that he's made over the years," the bartender said with a grump. "Mrs. Tutty is the only one who has a good sense of how the hotel should be run, but Abner Redder doesn't ever listen to what she has to say. He thinks he's the only one who knows how to run this hotel, which he's been running it into the ground lately. Plus, Mrs. Tutty is usually too busy trying to take care of Mama Lulu to do much around the hotel. You met Mama Lulu, haven't you?"

"Oh, yeah." Fred chuckled. "She's *definitely* quite a load."

When a guest signaled for a drink at the far end of the bar and the bartender went to serve him, an emcee suddenly came over the intercom in the bar and lounge area.

"Good afternoon to everyone who's relaxing inside the bar and lounge area here at the Lucky Jackpot Hotel," the emcee said in an energetic voice. "Hope you're having a wonderful day. Right now, we'd like to bring you some entertainment. Everyone, focus your eyes on the stage near the bar and give a round of applause to the wonderful Lucky Jackpot Showgirls!"

The few patrons in the bar and lounge area began to applaud as the shimmering gold curtain over the stage suddenly opened. A row of twelve showgirls with long gorgeous legs, wearing glittery, gold G-string bottoms, rhinestone-encrusted bras, and huge feathery headdresses began to dance in a horizontal line as a ten piece brass band, located below the stage, played a lively show tune number. Lots of bright smiles emanated from the showgirls as they danced in unison. The showgirls, all beautiful and talented, were very high spirited as they entertained the patrons.

While the showgirls entertained the guests as the brass band played, Joe suddenly came storming into the bar and lounge area like a wild tornado. He quickly jumped into an empty seat next to Fred at the bar, beaming his white as a cloud smile with his bellhop uniform on.

"Where in the devil have you been?" Fred quickly snapped.

"I've been out joyriding all over this wonderful city, my good dog," Joe said with a proud chuckle as he lit up a cigar.

"What have you done with that Mercedes? Please tell me you didn't wreck it?"

"Oh, I ran that baby into a telephone pole and smashed it to smithereens."

"You *what*?"

"Oh, don't get your tail all up in the air, you no talent mutt," Joe said as he blew a smoke ring in the air as he continued flashing his smile at Fred. "I didn't wreck the car, you stupid dog. It's sitting out front without a scratch on it. No harm done."

"No harm done!" Fred blasted. "You've caused all kind of trouble for Tango and the rest of us. Mr. Redder knows all about the car and Tango said he's mad as hell. You're going to get us fired and thrown out of here, you crazy ape!"

"Ah, stop your blabbering, dog, and lighten up," Joe said as he blew a cloud of smoke in Fred's face. "Who cares if we get thrown out of this flea bag dump. We should be performing in one of those nice, big, fancy hotels on the Strip anyway."

"Listen, you crazy ape. You're not going to—"

"Well, I see we have another one of your friends with us," the bartender said with a smile when he returned. "I'm Big Curly."

"Joe is the name, my good man," the boastful orangutan said in a brash voice.

"What's your pleasure, Joe? It's on the house."

"I want something with some fruit, so why don't you pour something that's going to make me holler and hoot," he said with a dynamite smile.

"Coming right up."

The bartender fixed Joe a Bahama Mama and placed it in front of him as he went to tend to another customer.

"Listen, you crazy ape," Fred said as he glared at Joe. "You're not going to get us into trouble. We got a good thing going here."

"What good thing?" Joe said in a mocking voice as he took a swig from his drink and chuckled as he puffed on his cigar. "We ain't performing here."

"We got to be patient, you stupid ape," he said in a riled voice. "And put that cigar out—you're on the job!"

"Ah, go chase a car or something, you no talent mutt."

"Listen, ape, we can't get Abner Redder upset or he'll—"

"Don't worry about old man Redder," Joe said calmly as he smoked his cigar. "I'll pay the old fart a visit tonight, charm him a little and keep him chilled."

"What do you mean *you're* going to pay him a visit tonight?"

"Not me," Joe said with a devious grin. "Mr. Beasley Upchurch is going to pay him visit."

"What in the devil are you up to, you scheming ape?" Fred said as he glared suspiciously at Joe.

"Business, my friend," Joe replied in a smug voice as he suddenly blew a big smoke ring around Fred's head. "Strictly business."

Later that afternoon, the five members of the Wonder Gang were in the room that Tango had finally assigned to Chipper getting the room ready for him to occupy. Three members of the Wonder Gang were busy putting up strobe lights and all kind of exotic, psychedelic paintings all over the walls, while the other two members constructed a device for Chipper to smoke his kerweekee from.

As the members of the Wonder Gang worked, they constantly argued, fussed, and complained with one another over which Wonder Gang member was dallying and playing around too much. Time was imperative. Plus they still had Elvyra's room to get to, and beer time was certainly calling.

While Tango, Zimmy, and Elvyra watched the Wonder Gang hard at work, Chipper flew above them in the room in circles waiting impatiently for the work to finally be completed. It had been nearly three weeks since he'd last smoke any kerweekee, and he desperately wanted to be left alone so he could finally be free to indulge in what he was meant to do.

"Hey, are you stupid boneheads finished, yet?" he said impatiently to the Wonder Gang as he continued circling slowly above everyone. "I need to go see Dr. Glittermoon. It's been three weeks since I last seen him, you know."

"Well, we'd be finished if Eddie would stop lagging around over there in the corner and come help me put this painting up," Lou said angrily as he stood on top of a ladder, struggling to put one of the psychedelic paintings onto the wall. "This painting is as heavy as hell."

"Hey, don't blame me if you got short legs and can't reach up there." Eddie shot back.

"What kind of statement is that?" Lou said in a riled voice. "We all got short legs, you idiot!"

"Well, I know we would've been finished a long time ago if Sammy and Mike would stop sneaking into the beer cooler every ten minutes getting a beer!" Frank yelled as he glared at his two comrades. "And you two morons better save me a beer, you drunk ugly bums!"

"Hey, I'm the only one who's been working around here." Frank snapped as he welded an empty picture frame onto a stool. "The rest of you douche bags ain't been doing nothing the entire time."

"What in the world are you talking about?" Eddie shouted from the top of his ladder. "You got the easiest job, you lazy schmuck."

"Hey, don't get smart with me," Frank yelled back. "I'll come up there and beat the crap out of you!"

"I'd like to see you try, buddy!"

"Oh, you would, huh?"

"Fellows, let's try to cut out all of this stupid nonsense," Tango said as he shook his head and began to laugh. "You guys still got Elvyra's room to get to, remember?"

"That's right, boys," Elvyra suddenly replied in a haughty tone as she swished her tail. "And this very fine, sexy cat here has got a *whole* lot of stuff that she wants done, too."

"Hey, who died and made you king, buddy," Lou said from his ladder as he glared at Tango. "Just because you tricked the owner of this crummy hotel and you got that suit on, don't mean nothing to us. We only work for the Big Chief."

"The Big Chief?" Zimmy said with a smile as he looked over at Tango.

"Yeah." Tango chuckled. "That's what they call Fred."

"Why?"

"Well, when we were down in Mexico on the road a couple of months back, Fred and the Wonder Gang made this huge bet one night of who could drink the most beer," he said as he explained. "After Fred had lapped up two whole kegs of beer and he left the Wonder Gang sprawled all over the floor and they couldn't drink another ounce, well, they lost the bet and were indebted to him. So, to pay back the bet, they have to work for Fred for an entire year."

"You mean Fred *actually* drunk two kegs of beer in one night?"

"Yep." Tango nodded. "Hey, Fred can go with the best of them when he's challenged."

"Ah, he was just lucky that night," Lou said as he complained. "But we certainly learned our lesson. We want ever challenge Big Chief anymore."

"Hey, enough with all the talk!" Chipper said in a pesky voice as he continued circling over the room. "Will you morons just shut up and finish my room!"

"Can't wait to see Dr. Fruitcake, can you?" Elvyra giggled.

"That's *Dr. Glittermoon* you stupid, silly cat."

"Hey," Zimmy said to Tango with a huge smile. "Have you ever tried any of that stuff?"

"What? You mean Chipper's kerweekee?"

"Yeah."

"No way, man. That stuff is *way* too powerful." Tango laughed. "Man, that stuff will zap your mind."

"That's why Chipper has to go see Dr. Fruitcake." Elvyra giggled. "He has to go find his brain."

"Shut up, you silly, dimwitted whore," Chipper said in a sour voice as he continued circling.

Fred suddenly entered the room as he joined the ongoing process.

"Fred, have you seen Joe since he's returned with that car?" Tango quickly asked in a concerned voice. "Mr. Redder wants to see me about that whole situation in a few minutes. And for the life of me, I don't know what I'm going to tell him."

"I haven't seen that moron ape since he came storming into the bar and lounge area about an hour ago," Fred said. "Who knows where he is. Knowing that crazy ape, he's probably roaming around right now causing even more problems."

Zimmy's cell phone suddenly rang as he answered it. When he finished his quick phone conversation, he looked at Tango with a huge smile.

"Hey, that was Chloe," Zimmy said as his smile radiated even more. "She and Maria want us to go with them skating when they get off their shift in thirty minutes."

"You mean the two girls in the concierge department who we met the other night?"

"Yep. And Chloe said Maria really digs you. She thinks you're cute, man."

"Oh, really," Tango uttered as he blushed.

"Who's Maria?" Elvyra suddenly said in a somewhat jealous voice.

"Yeah, man, Chloe said she's *really* been talking about you a whole lot lately."

"Well," Tango said as he continued to blush, "I kind of like her, too."

"Who's Maria?" Elvyra said in a persistent voice as she strolled over to Tango and rubbed her furry body up against his leg, trying to get his attention.

"Hey, let's head on up to the employee cafeteria and wait for them. They said they'll meet us there," Zimmy said. "When they get off their shift, we can go skating with them."

"Tango—*who's Maria?*"

"I can't. I got to go meet Mr. Redder in a few minutes and it's no telling how long the meeting is going to last," Tango said as he ignored Elvyra's persistence. "Anyway, I got to head back up to the office first before I meet with Mr. Redder. After I meet with Redder, then we can hook up with Chloe and Maria."

"Sounds good."

"Say, why don't you walk up to the office with me right now. We can talk about our plans with Chloe and Maria after we leave skating," Tango said with a wink and a smile.

"Cool, let's go."

"Who's Maria?" Elvyra said as she began to follow Tango and Zimmy on their heels as they were leaving. "Tango!"

Elvyra suddenly stopped dead in her tracks in the doorway when Tango and Zimmy had exited the room. After a couple of seconds, she slowly turned back around. Her emerald green eyes suddenly had a cold, envious glare that could literally shatter glass.

"Who is this Maria bitch!" she spewed out like hot venom.

"Looks like a certain Siamese cat ain't too happy," Chipper said from above as he continued circling. "Hey, Fred, I think you better go over and calm your *girlfriend* down." He chuckled. "I think the poor little feline is about to have a tantrum."

"Cut it out, Chipper," Fred said in a slightly embarrassed voice. "Just cut it out."

The Wonder Gang had finally completed Chipper's room and now Chipper was left all alone. The aura and ambience around the room was just the way Chipper wanted it. His room was a mixture between a hip, swinging nightclub and a swank art museum. Colorful strobe lights flickered constantly around the semi-dark room as glimpses of the psychedelic paintings that hung perfectly along the walls, gave the impression of pure artistic freedom. Chipper's mind was now free to go wherever it wanted to go, and the kerweekee was the vehicle that would take him there.

Chipper's room contained no furniture at all. The only piece of real furniture was a lone five foot red stool in the center of the room. Welded to the seat of the red stool was an empty, large picture frame. The empty picture frame was the pathway that Chipper would journey through to go on his wandering voyages and the retreats of his mind. But more importantly, it was a direct pathway that would lead him straight to Mystical Lake, where the great Dr. Glittermoon resided.

Attached to the wall of Chipper's room between all of the psychedelic paintings was a large bird house with a chimney. Rigged by the ingenuity of the members of the Wonder Gang, the bird house was nothing but an elaborate smoking device for Chipper to smoke kerweekee from.

A small chain hung down the side of the roof of the bird house like a rain gutter. Whenever Chipper felt the need to have a smoke, he'd pulled the chain with his beak. The chain ignited a fire to the kerweekee stored inside the bird house, and from a pipe that protruded from the bird house, Chipper would have his smoke.

Crammed with at least a pound of kerweekee stored inside the bird house like hay stuffed in a barn, Chipper now rested on a perch connected to the birdhouse as he pulled the chain with his beak and began to have a smoke.

As he indulged, smoke started puffing out of the chimney of the bird house like heavy smoke churning out of a smokestack of a busy factory. Chipper's mind, as it became captivated by the allure of the kerweekee, slowly began to float further and further away.

Soon, thoughts of his homeland along the Amazon rainforest began to take over his every thought, sound, and smell. It was paradise. The sweet smell of the rainforest and all of the wonderful creatures that inhibited it was an aroma that he knew so well. It was like fresh baked bread coming straight out of the oven to a soldier returning home from war.

Now feeling totally free and uninhibited from all constraints, Chipper decided it was time. Like a bird leaving his nest to find greener pastures, Chipper suddenly took flight as he circled once above the red stool in the center of the room, then he flew straight through the empty picture frame.

Chipper suddenly arrived at his destination in a blink of an eye. Mystical Lake, which was a shimmering, clear lake that stretched as far as the eye could see, was not only beautiful, but it was literally mesmerizing. Chipper had been to this beautiful, wondrous lake many times and he knew what to do. He slowly began to circle high above the shimmering lake as he waited for Dr. Glittermoon to appear.

Suddenly a great, gigantic golden moon appeared below the surface of the water. The huge glittering moon had a face that radiated like the sun itself. The great, golden moon was none other than Dr. Glittermoon. Deep below the surface of the water, he looked up at Chipper and began to speak.

"State your reason for coming to the great Mystical Lake, my feathered one," he said in a deep, mighty voice from below the surface of the water as stars and comets began to shoot out of the shimmering, clear lake as he spoke.

"Dr. Glittermoon, so glad to see you once again," Chipper said as he slowly circled above the lake. "I've come to be granted access to the second domain."

"How has your state of mind been, my feathered one?" he said as thousands of roses began to ascend slowly out of the shimmering, clear lake as they hung in the air like helium balloons.

"Most unfortunate," Chipper said in a dismal voice as he continued circling. "I desire to have many treasures and to seek new horizons, but I can't seem to fly over the great mountain where the land of fruit abounds plentiful. What does this mean and what should I do?"

The great, golden moon below the surface of the water suddenly began to turn red, green, orange, blue, and purple as if he were brooding heavily over Chipper's question. After a long silence, he finally returned back to his golden color.

"One's journey through the orbit of time has many hurdles," the golden moon began to speak. "But if one fuels oneself with the treasure that one seeks in one's mind, then that one will have already conquered many treasures and new horizons will certainly come. Once you do that my feathered one, your journey over the great mountain will be just a mere flight away."

"And once over the mountain, will I be free?"

"You're already free, my feathered one. Don't let the distance of the perceived treasure hold the spirit of your creativity bondage," the golden moon spoke as stars and roses continued to ascend from the great, shimmering lake. "You are a superior being from the land of the tropics. The orbit of the great space is always yours, my feathered one."

"I'll remember that knowledge."

"Very well. Now take flight and go on to the second domain," the golden moon spoke. "But remember, when the magic rainbow appears you must leave, my feathered one, or you'll forever be stuck in the second domain."

The great, golden moon quickly dissolved away below the surface of the water as the massive, shimmering lake suddenly began to part. As the water was held back, Chipper, with the gusto of life flowing through him, took flight and flew straight through the open space.

After traveling many miles in the second domain, Chipper finally arrived at a rest area. The rest area was called the Hypnotic Café, a place he'd been many times. There were other rest areas located in the vast second domain such as the Wonder Sky Stop, Dreamers Layover, and the Seven Heaven Joint, but Chipper preferred the Hypnotic Café the best. It was a place where the mind was treated with the upmost respect.

Chipper suddenly flew through the open doors of the Hypnotic Café as he immediately transformed into a six-foot man. Now wearing a polo shirt, nice slacks, and loafers, he now looked like a casual everyday man stopping to have a drink after a long day at work. The transformation was natural. Everyone who entered through the doors of the Hypnotic Café immediately transformed into what his or her mind wanted them to be. There weren't any restrictions. If your mind possessed the will, then the spirit was willing to submit.

The Hypnotic Café, as always, was packed. Fifty or so artists, thinkers, dreamers, wanderers, and loners filled the tables of the café as they communed with one another in their own way about the topic that brought all of them together, which was life, liberty, and the pursuit of happiness. Incense burned all around the place as the walls were filled with all sorts of strange, yet wonderful graffiti that made one's mind spin on its axis and fly away. Freedom of thought and freedom of expression were like happy hour at the Hypnotic Café, and everyone in the place seemed to be filled with the merriment of their creativity.

The Hypnotic Café was run by a host named Superkite. The great wanderer of many places, Superkite had started the Hypnotic Café many years ago when he was in search of a higher plateau of the mind. When he refused to leave out of the second domain when the massive rainbow appeared one time when he was a young man, he had no choice but to adapt to his new, artistic surroundings. Stuck in the second domain with no chance of ever returning, he decided to make all of those whom ventured through his hemisphere of the second domain a journey that they'd never regret.

Superkite, dressed in an orange and white suit that radiated like a gleaming jewel, met the six-foot man who was now Chipper at the entrance of the Hypnotic Café. The cordial host was all smiles as he was with everyone who ventured through the doors of his miraculous establishment.

"Chipper, my man, so glad to see you once again at the Hypnotic Café. And I really do mean—*man.*" He laughed as he gave Chipper a hearty handshake.

"Good to see you, too, Superkite," Chipper said with a smile. "The way things have been going lately, I didn't know if I'd ever get back here."

"Where have you been, my good man? You've been busy down in the tropics or something?"

"Far worse. You just wouldn't believe where I'm dwelling at now, Superkite," he said with a disheartening sigh. "You just wouldn't believe it."

"Well, come in and free your mind and your spirit."

"I see the place is filled, as usual," Chipper said as he gazed around the joint.

"Yes, we have a lot of mind seekers, writers, and dreamers who are searching for their creative plateau. And the vibe going around today is real good, too."

"Superkite, I've been wondering something."

"What's that, my good friend?"

"How long have you been in the second domain?"

"Oh, my good friend, I've been here so long, I can't even remember when the last time I've been back."

"That long?"

"We all know the second domain is nothing but a state of mind. Why the last time I remember coming here, I was a young man who'd just finished college. When the rainbow appeared and I didn't leave, I've been here ever since."

"You're fooling me?"

"Not at all, my feathered one. And what's further, an old childhood friend who I grew up with back in Wichita, Kansas came through here not so long ago and told me that I was now a ninety-five-year-old man living in a nursing home back in Wichita. Can you believe that?" He laughed. "My body is in some nursing home being fed cold oatmeal every day, while my mind is here in the second domain living the supreme life."

Chipper laughed as he strolled on further into the Hypnotic Café. The entire place was surreal. There was an artist sitting at a table painting on a canvas who suddenly dove into the painting when it was finished as he disappeared.

At another table, a lady strummed a guitar as she sung a beautiful, romantic song. The lyrics that came out of her mouth suddenly transformed into live visual pictures of the romantic rendezvous that the two lovers in the song encountered.

And at another table, a guy was busy writing a story in a notebook as a miniature hologram of the actors played their parts of the story on the side of his notebook as he wrote. When the writer suddenly had a change of mind and erased something, the director shooting the scene in the hologram yelled "cut" as a staffer quickly ran a revised script to the director when the writer wrote a new scene as the action continued on.

Enthralled by all of the fascinating happenings and intriguing activities that took place all around the crowded café, Chipper finally found an empty place at the bar as he had a seat. The Hypnotic Café served a long list of various teas that had a special herbal component that brought out the extraordinary quality of what each brand of tea contained. Chipper glanced up at the menu board behind the bar of the various herbal teas that they had to offer and he ordered his favorite tea, Sunrise Over The Mountain.

When the bartender served him his hypnotic tea, Chipper sipped his tea and began to watch all who ventured through the doors of the Hypnotic Café.

Everyone who arrived at the café had a unique way of entering the establishment. One person suddenly transformed from a toad into a prince, another person transformed from a weak, tired old man into a young, strong athlete, while another person transformed from a ragged bum into a well-dressed movie star. The second domain was a place of freedom of mind and freedom of desire, and Chipper, during his many times of coming to the Hypnotic Café, had seen just about every entry there was.

Just as Chipper thought he'd seen all that there was to see, he suddenly spotted an entry coming into the Hypnotic Café that he'd never seen before. From above, a dark cloud suddenly approached the entrance of the café. A thunderbolt flashed through the dark cloud as a multi-colored rain shower began to fall gently from the cloud. As if the sea had just given birth, a mermaid suddenly evolved from the multi-colored rain shower as the mermaid instantly transformed into a fully-fledged beautiful woman.

Chipper immediately became captivated by this beautiful, mysterious woman. His heart began to pound more and more as she strolled into the Hypnotic Café and headed straight over to the bar. When she suddenly had a seat next to him and gave him a pleasant smile, he thought his heart was going to float all the way back to the Amazon rainforest.

"Hello," she said to him in an alluring voice.

"Wow," Chipper uttered as he stared in awe at this magnificent woman. "I've never seen anybody like you come in here. My name is Chipper," he said as he extended his hand to her.

"I'm Aquaflower."

When he shook her creamy, soft hand, he noticed an engraved tattoo of a mermaid on the back of her right hand, just as he had a tattoo of a scarlet macaw parrot on the back of his hand. Everyone who entered into the second domain, their true nature and true being were always engraved somewhere on their body.

"I've never met a mermaid in the second domain before," he said in awe.

"And I've never met a parrot in the second domain, either."

They both looked at each other and suddenly laughed.

While Chipper's new friend ordered a brand of hypnotic tea from the menu board, Chipper couldn't help but to become even more entranced with the beautiful woman sitting next to him.

Her unusual name, Aquaflower, seemed to fit her perfectly. The longer he stared at her and took notice of her shiny, blue hair that flowed in curls all the way to her waist, of her sparkling, golden eyes that twinkled like stars, and of her beautiful, smooth face that radiated like an angel, the more he was convinced. Yes, she indeed *did* seem like some rare, exotic flower that had come straight from the bluest sea.

"So, Aquaflower," he said with his heart still thundering in his chest. "What brings you to the Hypnotic Café?"

"Well, I've tried all of the other rest areas in the second domain. I've been to the Wonder Sky Stop, Dreamers Layover, and the Seven Heaven Joint, but I've never been to the Hypnotic Café. I heard they have an incredible VIP room here."

"Oh, they have the best VIP room here." Chipper smiled as he gazed into her shimmering, golden eyes. "No doubt about that. I've been through it many times."

"You know, I detect a certain sadness in your voice," she suddenly said with concern. "Your voice sounds like you haven't been to your homeland in the Amazon in quite a while. There's a certain despondency in the way you talk. I detect somewhere deep within you, that you're searching for something that you can't quite find."

"Wow, that's incredible," he responded in awe. "I was just telling Dr. Glittermoon before I entered the second domain, that I desired to have many treasures and to seek new horizons, but I can't seem to fly over the great mountain where the land of fruit abounds plentiful. How did you detect that?"

"Out in the deep sea where I live, dolphins and whales sometimes cry out in their need and pain. It's a certain sound in their cry that's so distinct that I hear, sometimes from many miles away. So, I swim to them and comfort them and be with them to try to make them feel whole again until they can finally be free to go on their journey. I detect the same in you," she said as she suddenly touched his hand. "I detect that same want that you have."

As she spoke her warm, kind words, Chipper could tell that the hypnotic brew of tea he'd been drinking, Sunrise Over The Mountain, was starting to work its stuff. Everyone else in the café faded away as the sun suddenly began to rise through a thick pack of clouds. Chipper could clearly see the sun now. The sun was in Aquaflower's face, and it blazed brighter than it ever had.

"May I ask you something?" Chipper said as he continued watching the sun rise in Aquaflower's face.

"Yes."

"Will you go with me into the VIP room? I think together we'll have a wonderful time."

Aquaflower suddenly flashed a smile so brilliant, that the beautiful, exquisite ray of the sun radiating from her face almost blinded Chipper.

Hand and hand, Chipper and Aquaflower slowly got up from the bar and strolled over to a section in the Hypnotic Café that was roped off. Superkite, the curator of the VIP section, immediately smiled when the two approached.

"Ah, I see fate has brought a new union together?" he said with happiness in his voice.

Still holding hands, Chipper and Aquaflower looked at each other as they continued to smile.

"Yes," Chipper said with joy in his voice. "It seems that way."

Superkite unhooked the red, velvet rope as Chipper and Aquaflower entered into the section where only those seeking the highest mind experience were allowed to enter. In front of them stood a curtain made of long beads of shimmering diamonds and red rubies. Superkite smiled as he gave them an inquisitive stare.

"Are you ready for your supreme experience to begin?"

They both nodded.

"Then wait no more. Let your experience and the wonder it may bring you begin."

Superkite pulled a cord as the shimmering diamonds and brilliant rubies of the curtain opened wide. Within a flash of an eye, a heavy suction of wind pulled Chipper and Aquaflower into another dimension.

Chipper and Aquaflower suddenly went up an escalator into a sparkling, golden cloud. Inside the sparkling, golden cloud, a palace awaited them full of every refined amenity as they were pampered by servants in white suits who constantly served them champagne and fruit.

Soft music played all throughout the chamber of the cloud as they relaxed and watched the world go by below them from windows inside the cloud. The great cities of Paris, Rome, London, Tokyo, and Dubai were beautiful, shimmering gems beneath them. They saw red rivers, orange waterfalls, pink rolling mountains, and purple trees by the million. The world was simply their oyster. Like a bottle of good wine that had been stored away in a wine cellar for years and had now been uncorked, their minds had finally been liberated and freed.

Hours later after seeing the world from a different perspective of the mind, Chipper and Aquaflower finally came down from the sparkling, golden cloud in a huge, colorful helium balloon. The helium balloon, with the words the Hypnotic Café going around it, eventually landed on a secluded, isolated beach.

All alone and totally undisturbed, Chipper and Aquaflower began to make love on the edge of the beach. The tide, as it rolled back and forth to shore, christened their feet as they lay together. Time was an unimportant entity as they made passionate love. The only thing that really mattered was the beating together of their throbbing hearts.

When they'd finished making love, they lay cuddled in each other's arms in the sand as they watched the waves of the ocean roll back and forth to shore. The sun seemed as though it was directly over them, warming their love even more as they kissed and caressed each other.

"I had a wonderful time," Aquaflower said as she softly caressed Chipper's chest.

"So did I."

"You think it was fate that brought us together?"

"I know it was," he replied as he looked into her golden eyes. "We were destined to be together. I know it."

"A mermaid and a parrot?" she said with a smile.

"Absolutely."

"So where do we go from here?"

"Wherever love takes us."

All of a sudden, a majestic rainbow suddenly appeared as it hovered over the sky like a precious jewel from another world. The rainbow was so awesome and beautiful against the backdrop of the vast ocean that it glimmered for miles.

"Well," Aquaflower suddenly said in a somber voice. "I guess it's time for us to be leaving."

Chipper stared out at the massive rainbow that hung over the ocean as his heart began to sink. As beautiful and as majestic as the rainbow was, at the moment, he almost wished that it would just go away.

"I want to see you again," he finally said to Aquaflower with love in his eyes when he turned to her. "When will you come back to the Hypnotic Café?"

"You'll know," she said as she gently kissed his lips. "Don't worry. You'll know."

Aquaflower slowly rose from the sand and hovered over Chipper as she stared down at him for the longest. While Aquaflower stared at Chipper with misty eyes, Chipper began to study the contours of her lovely face and he glanced over every inch of her naked body, and he swore to himself that he'd never seen anything as beautiful as she was. She *was* the sunrise over his mountain and his heart wanted to follow her wherever she went.

When Aquaflower slowly turned and headed for the water, Chipper watched her as she evolved back into a mermaid when she dove into the ocean. Her allure, her charm, and her natural beauty were so resplendent and illuminated so much that the ocean itself began to change a flurry of colors as she swam away.

With Aquaflower now gone away to the deep sea, Chipper finally rose from the sand as he instantly changed back into a scarlet macaw parrot. With one great swoop, he took flight as he flew away through the arch of the massive rainbow.

Chipper finally returned to his room as he flew back through the empty picture frame. He landed on his perch and immediately pulled on the chain connected to the birdhouse as he had a fresh smoke. As the kerweekee once again began to stimulate his mind, Chipper began to reflect on the wonderful time he had with his new soulmate, Aquaflower.

The feeling he experienced was like none other he'd ever felt before. As he smoked and liberated his mind, he couldn't help but to sing out a melody; a sweet melody so rich and so robust, that the sound of his a cappella voice could probably be heard all over the Lucky Jackpot Hotel.

When evening rolled around, Joe went around to Abner and Tutty's residential suite and rung their doorbell. Joe, out of his bellhop uniform and now dressed in his usual faded brown suit with the red and white polka dotted tie on, had come to pay a social call to Abner Redder. He'd come to see the owner of the Lucky Jackpot Hotel not as Joe but as Mr. Beasley Upchurch, one of Tango's managerial assistants of the sham Parker Incorporated Agency.

After causing such a big uproar around the hotel when he took off in one of the guest's Mercedes and went joyriding earlier today, Joe wanted to try to smooth things over with the big boss and try to keep him cooled out. But Joe had even further ulterior motives in his reason for wanting to chummy up with the big boss. If he could somehow charm the big guy and win over his trust, then Joe knew he could eventually set his ultimate plan into action.

When Tutty finally opened the door to their residential suite, Joe stood there in the hallway smoking on a hefty cigar as he flashed his dynamite smile at her. Tutty immediately glared at Joe as if he were some wild, roguish thug that had the nerve to show his face after stealing money from the church collection plate.

"You!" she suddenly said with fire in her eyes. "What in the world do you want?"

"Ah, good evening, my fair lady," he said with grace as he continued smiling. "I wonder if it wouldn't be any trouble if I may have a word with your dear, wonderful husband."

"Listen you crazy, wild ape." She pointed her finger as she gave him a vicious sneer. "You ever pull a stupid stunt again like you did today, and I'll personally throw your hairy tail all the way back to that stinking jungle that you came from. I don't care how talented you *or* the rest of those other animals are. This hotel always respects its guests. Do you comprehend?"

"Most definitely, my dear lady," he said in an apologetic voice. "Please, madam, forgive me of my childish, careless ways. I promise, it'll never happen again."

"Oh, I know it won't happen again, because you certainly won't be working as a member of this hotel staff ever again."

"That's quite understandable, my lady."

"What do you want with Abner anyway?"

"Just a friendly social call, madam."

"Well, right now, he's busy in his office talking with your owner."

"My dear, sweet lady, I have no owner," he said with a mischievous smile as he puffed on his cigar. "I do as I please."

Tutty suddenly gave the charismatic orangutan a hard, critical look as she slowly glanced over his faded brown suit with the red and white polka dotted tie that he had on. Eventually she shook her head as she began to smirk.

"An ornery, old ape with the gift of gab." She chuckled. "Oh, I think I better hurry up and convince Abner to put you and the rest of that gang of talking animals on stage so we can all see what you guys can *really* do."

"Oh, most definitely, my dear lady," he said in a pompous voice as he blew out a big smoke ring. "Most definitely."

Joe followed Tutty into their residential suite when she finally allowed him to enter. After closing the door, Tutty led Joe into the parlor of their suite. Mama Lulu, Abner's dimwitted eighty-year-old mother, was sitting in her usual armchair in the parlor when they entered. She immediately became riled as an alligator when she saw Joe, the orangutan who'd caused her so much distress that night when Tango and his array of animals first arrived.

"What's that mangy ape doing here?"

"Mama Lulu, now you just calm down," Tutty said in a pacifying voice. "He didn't come here to disturb your peace."

"I want that mangy ape out of here right now!"

"Well, good evening to you, my very beautiful lady," Joe suddenly said to Mama Lulu in a chivalrous voice as he beamed his radiant smile at her. "And how are you feeling on this wonderful night?"

When Joe bent over and tried to give Mama Lulu a kiss on her hand, she quickly gave him a vicious smack.

"Don't you dare try to bite my hand, you mangy ape!"

Tutty quickly covered her hand over her mouth as she hid her smirk.

"Sit down ape and don't you dare mess with Mama Lulu," she said to Joe with a scathing look. "Abner is still busy talking with your owner in there in his office. Now I got to go into the kitchen and take care of some things. So you mind yourself, ape. You hear me?"

"Most understood, my fair lady. You definitely can trust me," he said with a hefty smile as he suddenly gave Tutty a respectful bow. "And may I add, madam, how gracious of you to let me visit your beautiful suite that you have here."

Tutty slowly shook her head as she left out of the parlor.

When Joe and Mama Lulu were all alone, Joe had a seat in an armchair next to the coffee table directly beside where Mama Lulu sat. He leaned back in his armchair and puffed on his cigar as he looked over at Mama Lulu, flashing his pompous smile at her. While Joe continued to smile at Mama Lulu in a mocking fashion, Mama Lulu stared back at him with a look that could kill a rattlesnake.

"Don't you dare smile at me, you mangy ape," she finally uttered in a fiery voice.

"You know," Joe suddenly said as he slowly took his cigar from his mouth. "You remind me of an old saying that we used to have back in the Sumatra jungle where I'm from."

"What are you talking about, you mangy ape?"

"Well, back in the Sumatra jungle, we used to have a saying that an orangutan who was too dumb and too stupid to remember where he'd last left his banana at was called a mooly-mooly. And that's what you are, a mooly-mooly."

"What did you call me?"

"You're a mooly-mooly."

Mama Lulu suddenly balled up her fist. "You call me that one more time, and I'm going to put a knot on that hairy head of yours!"

"Mooly-mooly, mooly-mooly—*MOOLY–MOOLY*." Joe teased her as he let out a hearty chuckle.

"Get up, you mangy ape, so I can knock that silly smile off of your face." Mama Lulu quickly rose from her armchair, waving her fist in the air as she was ready to fight. "GET UP!"

Tutty quickly stormed out of the kitchen as she came back into the parlor. "What's going on in here?"

Abner's office door also opened as Abner and Tango came out of the office.

"What the devil is going on out here?" Abner said with his dark shades covering his eyes and walking with his white cane. "Is mama out here dancing around with that bedsheet tied around her neck again?"

"No, Abner, it's not that."

"Well, then what the devil is going on?"

"Abner, someone is here to see you."

"Who?"

"Jo—" Tutty quickly corrected herself. "I mean, Mr. Beasley Upchurch is here to see you."

"You mean one of Mr. Parker's assistant managerial associates from the Parker Incorporated Agency."

"The what?" she said as she gave him a confused look. "Oh, that. Yes, the Parker Incorporated Agency. Yes, Mr. Beasley Upchurch from the Parker Incorporated Agency has come to pay you a visit."

"Is that so?"

"Abner, you get this mangy ape out of here this instant!" Mama Lulu said in a testy voice. She continued to stand over Joe, waving both of her fists in the air. Joe merely sat comfortably in his armchair smiling his arrogant, pompous smile at her as he casually smoked his cigar. "Abner, I'm warning you, if you don't get this mangy ape out of here, I'm going to crane his hairy head!"

"What ape is she talking about, Tutty?"

"Oh, Mama Lulu is just carrying on like she always does," Tutty said with a nervous laugh as she quickly guided Abner's mother away from Joe and placed her down in a nearby couch. "She's probably just talking about some ape she's seen in one of Madam Cureall's coloring books or something."

"I swear that woman gets loonier and nuttier every day," Abner said with a sigh as he had a seat in the armchair that Mama Lulu just sat in. "One minute she's going around here wearing bedsheets around her neck, and the next minute she's raving about that stupid Benny. What's next? I swear if you threw a ball in this room, she'd probably go running around here like a senile dog trying to fetch it."

While Abner raved on and on about his misguided mother, Tango quickly rushed over to where Joe sat as he desperately tried to get him to leave.

"What are you doing here?" he leaned down and whispered in Joe's ear.

"I've come to bamboozle the big, fat geezer," Joe whispered with a chuckle.

"Absolutely not. You get up right now and—"

"Tango, now you remember what I said about this Joe employee," Abner suddenly said in an authoritarian voice. "I don't want this Joe fellow around this hotel anymore. You fire him on the spot and send him packing. Is that understood?"

"Yes, sir," he answered nervously. "I will."

"Oh, he's already been fired, Abner." Tutty quickly came to Tango's defense. "He wasn't one of our regular employees anyway. He came from some temporary agency that we sometimes get workers from."

"Well, we certainly won't use any more of *their* employees."

"Mr. Redder, maybe it'll be best if Mr. Beasley Upchurch left with me," Tango said nervously as he gazed down at Joe as the charming, smooth orangutan continued to beam his bodacious, pompous smile and leisurely puff on his cigar. "He had no right just barging in on you like this, Mr. Redder. I know you're a busy man running this hotel and you don't have time for any frivolous conversations."

"Nonsense," Abner said with a smile of his own. "I like that a fellow member of your staff desires to get to know the head man a little better."

"But—"

"Now you go on about your duties of looking after this hotel, Mr. Parker, and just leave me and Mr. Upchurch here to have our conversation," he said with a smile. "I'd like to get to know the man a little better."

After staring at Joe for a long second, Tango finally turned and headed for the door as Tutty followed.

"Joe is going to ruin everything," Tango said in a low voice to Tutty.

"Don't worry," Tutty whispered. "I won't let anything happen."

When Tutty let Tango out the door and she came back into the parlor, Abner and Joe were beginning to have a cordial conversation.

"Well, Mr. Upchurch, how do you like working here at the Lucky Jackpot Hotel so far?"

"Please, call me Beasley," Joe said as he smiled over at Abner. "All my friends call me Beasley."

"Sure Beasley."

"And working here at this beautiful, wonderful hotel has so far been an extraordinary experience, Mr. Redder."

"Oh, call me Abner, likewise my good man," he said with a smile. "Tell me Beasley, did I hear you say that you worked as a butler over there in England at the queen's castle when you and the rest of your associates first arrived with Mr. Parker?"

"Buckingham Palace, that's correct, my good man." Joe quickly feigned up a British accent as he puffed on his cigar and beamed his cunning smile. "I can tell you some wild stories of my time over there working for the queen that you just wouldn't believe."

"Oh, really?"

"Take the time when I was serving the royal queen some soup and tea in bed one night when she wasn't feeling well."

"What happened?"

"The queen looked at me and said, 'Where are you from, my dear man?' I said, 'From the Sumatra jungle, Your Highness.'"

"What happened then?"

"The queen looked at me with lustful eyes and said, 'Is it true what they say about the sexual prowess of men who live in the jungle?' I said, 'I don't know, Your Highness. I haven't yet met a man who has a banana and a pair of coconuts quite like me.'"

"What did the old queen say then?"

"She said, 'well hop into bed my dear man and let me share my empire with the Third World.'"

Abner roared with laughter has his huge, medicine ball belly rumbled and tumbled as if it were suddenly tossed and shaken by a mighty earthquake. Tutty stood in the middle of the parlor with her arms folded, staring down at Joe as he sat in the armchair casually smoking his cigar. She could only shake her head as she smirked.

"Beasley, my good man," Abner said as he gushed a hefty smile. "Would you care for a drink? I have a bottle of some of the best rum in the world."

"Yes, indeed, by all means."

"Tutty, bring us some glasses and break out my best bottle of rum from the liquor cabinet."

Tutty brought the drinking glasses and the bottle of rum over as she poured both of them a glass of rum. She set the bottle of rum on the coffee table between Abner and Joe and glanced at both of them.

"Well, I guess I'll leave you two *men* alone so you can talk."

"That's a real good idea, woman."

Tutty suddenly gave Joe a hard, penetrating look and pointed her finger at him as if to say "watch it, ape" as she turned and left out of the parlor.

"Hey, Beasley," Abner said in a low voice when Tutty left the room. "Did the wife leave out?"

"Most definitely, my good man."

"Hey, how fine is that colleague of yours, that Ms. Romeno Mendez?"

"Elvyra . . . I mean—*Ms. Romeno Mendez,*" he said as he gleamed his witty smile at Abner. "Oh, she's gorgeous, my man. That woman is as fine as a cat."

"You know, I think that woman has got the hots for me. That woman was really coming on to me that first night y'all were here. I could tell."

"Ah, Ms. Mendez has been talking about you nonstop ever since that first night, my good man. She can't keep her mind off of you."

"Is that a fact," Abner said with a hefty smile.

"Abner, why you getting all chummy with that stinky, mangy ape sitting over there?" Mama Lulu said angrily from the couch directly across from where Abner and Joe sat. "You need to kick that old, filthy ape out of here this instant."

"Mama—stop it!" Abner yelled. "There ain't no ape in here."

"There is too!"

"Will you stop it!" He yelled even louder. "For the last time, there ain't no ape in this room!"

"THERE IS TOO!"

"You'll have to excuse my mama, Beasley," he said toward Joe. "She's eighty-years-old, but got a brain of a simple minded two-year-old."

"Oh, no apologies needed, my good man. I understand."

Joe suddenly pounded his chest twice with his fist and snapped his finger. Poof! A cloud of purple smoke mushroomed in the air as a flashing highway emergency road sign suddenly appeared in the air that said: DRIVE WITH CAUTION. A MOOLY-MOOLY IS ON THE LOOSE!

"That's it. I've had it with that smiley ape!" Mama Lulu quickly jumped up from the couch with her fists balled up. "I'm going to skin the hair off of that mangy head of his!"

"Mama—will you stop it!"

"Get up, you mangy, old ape!" Mama Lulu said with her fists balled up as Joe continued smiling at her. "Come on—GET UP!"

Tutty quickly rushed into the parlor as she pulled Mama Lulu away and quickly guided her to her bedroom. The entire time, Mama Lulu kept saying, "Let me at him! Just let me at him!"

When Mama Lulu was finally gone from the parlor, Joe pounded his chest twice and snapped his finger once again as the flashing highway emergency road sign that hung in the air suddenly disappeared.

"I tell you, Beasley, if that woman ain't worrying me to death about Benny and those cuckoo clocks of hers, then she's going on and on about some stupid coloring book that she likes to read. Now she's starting to rave about some imaginary ape," Abner said in a frustrated voice as he sipped his rum. "It's enough to drive a man crazy."

"Well, you ought to try to give the old mooly-mooly . . . I mean the dear, sweet lady a pet of some kind," Joe said as he sipped his rum and smoked his cigar. "You should get her maybe a dog, a cat, or something of that nature to help keep the old lady company."

"I HATE ANIMALS!" Abner suddenly shouted with a vicious rage as he started breathing heavily. "I hate *all* animals. I can't even *stand* to be around an animal, let alone smell of the foul beasts."

"Is that a fact?" Joe said with a sly smile. "Well at least you don't have to be around any animals around here."

"You got that right," Abner said in a scolding voice. "But I'd know if any were around. I can smell the stinking foul critters a mile away."

"Tell me, my good man, how did you attain this dump . . . I mean this beautiful, luxurious hotel?"

"Right before I went blind, I hit the lottery for eight hundred million dollars. And get this. On the very same day that I hit the lottery, oil was discovered on the land of my farm back in Texas that brought me another five hundred million dollars. So I quit my job as a tree logger the next day, moved here to Vegas and built this beautiful hotel casino," Abner said proudly. "And I've been running this magnificent hotel casino ever since for the last twelve years."

"You were once a tree logger?"

"Absolutely, my good man. Here, I have a picture that I always keep in my pocket of my younger days when I worked as a tree logger."

Abner dug into his pants pocket as he pulled out a wad of loose change, a couple of pieces of candy, a cell phone, a key ring with a bunch of keys, and an old photo as he dumped everything onto the coffee table next to him. He felt the contents on the coffee table until he finally felt the old, wrinkled photo of a younger version of himself dressed in overalls and holding an ax.

"Yeah, this is it," he said with a smile as he held the old, wrinkled photo over the coffee table for his guest to see. "That's me when I was a young tree logger back in Texas. Here, take a look."

Joe took the photo from Abner as he studied the picture. While he studied the photo, he reached out with his other long, hairy orangutan arm and snatched the ring of keys from the coffee table as he swiftly stuffed the ring of keys into the pocket of his suit coat.

"Oh, you looked most impressive, my good man," Joe said in a flattering voice. "You looked strong and very rugged, yet you had an air of charm and magnetism about you even back then."

"Yes, I did, didn't I?" Abner said with a smile as he sipped his rum. "It's been some years since I had my eyesight when I actually last saw that photo, but I remember it just like it was yesterday."

"You look even more distinguished now, my good man."

Abner and his guest had several more glasses of rum as they talked further and shared more hilarious stories. The cigars, the rum, the laughter, and the good camaraderie seemed as if they were never going to end.

By midnight, Joe finally rose from his armchair as he beamed his smile at Abner.

"Well, my good man, it's been a dashing occasion, but I've taken up enough of your time, and I thank you for your hospitality."

"Drop by any time, my good man, and we'll break out another good bottle of my special rum," Abner said in a chummy voice. "Maybe you can tell me some more stories about your time working at the great Buckingham Palace."

"Well, I'll leave you with this one, my good man," Joe said as he lit up a new cigar. "One night at Buckingham Palace we were having this big fancy ball with all sorts of dignitaries and luminaries from all over the world in attendance. Myself and the rest of the staff were busy serving all the guests this fancy champagne and caviar, while this symphony was playing this dull, boring music.

"After about an hour, we finally told the symphony to take a break and we pulled out a stereo system, hooked up some speakers and started cranking out some old, funky classics. We played a little bit of everything from David Bowie, Michael Jackson, Elton John, Donna Summer, Elvis Presley, The O'Jays, Stevie Wonder, and The Bee Gees. I mean we played all of the old, funky hits."

"What did all the dignitaries and luminaries do?"

"The whole Buckingham Palace suddenly turned into a wild party," Joe said as he smoked and gleamed his smile. "They soon dropped that fancy champagne and started guzzling down hard liquor like it was water. I mean those old, stuffy luminaries were partying up a storm."

"Sound like them dignitaries were loving those old disco hits."

"Oh, later on that night, the ball *really* got wild and loose when we started playing all of those current hip hop artists like Lil Nas X, Migos, Travis Scott, Megan Thee Stallion, Drake and a whole bunch of other stuff," Joe said with a hearty laugh. "Well, finally in the wee hours of the morning, we started running out of liquor. So, I went to go get some more cases of liquor from the back, when all of a sudden, I was pulled into this private room by this five-hundred-pound duchess who was totally naked."

"What did she say?"

"She smiled and said, 'The royal queen told me all about your banana and coconuts and I'd love to give you my empire."

"What did you do?"

"I looked at the duchess and started coming up with a million excuses not to get busy with that big, old fat whale."

"What did you say?"

"I said, 'I would, Duchess, but I'm getting ready to take one of the horses from the Buckingham Palace stable and ride down to *Old Town Road* on an errand that the queen has just asked me to go on."

"What did the duchess say?"

"She just smiled and said, 'I'd love to ride with you on that horse down to *Old Town Road*."

"What did you do?"

"I said, 'That's fine and all, Duchess, but you see after I head down to *Old Town Road,* I'm getting ready to wax my race car for this big *Motorsport* event that I'm about to enter."

"What did the duchess say then?"

"She just smiled and said, 'I'll go with you and help you wax it."

Abner chuckled. "Then what did you say?"

"I said, 'That's fine and all, but you see I got a ticket to the big *Astroworld* music festival in Houston that I'm heading out to when I finish waxing my race car."

"What did the duchess say then?"

"She just smiled and said, 'I got my ticket, too."

"Then what did you say?"

"Well, I got tired of coming up with all of these excuses. So finally, I just looked that fat *Big Ole Freak* straight in the eyes and repeated that Drake song to her."

"What's that?"

"I said, 'Sorry to tell you this, Duchess, but I'm just *Way 2 Sexy* for your empire and I flew out of that room."

Abner thundered laughing so hard that he knocked over the coffee table beside him.

"Well, you have a good night," Joe said as he blew out a double smoke ring and beamed his witty smile. "It's time for me to retire."

"Alright, Mr. Beasley Upchurch," Abner said with a hefty smile of his own.

Joe left out of Abner's residential suite as he closed the door. As he headed down the hallway, he patted the keys inside his faded brown suit coat that he'd swiped as he blazed a glorious smile.

"I got that fat rhino right where I want him," he said with jubilation. He suddenly took off running, yelping, and hollering as he began to climb the walls of the hallway like the wild jungle ape that he was.

It was almost one o'clock in the morning. Abner and Tutty were in their bedroom, still up after a long, busy day. Tutty was in bed watching one of her recorded daytime shows on TV, while Abner sat on his side of the bed and fed his favorite fish, a beautiful blue beta fish he'd had for years that he called Mr. Striper.

The fish was in a fishbowl on the nightstand next to the bed, and Abner, because of his blindness, spilled fish food all over the nightstand in his attempt to feed his favorite fish. It was a nightly occurrence. Mr. Striper usually got only half the food he needed, because the other half always fell wastefully on the nightstand.

"Tutty, you think I've fed Mr. Striper enough food for the night?" Abner said as he continued sprinkling fish food all over the nightstand as he kept missing the fishbowl.

"Yeah, Abner," Tutty said without taking her eyes away from watching TV. "You've fed him more than enough."

"You know, I must have the oldest Siamese fighting fish in the entire world," he said with a giant smile. "I've heard that Beta fish usually only live about three to five years in captivity. But Mr. Striper here must be a rare one indeed. He's been with me for over fifteen years, way before I went blind. That has to be a world record, Tutty."

"Not if he happens to be another Mr. Striper, he's not," Tutty whispered as she stifled a snicker.

"You say something?"

"Oh, nothing Abner. Go ahead and feed your fish."

"You know, Tutty, I don't know what I'd do if I ever lost Mr. Striper. He means the world to me."

"I wish I could say the same for you," she mumbled.

"What did you say?"

"Nothing."

Abner finally put the fish food on the nightstand beside the fishbowl as he got into bed. He had on his pajamas and his dark sunglasses were now off. Resting his head on two stacks of pillows, he began to chuckle as he thought of the wonderful time he had tonight with Beasley Upchurch.

"You know, Tutty, that Beasley fellow is a pure riot," he said as he chuckled. "I really like the fellow."

"Is that a fact?"

"Yeah." Abner smiled. "He's got a good sense of humor, he's a refined gentleman who's been all over the world, and he's smart too—*a real smart gentleman*."

"Oh, he's something else, alright," Tutty said with a smirk.

"That brings me back to the situation with this Joe character," he suddenly said with angst. "We've never had an employee who's worked at this hotel as a bellhop that got so many complaints in one day from our hotel guests as this Joe fellow did."

"Well, he's gone now, Abner, so you can rest your mind of that situation."

"Tutty, not only did he steal a car, but this Joe fellow got complaints that he hooked a whole pack of firecrackers to the back of a man's pants and set them off, snatched a woman's wig off her head and went running down the hall, spray painted blue paint all over a woman's brand new wedding gown, smacked a lady on the behind when he was taking her bags up to her room, and a whole bunch of other stuff, too."

"I know, Abner," Tutty said with a deep sigh. "I heard the complaints, too."

"Well, he better be gone from this hotel *permanently*!" Abner yelled heatedly. "They said he acted like a plum ape around here."

"Yeah, I know."

"You know, Tutty, a thought just suddenly came to me."

"Well, there's a first time for everything."

"This Joe fellow," he said with a frown, "he wouldn't by any chance be connected with Mr. Parker? You don't think that Mr. Parker hired him, do you?"

"No, Abner," Tutty quickly said. "I told you he came from this temporary agency that we sometimes get workers from when we're a little understaffed."

"Well, you just make sure they don't send over any more workers like this Joe fellow again."

"Don't worry, Abner. They won't."

"And speaking of Mr. Parker, I told him during our meeting today that he has until the end of this week to come up with a detailed report on how he plans to start bringing in some conventions to this hotel," Abner said with a snap. "He and his agency better produce some conventions to this hotel, and I mean real soon, or he and his entire staff will be out of here. But of course," he suddenly said with an aroused smile, "that Ms. Romeno Mendez can stay around as long as she likes."

"Abner, you've got to give that boy—" Tutty quickly halted her sentence. "I mean, you've got to give Mr. Parker time to get adjusted to his new role as assistant hotel manager around here. He needs time to get everything organized."

"This hotel doesn't have time to wait, Tutty!" Abner said harshly. "We need to start getting some conventions in here, and I mean soon. I just hope this Mr. Parker is up for the job. I know you said he has good qualifications and his résumé was impeccable, but quite frankly, sometimes he sounds like some damn blabbering teenager."

"That doesn't mean anything. Sometimes you sound like a dumbass, and a *lot* of times you are."

"Tutty, don't start with me. The profit margin of this hotel is going down and we need to do something to change that. We need conventions."

"The reason the profit margin is steadily going down is because we need some new and better entertainment around here, Abner. The stuff we're offering the people is getting tired and old."

"New and better entertainment," Abner said sarcastically. "Like what?"

"Well, how about putting on . . ." she uttered as she hesitated. "How about putting on an animal act?"

"What did you say?" he suddenly shouted as a ball of fire almost spewed from his mouth. "You know I hate animals. I don't want no animals around here, is that understood?" he said as he suddenly started breathing heavy and clutching his chest. "I DON'T WANT NO ANIMALS ANYWHERE AROUND THIS HOTEL! DO YOU HEAR ME—*I HATE ANIMALS*!"

"Alright, Abner, calm down, please," Tutty quickly said as she looked over at him with frightful eyes. "Please, just calm down. I don't want you busting a vein and having a heart attack. I'm sorry I even mentioned it."

"NO ANMIALS, DO YOU HEAR ME?" he shouted with rage. "NO ANIMALS!"

"Alright, Abner, alright," Tutty said in a conciliatory voice as she finally turned off the TV with the remote and rolled over. "I'm going to sleep. Goodnight."

Abner's anger slowly began to wane the longer he rested on his side of the bed in silence. Like a huge blowup doll filled with hot air, the big man slowly began to deflate.

When he'd finally calmed down, he soon became aroused. Wanting some love and affection, he slowly reached over and touched Tutty, and the mere touch of her body made him even more aroused.

"Hey, Tutty," he said with a lustful smile, "it's time to roll on over and do your duty."

"Abner," she said in a sleepy voice as she lay on her side.

"Yeah, my little cutie."

"You still ain't getting none of this."

When Abner finally began to hear Tutty's slight snoring, he couldn't help but to let out a frustrated sigh.

No sooner as he began to wallow in his sexually repressed misery, one o'clock suddenly struck. Above the headboard of his bed, he began to hear a commotion as he distinctly heard a voice. Abner's misery and frustration immediately sunk even lower, because he knew without a doubt who the voice belonged to.

On the wall right above the headboard of their bed was an automation cuckoo clock that resembled an elaborate big city police station. The three inch high mechanical policeman who came out of the police station at the top of every hour on a mechanical track was none other than Benny.

The police station cuckoo clock was one of five cuckoo clocks that Mama Lulu had scattered all around the house, and Abner hated the little, irritating weasel that came out each of the clocks. He wanted all of Mama Lulu's cuckoo clocks thrown out of the house, but he *especially* wanted the particular clock currently located on the wall above the headboard of his bed thrown out and demolished.

The only reason Abner even allowed the police station cuckoo clock to remain in his bedroom in the first place was because some time ago, Tutty had sided with Mama Lulu concerning the clock when one Christmas Mama Lulu had given the clock to Abner and Tutty as a gift. Tutty, not wanting to hurt Mama Lulu's feelings and to keep Abner's simple minded mother from throwing a tantrum, decided to go ahead and keep the clock in their bedroom. To get Abner to go along with her decision, she promised him all the loving and affection that he could handle if he just wouldn't do away with Mama Lulu's pride and joy; and like the horny sucker that he was, Abner gave in to her request.

With blue lights flickering from the police station cuckoo clock like emergency lights flashing from a police squad car, Benny, dressed in a spiffy blue police uniform and carrying a nightstick, suddenly came out of the police station on a mechanical track. The three inch high mechanical cop had a perpetual scowl. He looked like a mean, tough cop who didn't take any mess on his beat.

"Hey, you down there," Benny suddenly said in a surly voice as he held his nightstick. "What are you doing down there in the dark?"

"Go away, you little nuisance!" Abner snapped.

"Listen, you fat blimp, you're talking to the law here. We just got a call to this police station that some fat pervert was lying around in the dark performing some lewd sexual act. And that description fits you."

"Will you go away and leave me alone!"

"No can do, fat man. Ordinate 656 of our city statute states that no masturbation, indecent exposure, or any other illicit act of sex may be performed out in public. Just the other night, I had to run a couple of horny teenagers away from around here who were humping underneath a tree last night. It was totally inappropriate what they were doing, and it's totally unacceptable what you're doing down there, fat man."

"I ain't doing nothing, you little runt. Now go away and leave me alone!"

"You got some dirty pictures down there or something, because I don't allow no pornographic material on my beat, fatso?"

"WILL YOU GO AWAY!"

"Is that your wife, Tutty, lying down there next to you asleep?"

"You know who it is, you little, nagging twerp!"

"Well, I tell you what, big man. I might let you off this time with only a warning, but only if you'll answer this riddle."

"I ain't answering no stupid riddle!"

"Answer it, big man, or I'll stay out here all night long."

Abner finally sighed in frustration. "Alright, what's the riddle?"

"Here's the riddle. What do Noah's Ark and The Goose That Laid the Golden Egg have in common?"

"I don't know!" Abner said in an angry voice.

"Neither do I," Benny quickly replied. "But one thing I *do* know is that it's been forty days and forty nights since old Abner last got laid."

As Abner mulled and stewed in anger when Benny went back into the police station, the Magic Rainbow Hotel & Casino Orchestra suddenly began to play a closing melody.

The curtain closed on the main stage as ACT I ended.

INTERMISSION

ACT II

The curtain opened on the main stage. Abner and Tutty were in a meeting inside their residential suite office discussing the two upcoming conventions slated to arrive at the Lucky Jackpot Hotel. It was eight in the morning and the meeting was in high gear.

"So, Abner, the women's national sorority group, the Alpha Ladies Beta Society, will be checking into the hotel this morning for their convention and I'm pleased to report that all five hundred of our rooms for this weekend will be filled to capacity."

Tutty read from an itemized notebook like an efficient secretary as she sat in a chair in front of Abner's desk.

"Our banquet department is thoroughly prepared and ready with all the food and drinks that we'll be serving the Alpha Ladies Beta Society during their stay here at the hotel," she continued reading from her itemized notebook. "The guest speaker who'll be speaking to the ladies at their noon luncheon today, Dr. Phyllis Winslow, will arrive in a few hours. So we'll give her and the rest of the ladies in attendance for their banquet luncheon all the amenities they need to have a successful convention."

"Wonderful," Abner said with a hearty smile as he sat behind his desk with his black shades on. "Is the entire hotel staff ready for today?"

"Absolutely." Tutty nodded. "The entire hotel staff will be ready to serve."

"Sounds good," he said as he sipped from a glass of water.

"And next week, we have the Smith & Hirsch Brothers National Car Salesmen convention slated for here at the hotel, and all rooms will be filled to capacity for next week also. They've already sent in their deposit for their convention and their rooms, so everything looks alright for next week."

"Excellent," Abner said as his smile widened. "I have to compliment Mr. Parker. I told him I wanted some conventions at this hotel, and he and his crack unit staff got on the ball and made it happen."

"Now you know Mr. Parker had to slash room rates in half for all the conventioneers, don't you?"

"He did what?" Abner said as his fat cheeks suddenly began to swell like a boiling, mad owl. "He slashed room rates without my permission!"

"Abner, he had to slash room rates in order to attract anybody to come to this dump, let alone attract any conventions to come here," Tutty said in a pointed voice. "That's the only reason why we have these two conventions coming here is because of the slashed room rates. Why else would they come here?"

"Woman, the Lucky Jackpot Hotel is a refined, upscale Las Vegas hotel that anyone would be proud to come to."

"Please," she said with a snicker. "You must think this place is the Mirage or Caesars Palace."

"How *dare* he slash room rates without my knowledge!" he said like hot cannon fire. "I tell you, Tutty, that really steams me!"

Siren! Siren! Siren!

Flashing lights suddenly lit up from the fire station cuckoo clock on the wall behind the desk as a wailing siren began to shriek out. Benny, the three inch high mechanical fireman dressed in a red, shiny fireman suit, suddenly came out of the fire station cuckoo clock as he came sliding down the fire pole carrying a fire hose.

"What, big man steaming?" Benny said as he quickly shot a blast of water down on Abner's head from his fire hose. "I'll cool the fat man off," he said as he kept spraying the living daylights out of him. "Don't worry. Big man will be cooled off in a second."

Benny suddenly shut off the spigot of his fire hose and dashed back into the fire station. Abner sat behind his desk, dripping wet as his fat cheeks kept puffing in and out as if he were about to explode at any second.

"That stupid little twerp! I'm going to rip his head off!"

"I thought you already had your shower this morning." Tutty giggled.

"Never mind the sassy jokes, woman," Abner yelled. "You just get on that phone and call Mr. Parker and tell him and his staff to get in this office this instant!"

"Alright, Abner, alright."

When Tutty picked up the office phone and called Tango, Mama Lulu suddenly strolled into the office. She looked a pure mess this morning. Her uncombed white hair stood all over her head as if she'd just been shocked by a bolt of lightning and her blouse was on backwards. She had on some old shoes on the wrong feet, and the red lipstick she tried to put on, was smeared on one side of her mouth as it went down her chin in a crooked line.

"Abner," Mama Lulu said as she came over to his desk. "I want to do my part for the convention today."

"Mama, we're trying to have an important meeting here." Abner quickly snapped. "Don't come in here bothering me with your crazy, babbling talk this morning. Go read your stupid Madam Cureall coloring book or something."

"But I want to be a showgirl," she said like a whiny, little child. "You promised that you were going to let me dance with the showgirls."

"Are you nuts?" he shouted. "Why did I even ask that stupid question for? Of course you're nuts. I didn't promise you no such a thing."

"You did, too!"

"No, I didn't!"

Tutty hung up the phone when she got through talking as she looked over at Abner. "What's going on?"

"Mama is on one of her crazy rants again about being a showgirl," Abner yelled. "She must think I'm insane. Do I look like a fool or something?"

Tutty began to smirk. "Well, as a matter of fact—"

"Mama, you're eighty years old and you're too short to be *anybody's* showgirl!" Abner yelled as he suddenly interrupted Tutty. "How many times do I have to tell you that? You want to be a showgirl? Go twirl around in your room to some music. I tell you," he said as he shook his head, "that woman keeps telling me she wants to be a showgirl. Next she's probably going tell me she wants to be a dancer in some strip club so she can make it rain."

Siren! Siren! Siren!

Flashing lights once again lit up from the fire station cuckoo clock on the wall behind the desk as a wailing siren began to shriek out. Benny once again came out of the fire station cuckoo clock as he slid down the fire pole carrying a fire hose.

"Making it rain!" Benny yelled as he blasted Abner with a gush of water from his fire hose. "*Making it rain! Making it rain!*"

When Benny dashed back into the fire station cuckoo clock, Abner was soaking wet but mad as fire.

"That's what you get, you fat lard," Mama Lulu yelled as she pointed a finger at Abner. "You need to make me a showgirl so I can show off what I got."

"A hundred-year-old man in a nursing home wearing diapers don't even want what you got!" Abner yelled.

"You take that back, or I swear I'm going to whack that fat head of yours until it comes rolling off!"

"Mama Lulu, why don't you just forget all of this showgirl stuff and try to rest your mind," Tutty suddenly said in a comforting voice. "Dr. Leachman told you to not get too excited because it makes your psychosis even worse."

"You shut up, you home wrecker!"

Tutty sighed and shook her head as she looked at Mama Lulu. When the front doorbell to their residential suite suddenly rang, she left out of the office to go answer the door.

When Tutty opened the door, Tango, Fred, Elvyra, Chipper, Joe, and the Wonder Gang all stood outside. They indeed looked like some kind of weird freak show; it was Tango's animal kingdom and the five raunchy dwarfs.

"Oh," Tutty suddenly said with a look of shock. "I didn't expect the little Harley Davidson Hell Riders would be coming too."

"Lady, you got a problem with us being here?" Lou said in a gravelly voice.

"Yeah, lady," Eddie said as he smoked his cigarette. "What's the deal?"

"We're entertainers, too, you know," Frank replied.

"That's right," Sammy said. "Aren't we welcomed at the Lucky Jackpot Hotel?"

"You know, lady," Mike uttered as he glared up at Tutty. "I hope you're not like this warden at the last jail that I was serving time in, because she was one mean bitch."

Tutty looked at the Wonder Gang for a second, with their black leather jackets and their rough exterior, as she slowly began to shake her head. "This is just great. Now I have the little Sopranos to deal with, too," she mumbled to herself.

"What's that?"

"Nothing," Tutty quickly said. "Just come on in."

Tango and his gang entered the residential suite as Tutty brought them into the parlor.

"Now, before we go into the office, like I told you on the phone, Abner is upset about the slashing of the room rates for the conventioneers," she said to Tango. "But don't worry. I'll back you all the way when we go in there."

"Alright," Tango said with a nod. "Whatever you say."

"Now you guys," she said as she quickly pointed to the Wonder Gang, "you guys stay totally silent. Don't make a sound, not even a peep."

"No problem, Madam Warden," Eddie said in a flippant tone as he smoked his cigarette. "If that's how you want to run your jail, we won't break no rules."

"The name is Tutty," she said in an acid voice as she suddenly placed her hands on her hips and glared down at the five dwarfs who stood in front of her. "And you do well, gentlemen, to remember that."

"No problem, lady," Eddie answered as he suddenly blew a cloud of smoke up at Tutty.

"Yeah," Lou said in his gravelly voice. "No sweat."

Tutty gave all the members of the Wonder Gang a long, leery look, then she slowly turned her gaze toward Tango's animals. When the orangutan suddenly gave her a pompous look, flashing his bodacious smile at her in a mischievous way, she immediately glared at him like a judge getting ready to sentence a malcontent.

"And you," she said with a pointed finger. "You better watch yourself, ape. You comprehend?"

"Cheerio in the dealio, my good madam," Joe said in a mocking British accent. "This bloke has no problem with your rules, Your Majesty."

Tutty could only shake her head as she turned and led the group toward the office.

The contentious argument over Mama Lulu's desire to become a showgirl was still in heated progress when Mama Lulu suddenly became riled and agitated when she saw Joe entering the office.

"There's that old, mangy ape. Put 'em up," she said as she immediately began swinging her fists in the air as Joe beamed his smile at her. "I told you I was going to put a knot on that hairy head of yours. *Put 'em up!*"

"Mama Lulu, will you calm down."

"What in the devil is she talking about now?" Abner said angrily as he took another sip from his glass of water.

"She's not talking about anything. But, Abner, Mr. Parker and his staff have just arrived," Tutty announced.

"Parker!" Abner yelled. "Who gave you permission to slash room rates?"

"Well, sir," Tango nervously said as he quickly looked over at Tutty. "I just thought—"

"You thought what?"

"Well sir—"

"Abner, the boy—" Tutty quickly corrected herself. "I mean, Mr. Parker had no choice but to slash the rates to attract the conventioneers to come here. He's done a fabulous job. You should be happy that we even have the hotel filled to capacity."

As Abner and Tutty argued and fussed, Joe looked over at Mama Lulu as he gleamed his dynamite smile at her. He suddenly pounded his chest twice with his fist and snapped his finger. Poof! A cloud of purple smoke mushroomed in the air as a miniature flying saucer, with flashing lights all around the flying saucer, began to hover in the air.

The flying saucer suddenly came whizzing down as it landed on Abner's office desk. An automatic door quickly descended as two small Martian like space men came out of the flying saucer and held up a sign to Mama Lulu that said: WE'RE FROM THE PLANET MOOLY-MOOLY. WE'VE COME TO TAKE YOU HOME TO OUR PLANET!

"Abner!" Mama Lulu yelled hysterically. "This mangy ape just made this flying saucer land on your desk and these space men want to take me away!"

"Tutty, what the devil is she talking about now?" Abner roared like an angry lion.

"Oh, who knows," Tutty said as she suddenly glared over at Joe.

"First that woman wants to be a showgirl, then she's hollering about some stupid imaginary ape, and now she's talking about some space men in a flying saucer want to take her away. Well, I can't take it anymore," he yelled. "What the devil we been paying that Dr. Leachman for? Mama is as nutty and loony as she's ever been and getting worse!"

Fred quickly leaned over toward Joe. "Get rid of that flying saucer, you stupid ape," he whispered.

Joe once again pounded his chest and snapped his finger. Poof! The Martian space men and the flying saucer disappeared.

"Mr. Redder, sir, about the room rates." Tango began to explain nervously. "I'm sorry if I—"

"Never mind, Parker, I'll deal with you later," Abner said with an angry huff. "First I need to give some orders of how I want my managerial staff to operate while the Alpha Ladies Beta Society is here for their convention this weekend. And I *will* be roaming around the hotel today, so my orders better be implemented."

"Abner, the managerial staff already knows what to do and there's certainly no reason to go through some long—"

"Quiet, woman!" Abner quickly interjected. "There's only one boss of this esteemed hotel and you're looking at him."

"Sorry, sir," she said with an aggravated sigh.

"Bob, I want you to oversee the bellhop service and the room service, is that understood?"

"But—" Fred began to complain, but Tango quickly looked over at him and quickly shook his head. "Yes sir," he finally said with a sigh.

"Mr. Blue Hendrix, seeing that your background was once in concert promoting, I want you to oversee the entertainment of our house band during their nightly performances and the showgirl performances. Understood?"

"And I'll be one of the showgirls tonight, too," Mama Lulu suddenly said with a big smile.

"Never mind her, Mr. Hendrix," Abner quickly said. "Do you understand your duties?"

"Oh, no problem, sir," Chipper said as he suddenly took flight as he began to fly in circles above the office. "I can always find my way through the rainbow."

"Rainbow . . . what rainbow?"

"Oh, nothing, sir."

"Now, Ms. Romeno Mendez—"

"Yes, sir," the Siamese cat said as she quickly jumped onto the office desk and began to rub up against Abner's arm flirtatiously. "I'm *always* at your service, sir."

"Oh, how nice to hear." Abner began to blush as he chuckled. "My, I must say I feel a very soft furriness brush along my arm that's somewhat unique."

"That's my fine, fur coat, sir," she said in an alluring voice. "Do you like?"

"Indeed I do," Abner said with a huge smile. "My, you must be a very sophisticated lady to wear a fur coat to work."

"I try to be as presentable as I can for you, sir."

"How nice," Abner said as his huge, wide smile began to spread even further. "Well, Ms. Mendez, your duties will be to conduct a survey of all the convention guests while they're here. I want you to ask questions to see how they're enjoying their stay here at the Lucky Jackpot Hotel, and I want you to see if there's anything else that we can do to make their stay as comfortable as possible. I want you to keep precise hourly records of the overall atmosphere that the conventioneers are having here at the hotel, and I want you to bring your final report directly to me by the end of the day. Understood?"

"It'll be my pleasure, sir," Elvyra said as she suddenly sprayed a red, colorful scent onto Abner from her feline body that smelled like the most divine perfume ever.

"Oh, my, I can't wait for that report," Abner said with a dreamy smile as he sniffed the air.

"And I can't wait to *bring* it to you, sir."

"Now, Mr. Beasley Upchurch."

"Yes, my good man?"

"With your worldly self, with you having been working around royalty and with all your charm, grace, and personality, I want you to oversee the convention itself and to make all the conventioneers at all times feel welcomed," Abner said with a smile. "I'm making you the head point man of our public relations department to represent the face of this hotel."

"It'll truly be an honor, my good man," Joe said in a regal British accent as he flashed his cunning smile.

"Abner, I don't think that's such a good idea," Tutty quickly said as she glared over at the orangutan. "I think someone else should—"

"Woman, as president and CEO of this fabulous hotel, I've made up my mind," Abner said as he quickly cut her off. "There's no doubt about it. Mr. Beasley Upchurch is the man for the job."

"Excuse me, Mr. Redder," Tango suddenly said with an air of nervousness in his voice, "but I think Bob would serve perfect in that role. I think he'd be much better, sir."

"Bob," Abner said with a hearty chuckle. "No offense, Bob, but what does a former dog catcher know about public relations and dealing with people."

"What does a jackass know about running a hotel," Fred mumbled.

"Well, does everyone know their roles for the convention today?"

"Yes, we do," everyone answered.

"Good," Abner said as he suddenly grabbed his glass from the desk. He turned the glass up to his mouth for a sip of water, but quickly discovered that his glass was empty. "Damn, I'm all out of water."

Siren! Siren! Siren!

Benny once again came out of the fire station cuckoo clock as he slid down the fire pole with a fire hose in his hand.

"Water coming up! Water coming up!" Benny shouted as he sprayed a blast of water from his fire hose down on Abner's head. Within seconds, Benny turned the spigot off to the fire hose and dashed back into the fire station.

Drenching wet, madder than hell, and with snickering and laughter going around the room, Abner suddenly smashed his office desk with his fist like a wrecking ball crashing into a building.

"What the devil is everybody standing around snickering and laughing when there's work to be done?" he said with hot fire. "Let's make this convention the best in all of Las Vegas, people. Now let's get out there and roll out the red carpet—LET'S GO!"

A musical theatrical song began.

The Magic Rainbow Hotel & Casino Orchestra began to play an upbeat number as a large extravaganza began. A flood of showgirls, bellhops, concierges, casino workers, restaurant workers, and the rest of the Lucky Jackpot Hotel staff began to whirl and twirl in intricate choreography dance steps in the main hotel lobby as jubilant smiles radiated from everyone. One by one, Tango, Zimmy, Joe, Elvyra, and the Wonder Gang came strutting and dancing to the forefront of the extravaganza as Chipper flew overhead. A world of pomp and flair, like a Mardi Gras parade, ensued as confetti fell from overhead while everyone danced and sang.

"We're going to roll out the red carpet for you," half of the staff sung.

"Yes we are!" the other half sung.

"We're going to show you a real good time."

"Just wait and see!"

"So come on in."

"Just make yourself at home!"

"We got all the frills and thrills."

"That'll make you want to stay!"

"So unpack your bags and forget a motel."

"Because you're always welcomed at the Lucky Jackpot Hotel!"

The large extravaganza of hotel workers and showgirls suddenly began to part like the Red Sea. All of a sudden Fred came out of the hotel lobby elevator dressed in a king's red cape and wearing a golden crown on his head. Everyone immediately began to bow before his majestic presence as he strolled to the head of the great pyramid and stood like a mighty emperor.

With his entire kingdom bowing before his feet, the orchestra suddenly concluded the extravaganza. The musical number ended as the audience inside the Magic Rainbow Hotel & Casino Theater cheered and applauded.

By noon, Fred, with his dog vest on that said Welcome to the Lucky Jackpot Hotel, wandered through the lobby of the hotel checking everything out. The place was packed with people everywhere as guests from the Alpha Ladies Beta Society had arrived for their convention.

After checking out all the happenings going on inside the casino, Fred finally wandered over near the table that Chipper was performing at in the hotel lobby titled Chipper's Entertainment Booth. A large crowd of around thirty women or so huddled around the table as they watched the festivities take place.

As it was before, two showgirls helped assisted Chipper as he interacted with the guests, sung musical numbers, and performed his comedy skit. Today, however, Chipper entertained and amused the guests around the table as he showed off the rare power and capabilities that his miraculous left eye had.

"Folks, my left eye is like nothing you've ever seen before," Chipper said to all the people huddled around his table in a pompous, loud voice like a circus ring master getting all the people ready for a special act. "Being from the Amazon rainforest, the sun has enlightened my eye with special powers and gifts that no other creature that lives in the equator region of my part of the world has."

"What can your left eye do?" a lady asked.

"Funny you should ask that, my dear lady, because I believe everyone should see the light."

A red laser light all of a sudden began to beam from Chipper's left eye as he scanned the ultra, bright red laser light into the faces of all the guests huddled around the table.

"Wow, that's incredible!" a woman suddenly said in awe.

"It sure is!" another woman said.

"That's awesome!"

"Simply unbelievable!"

"How did you do that?"

"Well, it's not any computer-generated imagery or some optical illusion that you see in a movie, folks," Chipper said to the crowd. "It's all natural, as natural as the sun rises over the Amazon."

"Hey, you're alright, parrot," a lady said with a wondrous smile.

"Yeah, a fully grown talking parrot," another woman said. "I wish I could take you home with me."

"Are you married?"

"Yes, I am."

"Well, if I come home with you, then you better send your husband away."

"Why?"

"Because, my dear, I'm going to talk dirty to you all night and get you all hot and horny until you finally—"

Chipper suddenly shot a round of fireworks out of his left eye as a massive, colorful ball crackled and exploded in the air as it came raining down like the fourth of July.

"Oh, you naughty bird," the woman said with a smile as everyone around the table laughed.

"Say," Chipper said in an upbeat voice as he looked around. "Is anybody here at the Lucky Jackpot Hotel celebrating anything today?"

"I'm celebrating a birthday today," a lady quickly responded with a huge smile.

"Well, girls, let's get to it."

"*Happy birthday to you*!" the showgirls standing behind the table began to sing. "*Happy birthday to you! Happy birthday to you!*"

At the end of the song, Chipper winked his left eye at the woman as a small wrapped gift with a ribbon tied around it flew out of his large beak as the woman caught the gift.

"Wow," she said as everyone cheered and applauded. "You're amazing!"

Tango, dressed in his official assistant hotel manager's suit, suddenly came out of his office as he strolled over to Fred. They both watched as Chipper entertained and amused the crowd that surrounded his table as he kept attracting more and more people by the second.

"Wow, it looks like Chipper's Entertainment Booth is really taking off," Tango said with a smile. "Looks like I might need to find a bigger area for Chipper to perform at."

"No doubt about that." Fred nodded. "Chipper really knows how to pull the people in."

"Have you seen Joe around anywhere?"

"Yeah, I just saw the crazy ape outside standing on top of the building shooting off a cannon," Fred said frivolously.

"I wouldn't put it pass him if he were doing just that." Tango chuckled.

"I hope you ain't still got him working as one of the hotel bellhops, do you?"

"No way. In fact, Tutty just called up to my office and specifically instructed me that she doesn't want Joe doing *anything* around the hotel in a job capacity anymore."

"I guess she quickly learned her lesson about that crazy ape."

"Yeah, and I wish Joe hadn't fooled Mr. Redder so tough. He really thinks that Joe is this refined, worldly gentleman who actually worked for the queen of England over there at the Buckingham royal palace. Can you imagine that?"

"From one jackass to another jackass," Fred said with a deep sigh. "Anyone who would make Joe the head point man and the face of this hotel is definitely addled in the brain. I'm telling you, that fat blimp's elevator doesn't go all the way up."

"Well, I—"

"Good afternoon, everyone," Elvyra said in a rich, sophisticated voice as she suddenly came over the hotel intercom system to perform her afternoon announcements. "I want to welcome all the women of the Alpha Ladies Beta Society to the Lucky Jackpot Hotel," she said in a sexy, adorable voice. "While you're here for your convention this weekend, I hope you take full advantage of all the luxuries that our fabulous hotel has to offer.

"Come and visit our lovely swimming pool area, dine in our incredible restaurant, stroll over to our bar and lounge area and watch our beautiful showgirls perform, or spend some time in our marvelous casino. And don't be afraid to try your luck, either. Ladies, it's just like trying to win a good man. You may roll the dice and win that handsome Trojan horse, or crap out and find yourself with a dead beat mule," she said with a giggle. "Well, that's all for right now. So, *meow* to all you lovely ladies and ta-ta!"

Tango suddenly gazed down at Fred when Elvyra had finished her announcement and he saw the puddle of drool on the floor that had dripped from his mouth.

"She still gets to you, huh?" he said with a slight chuckle.

"Yeah," Fred answered with his head hanging down. "I guess I can't deny it."

No sooner when Fred admitted his lovesick guilt, Elvyra, wearing one of her beautiful red and green silk scarfs tied around her neck, suddenly came out of Tango's office swishing her long, beautiful tail as she strolled over to where Fred and Tango stood.

"Ooh, Freddy," she said with a giggle. "You've drooled all over yourself. You must be hungry or something."

"Yeah, I must be," he said sheepishly.

"Elvyra," Tango uttered as he gazed down at her. "Do you always have to talk in such a glamorous, superfluous way when you're giving the hotel announcements?"

"*Superfluous*," Elvyra said as she began to rub against Tango's leg in a sexually, suggestive manner. "Oh, sweetie, I'm so impressed. I just love the way this new job of yours keeps changing you every day. The suit, that tie, and everything else is *really* turning this cat on."

"Stop it, Elvyra," Tango quickly said as he gave her a stern look.

Suddenly Abner, dressed in a red suit coat, green slacks, a bright yellow shirt, and a fat necktie with huge giraffes engraved all over it, came ambling toward Tango and the rest of the gang with the aid of his white cane and black shades on. He looked like an overgrown, stuffed peacock strolling to a masquerade party.

"Here comes the psychedelic Goodyear Blimp." Fred snorted.

"Hello, Mr. Redder," Tango said respectfully when Abner approached.

"Who's that, Mr. Parker?"

"Yes, sir."

"Have you put my orders into action, Parker?"

"Yes, sir, I have," he answered nervously. "Everyone is carrying out your requests to the tee, sir."

"Very good," Abner said with authority. "I'm still going to have to dock your pay for that foolish, idiotic decision that you took by slashing the hotel room rates. That was a bumbling, stupid mistake on your part, Mr. Parker. I hope you learned a valuable lesson from all of this."

"Yes, sir," Tango said dejectedly. "I have, sir."

"Very well."

"Oh, I just *love* carrying out the assignment that you've given me to do, Mr. Redder," Elvyra stated in a flirtatious voice as she suddenly sprayed a pink fragrance from her feline body onto Abner. "I've already interviewed dozens and dozens of ladies, and they're all saying how much they love this wonderful hotel that you have here, sir."

"That must be the lovely Ms. Romeno Mendez," Abner said with a giant smile.

"The one and only."

"My, my, my," he said as he suddenly cocked his head back sniffing the air. "I must say, Ms. Mendez, that you do wear the most enticing perfume that I've ever smelled."

"You truly like it, sir?"

"Indeed, I do."

A well-dressed woman, who had on an expensive looking red hat, suddenly approached Abner as he stood talking with Tango and the gang.

"Sir, are you the owner of this hotel?"

"Yes ma'am," he said proudly. "I'm Abner Redder, the owner and CEO of the Lucky Jackpot Hotel. How can I be of service to you?"

"Well, I'm Mrs. Ellen Peters, chairwoman and president of the Alpha Ladies Beta Society."

"It's a pleasure to meet you, ma'am," Abner said cordially. "I'm so glad that your organization decided to have your convention right here at this hotel. I hope you and the rest of the members of your organization will have a fine stay here at the Lucky Jackpot Hotel."

"Well, we hope we will, too. I have to tell you, Mr. Redder, that at first we were a little reluctant to have our convention here at your hotel. The brochure we saw on the Internet of how the hotel looked from the outside wasn't too appealing to us, and the room rates were *definitely* too high," she said sharply. "However, a week later when I went back on the Internet and saw that you had slashed the room rates considerably, well, that made us go ahead and decide to have our convention here."

"Yes, indeed," Abner said with an affirmative nod. "I knew the room rates were *much* too high, so that's why I decided to go ahead and slash the room rates considerably."

"I must say that was very smart of you, sir."

"I appreciate the compliment."

Fred slowly let out a disgusted sigh as he mumbled, "Jackass."

"Oh, and furthermore, we have a little problem, Mr. Redder."

"What's that?"

"Our guest speaker, Dr. Phyllis Winslow, who's supposed to be our guest speaker today for our one o'clock banquet luncheon at the convention hall here at the hotel, just phoned and said she wouldn't be able to make it. It's most unfortunate, because we're not able to get a replacement speaker on such short notice. I was wondering could you recommend someone to replace her?"

"That's quite a shame," Abner suddenly said with a heavy frown. "Let me go back down to my office and call a few people and see if I can arrange a replacement speaker."

"We'd appreciate it very much, Mr. Redder," she said in a pained voice. "It's a shame that Dr. Winslow want be able to make it to the luncheon today. All of our five hundred members of our organization were very much looking forward to her speech today. Dr. Winslow has impeccable credentials in the field of medicine and she's such a highly gifted orator, that she'll be sorely missed. I do hope you can find someone on her esteemed level to replace her."

"Don't worry, Mrs. Peters," Abner said with a confident smile. "The Alpha Ladies Beta Society is in good hands. I'll take care of everything."

"Wonderful. Thank you, Mr. Redder." She returned his smile. "I must say also that this hotel may be a little somewhat on the shabby side for as Las Vegas standards go, but I do have to admit, that it has a certain special entertainment quality to it."

"Why yes," Abner said proudly. "Our house band and showgirls are some of the best in all of Vegas."

"No, I meant these animals that you have here around the hotel." She suddenly chuckled. "They're quite unusual, yet fascinating. Have you somehow programmed some kind of voice box or something to make it seem like that they're actually talking?"

"What did you say?" Abner said as he began to sweat. "What animals?"

"These animals standing right here," she said as she waved her hand toward Tango's animals. "They're quite fascinating."

"There are no animals at this hotel," he said as he all of a sudden started breathing heavily, sweating, and tugging uncomfortably at his collar trying to get air. "I absolutely don't allow *any* animals at all at this hotel, ma'am. And any guest who brings an animal into this hotel will be asked to leave immediately."

"Mr. Redder—" Tango quickly tried to intervene.

"No animals are allowed in here." He started breathing even harder and sweating profusely. "Did you hear me—ABSOLUTELY NO ANIMALS ARE ALLOWED AT THIS HOTEL!"

"Alright, sir, please, calm down," the woman quickly said as she suddenly stared at Abner with eyes of fright. "I didn't mean to cause you to get upset."

When the woman finally walked away, Tango, Fred, and Elvyra quickly jumped to the defense.

"Mr. Redder, she doesn't know what she's talking about," Tango nervously said. "They're no animals around here."

"That woman must've just hit the bar and already had herself a couple of happy hours," Fred said with a hearty chuckle.

"Yeah." Elvyra suddenly giggled. "I noticed that gin bottle that she was trying to hide in her purse was already near empty."

"Yeah, you're probably right," Abner said as he began to calm down and collect himself. "She probably did have a little too much to drink."

"Well, sir, I guess I better be getting back to work," Tango said to Abner. "With this big convention being here today and with the hotel as full as it is, there's a whole lot to do around here."

"And I must get back to conducting my survey, sir," Elvyra quickly stated. "I must keep a precise, up to the minute record of how the hotel guests are getting along as you've instructed me to do."

"Now you remember, Ms. Mendez, to bring your final report to me by the end of the day, you hear?" Abner said with a smile.

"Oh, it'll be my pleasure, sir."

When Tango and Elvyra walked away, Joe all of a sudden came strolling up to Abner and Fred as he flashed his huge, bombastic smile. Dressed in his usual faded brown suit with a red and white polka dotted tie on, he held a piña colada with a cocktail umbrella sticking out of his drinking glass. He looked like a vacationer relaxing with an alcoholic drink who was thoroughly enjoying his stay at the Lucky Jackpot Hotel.

"Well, my good man," Joe said with a brilliant smile. "I see you're out and about checking how your convention guests are enjoying your marvelous hotel?"

"Ah, is that Mr. Upchurch's voice that I hear?" Abner said with a smile.

"Just call me Beasley, my good man."

"Oh, yes." Abner continued smiling. "So, how are your duties coming along?"

"Simply marvelous, my good man," Joe said as he conned up a British accent. "I'm out and about shaking ladies' hands and showing them around your wonderful, exquisite hotel."

"And God knows what else," Fred mumbled.

"Very good," Abner said with a proud smile. "Keep up the good work, Beasley. I'm certainly glad I can count on a good, well-versed man as yourself to be the face of this establishment. It makes me sleep well at night knowing you're looking out for the well-being of this hotel."

"I'll certainly do my best, my good man. Maybe later on this evening, I can stop by your place and tell you some more stories of my time working at Buckingham Palace."

"Well, the wife is taking me out later on this evening. We're going to take in a show at one of the other hotels on the Strip. From time to time, I kind of like to know what performances that my competitors are putting out," he said with a chuckle. "Though I can't physically see the show myself, Tutty is my eyes and she has a good sense of the entertainment business."

"Will you be taking your lovely, sweet dear mother along?"

"Absolutely not," Abner quickly said. "We're putting her straight to bed."

"Well, have a good outing, my good man."

"We sure will."

Abner began to turn to leave, but he suddenly turned back around.

"Say, I'm supposed to get a replacement speaker for the women of the Alpha Ladies Beta Society for their banquet luncheon that they're having in the convention hall in about an hour, because their speaker had to cancel out at the last moment. A thought just came to me, Beasley."

"What's that, my good man?"

"Would you mind stepping in and being their replacement? I know with all your worldly charm, you'll be just what the ladies are looking for. Plus, you'll be doing me a huge favor, too, by presenting a good face for this hotel."

"No problem, my good man," Joe said with a dynamite smile. "It'll be my pleasure."

"Oh, my goodness," Fred mumbled.

"Swell," Abner said with an elated smile. "I'll inform the ladies to expect you at their luncheon."

Joe suddenly pounded his chest twice with his fist and snapped his finger. Poof! A cloud of purple smoke mushroomed in the air as Joe gave Abner a friendly slap on the back.

"Don't worry, my good man," Joe said as he kept patting Abner on the back. "I'll charm the good ladies with a speech they'll never forget."

"Wonderful." Abner smiled. "Well, I better be going."

When Abner began to walk away, a flashing neon sign was attached to the back of his suit that said: ATTENTION EVERYONE—I'M ABOUT TO LET OUT THE BIGGEST FART!

Fred immediately glared at Joe like a mad wolf. "What the devil you do that for, you crazy ape?"

"Just having a little fun with the fat lard." Joe chuckled as he watched Abner walk away with the flashing neon sign attached to his back.

"You're going to get us into big trouble, you stupid ape!"

"You know," Joe said as he lit up a cigar and beamed his cunning smile. "I think it's time that I introduce the women of the Alpha Ladies Beta Society to Little Joe."

Fred's eyes immediately went wide. "No way, you dumb ape! Don't you dare bring out Little Joe and do that stupid comedy routine!"

By one o'clock, the members of the Alpha Ladies Beta Society were in the midst of having their banquet luncheon inside the Lucky Jackpot Hotel's convention hall. Five hundred ladies sat at tables all around the convention hall listening to the host of their organization as she began to address their luncheon, while the hotel banquet staff served everyone their meals. The banquet luncheon was a dignified, esteemed affair. All throughout the convention hall, every member of the Alpha Ladies Beta Society was well-dressed.

"Good afternoon, ladies, and welcome to our annual convention," the host, Mrs. Ellen Peters, said from the podium as she began the proceedings. "While you're all being served your meals and dining on your lunches, I have to inform you of an important change to our luncheon schedule.

"Earlier today, I was notified that our keynote speaker, Dr. Phyllis Winslow, wouldn't be able to attend our luncheon today due to a misfortunate emergency," she said as she continued. "However, I've just been informed by the president of the hotel that we'll shortly be getting a substitute speaker to speak in place of Dr. Winslow. So, while we wait for our new keynote speaker to arrive, everyone just enjoy your meals and—"

With his faded brown suit and red and white polka dotted tie on, Joe suddenly waltzed into the convention hall flashing his booming smile. Shocked gasps began to ripple and echo around the convention hall as all the ladies stared in utter disbelief at the sight of the buffoonish, dressed orangutan who suddenly came marching into their banquet luncheon.

Joe immediately began to mess with a few of the ladies eating at their tables in the convention hall, as he started fiddling with their hats and dresses as he came prancing through. He was like some annoying, pesky intruder who'd suddenly barged into their banquet luncheon to disrupt the order of their meeting.

When Joe walked onto the stage and strolled over to the podium, the host, clutching her heart with her mouth hanging wide open in a horrified expression, immediately moved away from the podium. Joe took over the podium when she moved out of the way. He looked out into the crowd of ladies as he smiled.

"Good afternoon, ladies," he said into the microphone in a dignified manner. "My name is Dr. Spindle, the great renowned surgeon, chemist, inventor, and psychologist. I was asked to come speak to all of you dear, esteemed ladies, and I must say it is truly an honor to be here. I would like to introduce to you another fellow doctor who's a good friend of mine who I've brought along to speak to you also. Please welcome, Dr. Barry Bumwater."

Joe reached inside of his faded brown suit and pulled out a puppet that looked exactly like him. The puppet was dressed in a faded brown suit with a red and white polka dotted tie on, the same as Joe. Like a ventriloquist holding up his puppet for the audience to see, Joe and Little Joe began their act.

"Ah, Dr. Bumwater, welcome to the Alpha Ladies Beta Society banquet luncheon here at the Lucky Jackpot Hotel," Joe said to his puppet with an intriguing smile. "Say hello to all the wonderful, beautiful ladies that you see out in the crowd."

Little Joe, with a perpetual, grimacing frown, slowly scanned his head around as he looked out into the audience.

"What beautiful ladies?" Little Joe said harshly. "All I see are a whole lot of fat whales and ugly dogs sitting out there. Why did you interrupt me from a very important brain surgery that I was performing and haul me into this place?"

"Well, Dr. Bumwater, we were invited to come speak to the lovely women of the Alpha Ladies Beta Society banquet luncheon today," Joe said as he beamed his smile. "You have to admit, it's truly a great, stupendous honor to be here."

"Some great honor," Little Joe said with his perpetual frown. "Neither one of us are demolition or explosive experts."

"Why do we need to be demolition or explosive experts, Doctor?"

"Because we need a whole lot of dynamite, wrecking balls, and bulldozers to blast and haul away all the crud, filth, and ugliness that these scamps got caked all over their faces."

Loud gasps, shocked moans, and disturbed angry utterances suddenly began to circulate and reverberate from the women as a nasty overtone quickly started to build all around the convention hall.

"Well, Dr. Bumwater," Joe said hastily as he continued flashing his wily smile. "I think the ladies around the convention hall are starting to become a little feisty. I think we better cut our wonderful visit here today a little short. Wouldn't you say so, Doctor?"

"I believe you're right," Little Joe responded as he gazed out into the audience with his perpetual frown. "Just like Donald Trump once said, these women are starting to get so angry, that blood is starting to ooze out of their eyes or—*wherever*."

"Well, shall we give the lovely women of the Alpha Ladies Beta Society our usual special send off?"

"Yes, Dr. Spindle. Let's do that."

Joe suddenly stashed his puppet back inside of his faded brown suit as he jumped off the stage. He immediately began running around the convention hall like a maniac as he started jumping onto tables, hooping, yelping, and hollering out his jungle call. As all the women screamed and shouted in panic, Joe began smashing dishes, glasses, turning over tables, and throwing pies in women faces like a clown in a cartoon show. The scene inside the convention hall quickly turned into a pure melee mess.

As all the women went screaming and running out of the convention hall, Joe finally climbed onto the huge, beautiful chandelier hanging from the ceiling. With the entire place all in a mad upheaval, Joe dangled from the chandelier hooping, yelping, and hollering like the wild jungle ape that he was.

Abner, Tutty, and Mama Lulu were having their nightly dinner in the dining room of their residential suite. Abner was boiling mad. He sat at the head of the dining table with his black shades on, grilling three members of his banquet staff who stood in his dining room. He wanted some hard answers of who caused the massive disruption inside the convention hall when the Alpha Ladies Beta Society had their banquet luncheon there earlier today.

"Now, gentlemen, I want to know who it was that caused all of that ungodly commotion in the convention hall and insulted those women." Abner bellowed loudly. "I got a disturbing call from Mrs. Ellen Peters, the president of the Alpha Ladies Beta Society, and she said that this Dr. Spindle that he called himself, took over the podium and acted like a wild, boorish ape. In fact, she said he was an ape! Now what can any one of you tell me about this person? Who was this Dr. Spindle? What did he look like?"

Tutty, as she sat at the dining table, quickly shook her head and silently mouthed to the three banquet servers standing in the dining room to not divulge anything about Joe.

"Gentlemen, I'm sitting here waiting on an answer!" Abner said impatiently.

"Well, sir, we've never seen this person before," one of the banquet workers finally answered.

"Yeah, that's right," another worker quickly spoke up. "I believe it was someone who just came in off the street."

"That's right, sir," the other banquet worker jumped in and said. "I've never seen that person before."

"Is there anything you fellows can tell me that triggered that incident?" Abner said in an exasperated tone. "After all, you gentlemen were working the convention hall when all of this crazy madness took place."

Tutty quickly shook her head again to the banquet workers as she silently mouthed to them the word "no".

"No, sir, nothing at all."

Abner sighed as he suddenly pounded the dining room table with his fist in frustration. "A lot of help you gentlemen have been," he said angrily. "Alright, you're dismissed."

When the three banquet workers departed out of the residential suite, the doorbell rang again. Tutty got up from the dining table and went to answer the door. When she opened the door and saw Tango standing there, she quickly began to whisper to him.

"Now you watch what you say to him," Tutty said in a low whisper. "We've just returned from his doctor's appointment and the doctor just told him that his blood pressure was way up. Now don't you mention anything about that ape or the rest of those animals, because I certainly don't want him going into some explosive rant and have a heart attack in the middle of the dining room. Is that understood?"

"Yes, ma'am." Tango quickly nodded.

"Alright, come on."

Tutty escorted Tango into the dining room.

"Abner, Mr. Parker is here," she announced.

"Parker!" Abner quickly thundered. "What the devil happened to Mr. Beasley Upchurch? He was supposed to give the speech today to the women of the Alpha Ladies Beta Society during their banquet luncheon. What in the world happened to him?"

"I have no idea, sir," he said nervously as he quickly glanced over at Tutty as she sat back at her spot at the dining table. "In fact, I haven't seen him in a while."

"Did he go to the banquet luncheon at all?"

"I don't know, sir."

"Something very strange is going on around here," Abner said with a grump. "I can almost smell it."

"It's probably the smell of that old, mangy ape that be wandering around here," Mama Lulu said as she ate. "Going around here smoking cigars and doing all that hocus pocus stuff. And I swear," she said in a riled voice as she suddenly balled up her fist, "if it's the last thing I do, I'm going to get him. You just watch me. I'm going to get that mangy, old ape and skin his hairy hide!"

"What the devil is she talking about?" Abner snapped.

"Oh, Abner, it's just Mama Lulu going off on one of her delirious rants." Tutty chuckled. "You know how she gets sometimes."

"Yeah, she's just like some nut sucking a thumb at a lunatic asylum." Abner grumbled as he shook his head. "Alright, Parker, listen up," he quickly said as he got back to the subject at hand. "Me and the Mrs. are going to catch a show at one of the hotels on the Strip a little later on and we'll be back some time later tonight. Now, you'll be in charge of running the hotel while we're gone. I don't want any slip ups or problems like what happened in that convention hall earlier. Is that clear?"

"Yes, sir."

"Now as far as the women of the Alpha Ladies Beta Sorority, I want you to offer them free drinks in the bar and lounge area tonight to make up for all the trouble that they had to endure earlier today," Abner said with authority. "On second thought, just give them some of those complimentary tickets that we still have left over for that roller derby event that's going on over at that junior college out there in Henderson, Nevada. They might like that."

"Mister CEO, the cheapskate," Tutty said as she shook her head.

"Woman, be quiet," Abner quickly uttered. "Now, Mr. Parker, I want this hotel ran like a fine oil machine while we're away. Is that understood?"

"Totally, sir. You can count on me."

"Very well. You're dismissed."

Tutty rose from the dining room table to escort Tango out the door.

"Listen, you keep that crazy ape away from doing anything around here while we're gone," she whispered to him as her eyes bored into him like hot fire. "Is that understood?"

Tango quickly nodded. "Understood."

"And why can't you keep that lunatic ape of yours under control?" she said in an irritated voice. "I'm beginning to wonder if it's even worth having you and those babbling, talking animals around here at all."

"You have to understand that Joe, well, he's a little bit different from the rest of the gang."

"You don't say," Tutty said flippantly.

"But you got to also understand that he's an entertainer," Tango said with imploring eyes. "All of them are. They need to be doing what they're trained to do, and that's performing on stage."

"I know," Tutty said with a long sigh. "You keep saying that, and I keep telling you that I have to find a way to tell Abner about them without him having some kind of rant filled heart attack that's going to kill him, or at least find a way so he won't know what's going on."

"I know it's not easy, Mrs. Tutty, but please try."

"Yeah, I will."

When Tutty let Tango out of the door and she came back into the dining room, she was like a moviegoer who'd just arrived to the zany, whacky movie that was already in progress. Mama Lulu was now on her feet standing next to the dining room table with her fist balled up, glaring over at Abner like a vicious attack dog.

"Now you promised you were going to let me be a showgirl, and I'm going to be one even if I have to knock that fat head of yours off of that cliff!"

"I ain't promised you no such a thing, you dimwit!" Abner hollered.

"Yes, you did!"

"NO, I DID NOT!

"YES, YOU DID!"

"Woman, your light bulb up there in that head of yours has blown out a long time ago!" Abner yelled. "But it's too bad it blew out, because they don't make those type of light bulbs anymore!"

"Oh, I've had it with you—Mister Chubby Wubby!"

The bell rung as the feisty little fighter came out of her corner swinging, but the referee quickly disqualified the fight.

"Mama Lulu, sit down and finish your dinner," Tutty said as she quickly grabbed Mama Lulu and forced her back down in her seat at the dining table. "And little missy, if you don't mind yourself, I'm taking every one of those Madam Cureall coloring books out of your dresser drawer—permanently!"

With Tutty's proclamation, quietness began to reign over the dining room table as everyone continued eating in total silence. Abner finally broke the fleeting peace when he suddenly smashed his fist once again on the dining room table.

"What is this slop we're eating tonight," Abner exclaimed angrily. "This food ain't got no taste whatsoever, Tutty. It tastes as bland as trying to eat a rubber duck."

"Look, the doctor said your blood pressure was high, and he also said you needed to lower your cholesterol, too," Tutty said as she continued eating. "I thought we'd try eating a little healthier for now on around here."

"That stupid doctor don't know what he's talking about."

"Abner, you're over three hundred pounds," Tutty said in a guarded voice. "It's time you started eating healthier anyway."

"That's just great." Abner balked. "Anything would probably be better than this tasteless junk that we're sitting here eating."

"I bet Benny could probably fix you something that's real nice and tasty," Mama Lulu said with a smile.

"No!" Abner suddenly blasted with a fit of anger. "I don't want to hear *nothing* about that little, irritating cockroach. I got enough problems as it is sitting here listening to you and eating this tasteless garbage."

"Benny, come on out, sweetie," Mama Lulu said in a sweet voice toward the cuckoo clock on the dining room wall as she ignored Abner's wishes. "Mama wants to see you."

The cuckoo clock on the wall right next to the dining room table resembled a truck stop diner restaurant. It even had a neon sign above the diner that said *Benny's Down Home Diner*.

As Mama Lulu kept calling for Benny, the neon marquee sign above the diner suddenly started flashing. Within seconds, Benny, the three inch high short order cook, came out of the truck stop diner on a mechanical track wearing a big white chef hat and holding a spatula. He had a nasty, surly scowl as if he were backed up with multiple orders and didn't have time for unruly customers.

"What is it, lady?" Benny snapped. "I got a long line of customers in here and I got meatloaf in the oven."

"Benny, Mama wants you to fix us something really good for dinner," Mama Lulu said with a burst of a smile. "Can we come to your restaurant tonight? I can almost taste that good old meal that you're about to cook for us."

"I'm sorry, lady, but you can't enter *Benny's Down Home Diner*."

"Why not?"

"Some Joe fellow was just in here eating a minute ago and he said some mooly-moolys were on the loose around here. You look like the description of one of them that he described. I don't allow no mooly-moolys in my diner, lady."

"Why that old, mangy ape!" Mama Lulu quickly balled up her fist. "I'm going to get him!"

"Now as far as you, fat boy, what would you like? I know you're tired of eating that slop that's on your plate," Benny said to Abner as he waved his spatula. "I know you'd rather have one of my big, fat juicy steaks, or some of my good finger licking ribs, or a giant double cheeseburger with the cheese just oozing off the meat—"

"Will you shut up!" Abner yelled. "You're making me hungry, you little pest!"

"Well, you wouldn't have gotten into my restaurant either, fatso."

"And just why not?"

"I don't allow mooly-moolys in my diner, and I *certainly* don't allow fat hippos to come in here who'll eat up my entire diner—brick, mortar and all!"

Benny, the short-order cook, quickly dashed back into the truck stop diner.

"That's all I need is some stupid, little runt that comes out of a cuckoo clock who thinks he runs a diner." Abner protested. "Tutty, I'm telling you, I'm *real* close to getting a hammer and smashing *Benny's Down Home Diner* to smithereens once and for all."

"You lay one finger on my dear, sweet Benny," Mama Lulu said in a steamed voice, "and I'm going to take that fat bowling ball head of yours and sling it into the river. You hear me—*Mr. Gutterball?*"

"Oh, I wish I *were* a bowling ball." Abner countered. "Because I'd love to bowl a strike right through your raggedy teeth."

"You're just a mean, old rotten son!" Mama Lulu blasted. "You want to harm dear, sweet precious Benny and you've gone back on your promise, too?"

"What promise?"

"You promised me you were going to let me dance with the showgirls."

"I ain't *never* promised you no such a thing," Abner said in a scolding voice. "Only in your delusional, warped mind would you think that anyone would want to see a four-foot-eight wrinkly eighty-year-old showgirl dancing around."

"But you promised me."

"No, I did not!"

"Yes, you did!"

"NO, I DID NOT!"

"Well, I've had it with you, Mr. Wubby Chubby!"

Mama Lulu suddenly grabbed a handful of mashed potatoes from her plate and slung it across the dining table as it walloped Abner straight in the face.

"Mama Lulu, how dare you throw food across this dining table like some childish brat," Tutty said in a riled voice. "You stop that this instant."

"And, missy, I've had it with you, too!"

Mama Lulu quickly scooped up another handful of mashed potatoes from her plate and walloped Tutty dead in her face. After getting creamed, Tutty suddenly looked like she was ready for war.

"Oh, so it's like that, huh?" Tutty glared over at Mama Lulu, panting like an angry, rabid dog. "Well take this!"

An all-out food fight suddenly exploded at the dining table with mashed potatoes, green peas, chopped carrots, celery, fish sticks, and water were slung, thrown, and splashed around the table. Even Benny, the short-order cook with the white chef hat, soon got in on the wild food fight as he kept dashing in and out of the diner with cream pies.

"I got one takeout order here for a cream pie ready to go!" he yelled. He suddenly reared back and slung the cream pie as he smashed Abner dead in his face with it.

Benny quickly dashed back into the diner and rushed back out again.

"I got another takeout order here for a cream pie ready to go!" He slung the second cream pie and smashed Mama Lulu dead in her face.

Benny quickly dashed back into the diner and rushed back out again.

"Here's another takeout order for a cream pie ready to go." He suddenly walloped Tutty in her face with the third cream pie.

Soon, as the food fight at the dining table continued to escalate, Benny kept dashing into the diner and rushing back out with more cream pies so fast, that he was almost a blur.

"Keep the pies coming in there," he suddenly yelled inside the diner to his staff as he kept slinging cream pies at Abner, Tutty, and Mama Lulu. "IT'S BUSY AS HELL OUT HERE IN THE DINING AREA TONIGHT. WE MIGHT HAVE TO WORK OVERTIME. JUST KEEP THE PIES COMING!"

Tango was in his office going nuts. Left in charge of running the entire hotel, he had his hands full and tonight it seemed as if nothing was getting off on the right foot. One worker after another began calling in to inform the assistant hotel manager that he or she wouldn't be able to make it to work for one reason or another.

The biggest department shorthanded for the night was the custodial staff. Nearly every worker on the custodial staff had called in sick. Even Zimmy was down in his employee room suffering from the flu, and Tango was literally racking his brain trying to figure out what to do to solve his workforce shortage for the night.

Despite Tutty's firm instructions, with the Alpha Ladies Beta Society filling up the hotel all on the busiest night, Tango had no choice but to put Joe in a working capacity around the hotel for the night. He dreaded what that decision would cause, but his hands were simply tied. He had to find workers to tend to the hotel's needs, and that was all there was to it.

While Tango was busy in his office putting information into the hotel computer, Elvyra suddenly came over the hotel intercom system with her hourly update.

"Good evening to all of our wonderful, dear guests here at the Lucky Jackpot Hotel," Elvyra said in her sultry, sexy voice. "Tonight, we have a full house at our lovely hotel, and I want to invite everyone to come on down to our fabulous casino and play a few hands of poker, or try your luck at the slots, play some keno, craps, roulette, or whatever that suits your fancy. Just remember that your money is always good here at the Lucky Jackpot Hotel, and folks, we certainly don't mind taking it off of your hands," she said with a giggle.

"Now if the casino is not your fancy, then stop over to our movie theater and catch the latest showing of our featured movie tonight. It's in 3-D and we'll even provide you the glasses for a real freaky showing, but not the freaky showing you're probably thinking of you *naughty* people." Elvyra once again giggled. "Also, stop by our bar and lounge area tonight for a couple of drinks and catch our wonderful showgirls perform on stage. But just don't get too drunk. We don't have enough wheelbarrows here at the Lucky Jackpot Hotel to take everyone up to your room if you get too drunk to walk," she said with a hearty giggle. "Well, that's about all for now. So, everyone just enjoy yourself, and once again—*meow!*"

When Elvyra finished giving her promo updates over the hotel intercom system, she came down the stairs from the control room with her helpers, Eddie and Sammy of the Wonder Gang by her side.

The control room was connected to Tango's office. Tango had just gotten off the phone when the threesome came down the stairs as Elvyra, the prima donna, was busy giving Eddie and Sammy her special instructions.

"Now remember, boys, I want my teddy bear, Cuddly, hair immaculately brushed, my pillow fluffed out, my pink silk scarf ironed for tomorrow, and my bowl filled with warm milk when I get down to my room."

"We ain't your errand boys, Elvyra," Sammy said as he glared at the quibbling cat.

"Yeah, we're only here to help you whenever you come to the control room to give your hourly announcements," Eddie said with angst. "And anyway, we only take orders from the Big Chief."

"Plus we got a big party getting ready to start down in our room in a few of minutes." Sammy complained.

"And I'm getting ready to go to the casino and gamble," Eddie said in an irritated voice. "I ain't got time to be your flunky."

"Ah, come on boys." Elvyra began to beg with a whimper. "Please, do me this favor just this once—*pretty please*."

The two dwarfs suddenly looked at each other as they both sighed.

"Alright," Eddie said with a moan. "Come on, Sammy, let's get this over with."

When Eddie and Sammy left out of the office, now all alone with Tango, Elvyra weaved her way over to Tango as he worked. She began to rub flirtatiously up against the calf of his leg.

"How you doing tonight, cutie?" Elvyra said as she kept rubbing back and forth against his leg. "You look like you could use a break. Why don't you come on down to my room and let me play with you."

"Stop it, Elvyra," Tango said as he continued working at his computer. "I ain't got time for no foolishness, tonight. I'm too busy."

"You used to always make time for this sophisticated cat, remember? So come on, Mr. Hotel Assistant Manager," she said with an alluring, little giggle. "Let me make all of your problems and worries go away."

Two attractive girls, dressed in hotel uniforms, suddenly entered Tango's office. Smiling pleasantly, they were none other than Chloe and Maria.

"Hey, I see you all busy at work here," Chloe said amicably.

"Yeah, they got me all tied up here tonight." Tango began to smile as he stopped his work. "Mr. Redder and Mrs. Tutty are going to see a show tonight, and the big man left me in charge of running this place all alone tonight."

"How intriguing," Maria said as she suddenly fondled his necktie. "You know, that tie really looks good on you."

"Oh, thanks," Tango said with a modest grin. "I guess I'm still getting used to wearing the standard hotel suit and tie."

"Well, it *really* looks good on you," Maria said as she gave him a wink.

Elvyra suddenly jumped onto Tango's desk. The promiscuous cat immediately curled up next to Tango's arm as if she were trying to claim what was hers.

"Oh, what a beautiful Siamese cat," Maria said with a smile as she extended her hand to give the mysterious cat a gentle rub. "This must be Elvyra."

Elvyra quickly moved away from her hand. "Don't you ever put your hands on me, honey!" she snapped.

The two girls slowly looked at each other with baffled stares.

"Well, Tango, we're going to let you get back to your work," Maria finally said after the awkward exchange. "Maybe later on you and Zimmy can meet us down in the employee lounge and we can watch a movie or something."

"Zimmy is down in his room tonight under the weather a little bit."

"He is?" Chloe began to frown. "Oh, wow, that's too bad."

"Well, why don't you make it if you can," Maria said.

"Sure, that'll be great."

"Awesome." Maria smiled. "Well, we'll leave you alone so you can get back to your work."

When the two girls left out of the office, Elvyra immediately began to prowl back and forth along Tango's desk as if her temper had suddenly reached the red hot level.

"So, who was that, your new *girlfriend*?"

"Elvyra, don't start," Tango said as he went back to work.

"You don't need her," Elvyra said as she began to fondle and caress up to Tango once again as he worked. "You know I'm all the woman you'll ever need."

"No, Elvyra."

"Come on. It'll be just like old times."

"No."

Elvyra suddenly sprayed a pink mist from her feline body onto Tango as she nestled up against him. The aroma of her alluring perfume literally filled the entire office. "You know you can't resist me, don't you?"

"It won't work, Elvyra."

"Oh, yes it will."

"Why don't you go and imply your intoxicating perfume on Fred. You know he's crazy about you."

"I like Fred. He's like a dear, sweet brother that I never had," Elvyra said as she continued to rub flirtatiously against Tango's arms. "But you're the one I've always wanted."

"That's over with, Elvyra."

"It doesn't have to be."

"Better yet, why don't you go and seduce Mr. Redder." Tango suddenly chuckled. You know he *definitely* wants you."

"I don't want big teddy bear," she said as she kept nestling up against Tango. "I want you."

"No, Elvyra."

Elvyra suddenly emitted a green smoke from her feline body as she turned from a Siamese cat into a fully-fledged six-foot-tall gorgeous Latino woman. Her long, beautiful black hair fell to her waist and her curvaceous body was to die for.

"Come on, Tango, my dear sweet," she said with a giggle as she began to massage and kiss his neck as he continued working at his computer. "I'm not taking no for an answer."

"Elvyra, stop it."

"I can't," she said as she continued to slowly kiss his neck. "You taste too good to stop."

Fred suddenly walked into the office. When Elvyra saw him, she immediately stopped her fondling of Tango and quickly transformed back into a Siamese cat.

"Oh, hey Fred," she said with a sly, nervous giggle.

"Elvyra."

"Well, I think I'll wander around the hotel for a while," Elvyra suddenly announced as she swished her tail. "You know a cat has to stretch her legs sometimes if she wants to get the most out of life."

Elvyra began to leave out of the office when she suddenly stopped in the doorway and turned back around. "Oh, about Big Teddy Bear," she said to Tango with a giggle. "I think I might just take your advice on that."

When Elvyra finally strolled out of the office, Fred ventured over to Tango's desk.

"Big Teddy Bear?" he said in a confused voice. "What was she talking about?"

"Nothing." Tango smirked. "Elvyra was just being silly."

"So . . . how's it going tonight?"

"It's been murder." Tango sighed as he finally leaned back in his chair and rubbed his forehead. "With the hotel as packed as it is tonight with this big convention going on here, it's been triple the work. And with so many workers calling in, I've been having a hard time trying to put people in the right spots. Along with that, Mr. Redder and Mrs. Tutty are going out tonight to catch a show, so I've been left in total control."

"You're still nervous about trying to run this hotel, huh?"

"Absolutely."

"Well, Chipper has got a big crowd over at his entertainment booth and he's doing his thing, Elvyra is taking care of all the hotel announcements, and I've been wandering around greeting the guests and trying to make them feel as comfortable as they can be. So that just leaves Joe and the Wonder Gang, the two misfits.

"For as the Wonder Gang, they're going to be locked away down in their room tonight having some wild party, so they'll be out of the way. That just leaves that crazy, moron ape. And at least you won't have to worry about him screwing anything up on the job tonight."

"Wrong," Tango said with a heavy sigh. "He's over in the movie theater right now working the concession stand."

"He's what!" Fred bellowed out. "I thought Tutty told you not to assign that crazy ape no more jobs around here."

"Yeah, she did." Tango rubbed his forehead even harder. "But we've been so short of workers tonight, I didn't have any choice."

The phone on Tango's office desk suddenly rang as he quickly picked it up and answered it. When he hung up, he was even more distressed.

"Who was that?"

"That was the front desk." Tango sighed. "They said a couple of ladies up in room 317 just called and said their room wasn't cleaned today and their bed sheets hadn't been changed. So now I've got to find somebody to go up there and clean their room."

"I can go down and tell one of the boys from the Wonder Gang to go up there and tend to it."

Tango slowly shook his head. "No, they're probably already getting plastered drunk down in that room. No telling what they might do if I sent one of them up to a guest room being as drunk and wild as they are," he said with a heavy sigh. "Go over to the movie theater and tell Joe to take a cart from housekeeping and go up to room 317 and clean the room. That movie has been in progress for over an hour now. Most of the people over in that movie theater probably have already bought all the refreshments they're going to buy at this point anyway."

"Are you kidding?"

"Hey, he's already somewhat familiar with the guest rooms by being a bellhop. Maybe disaster won't strike."

"That's what they said when Covid first came out."

"Yeah, I know."

"Are you *sure* you want me to go get that moron ape?"

"No, I'm not," Tango said with a heavy sigh. "But go tell him anyway."

Joe, running the concession stand at the movie theater, served a woman a box of popcorn and a Coke when she came to the concession stand and ordered. When the customer paid for her items and opened the box of popcorn, Joe quickly pounded his chest twice with his fist and snapped his finger. Poof! A cloud of purple smoke mushroomed out of the box of popcorn as all the popcorn suddenly turned into worms. When the woman was about to eat a handful of popcorn and made the horrified discovery of what she held in her hand, she quickly dropped the box and went running away screaming.

With sheer delight, Joe stuffed the money into his pocket when the woman went running away screaming. In fact, nearly all of the money that the customers paid for their concession items went into his suit coat pocket and not the cash register. He'd made a good wad of dough tonight, thanks to the Lucky Jackpot Hotel.

When there were no more customers coming to the concession stand for refreshments, Joe grabbed a broom and a dustpan as he went inside the movie theater to do a little cleaning. While the fifty or so people sitting inside the darkness of the theater watched the movie playing on the big screen with their 3-D glasses on, Joe began to sweep up the few pieces of trash in the aisle of the movie theater.

As Joe tended to his sweeping duties, he began to watch the movie taking place up on the big screen. Two flying superheroes were fighting out in space as they shot lasers and all sorts of other intergalactic weapons at each other as they fought a duel to the death.

While Joe watched the movie, he began to smile. With glee pumping all through him like a wayward troublemaker who suddenly spotted an opportunity to cause havoc, he quickly dropped his broom and dustpan as he ran and jumped onto the movie screen.

Joe instantly became part of the intergalactic duel between the superheroes as the 3-D moviegoers inside the theater laughed hysterically. Joe began to do all sorts of wild, silly stunts on the movie screen as the superheroes continued to fight. Within seconds, he'd suddenly turned an action adventure movie into a hilarious, goofball comedy.

As Joe had everyone rolling in their seats, Fred suddenly entered the dark movie theater. He quickly strolled down the movie theater aisle as Joe continued his wild antics up on the screen.

"Hey you crazy ape, get down from that screen!" Fred yelled up at Joe when he got close enough to him. "Get off of there this instant!"

Joe finally jumped off the movie screen as the people were still laughing hysterically. He was all smiles and full of gaiety as he approached Fred.

"What in the world were you doing up there on that movie screen, you stupid ape?"

"Just giving everyone a different twist to the movie," he said with a hearty chuckle.

"You need to straighten up and act right, you dumb ape," he said heatedly. "You're going to get all of us thrown out on the street. You better—"

"Ah, hush all of your blabbering, dog," Joe quickly said as he cut him off. "Why did you come in here for anyway?"

"The people up in room 317 are complaining that their room hadn't been cleaned today. So, Tango wants you to go to housekeeping, get a cart, and go clean the room."

"I ain't no housekeeper, you no talent mutt."

"You're a housekeeper if Tango wants you to be one!"

"Still licking that kid's butt, huh?" Joe said in a snide tone.

"You just go to housekeeping, get a cart, and go on up to room 317 like Tango wants you to."

"And who's going to make me?"

"Oh, I'm going to make you," Fred said with a vicious growl as he suddenly moved within inches of Joe. "I've been wanting to taste some of that red jungle juice for a long time, buddy."

"Alright, dog," Joe said as he slowly moved away from Fred. "Put your fangs back in. I'm going . . . I'm going."

"And you bet not cause any trouble while you're up there, you stupid, crazy ape!"

Joe headed out of the theater as he went over to the housekeeping department and grabbed a cart that contained clean bed sheets, dust broom, cleaning supplies, and a vacuum cleaner. He got on the elevator with the cart and punched for the third floor.

When Joe got off the elevator on the third floor, he strolled down the quiet hallway with his cleaning cart whistling away as if he were taking a leisurely stroll through the park. With each step he took, his little tune he whistled became livelier and livelier. He was like a salsa singer, dancing and strutting to his lively tune as he strolled down the hall.

When Joe reached room 317, he thumped on the door like a pair of bongos as he continued dancing and whistling his lively tune. As soon as a woman opened the door, Joe immediately pushed his way inside the room with his cart. Two other ladies, also in the room, stood gawking at the wild orangutan who'd suddenly intruded into their room.

"Good evening, my dear ladies," Joe said in a cheerful voice as he flashed his glorious smile. "I've been summoned up here to tidy up your room a bit, so you dear, wonderful ladies can have a most comfortable stay here at our lovely hotel."

"It's you!" one of the women said with a vicious glare.

"You're that ornery, foul mouth orangutan who insulted us today at our banquet luncheon!" another lady said heatedly.

"How dare you have the nerve to just come waltzing in here, you rude beast!" another lady said angrily.

There was a sudden knock at the door. When one of the ladies answered the door, four more ladies suddenly entered the room also.

"Hey," one of the women who just entered the room said with a sneer, "isn't that the orangutan that barged into our banquet luncheon today?"

"It sure is," the other woman said in a steamed voice, "and he's still wearing that old, stupid faded brown suit and that red and white polka dotted tie, too."

"What kind of hotel is this that let some gutter bum talking ape just wander around here, disrupting our convention?"

"Ladies, let's teach this orangutan a lesson he'll never forget," another woman said in a hostile voice. "We'll show him he can't mess with the Alpha Ladies Beta Society. Let's get him."

"YEAH!"

"My dear, sweet ladies, please forgive me for that intrusion today," Joe hastily said as the women quickly surrounded him with blood in their eyes. "I only came to entertain you wonderful, beautiful ladies at your brunch today."

"*Beautiful?*" one of the women said sarcastically. "That's not what that puppet of yours said today."

"He's full of it," another woman said in a surly voice. "Let's get him!"

Joe quickly pounded his chest twice with his fist and snapped his finger. Poof! A cloud of purple smoke mushroomed in the air as a bouquet of roses and twelve boxes of chocolates suddenly fell into his hands. Joe quickly distributed a long stem rose and a box of chocolates to each lady in the room as he continued to extend his heartfelt apologies.

Joe suddenly began to pour on the charm and charisma so much that he soon had all the ladies in the room virtually eating out of the palm of his hand. They soon began to adopt a more festive mood as Joe steadily poured on the charm like a used car salesman trying to sell every clunker on his lot.

The roses and chocolates quickly followed with several hilarious stories and humorous tales that began to tickle the women's fancy. Within ten minutes, he'd gone from hated to adored as he held an impromptu stand-up comedy special as the women surrounded him.

"You know, ladies, I was once a contestant on the live airing of the show *America's Got Talent*," Joe said with a flamboyant smile. "Did you lovely ladies know that?"

"An orangutan was once a contestant on the show *America's Got Talent*," one of the ladies said as she gave a glib chuckle. "You've got to be kidding me."

"Oh, it's true. When I walked on stage with those cameras rolling and with millions of TV viewers watching, the panel of judges asked me what was I getting ready to do for the folks and I told them I was going to perform the moonwalk."

"Wait," the lady said with a chuckle. "You mean you, an orangutan, actually did the moonwalk on TV?"

"I sure did, sweet thing," Joe said with a flashy smile. "I mooned everybody in that place and walked right off the stage!"

The women exploded with laughter.

"You know, ladies, one day I was asked to be a conductor of a banana boat ride for a group of women on vacation who were very much similar to you beautiful, lovely ladies."

"That's hard to believe," a woman said with a snicker.

"Oh, it's true. In fact, they enjoyed the banana boat ride so much, when it was over, they asked to go again."

"Did you take them again?"

"Once my banana was ready to go again, I sure did!"

"You beat all, ape." The women roared with laughter.

After doing a couple more comical gags for the ladies' entertainment, Joe suddenly excused himself from the women surrounding him as he tended to his housekeeping duties.

As he began to vacuum, clean the dresser mirrors, change the bedsheets, and do a little dusting, the seven women in the room began to discuss where they wanted to go to have some fun for the night. All agreed that nothing worthwhile was happening at the Lucky Jackpot Hotel, so they all agreed the best place was to hit the Las Vegas Strip so they could hang out and party all night long.

While Joe was busy whistling a lively tune as he cleaned the room, he suddenly spotted out of the corner of his eye something that nearly made his head spin around like a top. One of the women suddenly took off a huge, expensive looking diamond ruby necklace as she opened the safe on the dresser by her bed, put the necklace into the safe, and locked the safe back.

Joe suddenly began to smile a lustful smile so wide, that one would've had to buy a cross country plane ticket to get from one end of his mouth to the other. For the first time ever Joe was in love, and his object of desire lay locked secured behind a small steel door of a safe.

When Joe finally finished his housekeeping duties, he addressed the seven ladies in the room who were about to go out partying for the night.

"Ladies, it's been a most exuberant experience meeting with all of you, but I must go now to tend to my other duties," Joe said in a chivalrous voice. "My name is Joe, and if there's ever anything that you wonderful ladies ever need, please feel free to call on me. But before you lovely ladies go out tonight, there's something that I want you to remember."

"What's that?"

"A fox may approach you with a silver tongue wanting to get into the chicken coop, but he better have a skin of a lamb before you the set the chickens loose."

The ladies rolled with laughter.

"Good night, ladies."

Joe left out of room 317, jubilantly whistling as he quickly pushed his housekeeping cart down the hallway. His mind raced faster than a statistician trying to compute a flurry of numbers in a hurry as he contemplated how he was going to get his hands on that big, beautiful diamond ruby necklace. He'd never seen anything as gorgeous as that rare, beautiful necklace, and no matter what it took, he was going to get his hands on it.

When Joe put away the housekeeping cart, he strolled over to Chipper's Entertainment Booth. Chipper had so many people crowded around his table watching him perform, there was virtually no room for anybody to move. Joe knew he had to think of something to get rid of everybody so he could be alone to talk to Chipper.

Joe quickly pried and pushed his way through the thick crowd of onlookers as he suddenly jumped onto Chipper's table. He flashed his broad smile at everyone as he held up his hand.

"Folks, the most unbelievable thing is happening right now inside the casino," Joe said with a bubbly smile. "A woman just won a hundred thousand dollars playing the roulette, and now she's giving all the money that she just won away to everyone in the casino."

The mass of people surrounding Chipper's table immediately vacated the area as they went storming toward the casino. Joe, proud of his quick wit, immediately jumped down from the table and confronted Chipper who was now all alone.

"Chipper, old buddy, let's head over to the bar and lounge area," he said with his bubbly smile still radiating. "I got a proposition that I want to discuss with you."

"I wonder what idiot woman in the casino is giving away all of her money?"

"Nobody. I made it up," Joe quickly said. "Now come on, let's go."

Chipper took flight as he began to follow Joe as they headed for the bar and lounge area. When they entered the bar, the place was packed. People sat all around the bar and at the tables enjoying drinks and listening to the house band perform.

Joe finally found a space at the very end of the bar as Chipper landed on the bar next to him. The bartender, Big Curly, immediately made his way down to where they were.

"Joe and Chipper, my favorite orangutan and my favorite parrot," he said with a hearty smile. "What will it be tonight? For you two, it's all on the house."

"Big Curly, bring me something fruity that's going to make me feel like I have all the riches, or at least tipsy enough that'll split my britches," Joe said his little jingle as he flashed his smile.

"And what would you like to drink, Chipper?" Big Curly asked with a chuckle. "I can put a straw in a glass for you if you'd like."

"I'll just take a bowl of nuts."

Big Curly served Joe a piña colada and set a bowl of nuts in front of Chipper as he went to take care of some other customers at the bar. As soon as the bartender served Joe his drink, Joe quickly turned up his glass and down the drink in three seconds flat as he flashed a wondrous smile at Chipper when he'd finished.

"So, what's this big proposition you're talking about, ape?"

"I want to know just how good that left eye of yours is that you're always claiming is so great?"

"Ape, you know what my miraculous eye is capable of doing," Chipper said in annoyed tone. "I don't question your abilities, do I?"

"Can that laser eye of yours cut through a steel door of a safe?"

"It can cut through the steel doors of Fort Knox if it had to."

"Well, here's the proposition," Joe said in a low voice. "I was just up in room 317 cleaning the room when I noticed that this woman had this huge diamond ruby necklace that she just put into this safe up in her room. I mean this huge necklace is probably worth about fifty or sixty grand easily. Now, she and her friends just left to have some fun on the Vegas Strip and they'll be gone for probably most of the night. So, why don't we go up to room 317, break into that safe and snatch that necklace."

"Nope, can't."

"What do you mean you can't?"

"Look, my shift for the night at the entertainment booth is about to end in thirty minutes, and when it's over, I'm flying straight down to my room and smoke some kerweekee," Chipper quickly said. "Then I'm going to see Dr. Glittermoon, and if all goes well, I'm going to be lying on the beach with Aquaflower making love."

"Aquaflower . . . who in the world is that?"

"She's my new lady friend," Chipper said in a revered voice as he picked a couple of nuts out of the bowl with his beak. "I mean she's *very* special."

"Aquaflower, huh?" Joe suddenly said with a laugh. "Sounds like something that comes from smoking too much kerweekee."

"She's all real, ape," Chipper said in a slightly peeved voice. "See, I knew you wouldn't understand."

"Hey, if this Mayflower chick rocks your boat, then it's all cool with—"

"That's *Aquaflower* you dumb ape."

"Whatever," Joe said as he lit up a cigar. "Just come on up to room 317 and let's do this. I need that laser eye of yours to cut through that steel door of that safe."

"What's in it for me?"

"I'll cut you in on half of whatever I get once I hock it."

"What do you mean once *you* hock it?" Chipper said in a wary voice. "You ain't going to pull that one on me, you conniving ape. You go hock it, and the next thing I know is you've run off back to the jungle someplace. No, if I do this, we'll *both* hock it together."

"Sounds even better."

"Why do you want to snatch this diamond necklace anyway?"

"We can hock it, take the loot we get from it, and scram out of this place," Joe said as he blew a smoke ring into the air. "We can head down to South America together, get a few gigs down there in some of those fancy night clubs and really live it up. Ain't nothing happening around here, and we certainly don't need no one managing us. Plus that kid, Tango, can't take us to the top anyway. He's all washed up in the entertainment business as a trainer and a promoter. We ain't never going to make it with that kid controlling us."

"I don't know, ape."

"Come on, Chipper, let's do this." Joe implored. "With the money we get from that necklace, we can finally scram out of this dump and get back to performing on stage as we were meant to do. And we can once and for all finally get away from this hotel work staff stuff that we've been doing around here lately. So, what do you say?"

"I don't know, Joe," Chipper said hesitantly as he picked a few more nuts out the bowl with his beak. "I mean what I'm doing performing at this entertainment booth table ain't so bad, really."

"Yeah, but it ain't performing on stage, is it?"

"Well, that's true," Chipper said reluctantly. "Alright, Joe, I'll help you."

"Good," Joe said as he lowered his voice even more. "Now in exactly an hour, you meet me by the left stairwell and we'll go up together to room 317, crack that safe, and snatch that diamond ruby necklace."

"How are we going to get into the room?"

"I'm going to distract the front desk clerk and swipe an extra key to room 317. And once we get the necklace, I'm going to stash it in a place where no one in the world would suspect it to be."

"And where's that?"

"I snatched the big boss' keys a couple of nights ago when I went to spend some time with him," Joe said in a low voice with a chuckle. "I know him and Tutty are going out tonight to catch a show on the Strip, which means it's just going to be that old mooly-mooly there all alone asleep. So, I'm going to stash the necklace in her room. Nobody in the world will suspect the necklace to be in her room. And after a couple of days when the coast is finally clear, I'll get the necklace and we'll go hock it and scram out of here."

"I see you've already been doing a lot of scheming, ape."

"Exactly," Joe said as he flashed his smile. "So, are you still in?"

"Yeah, ape," Chipper said with a heavy sigh. "I'm in. But first I'm going down to my room and smoke me some kerweekee."

"Don't be going off to see no Dr. Glittermoon."

"Yeah, yeah," Chipper said as he took off from the bar and began to fly away. "See you in an hour, ape."

Fred, with his Welcome to the Lucky Jackpot Hotel vest on, had been wandering around the hotel lobby greeting guests and making them feel welcome for hours. He needed a break and decided to head outside to get a breath of fresh air. Fred's two favorite showgirls, Cassie and Lonnie, were at their usual posts at the front entrance of the hotel doors dressed in their full elaborative showgirls' costumes. On his way outside, Fred stopped to have a few words with them.

"Cassie and Lonnie, my two lovely showgirls, how's your night going?"

"Great, Freddy," they said with a bubbly smile. "How's yours?"

"Oh, not bad."

"Have you gotten accustomed to the Lucky Jackpot Hotel yet, Freddy?" Cassie asked with a smile.

"Well, being here with you two beautiful ladies certainly helps."

"Ah, Freddy, you're such a Casanova," Lonnie said with a smile.

"I wonder if Casanova ever had the wonderful privilege of working with such incredible beauties as the two of you," Fred said with a wag of the tail. "I'd bet you he'd never call in sick to work."

"That compliment might just get you a nice hot bath," Cassie said with a smile and a wink.

"Well, I'll make sure I'll go get good and dirty, then."

Fred left Cassie and Lonnie as he headed outside. He left from underneath the hotel awning as he strolled down the sidewalk of the hotel. It was a clear, warm night with plenty of stars shining brightly. Fred finally stopped his little stroll when he reached the end of the building.

In the far distance the skyline of the Las Vegas Strip, with all of its magnificent hotels, could clearly be seen gleaming and twinkling in the night. It was a sight to behold with thousands of the neon lights illuminating all of the grand, luxurious hotels on the Strip.

Fred just stood there for a moment and took in the splendid view before him. He and the gang had seen many places during their traveling and performing around the world, but Fred knew that the sight before him was like no other. It could literally take one's breath away, and the longer one stared at the magnificent sight before him, one would probably have to conclude that the Las Vegas nighttime skyline had to be one of the great wonders of the world.

After Fred had gotten enough fresh air, he finally turned to head back into the hotel. But when he suddenly gazed up, he was amazed at what he saw. Sitting forty feet up on top of the hotel on the edge of the building was Elvyra. She sat all alone on top of the building gazing up at the stars. Fred could hardly believe that she was sitting all alone so high up.

"Elvyra," Fred suddenly called up to her. "What are you doing way up there?"

"Oh, hey, Freddy," Elvyra said with a laugh. "I'm just enjoying the view. Hold on, I'm coming down."

With great swiftness, Elvyra quickly jumped from window to window as she began to scale down the hotel building. Within five seconds, she'd scaled the hotel building all the way down to the ground.

"Wow, Elvyra, you have skills," Freddy said with admiration.

"Well, this little cat girl can get around when she really wants to," she said with a giggle.

"So, you were just up there gazing at the stars, huh?"

"Yep. I climb up there every night about this time just to gaze at the stars in the sky."

"Why?"

"Well, it kind of reminds me of the star that I still want to be," she said like a star struck girl. "Someday I want to be a huge, big star, just like one of those stars that you see up there in the sky."

Fred suddenly glanced toward the skyline of the Las Vegas Strip in the far distance. "I guess you wish you were in one of those fancy hotels over there on the Strip performing under the big lights, huh?"

"You know I would." Elvyra giggled. "It's all I ever dream about."

"Well, you know, Elvyra, just be patient," Fred said in a consoling voice. "Tango is going to get us to the top. Don't worry. And who knows, you may get what you've been looking for at this very hotel right here."

"You mean right here at the Lucky Jackpot Hotel?"

"Absolutely."

"You really think so, Freddy?"

"It could happen."

"How?"

"We just have to make it happen."

There was a sudden silence in their conversation that began to drag on and on as they both looked at one another. During the awkward silence, Fred couldn't help but to look affectionately into Elvyra's green, alluring eyes. Her beautiful green eyes could always hold him captivated. It was as if a witchdoctor had suddenly waved a watch in front of him and had put him into a deep spell. That spell always tugged hard at his heart. No matter how hard he tried to avoid them, he was always at the mercy of those enchanting, lovely eyes.

Suddenly the violin section from the Magic Rainbow Hotel & Casino Orchestra began to play a soft melody as Fred continued to stare deeply into Elvyra's green eyes. He'd been wanting for a long time to tell Elvyra how he felt about her and now seemed a good a time as ever. But somehow the words just wouldn't come out. They were lodged in his throat like cement that had hardened over.

The longer Fred stared into her eyes, the harder it was to say what he had to say. It was sheer torture, but Fred was determined to say what was on his mind.

"Elvyra . . ." After one word, Fred suddenly started to gag and choke.

"What's the matter, Fred?" Elvyra suddenly giggled. "I thought cats were the only ones that got fur balls."

"It's nothing. I just had a little something stuck in my throat," Fred said sheepishly. He finally collected himself as he looked into her eyes. This time he was finally going to do it. "Elvyra, I've been wanting to tell you something for a long time. You see, I'm in lov—"

"Oh, Fred, I almost forgot. It's almost time for me to do my promo over the hotel intercom again," she said as she suddenly interrupted him. "We better head on back inside."

"Yeah," Fred uttered in a dejected voice. "I guess we better."

"Come on."

Fred and Elvyra began to head back for the hotel. When they got back inside the lobby of the hotel, Elvyra quickly hustled toward the assistant manager's office.

"I better hurry up," Elvyra said as she quickly strolled for the office. "I see Mike and Frank of the Wonder Gang are already headed for the office to help me. I see you later, Freddy."

"Bye."

When Elvyra disappeared into the office, Fred decided to check out what was going on inside the bar and lounge area.

The place was totally packed. Members of the Alpha Ladies Beta Society, along with others, had filled the place and there wasn't a single vacant space at the bar or any of the tables. The house band was busy performing a couple of jazz numbers as they entertained the guests.

As Fred scanned around the bar and lounge area to see what was going on, he suddenly spotted Tutty sitting at a table in the far back. With nothing to do at the moment, he decided to go over and have a few words with the boss' wife.

"Why, hello, Mrs. Redder," Fred said when he approached her table.

"It's Tutty."

"Oh, yeah, I almost forgot."

"You know, it still seems a little strange having a conversation with a four legged dog." Tutty chuckled. "Well, Mr. Fred, tell me. Just how do you like the Lucky Jackpot Hotel?"

"I've come to like it quite well."

"You not only speak eloquently, but you're also a hell of a liar." She chuckled again.

"No, really, I kind of like it here."

"Well," she said with a smile, "I guess that's good to hear."

"I thought you and your husband were going out to catch a show on the Strip tonight."

"Yeah, we are. But first I'm waiting for the showgirls to come out and perform."

"Is there something special going on tonight with the showgirls?"

"Yep, you can say that," Tutty said with a deep sigh. "Abner's mother, Mama Lulu, is performing tonight with the showgirls."

Fred almost had to bite his tongue to keep from saying something harsh. "Well, that's *really* intriguing," he replied rather nicely.

"Dog, you don't have to be so courteous," Tutty said with a laugh. "I know it sounds totally ridiculous and stupid. And you know what, that's because it is."

"Well, pardon me for asking, but how did this all come about?"

"Abner's mother has been pestering Abner for the longest to be a showgirl. Well, Abner finally caved in tonight and decided to go ahead and give her this one and only shot at being a showgirl so she'll stop pestering him to death about it."

"Well, I guess mother Mama Lulu must've said the right words tonight to convince your husband to let her perform with the showgirls."

"It wasn't what she said, it was the food fight we had at dinner tonight that finally did it."

"Food fight?"

"Yep." Tutty chuckled. "And it was a big one, too."

When loud, rowdy laughter began to erupt over at the bar, Fred and Tutty began to take notice. Joe had suddenly become the center of attraction. A large group of people surrounded him over at the bar as he entertained everyone with a round of jokes.

"Folks, did you know I was once a traffic cop?" Joe said loudly with a flamboyant smile as he puffed on a cigar.

"An orangutan that was a traffic cop," a guy suddenly said with a hearty chuckle. "Now that's hard to believe."

"Oh, it's true. One day I caused a fifty car pileup collision right in the middle of this busy intersection."

"I bet you did when they saw *you* directing traffic."

"Well, you see, while I was directing traffic, I was also warming up for my night job, too."

"Your night job?"

"That's right. I was conducting this big symphony that night and I had to practice my baton strokes!"

Laughter exploded over at the bar as Joe started telling another joke.

"You know, folks, one time I took my car to this mechanic to get a lube job done."

"What happened?" someone asked.

"Either the mechanic was stupid or thought I said a boob job, because an hour later, my car had two big, giant tits hanging off the front!"

A burst of laughter exploded once again as Joe kept reeling off the jokes.

"Well, I see your friend has become quite the fan favorite around here," Tutty said as she continued to watch the activity over at the bar.

"Yeah," Fred said with a groan. "He's definitely a nut case."

"He's a wild, crazy nut case to be more exact."

"You know, Tutty, as much as I hate that moron ape, he and the rest of us belong up on stage you know. I was just wondering when we'll finally get the opportunity to perform for the guests."

"Yeah, I know y'all belong on stage," Tutty said with a heavy sigh. "But I'm still trying to convince my husband of what we have here with the four of you. As soon as I can somehow convince him of that, then maybe we can get something accomplished."

Tango suddenly entered the packed bar and lounge area as he came over to where Fred and Tutty were at.

"Ah, Mrs. Redder, I just got your text that you sent me. You wanted to see me?"

"It's Tutty, remember?" she said with a smile.

"Oh, sorry about that."

"And, yes, I wanted to see you," she said in a more serious tone. "I just wanted to remind you that Abner and I are getting ready to go see our show in a little bit and you'll be in charge until we get back. Now I want you to look after things while we're gone and make sure everything is running smoothly around here. Got it?"

"Sure thing," Tango quickly said. "I'll look after everything and make sure the guests are having a good time."

"And make sure you *definitely* keep that crazy orangutan in line," Tutty said as she pointed toward Joe over at the bar. "I don't want to come back and hear about any disturbances that he's caused. Understand?"

"Yes, ma'am."

"You know, compared to that lunatic orangutan over there, this one here seems quite special," she said as she pointed at Fred. "He's quite an astute, shrewd St. Bernard dog I might add."

"Oh, Fred is definitely one of a kind." Tango smiled as he patted Fred on the head. "I don't know what I'd do without him."

"And another thing," Tutty said with a teasing smile. "Word is going around that you and Maria over in the concierge department are starting to become quite an item. Is there something special brewing there?"

"Oh, we're just friends," Tango said with a slight blush.

"Alright, I was just wondering."

"Well, I better be getting back to the office. I'll see you."

When Tango left Fred and Tutty, an emcee suddenly came over the intercom system inside the bar and lounge area.

"Good evening everyone and welcome to the Lucky Jackpot Hotel," the emcee said in a rich baritone voice. "For your entertainment, focus your eyes on the stage and give a warm welcome to the Lucky Jackpot Showgirls!"

Everyone in the packed bar and lounge area applauded as the curtain over the stage suddenly rose. Standing front and center in the horizontal line of the twelve smiling showgirls was none other than Mama Lulu. She was dressed in a glittering gold G-string bottom, rhinestone-encrusted bra, and a huge feathery headdress just as the other showgirls were. She began to smile and dance with all the other showgirls as the house band played an upbeat jazz number for the showgirls to begin their dance routine.

Standing nearly a foot shorter and looking a hundred years older than the rest of the young, beautiful showgirls, Mama Lulu was all over the place. She was all off key, bumping into the other showgirls as she danced, and was as slow as molasses. She looked like a total joke as she tried to twirl and whirl with the rest of the young, energetic showgirls.

Fred, as he stood beside Tutty's table, could hardly stand to watch what was happening. He felt the pit of his stomach suddenly turn vile as if he were about to throw up at any second. During the entire fiasco, his only hope was that the showgirls' dance skit routine would hurry up and finally end.

"God, this is painful," he muttered to himself.

As the dance skit continued, Joe suddenly broke away from the group crowded around him as he dashed from the bar and jumped onto the stage. He immediately began to disrupt the showgirls' routine.

The crowd laughed hysterically as he started circling Mama Lulu like a wild savage Indian going around a totem pole doing a war dance. As he kept going around her, he suddenly pounded his chest twice with his fist and snapped his finger. Poof! A cloud of purple smoke mushroomed in the air as a neon sign hovered over Mama Lulu that flashed the words *The Mooly-Mooly Show*.

Mama Lulu became so mad and infuriated she began to swing repeatedly at Joe, but she was unable to catch the fast, lightning orangutan that kept circling her.

"You mangy, stinking ape!" she yelled heatedly. "I'm going to crane that head of yours!"

Joe kept taunting Mama Lulu as he continued skirting around her even faster. "Mooly-mooly!" he shouted with a hearty laugh as he kept circling her. "*MOOLY-MOOLY!*"

Mama Lulu chased Joe all over the stage, trying her best to club the pesky, irritating orangutan. The crowd rocked and laughed so hard at their antics on stage that the entire event had become nothing but a wild lampoon.

As the house band played on and the rest of the showgirls tried to continue their performance, Joe kept skirting all around Mama Lulu making a mockery of her as she kept trying to crane his head. Finally, Joe's luck ran out. He slipped and fell off the stage as he crashed into the house band and got his head stuck inside of a tuba.

Mama Lulu was lying in bed with her nightlight on. Unable to go to sleep because she was so angry and upset with that mangy ape for messing up her debut performance tonight with the Lucky Jackpot Showgirls, she decided to read one of her coloring books to try to give herself some sort of solace and comfort.

The one she read tonight was called *The Wooly Rabbit Outsmarts the Grubby Bear*. She'd pick this particular coloring book out of the mounds and mounds of coloring books stuffed inside her dresser drawer, because the rabbit outsmarted the bear and had finally gotten revenge against his tormentor. Mama Lulu desperately wanted revenge against that mangy ape, and at the moment, reading *The Wooly Rabbit Outsmarts the Grubby Bear* was the best way that she could get it.

"The rabbit laid a trap for the grubby bear deep in the woods," Mama Lulu read with a wicked smile. "The grubby bear stumbled upon the trap and—"

"Mooly-mooly!" Mama Lulu suddenly heard the sound of Joe tormenting and mocking her as it came from the pages of the coloring book.

"What? I heard that mangy ape," Mama Lulu said testily. "That just can't be."

Mama Lulu quickly turned the page. When she only saw a picture of the wooly rabbit and the grubby bear, she continued on with the story.

"The big dumb bear had no idea the trap was set for him," she read as she began to smile once again. "So, when he stepped his big foot into the trap, he cried out in agony with a loud shout—"

"*MOOLY-MOOLY!*"

"Why that mangy ape!"

Mama Lulu quickly closed the coloring book, shoved it back inside her nightstand drawer, and slammed the drawer shut. Seething with anger, she lay in bed thinking of nothing but revenge against the mangy ape that had ruined her special night.

Needing some solace and comfort from somewhere, Mama Lulu glanced over at the old, shabby farmhouse cuckoo clock on the wall in her bedroom and saw that it was ten minutes before 11 p.m. Not wanting to wait until the hand struck on the hour until Benny came out of the farmhouse on his mechanical track, she suddenly began to smile as she called for him.

"Benny, sweetie, it's Mama Lulu," she said in a sweet, cajoling voice toward the cuckoo clock. "Mama wants to talk to you. Come on out."

When there was no movement, Mama Lulu tried once again.

"Come on out, Benny. Mama desperately needs to talk to you, tonight."

Benny, the three-inch-high mechanical farmer wearing old dingy overalls and a big floppy straw hat, suddenly came out on the mechanical track with a pitch fork in his hand. He looked over at Mama Lulu with his menacing, perpetual scowl.

"Woman, what do you want? I ain't got time just to be out here lollygagging with you."

"Oh, Benny, I need some company tonight," she said in a whiny voice. "I feel so down and depressed. I feel just awful."

"You look awful, woman, but don't be coming bothering me with that."

"Please, Benny, you're supposed to talk to me and comfort me when I need you."

"Woman, I only plant and take care of tomatoes, corn, turnip greens, and carrots. I don't plant *nor* take care of nuts."

"Benny, you watch your mouth," she said as she pointed a firm wrinkled finger at him. "I got a notion to straighten you out if you don't behave yourself."

Benny gave an irritating sigh. "Alright, woman, what the hell is your problem tonight?"

"Well, you see, Abner finally let me dance with the showgirls tonight," she said in a pitiful voice. "Tonight was going to be my big night. I was all dressed up in my showgirl outfit and everything. Then when the curtain came up and we started dancing, that mangy, old ape I told you about came rushing onto the stage and disrupted everything. He started circling and making fun of me in front of everybody. He ruined my night as a showgirl. It was just awful," she said in a pathetic, withering voice. "Just awful."

"So, you're hurt and upset?"

"Yeah."

"You feel like your big moment in the sun was ruined?"

"Yeah."

"And you want revenge against that mangy ape, too?"

"Yeah."

"Well, you should go to the police."

"You think so?"

"Absolutely. They're used to hearing complaints from nut cases like you."

"Why you—"

The bedroom window to the old, shabby farmhouse suddenly raised as Edna stuck her head out.

"Mama Lulu, you still up? How are you doing tonight, girl?"

"Not too good, Edna," Mama Lulu said in a sour voice.

"What's wrong, honey?"

"Edna, don't be trying to figure out this woman's problems!" Benny snapped angrily. "All the scientists at NASA probably couldn't figure out what makes this dimwitted woman tick."

"Benny, you be quiet," Edna said with a sharp tongue. "Mama Lulu, you go ahead, sweetie. Tell Edna what's bothering you."

"Well, I was supposed to dance with the showgirls tonight," she said in a dismal, somber voice. "I was all dressed up in my showgirl outfit and everything. Then when the curtain rose and we started dancing, this mangy, old ape suddenly came onto the stage and ruined everything."

"Ah, that's terrible," Edna said in a consoling voice. "And I bet you would've been just wonderful dancing with the showgirls, too."

"I'm pretty sure I was, too," Mama Lulu said once again in a somber voice. "It was going to be my big night and everything."

"Well, don't worry about it Mama Lulu. In my book, you'll always be a star."

"Thank you, Edna."

"Some star," Benny said with a grouch. "The only star that dimwitted woman will ever know about is *Twinkle, Twinkle, Little Star*."

"Benny, you stop talking about sweet Mama Lulu like that," Edna said with a huff. "You're the reason why this farmhouse is in such a bad shape as it is."

"It ain't my fault." Benny complained. "It's that dimwitted woman's fault over there and that stupid bat she has. The loony woman must think she play for the New York Yankees or somebody."

"I don't care," Edna said with a gruff. "You just watch what you say before we end up homeless. Good night, Mama Lulu, and sweet dreams."

Edna pulled down the window.

"That's just great. I got a nagging wife and a nut case as a neighbor," Benny said with a deep sigh. "What a life."

Benny turned to head back into the farmhouse.

"Where are you going?" Mama Lulu desperately asked.

"I'm going to bed," Benny said with a grump. "I ain't got time to stand around all night and yap with you."

"But I need you to keep me company, Benny." Mama Lulu implored. "I can't go to sleep. Maybe you can tell me a bedtime story or something."

"Yeah, I got one for you. When Christopher Columbus crossed the ocean and found the new land, what did he call it?"

"America."

"Wrong. He took one look at you and called it Nutville, U.S.A."

"Why you—"

When Benny dashed back into the farmhouse, Mama Lulu grabbed the baseball bat next to her bed and started hitting homeruns.

Fred went down to the hotel employee residential rooms. He approached the residential room at the end of the hall where the Wonder Gang stayed. The door was closed, but Fred could clearly hear the sound of loud music going on inside. He knew the Wonder Gang was having a wild, raunchy party with all the whooping, hollering, and the sound of glass shattering on the other side of the door. It was one of the Wonder Gang's typical parties; the louder and wilder it got, the better they seemed to like it.

"Hey, in there, open up!" Fred yelled toward the door. "HEY, YOU STUPID MORONS IN THERE, OPEN UP!"

When a hotel worker suddenly strolled by, Fred quickly got his attention.

"Hey, John, would you mind banging on this door for me. I can't seem to get their attention in there."

"Sure."

"I guess that's one of the problems of having no hands," he said with a chuckle.

When the hotel worker banged on the door several times, the door suddenly swung open as one of the Wonder Gang members stood in the doorway with nothing on but his underwear and a red and green party hat on his head.

"Thanks, John."

"No problem," the hotel worker said as he took off down the hallway.

"Hey, Big Chief," the Wonder Gang member said with a drunken slur and a smile. "Come on in, baby, and join the party."

When Fred entered the room he saw the Wonder Gang, along with eight half naked dwarf women who the Wonder Gang had invited to party with them, all dressed in red and green party hats and skimpy outfits. The music was blasting as liquor and beer bottles were strewn all over the place. The smell of kerweekee drifted in the air and the entire room was decked out in party attire. A huge banner on one of the walls in the room said: DWARF NATION, WHAT'S UP? WE GOT THE PARTY GOING ON AND THE KERWEEKEE IN THE AIR!

"Hey, ladies," Lou, the leader of the Wonder Gang, said to all the women in the room as he came over to Fred. "I want you all to meet the baddest St. Bernard dog in the entire world. His name is Fred, but we all call him Big Chief."

"Say, big boy, how'd you like to take a stroll to the bedroom and party with me," one of the half-naked dwarf ladies said as she suddenly came over and wrapped her bra around Fred's neck. "You know, I've never made it with a big, husky St. Bernard before."

"And you won't tonight, either, sweetie," Fred said to the promiscuous woman.

"Don't knock it till you try it."

"I'll keep that in mind," Fred said as he rolled his eyes. "Lou, could I speak to you for a minute."

"Sure, Big Chief."

Fred and Lou strolled away from all of the wild festivities taking place in the room.

"What's happening?" Lou said when they were all alone.

"Lou, I need one of the boys in here to follow Joe around the hotel from a distance and see what he's doing. Abner and Tutty have gone out for the night, and I don't want that ape moron to cause any problems while they're away that can get us into trouble."

"You mean perform a clandestine operation?"

"Exactly, and it has to be done pronto."

"I don't know, Big Chief." Lou said with a grimace. "None of the boys are going to want to leave the party and all of these gorgeous women to go do something like that."

"You horny, drunk lowlife bums can party with these sluts and whores anytime. I need a job done and I need it done right now."

"But—"

"Lou, don't forget, I drunk you and the boys under the table the last time we had our bet and left all of you knot heads with an unbelievable hangover for days. Do we have to do our little famous bet all over again? When I win this time, I'll tack on *two more years* of servitude for you and the boys," Fred said with a little chuckle. "And you know I'll win, don't you?"

Lou looked at Fred as his shoulders began to slump. He slowly let out a deep sigh. "Alright, Big Chief, I guess you win. Hey fellows," he called over to the rest of the Wonder Gang members in the room. "Y'all get your butts over here."

Sammy, Mike, and Frank left the women they were with as they strolled over to where Lou and Fred stood. They all had liquor bottles in their hands that they were swigging from.

Lou suddenly looked at his comrades suspiciously. "Where's Eddie?"

"Don't you remember that stupid putz left the party thirty minutes ago and went up to the casino," Mike said as he took a swig from his liquor bottle. "You know Eddie's got a serious, bad gambling problem. His second wife left him two years ago when he gambled their house away."

"That was his third wife, you idiot," Frank jumped in and said.

"No it wasn't, you moron, that was his fourth wife," Sammy replied.

"Who cares," Lou quickly said. "Alright, boys, listen. Big Chief wants one of us to follow Joe around the hotel tonight to see what he's up to since the big boss and his wife have gone out for the night. And he wants us to do it sort of clandestine like. So . . ." Lou looked at the three of them. "Which one of you is it going to be?"

"Don't look at me," Sammy quickly said.

"I'm too drunk to be following anybody around," Mike said with a slur.

"And me and the Della twins are going to be humping in the bedroom in a few minutes," Frank said with a hefty smile. "So, you can count me out."

"Hey, the Della twins are with me, you cruddy louse." Mike suddenly gave Frank a vicious glare. "They ain't going to be doing no humping with you."

"What are you two talking about?" Sammy quickly jumped in. "They just said they were going to be riding *me* in a few minutes. You two bozos can have Ethel, Mary Lou, and the rest of them."

"Don't nobody want Ethel and Mary Lou!"

A scuffle quickly broke out over the women as Sammy, Mike, and Frank rolled around on the floor throwing fisticuffs, biting, and kicking one another.

"Hey, break it up!" Lou hollered. "Break it up I said!"

When the boys finally ended their shenanigans and got up from the floor, Lou glared at them and said, "Alright, here's how we're going to do this. I'm going to think of a number from one to a hundred, the one who gets the closes to the number in my head is the one who'll have to go do the surveillance on Joe. So, Sammy, we'll start with you. What's your number?"

"Forty-five."

"That's the number!" Lou said with a chuckle. "You're it."

"What?"

"Well, you got your man, Big Chief." Lou gave Fred a hefty smile. "Now we can get back to the party."

Lou, Mike, and Frank quickly scattered as they rejoined the party with the ladies in the room.

"Hey, that ain't right, you scumbags!" Sammy yelled at the three fleeing members of the Wonder Gang.

"Come on, Sammy," Fred said without pretense. "You've got a job to do."

Sammy, with great consternation, hastily put on a pair of jeans, a shirt, and shoes as he headed for the door with Fred. But before they could leave out of the room, Fred's admirer caught him at the door as she once again slipped her bra around his neck.

"Where are you going, big boy?" she said as she rustled up against Fred. "The party in here is just getting started."

"We've got a little business to tend to," Fred said to his admirer.

"I'd love for you to get into my business, big boy," she said in an alluring voice.

"Excuse the pun, ma'am, but I got a feeling you've already been giving the business to every Tom, Dick, and Harry."

"Ah, come on, sweetie," she said as she rustled up to him even closer. "Come on to bed with me, big boy. I'll treat you right and put you to sleep, honey."

"One night with you, honey, and tomorrow the veterinarian will probably tell me there ain't no cure and I *will* be put to sleep."

Fred and Sammy left the promiscuous admirer standing at the door as they left out of the room to tend to their business.

Joe stood outside of room 317 eager and ready. The flamboyant orangutan had managed to swindle a key to room 317 from the front desk and now he was ready to put his master plan into action. His accomplice and lookout, Chipper, circled above his head in a languid fashion waiting for Joe to unlock the door to room 317. With Joe dressed in a faded brown suit, red and white polka dotted tie, and with Chipper being a colorful scarlet macaw parrot, they both looked like two shyster crooks whose wardrobe wasn't quite suited for such a secretive, undercover operation.

"Will you hurry up and unlock that door," Chipper said impatiently as he continued circling above Joe's head. "I thought I just saw a little guy peek around the corner with a red and green party hat on."

"A red and green party hat on?" Joe said with a chuckle. "Like a little leprechaun or something?"

"I don't know. You just hurry up and open that stupid door."

"Have you gone to see Dr. Glittermoon already?" Joe chuckled again.

"Just hurry up and open the door."

Joe unlocked the door to 317 as he and Chipper went inside the room. As expected, no one was in the room. Joe immediately went over to the safe on the nightstand and stared at it enticingly as Chipper landed on the nightstand beside the safe. They both stared silently at the safe.

"So, you think you can bust open that safe?" Joe finally asked.

"Piece of cake."

"I hope that famous eye of yours can cut through steel, or was that just a bunch of talk you were doing at the bar?"

"Please," Chipper said with a huff. "Ape, you're about to witness what my left eye is capable of."

Chipper suddenly flipped a pair of protective glasses from his head over his eyes with his wing. Like an eye on a stove, Chipper's left eye slowly became redder and brighter until a powerful red stream of light began to beam from his left eye. His left eye blazed like burning fire as the intense red light beamed straight at the bolts riveted to the side of the safe door. After nearly a minute, the red intense light beaming from his left eye burned off the two steal bolts connected to the side of the safe door as the door suddenly fell off.

The entire room was all smoky from the intense heat that Chipper's left eye had created. When the door of the safe finally fell off, Joe, with glee all over his face, quickly reached into the safe and grabbed the expensive diamond ruby necklace.

Joe blazed his brilliant smile as he admired the necklace in his hand. "Good work, bird."

"Like I told you, ape," Chipper said as he removed the protective glasses from his eyes with his wing, "piece of cake."

Joe quickly stuffed the diamond ruby necklace into the pocket of his faded brown suit. "Let's go, bird. Time for phase two of the plan."

Joe and Chipper headed down to Abner and Tutty's residential suite. As Joe fumbled around in his suit coat pocket trying to retrieve the keys he'd stolen from Abner, Chipper circled above his head waiting for him to unlock the door.

"Will you hurry up, ape," Chipper said impatiently. "I could've sworn I just saw a little man wearing a red and green party hat just peek around the corner again."

"Chipper, I believe all that kerweekee is starting to mess with your head," Joe said with a chuckle.

"Just hurry up and open the door."

Joe finally found the key to Abner and Tutty's residential suite. He unlocked the door as he and Chipper went into the owner's suite.

After a couple of unsuccessful attempts, they finally found Mama Lulu's room as they entered her room. The nightlight on the nightstand was on as Mama Lulu slept soundly under the covers of her bed. Joe and Chipper lingered for a moment in her room as they watched her sleep.

"Alright, let's do this and get out of here, ape," Chipper said in a low voice as he circled overhead.

"Hold on, bird," Joe said as he scanned around the room. "I'm trying to figure out where's a good place to stash this necklace."

"Well, find it and let's go."

As Mama Lulu slept, Joe finally went over to one of her old dresser drawers. Trying not to wake her, he eased the bottom drawer open, pulled out the stolen diamond ruby necklace from his coat pocket and stashed the necklace into the bottom of the drawer under some old clothes of hers. He then eased the drawer back shut, took a glance over at Mama Lulu to make sure she was still asleep, then he slowly turned as he and Chipper began to head out of the room.

"I saw what you did, ape."

Joe stopped dead in his tracks when he suddenly heard the voice. Not knowing where the unidentified voice came from, he finally glanced over at the old, shambled farmhouse cuckoo clock on the wall and saw the three-inch-high mechanical farmer with the pitch fork in his hand. Joe immediately flashed his smile at the mechanical farmer; a smile of true guilt as his heart began to thunder.

"You saw what, my friend?"

"You know what I'm talking about, ape," Benny said with his perpetual scowl. "That necklace you and that bird circling overhead tried to sneak in here to hide. Are you two buffoons some kind of jewel thieves or something?"

"We didn't come in here to hide no necklace, farmer man," Joe said as he continued smiling. "We just came to—"

"Stop your lying, ape." Benny quickly interrupted him. "That old cheesy smile of yours gives you away. I know a no-good con artist when I see one. You ain't fooling me, ape."

"Listen, old farmer, I ain't stole no necklace," Joe said as he continued flashing his guilty smile. "I just came in here to—"

Joe suddenly went silent as he glanced over at Mama Lulu in her bed when he heard her mumble something in her sleep.

"You don't have to worry about her," Benny quickly said. "That old senile woman can sleep through an earthquake. That's why you and that bird came in here. You knew the Mr. and the Mrs. were away and you knew that dumb lump sleeping under them covers over there would probably be sound sleep. Well, you guessed right. And even if she were awake, she so dumb and stupid, the only thing you'd have to do to fool her is to tell her you were sent by Madam Cureall or something and that dumb stupid woman would believe it."

"Well, that's good to know, old farmer," Joe said as he beamed his smile. "We'll be seeing you."

"Not so fast, ape. Where you think you're going?"

"Well, we were just—"

"Stop your lying, you scheming ape and cough up some money or I'm telling all about that necklace when the fat man gets back."

"Some what?"

"You heard me, ape. Now start digging into that suit coat of yours and pull out some cash before I call the police on you two jewel thieves."

"Farmer man, how about I give you a brand new pitch fork instead," Joe said with a radiant smile as he performed his magical ritual and produced a brand new pitch fork.

"What in the world do I need a pitch fork when I already got one?" Benny said as he glared at Joe. "I want cash, you stupid ape, cash. I need to buy more seed for the farm, my mule is going lame, plus I've got to fix the roof to my house."

"I'll tell you what, old farmer. I'll give you a hundred dollars tomorrow," Joe said as he blazed his smile. "I promise."

"You expect me to believe a promise from a scheming ape?" Benny said in an irate voice. "Hell, I'd believe that senile woman lying in that bed over there if she said she was once Queen Victoria before I'd believe a lying scheming ape like you."

"Alright, Mr. Farmer," Joe said as he dug into his suit coat. "Here, I got a twenty."

"I'll take forty, ape."

"Twenty is all I got, old farmer."

"Alright," Benny said with a huff. "Drop it down my chimney."

"What?"

"I got a pitch fork in my hand, you stupid ape," Benny said heatedly. "You're going to have to drop it down the chimney."

Joe went over to the old shambled cuckoo clock on the wall and dropped the twenty dollar bill down the chimney of the farmhouse.

"Nice doing business with you, ape," Benny said as he quickly went back into the farmhouse.

When Benny disappeared, Joe began to flash his giant, luminous smile as he stared down at Mama Lulu as she slept in her bed.

"What you lingering around watching her sleep for?" Chipper said as he continued to circle overhead. "Let's get out of here."

"Hold on, bird," Joe said as his smile became even brighter. "I just got a marvelous idea."

Joe pounded his chest twice with his fist and snapped his finger. Poof! A cloud of purple smoke mushroomed in the air as he turned into a sea captain wearing a white captain's uniform and a spiffy white skipper hat. He suddenly pulled a long pipe from his suit coat as he quickly filled the bowl of the pipe with kerweekee.

"Hey, ape, you stole my kerweekee!" Chipper said with a gruff.

"Relax, bird," Joe said with a hearty smile. "The Wonder Gang brought forty pounds of the stuff."

Joe lit the bowl of the pipe as he softly placed the end of the pipe between Mama Lulu's lips as she slept. He watched with glee as Mama Lulu began to breathe in and out as she huffed and puffed from the pipe.

"That's right, mooly-mooly, keep taking those big puffs," he said with a laugh. "Welcome aboard my ship. I'm your captain, the one and only Captain Joe, and it's time that we drop anchor and head for Jamaica!"

"You're insane, ape."

"Most definitely, my tropical bird," Joe said with a hefty smile. "Most definitely."

Joe finally took the pipe from Mama Lulu's lips as he and Chipper left Mama Lulu all alone to her peaceful sleep.

Fred strolled around the packed casino as he intermingled with all of the people as they played the slots, the roulette, and took their chances at the crap table. With his dog vest on that said Welcome to the Lucky Jackpot Hotel and with his uncanny ability to speak, he constantly got a lot of attention from the hotel guests. Fred was certainly used to all of the recognition by now. He took great pride in being the hotel's spokesperson and making sure all the guests felt welcomed.

When Fred suddenly spotted a woman sitting all alone at a slot machine with a sad face, he became concerned as he stopped to have a few words with her.

"Enjoying your stay here at the Lucky Jackpot Hotel?" he said in a friendly voice.

"Oh, I guess so," the woman said in a dreary voice. "You're one of those talking animals they have here at this hotel, aren't you?"

"I guess you noticed." Fred chuckled.

The woman kept pouring more money into the slot machine as she continued to lose.

"I've had it playing this machine," she finally said with a heavy sigh.

"Hoping to win big, huh?"

"I guess we're all," the woman said in a gloomy voice. "It's just that I've spent everything that I had to come on this trip and now I'm going to return to Virginia in a few days flat broke with a stack of bills to pay when I get back. And on top of that, now I'm down to my very last quarter."

"That's a shame," Fred said in a caring voice. "But just remember, ma'am, there's always hope."

"I'm all out of hope," the woman said dejectedly as she let the quarter slip from her hand as it dropped to the floor. Fred picked the coin up from the floor with his mouth.

"Don't ever give up hope, ma'am," he said as he dropped the coin into the woman's lap. "There's always that next chance."

The lady looked at Fred as she gave him a long, pitiful sigh. She then slowly took the coin from her lap, put it into the slot machine, and pressed the button. The fruit immediately began to spin. When the fruit finally came to a stop, three cherries were lined up in a row as the slot machine rung—$5,000 Jackpot!

As the woman jumped and celebrated, Fred continued his tour around the casino. When he came to the blackjack tables, he suddenly saw a familiar face. Eddie, the compulsive gambling member of the Wonder Gang, was at a blackjack table with three large towers of chips sitting in front of him.

"Well, Eddie, I see you've been doing pretty well at the blackjack table," Fred said as he came over to him.

"I'm on a roll, Big Chief!" Eddie spoke with a smile. "Nothing can stop my luck tonight."

"Eddie, you know employees are not supposed to be gambling in the casino, don't you?"

"I ain't no employee," he said with a huff. "We're just here working for you."

"Big Chief, I've been looking all over for you," Sammy said as he suddenly rushed over to Fred when he entered the casino. "Joe and Chipper have just swiped this diamond ruby necklace out of the safe of room 317."

"They what?"

"I followed Joe like you wanted me to," Sammy said as he continued. "They broke into room 317 and Chipper used his left eye to burn off the bolts of the doors to this safe in the room. When they finally broke into the safe, that's when Joe snatched the necklace. I saw the whole thing when I sneaked inside the room while they were preoccupied trying to break into that safe."

"You mean to tell me that Chipper and that moron ape stole a hotel guest's necklace out of a safe?" Fred said in an alarmed voice.

"Yep."

"What did Joe do with the necklace?"

"Well, I followed him and Chipper all the way down to Abner and Tutty's residential suite. Somehow the ape already had a key to their suite. Him and Chipper just waltzed inside their suite, then they came back out about ten minutes later."

"He broke *inside* Abner and Tutty's residential suite?"

"No. He had a key, Big Chief," Sammy said with a chuckle.

"How in the world did that ape moron get a key to their suite?"

"I don't know. But it seems like that's probably where they stashed the necklace at, inside Abner and Tutty's residential suite."

"Good heavens," Fred said like a dog getting ready to collapse from a massive heart attack. "We've got to get that necklace back. Let's go."

"Hey, no way. I did my part, Big Chief," Sammy said as he took a seat next to Eddie at the blackjack table. "I want to get in on some of the action that my man Eddie's got going on," he said with a hefty smile. "My man looks like he's racking up at this table."

"You damn gambling addicted, whore chasing morons!" Fred said in an irritated voice.

Fred quickly scurried out of the casino as he dashed back down to the employee residential rooms. When he reached the Wonder Gang's room, to his dismay, he once again found their door closed as he heard the loud music blasting from inside the room.

"Ah, no. Here we go again," Fred said in frustration as he stared at the door. "Hey in there, open up!" he yelled toward the door. "HEY YOU MORONS, OPEN THIS DOOR!"

Fred was surprised when the door suddenly swung open as one of the members of the Wonder Gang stood there in the doorway in his birthday suit. It was Lou. He was in the arms of three women as they cuddled and fawned all over him.

"Lou, we got a serious problem," Fred said in an urgent voice.

"You're telling me," Lou uttered as he laughed and turned up his bottle of whiskey. "I don't know which one of these lovely beauties I want to have a fun with, or maybe I should just do all three of them and call it a night."

"Lou, excuse yourself from the ladies, get dressed, and put the bottle down." Fred lashed out. "We've got a big problem and I need your help."

"Oh, Big Chief, can it wait until the morning?"

"Now, Lou!"

"Well, ladies, you heard him," Lou said to his harem. "Why don't you three ladies go play amongst yourselves while I have a little talk with Big Chief here. But don't have too much fun without me if you know what I mean."

When the three ladies wandered off, Lou motioned for Fred to come in as he took him all the way to the far back of the room. Lou put on some jeans, a t-shirt, and shoes as he put his whiskey bottle down.

"What's so important this time, Big Chief?"

"Lou, Joe and Chipper broke into room 317 and stole a diamond ruby necklace from the safe in the room," he said in a panic voice. "They took the stolen necklace and stashed it in Abner and Tutty's suite. Lou, we need to get that necklace back before the guest in room 317 gets back to the room and discovers that the necklace has been stolen. And we *definitely* need to get that necklace out of Abner and Tutty's suite before they come back from their show."

"How in the world did they get into the big boss' suite?"

"Sammy said Joe already had a key."

"Man, Joe has skill," Lou said with admiration.

"Lou, now is not the time to be admiring that ape moron for the skill of his criminal activity!" Fred yelled. "You don't seem to understand the seriousness of this."

"Alright, Big Chief, what do you want me to do?"

"Are you still any good at hacking into computer systems?"

"I haven't done any of that stuff since I last went to jail for hacking into the payroll department of that Fortune Five company a couple years ago. I only took two grand," he said with a laugh. "Why do you ask?"

"Because I need you to hack into the hotel system computer and see if you can find the code to Abner and Tutty's suite. We can get another key from the front desk to room 317 with no problem, but there's no way we can get into Abner and Tutty's suite without making another key to their suite. And that requires knowing the code to their room."

"I thought the owner's suite required a traditional physical metal key to get in."

"The last time we were there, I noticed that their door had both the traditional pin tumbler lock and the modern type Radio Frequency Identification card option. So, if you can hack into the hotel computer system, we could get the code to their room and make a key card."

"Alright, Big Chief, if it's that important to you I'll see what I can do."

"It is important, Lou!"

Lou and Fred went over to a section of the room cornered off into an office workstation. Lou sat down at a computer behind the cubicle as he began to try to hack into the hotel computer system. Fred, nervous and worried, began to pace back and forth like a dog that had gone mad as Lou pecked away at the computer.

"How's it coming?" Fred asked after fifteen minutes.

"Big Chief, it's been a while since I've last done anything like this. I'm a little rusty, so you're just going to have to be patient."

"We don't have time to be patient, Lou!"

Thirty minutes later, Lou finally looked at Fred with a giant smile.

"I did it."

"You got the code?"

"Yep."

"Good. We can get the front desk to make us some key cards for the two rooms and get two telephone headsets. Let's go."

"Hey, I got a party going on here and women who are horny, Big Chief." Lou complained. "Get Sammy to do it."

"Sammy is up there in the casino with Eddie gambling away. It's your turn, Lou."

"But—"

"Lou, I'm about to add another year of servitude if you don't get your butt up and let's go."

"Alright, Big Chief."

As Fred and Lou headed for the door, Fred's promiscuous admirer suddenly roped her target once again with her bra.

"Where are you going, Big Daddy?" she said in a seductive voice. "I've got some cherry pie I desperately want to serve you."

"I don't have the time, Ms.," Fred said to his admirer. "I have to leave."

"Well, when you come back, that cherry pie will still be waiting for you."

"I can't wait."

"Neither can I, Big Daddy."

Fred and Lou headed on for the door.

"That damn cherry pie probably rotten as hell," Fred said as he and Lou headed out the door.

Lou, wearing a telephone headset, opened Abner and Tutty's residential suite door when he pressed the room card key he'd just attained to the key base on the door. He entered their suite and immediately started searching around the parlor in different desk drawers and shelves trying to find the stolen necklace that Joe and Chipper had stashed.

Not having any luck, he finally went into the kitchen and started searching there. Coming up empty and beginning to get hungry, he opened the refrigerator, fixed himself a ham sandwich and had a seat at the kitchen table.

Lou was enjoying his ham sandwich when he heard Fred's voice suddenly come over his headset.

"Lou, have you found it yet?"

"No, Big Chief," he said into the microphone of his headset. "I ain't had any luck yet."

"You sound like you're eating something."

"I am." He continued to eat his sandwich. "I'm sitting in their kitchen right now munching on a ham sandwich."

"You mean you went into their refrigerator and made you a sandwich?"

"Sure did. They got some good ham, too."

"Lou, put that sandwich down and get to looking for that necklace right now!"

"I'm having a hard time finding it, Big Chief. Hell, I don't know where to look."

"Look everywhere! It's got to be in there someplace."

"But where?"

"Look in the closets and look . . ." Fred suddenly went silent. "On second thought, Lou, a thought just came to me. Knowing that ape moron, try looking in Mama Lulu's room. He knows she's kind of ditzy and half off her rocker. He probably knows that hiding that necklace in her room will probably be the perfect place until he can come back and retrieve it."

"Alright, I'll—" Lou stopped in midsentence when the sound of the front door opened as he heard Abner and Tutty's voice. "Big Chief, the big boss and his wife just came back!"

"Get out of that kitchen, you moron!"

Lou quickly grabbed his ham sandwich and dashed over to the coat closet in the parlor as he went inside and closed the door. He sat on the floor and listened as Abner and Tutty made their way into the parlor.

"I'm going to check on Mama Lulu and see how she's doing," he heard Tutty say.

"She's probably got that stupid bed sheet tied around her neck pretending to be Madam Cureall or something." He heard Abner grumble.

Lou suddenly froze when the closet door swung open. Crouched down on the floor, he saw it was Abner trying to hang up his suit coat. When the coat fell from his hands, Lou picked it up and handed it back to him.

"Thanks," Abner said.

"No problem."

Lou immediately cringed when he realized he'd spoken. Abner, with his dark glasses on, stood in the doorway of the coat closet with a puzzled, mystified face as if trying to figure out if he really indeed hear someone speak. When Lou thought he was about to get busted, the phone suddenly rang.

"Abner, you got a phone call," he heard Tutty say.

Abner closed the coat closet as Lou, in the darkness of the closet, listened as Abner answered the phone.

"Hello?"

There was a pause.

"What, there's been a robbery of a thirty-thousand-dollar necklace out of the safe of room 317?"

There was another pause.

"The police are waiting down at the front desk?"

There was another long pause.

"Good heavens. I'll be down there immediately."

Lou heard Abner hang up the phone. Abner quickly told Tutty the situation as he departed the residential suite.

"Big Chief," Lou said quietly into his microphone as he sat crouched in the darkness of the coat closet.

"Yeah?"

"I just heard the big boss on the phone. Someone has just reported to him about the stolen necklace and the police are at the hotel front desk. The big boss is on his way to the front desk right now."

"Where are you now?"

"I'm hiding in the coat closet of their parlor."

"Lou, get in Mama Lulu's room right now and find that necklace!"

"I'm on it, Big Chief. I'm on it."

Lou slowly opened the door of the closet as he peeked out. When he didn't see anyone, he scampered out and began to carefully peek into rooms. When he finally wandered into Mama Lulu's room and found her asleep with her nightlight on, he began to quietly check around the room for the stolen necklace.

"I know what you're looking for."

Lou quickly spun around when he heard the voice. When he saw that Mama Lulu was still asleep, he began to scan the room searching for the location of the voice.

"Up here, little man."

Lou finally peered up at the old, decrepit cuckoo clock on the wall and saw the three-inch-high mechanical farmer with the pitchfork in his hand.

"Yeah, I'm the one talking to you," Benny said with his perpetual scowl. "I know what you're looking for."

"You do?"

"You're looking for that necklace that ape and bird came in here to hide."

"Where is it?"

"Not so fast, little man. I'm a farmer in need, and I need cash money."

The window to the farmhouse suddenly flew open as Edna stuck her head out.

"Benny, what are you doing out here at this time of night with that fellow down there?"

"Nothing, Edna. Go back to sleep."

"Benny, if you think I'm going to let you sneak off and go to some strip club with that fellow, you got another thing coming, mister!"

"Woman, will you shut that mouth of yours, close that window and go back to sleep."

"Not until you tell me what you're doing with that fellow down there at this time of night."

"Woman, it's strictly business!"

"Business?" she said incredulously. "The only business you need to be tending to, mister, is fixing the roof of this house!"

"Woman, will you stop nagging me about that roof!"

"No, I'm not going to stop nagging you about that roof, because it's all your fault!" she yelled. "Now say goodbye to your little friend and come to bed so you can get up in the morning and start repairing that broken down, crumbling roof!"

Edna slammed the window down as Benny let out a long sigh.

"That woman is always nagging me about that roof," he said with a grouch. "Now, back to you, little man. Pull out some cash or you'll never find that necklace you're looking for."

Lou reached into the pocket of his pants and pulled out a twenty-dollar bill.

"The ape paid me twenty bucks to hide that necklace. If you want that necklace back, little man, it's going to cost you double."

Lou grudgingly dug back into the pocket of his pants as he pulled out two ten-dollar bills and added it to the twenty he already held. "Alright, here's forty, farmer man," he said as he held out the forty dollars for Benny to take. "Now where's the necklace?"

"Dumbass, I got a pitch fork in my hand." Benny snapped. "You're going to have to drop it down my chimney."

Lou gazed up at the chimney of the farmhouse cuckoo clock. Standing from his viewpoint, the chimney looked like scanning up at a tall skyscraper. "How am I supposed to get way up there?"

"That's your problem, little man."

Lou sighed as he tried to figure out how he was going to get up there. Finally, he climbed onto the nightstand next to Mama Lulu's bed. Standing on his tiptoes, he reached up as high as he could, barely getting his hand over the top of the chimney as he dropped the money down the chimney. When he let go of the money, he suddenly lost his footing and fell off the nightstand as he crashed hard to the floor.

"Fell on your ass, didn't you?"

"Enough with the wisecracks," Lou said angrily. "Just tell me where the necklace is at?"

"The ape hid it in the bottom drawer of the dresser underneath the clothes."

Lou quickly opened the bottom drawer of the dresser as he rummaged underneath all the clothes. He suddenly grabbed onto the necklace as he pulled it out and admired the gleaming, shiny diamond ruby necklace.

"Wow," Lou said with a giant smile, "the ape certainly knew what he was doing when he snatched this beautiful gem!"

Mama Lulu suddenly shuffled and groaned under the sheets of her bed as she woke up. She rolled over and slowly opened her eyes as she gazed over at the dwarf holding the diamond ruby necklace.

"Are you Madam Cureall's little helper?" she said with a childish smile. "Did you come to bring me a present from her?"

"No, sweetie, I'm the tooth fairy," Lou quickly said. "This here was a mistake, but I've come to bring you your real present. So, close your eyes and go back to sleep, and when you wake up in the morning, your *real* present will be waiting for you underneath your pillow."

"Oh, goody," Mama Lulu said with a childish smile as she lay her head back onto her pillow and closed her eyes. As she drifted back to sleep, she suddenly mumbled, "Why do I feel so hungry?"

Lou took the necklace and scrammed out of the room as he made a quick exit out of Abner and Tutty's residential suite. As soon as he exited the suite, Fred came over his headset.

"Lou, I'm down here at the front desk," Fred said in a panic voice. "The police, Abner, Tango, and the lady whose necklace was stolen are heading up to room 317 this very second. Please tell me that you found the necklace?"

"I got it, Big Chief."

"Well, hurry as fast as you can to room 317 and put that necklace back into that safe before they get up there!"

"I'm on it!"

Lou ran as fast as he could as he hurried to get to the room. He skipped going up the slow elevator and took the stairway as he climbed the stairs like a speed demon.

When Lou finally reached the third floor, panting and gasping for air, he scampered down the hallway until he reached room 317. He used the key he and Fred had gotten from the front desk as he quickly opened the door. Once in the room, he dashed over to the safe that had been busted open by Chipper's left eye as he tossed the diamond ruby necklace inside of it.

With the job completed, he headed straight for the door. But as soon as he placed his hand on the doorknob to leave out of the room, he heard voices on the other side of the door. Not wanting to get caught inside the room, Lou quickly ran over and crawled underneath the bed as he stayed as silent as he could.

"Now, ma'am, you said there was someone from the hotel staff cleaning your room when you last put the necklace into the safe?" Lou heard someone say when the hotel room door opened.

"That's right, officer," a lady said. "There was this talking orangutan ape in here cleaning the room when I last locked my necklace into the safe before me and my girlfriends left the hotel. I believe he called himself Joe."

"Joe!" Lou heard Abner say. "What did this Joe fellow look like?"

"He was an orangutan ape."

"An ape!"

"That's right. You see I put my necklace over here into this safe and—"

There was a sudden silence.

"Hey, there's my necklace!"

"Ma'am, you're sure that your necklace was stolen from this safe?" the police voice said.

"Yes, it was locked into this safe, officer."

"And are you sure there was an *ape* cleaning your room?" Lou heard Abner say with a slight chuckle. "Ma'am, I don't allow animals of any kind at my hotel, and I *certainly* wouldn't allow any animals or beasts to be working on my hotel staff," he said with a hearty chuckle. "You know this is Las Vegas where all the partying, alcohol, and all the other stuff can sometimes make you see funny things, ma'am."

"That's right, ma'am," Lou heard Tango suddenly say. "There are no apes here at this hotel."

"I'm telling you there was an orangutan in here cleaning—" the woman said as she suddenly hesitated. "Oh, never mind. I'm just glad I got my necklace back."

"Well, I guess we'll call this investigation closed," the police voice said.

"And, ma'am, please enjoy your stay here at the Lucky Jackpot Hotel," Lou heard Abner's voice say. "And if there's anything further I can do to make your stay more comfortable, please don't hesitate to ask. Goodnight."

When Lou heard the police officer, Abner, and Tango leave out of the room, he waited for a good opportunity to sneak out without the occupant of 317 getting a shock seeing him crawling from out under the bed.

"Lou, did you put that necklace back into the safe?" Fred's voice suddenly came over the headset once again.

"The necklace is back into the safe," Lou whispered into the microphone.

"Are you still in that room?"

"Yeah, I'm hiding underneath the bed," he whispered once again into the microphone. "I'm just waiting until the coast is clear before I scram."

When Lou heard the woman go into the bathroom and the shower began to run, he figured it was time to make a move.

"I think I found my chance," he whispered into the microphone. "I'm out of here."

Lou quickly slid from underneath the bed as he got up from the floor and headed for the door. Just as he was about to turn the doorknob to leave out of the room, he suddenly heard a scream. Lou quickly whirled around and saw a naked lady with the biggest boobs ever staring directly at him.

"Hot damn!" he said with a giant, lustful smile. "You got some nice jugs, baby!"

Lou quickly turned and scrammed out of the room as he hightailed it down the hallway.

Tutty sat at the head of the kitchen table having a late-night snack and doodling over some notes of hers in preparation for tomorrow's business meeting with Abner. It was late and Tutty didn't want to stay up too late because she was tired and tomorrow promised to be a long day of dealing with matters concerning the hotel.

Suddenly Mama Lulu stormed into the kitchen like a wild twister as she went straight for the refrigerator.

"Mama Lulu, what in the world are you doing up at this time of night?" Tutty said as she looked up from her notes when Mama Lulu stumbled by her. "When I looked in on you when we got back, you were sound asleep."

Mama Lulu didn't say a word as she opened the refrigerator and started pulling out stuff like she was getting ready to clean out the entire refrigerator. She pulled out a ham, left over beef stew, a pot of baked beans, a pack of hot dogs, half of a pizza, and a sweet potato pie. She opened the freezer and yanked out a carton of chocolate ice cream. She then began to rummage through the kitchen cabinets and started yanking down donuts, potato chips, pop tarts, popcorn, and cupcakes.

Mama Lulu took all of the collected stuff, plunged herself down at the kitchen table and began to have a pig fest feast. Tutty watched her go to work tearing into all of the food with a flabbergasted expression.

"Mama Lulu," she said in shock, "are you alright?"

Mama Lulu had nothing to say. The only sound that came from the kitchen table was the sound of munch and crunch.

Twenty minutes later when Mama Lulu had gorged herself with enough food to feed an army and there was nothing left to eat, she sat back in her chair at the kitchen table with a satisfied, dazed look. Her nightclothes were a pure mess from all sorts of food stains and chocolate ice cream smeared down her pajamas.

Abner suddenly strolled into the kitchen on his white cane.

"Tutty, I tell you, there's something strange going on," Abner said as he went over to the refrigerator and opened it. "That woman in room 317 whose necklace was supposedly stolen, said some talking orangutan ape cleaned her room and had stolen her diamond necklace. And she said his name was Joe. Something funny is going on, but I don't know what it is."

"Oh, Abner, that woman probably had too many daiquiris to drink tonight," Tutty said with a chuckle. "Ain't no telling what she thought she saw in her room."

"That's what I said. But she said his name was Joe," Abner said in a baffled voice. "We don't have anybody new working here name Joe on the hotel staff, do we? I thought you said that last Joe fellow was let go."

"Abner, that woman must've been blitzed out of her mind when she came back to the hotel." Tutty chuckled again. "There are no Joes working around here."

"Yeah. That's what I thought. The whole thing has given me nothing but a headache and made me hungry," he said as he felt around inside the refrigerator. "Hey, I don't feel that sweet potato pie on the shelf in the refrigerator. What happened to it?"

Tutty suddenly sighed as she glanced over at Mama Lulu sitting at the table. "Well, Mama Lulu came in not too long ago and ate it."

Abner felt around some more in the refrigerator. "I don't feel that pot of left over beef stew. What happened to it?"

Tutty sighed once more. "Mama Lulu ate it."

Abner opened the freezer and felt around. "I don't feel that carton of chocolate ice cream either. What happened to it?

Tutty groaned again. "Mama Lulu, she ate it."

"What about those box of donuts?"

"Mama Lulu ate it."

"Where in the world are those cupcakes?"

"Mama Lulu ate it."

"Where is she at?"

"Abner, she's sitting right here at the kitchen table."

"Woman, I know you're as nutty as those stupid cuckoo clocks of yours," Abner bellowed angrily, "but did you have to eat up the whole entire house?"

"I couldn't help it!" Mama Lulu yelled. "I got hungry!"

"Well, I'm hungry too! What the devil am I supposed to do for a late-night snack?"

"Your fat butt need to go on diet anyway!"

"Tutty, I swear we need to go ahead and commit that woman to a funny farm as soon as possible!" Abner bellowed as he began to head out of the kitchen on his white cane. "I'm going to bed."

Tutty began to snicker as Mama Lulu got up from the table as she sauntered out of the kitchen also. In the forty years she'd been married to Abner, she'd never seen the little woman have the type of appetite that she'd just portrayed.

As Tutty sat at the table and began to skim over her notes once again, the doorbell suddenly rang. Not knowing who it could be at such a late hour, Tutty got up from the kitchen table as she went to see who was at the door.

When she opened the door, she was a bit confused because no one was standing there. After a second, she happened to glance down and noticed the white and black striped Siamese cat known as Elvyra at the foot of the door. Tutty was totally perplexed of how the small, diminutive cat could've possibly rang the doorbell by herself.

"Yes, can I help you?"

"I'm here to report to Mr. Redder on the survey of how well the convention guests enjoyed their stay here at the hotel today," Elvyra said in an efficient secretarial voice. "I was told by the boss to report my findings to him by the end of the day."

"Well, it's kind of late and my husband is getting ready to go to bed," Tutty responded. "He's had a very long day. Maybe you should just come back in the morning."

"But the boss implicitly told me to come and report my findings by the end of the day."

Tutty chuckled as she stared down at the Siamese cat. She thought it was cute that the Siamese cat was so persistent and dedicated to her job. "Alright, come on in. The bedroom is right down the hall."

"Thank you."

When the Siamese cat headed for the bedroom, Tutty couldn't help but to shake her head and chuckle as she went into the parlor. She went over to the bar and fixed herself a nightcap as she had a seat on the couch and sipped her drink.

Five minutes later, Tutty was totally stunned beyond belief. A beautiful six-foot Latino woman suddenly came out of their bedroom dressed in a skimpy Playboy Bunny outfit arm and arm with her husband. Abner was smiling from ear to ear as he and his beautiful sexy escort headed for the door.

"Big Teddy Bear, don't you worry about a thing," Elvrya said in a sensuous voice. "I'm going to take care of your *every* need."

"Oh, Ms. Mendez, I can't wait," Abner said as his bodacious smile began to spread even further.

As Elvyra and Abner passed Tutty sitting in the parlor as they headed for the door, the sultry six-foot beauty suddenly glanced over at Tutty, gave her a wink and a smile as she headed arm and arm with her husband out of the door. Tutty, in total shock, could only sit and watch with her mouth hanging wide open.

It was early Wednesday morning. Abner and Tutty had just had a business meeting inside Abner's office and Abner was highly upset. He'd just been informed that the five hundred members of the Smith & Hirsch Brothers National Car Salesmen Organization scheduled to have their convention at the Lucky Jackpot Hotel this Friday, had just canceled their convention and their entire deposit was due to be returned.

Abner was boiling mad that Tango had written up the contract, and he didn't stipulate in the contract that no deposit money would be returned in case of cancelation. Abner instructed Tutty to summon Tango over to his office immediately. There were a million things he wanted to yell and fuss at Tango about, and the sooner he got there, the sooner he could start his venting.

After phoning Tango and telling him that the head CEO wanted to see him immediately in his office, Tutty finally ventured out of Abner's office to get a much needed break from all of her husband's wolfing and yelling. When she strolled through the parlor, she suddenly heard a bell chime indicating that today's mail had arrived.

The mail was delivered by none other than Benny from the cuckoo clock located on the wall in the parlor that resembled a post office. Every day Benny, dressed as a three-inch-high mailman, would come out of his post office cuckoo clock on a mechanical track and deliver the mail. He was always a fussy, disgruntle mailman who *always* had a million things to gripe and complain about. The heavy workload of his job or the people on his mail route was usually what all of his complaining and griping were all about.

Benny, dressed in his blue mailman uniform and hauling a big sack of mail over his shoulder, suddenly came out of the post office cuckoo clock on a mechanical track. He had a mean, nasty snarl on his face, as he did every day, as if he didn't want to be bothered with any nonsense.

"Why hello there, Benny," Tutty said in a pleasant voice as she went over to get today's mail. "How's your day been? Good, I hope?"

"It's been terrible, woman, that's how it's been!" Benny snapped.

"Didn't you just start your mail route? What could've happened already?"

"This dog just bit me in the ass when I was delivering mail at this house over on another street," he said in a hostile voice.

"Oh, I'm so sorry to hear that, Benny," Tutty responded in a concerned voice. "Did it hurt?"

"What kind of question is that?" Benny yelled. "Hell, yeah it hurt, woman!"

"Excuse me for even asking."

"Plus this drunk wandered over to me and asked could I give him a dollar so he could go get him some cheap wine?"

"What did you tell him?"

"I told him to go drink his own piss and get out of my face."

"Oh, Benny," Tutty said with a chuckle as she shook her head. "You're certainly a character, did you know that?"

"Here's your mail, woman," Benny said with a heated grouch as he suddenly handed her a big stack of mail. "I tell you, I *hate* delivering to this hotel. Y'all get so much mail here every day, and I always get a hump in my back when I go home in the evening from carrying around so much mail."

"Oh, that's a real shame, Benny." Tutty emphasized. "And believe me, I really do apologize for your discomfort."

"What's your apology going to do for the hump in my back, woman?"

"I didn't mean—"

"I'm used to getting a hump in my back when I go home and me and the old lady get busy at night," Benny said in an aggravated tone as he interrupted her. "But dealing with this job will put a hump in your back permanently!"

"Well, I'm so sorry—"

"There goes that word again—*sorry*," Benny said as he glared at Tutty. "If you were really sorry, woman, you'd give me a couple of bucks so I can get me a bottle of liquor when I get off work today."

"You're absolutely right, Benny." Tutty suddenly pulled out two bucks and handed it to him. "There you go."

"What am I supposed to buy with two bucks, woman?" Benny complained. "I might as well go hook up with that drunk when I get off work. Hell, with both of us going around begging, maybe we can scrounge up enough money and get us some *real* good wine to drink tonight. Bye, woman," he finally said with an angry huff. "I got to go. I still got a whole lot of mail to deliver."

Benny, with a heated gruff, all of a sudden dashed back into the post office cuckoo clock as Tutty began to snicker.

When the doorbell suddenly rang, Tutty was reminded that she'd just called Tango over because Abner was fuming mad. After glancing at the time on the cuckoo clock, Tutty went over to answer the front door. She opened the door and saw Tango standing there dressed in his usual gold blazer, starched white shirt, black tie, and black slacks. Tutty quickly motioned for Tango to come in as she gathered with him in the parlor.

"Before we go into the office, I just wanted to warn you that Abner is storming mad this morning?"

"Why?"

"We just got a call from the Smith & Hirsch Brothers National Car Salesmen Organization and they've canceled their convention for this weekend, and Abner had to return their entire deposit."

"Oh, no," Tango said in a dismal voice as he slowly lowered his head. "I guess I didn't think to put a no deposit return clause in the contract. I'm sorry."

"It's not your fault," Tutty said in an understanding voice. "You're not used to writing those types of contracts and I forgot to scan over the contract before you sent it off to Smith & Hirsch."

"How mad is he?"

"*Very mad.*"

"So, I guess I should get ready for a vicious yelling and tongue lashing."

"That's putting it mildly," Tutty said with a sigh. "But I'll have your back, don't worry."

"Thanks."

"Oh, there's something else I wanted to talk to you about," Tutty said as she suddenly looked at Tango with trepidation.

"What's that?"

"The other night, Elvyra came over to our suite to report to Abner on how well the Alpha Ladies Beta Sorority guests were enjoying their stay at the hotel. So, when I sent the Siamese cat on back to our bedroom to talk to Abner, she came back out of the bedroom a couple of minutes later a fully grown sexy woman. She was arm and arm with Abner like she was some prostitute escort, and she just hauled Abner right out of here and didn't return with him until two hours later."

"Sorry," Tango said with remorse. "I guess I forgot to tell you."

"Forgot to tell me what?"

"Elvyra is a werecat."

"What's a werecat?"

"She's able to change from a Siamese cat into a woman and vice versa."

"You mean she—"

Tango quickly nodded before Tutty could even finish her sentence.

"Well, did she tell you what happened between her and Abner, because Abner won't tell me a thing? Every time I mention anything about what went on between them that night, he just smiles like the whole world is his."

"Elvyra told me she just took him for a late-night stroll that night and talked sweet to him. She said nothing else happened."

"Oh . . . I see," Tutty said in a somewhat relieved voice.

"But I must tell you that Elvyra is known to lie sometimes, too," Tango said somewhat reluctantly.

After Tutty gave him a wary, uncomfortable look, she and Tango headed on into Abner's office. Abner was sitting behind his desk with his dark glasses on listening to a tape recording of the notes that Tutty had recorded for him concerning the hotel's financial obligations when they walked in.

"Abner, Mr. Parker is here," Tutty announced.

Abner turned off the tape recorder as his anger button went red. "Parker, why in the world didn't you put a no deposit return clause in that contract for the Smith & Hirsch Brothers convention?"

"I'm really sorry, sir," Tango answered in a petrified voice. "It just didn't occur to me at the time I was writing the contract to put that in there. It's totally my fault, sir."

"I know it's your fault!" Abner shouted. "Even a teenage kid with no experience in writing contracts would know to put a no deposit return clause into a contract. I certainly wouldn't expect that from a seasoned hotel manager as yourself. It makes me wonder if I made a mistake in hiring you, Parker!"

"Calm down, Abner," Tutty said as she jumped in. "The boy . . ." She quickly caught herself. "I mean Mr. Parker has done an admirable job since he's come to work here. After all, he brought the Alpha Ladies Beta Society here for a big, successful convention last week and the hotel did very well financially. You ought to be grateful for what Mr. Parker has been able to accomplish."

"That was last week, woman!" Abner said in a hot tone. "And the old saying in the hotel business goes, 'What have you done for me lately?'"

"Oh, Abner—"

The phone on Abner's desk suddenly rang as Abner picked up the phone and answered it.

"Hello, this Abner Redder speaking," he said with authority. "You're speaking with the CEO, owner, and the president of the Lucky Jackpot Hotel."

Tutty shook her head as she glared at Abner. "What a pompous jackass."

"Buford, is that you?"

"That's his dumb brother from St. Louis," Tutty whispered over to Tango as Abner continued his phone conversation. "He's about as lamebrain as Abner."

"What?" Abner said as his face suddenly contorted. "Your place of business caught on fire last night?"

Siren! Siren! Siren!

Flashing lights suddenly lit up from the fire station cuckoo clock on the wall behind the desk as a wailing siren began to shriek out. Benny, the three-inch-high mechanical fireman dressed in a red, shiny fireman suit, suddenly came out of the fire station cuckoo clock as he slid down the fire pole with his fire hose clutched in his hand.

"Someone's business is on fire around here, huh?" Benny said like a conscientious fire fighter. "Don't worry, Benny's Fire Department will take care of that fire for you, sir."

Benny started blasting water from his fire hose down on Abner's head as Abner was talking to his brother. "Don't worry, folks, the fire will be put out in a second. Benny's Fire Department will make sure the fire is all out."

When Benny finally shut off the spigot of his fire hose and dashed back into the fire station, Tutty couldn't help but to snicker as Abner sat behind his desk dripping wet.

"THAT STUPID LITTLE TWERP!" Abner shouted as he held the phone. "I SWEAR I'M GOING TO KILL HIM!"

A couple minutes later when Abner finally finished his conversation with his brother and he hung up the phone, he sat behind his desk shaking his head.

"That was Buford."

"What's that dumb brother of yours been up to now?" Tutty said with a sigh. "Has he been playing with matches or something?"

"Last night his place of business caught on—" Abner suddenly hesitated.

"What, you're afraid to say the word?" Tutty laughed.

"No, I'm not!" Abner said with an angry huff. "Anyway, his place of business burned down last night and he wants us to come to St. Louis this Friday to help him with some banking issues and with the fire insurance policy."

"I don't know why that dumb brother of yours even started that signage business of his. I can't even keep up with the number of times we've had to help bail him out of so many lawsuits and money problems."

"Tutty, don't start in on my brother."

"Your dumb brother don't need to be in the sign making business," Tutty said in a scathing voice. "For one thing, the dumb moron can't even spell. It was just a couple months ago that we had to get him out of that legal jam he was in when he made all those signs for that election headquarter center. The moron spelled vote here on all the signs he made for them—FOTE HERE."

"Tutty, I'm warning you."

"And another time his dumb brother got sued by this college for a sign he made them," Tutty said to Tango with a snicker. "The ignoramus made a sign for their financial aid department that was supposed to say Get Aid Here, but he spelled it on the sign—GET AIDS HERE."

"Tutty!"

"Alright." She chuckled. "I'll stop."

"Now, back to why you're here, Mr. Parker," Abner said with authority once more. "You've cost this hotel a great deal of money by not putting a no deposit return clause into that contract you wrote. I've already ordered additional liquor, food, and other amenities in anticipation of the Smith & Hirsch Brothers convention being here this weekend, and now that's money flushed down the toilet."

Siren! Siren! Siren!

Benny once again came out of the fire station cuckoo clock on the wall above Abner's desk as he slid down the fire pole with his fire hose clutched in his hand.

"Need water flushed down the drain?" Benny pronounced as he began to spray Abner's head once again with a heavy stream of water from his fire hose. "No problem. Benny's Fire Department has plenty of water for flushing water down the big man's head. *Plenty of water.*"

Seconds later, Benny shut off the spigot of his fire hose as he once again dashed back into the fire station. Abner was so mad he was about to explode. Tutty had to literally slap her hand over her mouth to keep from laughing.

"THAT STUPID LITTLE PIPSQUEAK!" Abner said with rage as water drained down his face and neck. "He's made me so angry that I forgot what I was talking about."

"I believe you were saying something about flushing water down the drain," Tutty said with a smirk.

"Don't get sassy, woman!"

"Oh, sorry, sir," she said as she stifled her laughter.

"Now, Parker, since you caused this entire fiasco mess," he said in a hot, simmering voice, "I want you and your staff to get busy immediately to bring another organization here in Smith &

Hirsch Brothers' place to have a convention here by this Friday. And if you don't get a replacement organization to come here and hold a convention this weekend, then I'm docking your pay for an entire month. Is that understood?"

"Yes, sir," Tango answered nervously.

"Abner, you can't be serious," Tutty said in an admonishing tone. "You can't expect the boy . . . I mean Mr. Parker and his staff to get an organization to commit to come here and have a convention by this weekend. That's impossible."

"That's what I expect and that's what I demand."

"But Abner—"

"The CEO and president of the Lucky Jackpot Hotel has spoken, and that's final," Abner said in a scolding voice. "Now, there's another matter I need to address with you, Parker."

"What else do you want him to do?" Tutty said derisively. "Get the President of the United States to come stay here for the weekend also?"

"Mr. Parker, this is sort of unexpected, but me and Mrs. Redder are going to have to fly to St. Louis this Friday to deal with my brother's situation."

"One lamebrain trying to take care of another lamebrain," Tutty mumbled. "What's the world coming to?"

"Now, we're going to have to leave my mother here because we're going to be on the run taking care of a lot of business in St. Louis and she's just not up for a lot of traveling and she's just going to be in the way," Abner said as he spoke. "So, I want you to look after her while we're away. We'll only be gone for the weekend. So put an extra cot in your room and make sure her well-being is looked after and taken care of. Understood?"

"Uh, yes sir," Tango said with hesitation. "I'll make sure she's looked after and taken care of."

"Abner, we can't ask Mr. Parker to take on such a responsibility." Tutty snapped as she glowered at Abner. "That's too much of a burden."

"I've already made up my mind, Tutty. She's staying here and Parker is going to look after her."

"That's not a good idea, Abner!"

"My decision is final, woman."

"Oh, my God." Tutty sighed as she slapped her hand on her forehead.

"Well, Parker, what are you standing around here for?" Abner said with authority as he suddenly pounded his desk with his fist. "You've got your instructions. Now let's get to work!"

"Yes, sir. Right away."

Tango quickly turned and shot out of the office.

It was twelve noon and Tango was in his office making a flurry of calls. He was desperately trying to get any group or organization he could find to come to the Lucky Jackpot Hotel and hold a convention there by this weekend. As expected, he quickly found his mission nearly hopeless to achieve.

No matter what he offered in the form of room rate discounts, reduction in the convention fee, or other amenities, no one was taking the bait and signing up for a convention on such short notice. It was an impossible task and Tango knew he was virtually wasting his time even bothering to try.

As Tango was at his desk busy flipping and scanning through a thick phone book of businesses, companies, organizations, unions, and institutions listed across the country, Fred suddenly strolled into the office wearing his customary hotel dog vest. He sauntered over to Tango and immediately engaged with him in a conversation.

"Say, you look like you in a deep pile of work over here. What are you busy doing?"

Tango sighed as he finally closed the thick phone book in frustration. "Oh, I've just been sitting here all morning trying to get some organization to come here and have a convention here by this weekend."

"Why this weekend?"

"Because the Smith & Hirsch Brothers National Car Salesmen Organization canceled their convention that they were supposed to have here this weekend, and their entire deposit that they'd already given the hotel had to be returned to them. Now the big boss is upset with me because I didn't think of putting a no deposit return clause into the contract that I wrote up for the Smith & Hirsch Brothers convention."

"So, he's blaming you?" Fred asked with sympathy.

Tango slowly nodded. "Yep, and he said if I didn't get another convention to come here by this weekend to fill the Smith & Hirsch Brothers place, he was going to dock my pay for an entire month," he uttered with remorse. "So, I've been on this phone all morning trying to get any organization I can find to come here and have a convention here by this weekend, which I've found is a total impossible feat to achieve," he said with a deep sigh. "I guess I should just be happy that he didn't fire me on the spot and throw us all out onto the street."

"Wow, what a bummer," Fred said in a grim voice.

"Yeah, exactly."

Joe suddenly swaggered into the office in his usual faded brown suit with the red and white polka dotted tie on as he puffed generously on a cigar. He sauntered straight over to Tango, flicking ashes from his cigar onto Tango's desk.

"Say, when are we going to finally do some performing and entertaining around this crummy hotel instead of doing all of this manual labor crap that we've been doing around here lately?" Joe said with an attitude. "Because I'm telling you, I'm getting *real* fed up with the stuff we've been putting up with around here these last few weeks."

"Joe, please don't start nagging me about that again," Tango said as he yanked opened the thick phone manual on his desk once again and began flipping through it. "I've got a whole lot on my mind today and I'm just too busy trying to run this hotel."

"You've got a lot on your mind," Joe said as he gave a scornful chuckle. "What, you *really* think you're a hotel manager now or something?" he said as he continued to chuckle. "The only thing that needs to be on your mind is getting us back to performing on stage. Because I got to tell you, buddy, you've been the worst handler we've ever had."

"Hey, Tango is under a lot of pressure trying to run this hotel and he doesn't need to hear any stupid nonsense from a moron ape like you," Fred yelled. "So, just go somewhere and annoy somebody else."

"This kid couldn't run anything if his life depended on it," Joe said to Fred with a snap.

"You think you could do better?"

"I could run this place way better blindfolded than he ever could with 20/20 vision."

"Yeah, you'd run it right into the ground." Fred snapped back. "It's because of you and Chipper trying to steal that diamond ruby necklace from room 317 that could of have gotten us into a whole world of trouble."

"Hey, I would've been long gone from this dump, chilling someplace down in South America by now if you wouldn't have stuck your nose into my business, you no talent dog."

"Guys, just stop it," Tango said as he scanned through the phone book searching for organizations to call. "You're both giving me a pounding headache."

"You don't realize the pressure that Tango is under, you stupid ape." Fred snapped back. "The big boss wants him to find a replacement organization to have a convention here by this weekend, because the original people who were supposed to have their convention here this weekend had to cancel and Abner had to return their deposit money back to them. Now he's laid the entire burden on Tango to find someone to take their place by this weekend or he's going to dock Tango's pay for an entire month."

"That ain't nothing," Joe said in a cocky voice as he took a huge puff from his cigar. "Give me the telephone. I bet I can find an organization to fill their place in no time."

"You couldn't find your hairy ass if you stuck your hand back there."

"Oh, so you don't think I can't go out there in them streets and find an organization to have a convention right here at this hotel by this weekend?"

"Please, you stupid ape. Don't make me laugh."

"Well, when I get back, dog, I'm going to make you eat them words."

"I'm going to eat a bite out of your hairy ass just for the hell of it, and I'm thinking about doing it right now."

"You want to try it, dog?" Joe snapped.

"Oh, I ain't going to try, ape," Fred said as he started growling. "I'm going to do it!"

"Hey, I've had it with both of you," Tango said as he crashed his hand down on his desk. "I want both of you out of here."

"But Tango—"

"OUT!"

Fred slowly lowered his head in dejection as he and Joe scampered out of the office.

Early Friday morning, Abner held a meeting once again with his entire hotel staff in the conference hall before he and Tutty left on their flight for St. Louis. Restaurant servers, casino workers, showgirls, the house band, laundry workers, bartenders, gift shop workers, and other important hotel personnel stood in a long horizontal line as Abner paced back and forth on his white cane as he lectured them.

Abner wore one of his outrageous, bright colorful suits that Tutty had picked out for him to wear this morning. Whenever she had the chance to stick it to him and make him look like a total pompous fool, Tutty always took that shot. It was her way of getting back at him for all the arguing and bickering that they often engaged in.

Instead of berating his workers as he often did whenever he called the entire hotel staff together for a meeting, this morning Abner was actually praising and extolling one group in particular: The Parker Incorporated Agency.

Tango had pulled off an incredible feat. Overnight, he'd managed to secure the World Circus Association to have their annual convention at the Lucky Jackpot Hotel. Nearly a thousand clowns and their entire circus outfit would be descending on the Lucky Jackpot Hotel later on today and Abner was thrilled to death.

Not only did Tango get it right this time by placing a no deposit return clause into the contract that the World Circus Association signed, but the Lucky Jackpot Hotel would actually receive double the convention fee than it would've received had the Smith & Hirsch Brothers National Car Salesmen Organization not canceled and showed up for their convention.

Tango along with Fred, Chipper, Elvyra, and the Wonder Gang stood next to Tutty as Abner lectured everyone and gloated over the Parker Incorporated Agency. At the moment, it was definitely great to be a member of the sham Parker Incorporated Agency.

"Well, Mr. Parker," Tutty whispered to him with a generous smile as Abner continued lecturing the hotel staff. "You should feel right proud of yourself. Abner doesn't normally call a hotel staff meeting to gloat over any of his employees. He's usually fussing and demanding more efficiency."

"Thanks," Tango said with a hefty smile. "I was just as shocked and surprised when the World Circus Association accepted the offer to have their convention with only twenty-four hours prior notice. I guess it helped that they were already here in Las Vegas performing at a circus event and they just decided to stay over to have their annual convention. I guess some days you just wake up and get a little lucky sometimes."

"Luck had nothing to do with it," Tutty whispered to him with a smile. "It was all your hard work and ingenuity that made it all happen. I don't know too many fifteen-year-olds who have your hard work ethic and values. Well done, Mr. Parker."

"Thanks," Tango said with a blush.

"Now I know this is a burden that you didn't ask for, but I want you to really keep an eye on Mama Lulu and take really good care of her while we're gone. She can be a handful sometimes, so just keep your eyes open and make sure she gets to bed at a decent hour."

"Don't worry, I will." Tango reassured her. "I'll take real good care of her."

"And whatever you do, please keep that crazy ape away from her."

"I'll certainly do that."

"By the way," she glanced down at Tango's crew who stood next to him. "Where's that crazy ape of yours?"

"I don't know," Tango suddenly said with a heavy sigh. "He took off two days ago claiming that he was going to bring some conventioneers to the hotel by this weekend, if you can believe that," he said as he shook his head. "It's no telling where he's at."

"Well, you just make sure you keep that maniac, lunatic ape in line."

"Don't worry. I'll keep him in line whenever he comes back."

"Good, because I don't have to worry about you running the hotel while we're gone anymore," she said with a smile. "You've thoroughly proven yourself as a good, reliable assistant hotel manager."

"Thanks, Mrs. Redder."

"Now what did I tell you?" she said as she beamed her smile.

"I mean Mrs. Tutty."

"You just remember that," she said with a nod. "And when Abner and I return from St. Louis Monday morning, you and I are going to finally start planning how to get these animals performing up on stage. I think it's high time that I kept my promise to you."

"That's what I've been waiting on," Tango said with a smile.

Tango and Tutty suddenly became silent as they listened as Abner ranted on with his lecture.

"Now I've been going on gloating over the accomplishment that the Parker Incorporated Agency has been able to pull off without mentioning the real reason why I've gathered all of you here this morning," Abner said proudly to everyone. "Tomorrow will be exactly twelve years since the Lucky Jackpot Hotel has been in existence, and to celebrate that awesome achievement, I'd like to ring this bell on this stool twelve times in commemoration of that great achievement."

"No bonus for the employees," Tutty mumbled to herself. "The cheapskate."

Elvyra suddenly left her place in the line of employees as she ran and jumped onto the stool. "Please, Mr. Redder," she said in an endearing voice. "Please let me do the honors, sir."

"Ah, is that Ms. Mendez's voice?" Abner said with a hefty smile as he chuckled. "Please, Ms. Mendez, be my guest."

Elvyra took her cat paw and rung the desk call bell twelve times as the entire hotel staff applauded. When she finished the little ceremony, she jumped off the stool and sauntered back over to her place with the other employees. But before she returned to her place, she suddenly glanced over at Tutty with her green emerald eyes and gave her a teasing wink.

"So, it's like that, huh?" Tutty mumbled to herself as she eyed Elvyra. "Alright *Ms. Thang*. I better keep a real close eye on you from now on."

By Friday night, the Lucky Jackpot Hotel was filled with all sorts of spectacle and display of circus exhibition. The World Circus Association, with their thousand members of clowns, acrobats, jugglers, unicyclists, and other circus personnel, had descended upon the hotel for their three day convention. The lobby of the hotel was decked out and littered with hundreds of balloons as if the circus convention was open to the public as an assortment of festivities took place.

Clowns performed a variety of gags and tricks, sword swallowers practiced the craft of sword swallowing, fire breathing artists blew out balls of fire, jugglers juggled, stilt walkers walked on poles thirty feet in the air, acrobats performed their incredible stunts, and unicyclists rode their bikes. Daredevil stunt artists were over in the convention hall performing human cannonball acts, knife throwing, and tightrope walkers practiced the fine art of tightrope walking. Circus music played all throughout the entire lobby of the hotel and convention hall as the festivities went on through the night.

Fred wandered around the hotel lobby with his hotel vest on watching all of the amazing stunts and displays of incredible showmanship with a wag of his tail. He was thoroughly enjoying all of the circus activities, clowns, and pomp that presented itself around the hotel. It was a different atmosphere than what they'd been accustomed to at the Lucky Jackpot Hotel over the last several weeks and Fred sort of liked the new change.

Elvyra suddenly came over the hotel intercom system as she gave her update on all the activities to do at the hotel.

"Good evening, everyone," Elvyra said in a charming, sophisticated voice. "I want to welcome the World Circus Association to the Lucky Jackpot Hotel for your annual convention. All of you wonderful, smiling clowns, you've come to the right place for laughter and amusement. Just take a good look around the Lucky Jackpot Hotel and you'll laugh your head off," she said with a hearty giggle.

"But we do have a marvelous casino, a cozy bar and lounge area for you to relax in, a great gift shop to pick up souvenirs, and a lovely restaurant to dine in," she continued in her festive voice. "If you get tired of playing games with yourself, then hop on over to our movie theater and catch a late-night movie. Tonight's late night special feature we're showing is a good one. It's called *Clowns Always Make Love With A Smile*," she said with a giggle.

"Well, that about does it for now. So, all you clowns just enjoy yourself tonight at the Lucky Jackpot Hotel and don't stop laughing and joking around, because I certainly won't," she said with a hearty giggle. "Well everyone—*meow and tah-tah!*"

Fred gave a hearty chuckle when Elvyra finished her announcement. "Clowns always make love with a smile," he said to himself as he chuckled again.

Suddenly Tango came out of his office and strolled over to where Fred was at.

"So, how's everything going in your department?" Tango asked Fred.

"Couldn't be better," Fred said as he wagged his tail. "Just look around you. This is marvelous. You really out did yourself, Tango. All of these clowns and this big circus convention being here might be the best thing that ever happened to this hotel."

"You really think so?" Tango said with a smile as he gazed around at all of the festivities.

"Absolutely. You're a genius, Tango."

"Please," he said with a slight laugh. "Let's not go that far."

"You are. Just look at all of this stuff."

"This is not everything, you know," Tango said with a smile. "The World Circus Association brought four elephants with them also."

"They brought elephants, too?"

"Yep. They're outside in the back parking lot locked up in cages."

"Wow, I got to go check that out," Fred said with admiration. "Well, I guess the only problem out of all of this is that you got stuck with looking after Mama Lulu for the entire weekend."

"Yeah, unfortunately so." Tango sighed. "She's down in our room right now asleep. I told the Wonder Gang to check in on her from time to time."

"Good luck with that." Fred chuckled. "They've got another one of their wild, raunchy parties going on down in their room tonight. They're playing poker with some friends of theirs that they've invited over, so they'll probably going to be too preoccupied with their poker game to look in on Mama Lulu."

"Don't worry. I'll go down and check on Mama Lulu after a while. She'll probably just sleep all night anyway."

"Yeah, probably will."

Tango suddenly went silent as a concerned look crept over his face.

"You look worried about something," Fred said as he gazed up at Tango. "What's the problem? Mama Lulu ain't going to be that big of a problem to take care of."

"No, it's not that," he said in a dismal voice. "I couldn't help for thinking about Joe. He's been gone for two days now. I was just wondering if he was alright."

"I don't know why you're worried about that ape moron for," Fred said in a peeved voice. "Frankly, I hope he never comes back. We'll be better off without him if he doesn't come back."

"Look, I know Joe is wild and crazy and he liked to gotten us into serious trouble trying to steal that necklace and all. But he's still one of us, you know," Tango said in a drab voice. "He's still a member of the Magnificent Four and I wouldn't want anything to happen to him."

"Well, that was the dumb ape's own fault leaving here claiming he was going to bring some conventioneers back with him, of all the stupid, idiotic things to do." Fred chuckled. "I'll tell you, the only thing that stupid ape is capable of bringing is trouble and *more* trouble. Trust me. I won't lose any sleep if the dumb ape never comes back."

Fred finally took off as he strolled throughout the lobby speaking and interacting with all the clowns as they performed their various tricks and gags. This was one night he was truly happy to be a greeter and host of the Lucky Jackpot Hotel. Everywhere he turned and looked, there was nothing but smile after smile from one clown after another.

After speaking and fooling around with a dozen or so clowns, Fred headed out the front entrance where Cassie and Lonnie, Fred's two favorite showgirls, were at their usual posts by the door. They were in their full showgirl attire and smiling like angels.

"Well, Freddy, by the look of that tail of yours wagging like that, I'd say you were in a very good mood tonight," Cassie said with a wondrous smile.

"Isn't that the truth," Lonnie said with the same captivating smile. "I haven't seen that beautiful tail wag like that since you've been here, Freddy."

"Oh, I'm feeling great tonight, girls," Fred replied. "We've got all of these wonderful clowns here at the hotel tonight from the World Circus Association. What could be better?"

"So, you like clowns, Freddy?"

"Oh, you bet I do. They'll always keep a smile on your face, or in my case, keep my tail wagging."

"They are very funny and wonderful to be around."

"Yeah, and what makes this night even better is Joe is nowhere around," Fred said as he kept wagging his tail. "In fact, I hope that moron ape never comes back. We'll all be better off if that stupid ape never returns."

"Oh, you don't mean that, Freddy, do you?"

"I sure do, Lonnie. I can't stand that ape. I hope the moron runs out in front of a truck on a highway and gets smacked all the way back to that stinking jungle that he came from."

Fred left Cassie and Lonnie by the door as he wandered out beyond the awning of the hotel as he took in the fresh evening air. It was a beautiful, warm night with the stars all glittering and shining. The night was simply perfect; it seemed that nothing in the entire world could go wrong.

Suddenly, as Fred enjoyed the peace and tranquility of the night air, he began to hear a huge, rumbling roar as hundreds of lights began to fill the nighttime sky in the far distance. The sound of the rumbling roar began to grow louder and louder as the pack of lights became brighter and brighter. Fred, trying to figure out what was causing the loud rumbling and the massive bright lights, ventured out a little further in the parking lot to get a closer look at what was approaching the hotel.

"What in the devil is that?" he said to himself.

Within seconds, Fred got his answer.

Nearly two thousand Harley Davidson motorcycles came rumbling into the Lucky Jackpot Hotel parking lot. A rowdy motorcycle gang, dressed in leather black jackets, hooped and hollered like wild savages when they turned off their motorcycles.

One of the motorcycles suddenly broke away from the massive pack and pulled right up to the doors of the hotel. Fred, totally baffled and mystified, didn't know what to make of this massive intrusion when he suddenly saw someone with a black helmet and black leather jacket hop off the back of the motorcycle that had pulled up to the door.

"What's up, *dog*?" Joe yelled with glee when he yanked off the bike helmet. He was dressed in a black leather jacket that said the Hell Avengers and had a red bandanna tied around his head. "I told you I'd be back with some company, didn't I?"

"Joe," Fred uttered in a stunned voice, "what in the world is this?"

"It's the answer to all of our problems. Dog, meet the two thousand members of the Hell Avengers—the baddest motorcycle gang in all of America!" he said with great pomp as the motorcycle gang hooped and hollered as they fired off their sawed-off shotguns into the air.

"Joe, what did you bring them here for?"

"To celebrate."

"Celebrate? What are you talking about?"

"I went on the outskirts of Vegas to this bike bar and met the Hell Avengers. We've been hanging out for the last two days. We've just come from the desert where the Hell Avengers just had this big rumble. They just annihilated and beat the mess out of the Devil Guardians."

"Who are the Devil Guardians?"

"This opposing biker gang the Hell Avengers had gotten into a rumble with. So, to celebrate the Hell Avengers great victory, I brought them all here to have a big party."

"You did what?" Fred said in a stunned voice.

Joe suddenly turned to the two thousand bike members of the Hell Avengers in the parking lot.

"EVERYBODY, COME ON IN AND LET'S PARTY!" he yelled.

A thunderous cheer erupted as the two thousand members of the Hell Avengers stormed the entrance of the Lucky Jackpot Hotel like a bunch of wild hooligans. They hauled in cases and cases of beer as a hard rock band lugged instruments in as they headed for the main showroom to set up and play.

When the Hell Avengers had all stormed into the hotel, Joe flashed his brilliant smile as he calmly lit up a cigar.

"You crazy, stupid ape, why did you bring those wild hooligans here?" Fred yelled. "We've got a convention going on right now."

"Hey, you and Tango both said you needed some conventioneers. Well, here they are," Joe said as he leisurely puffed on his cigar and gushed a huge smile. "You can consider it my gift to the Lucky Jackpot Hotel."

When Joe swaggered on into the hotel, Fred immediately ran into the hotel and galloped as fast as he could to Tango's office. Tango was already at the door of his office gawking at all the wild hooligans and thugs that had stormed into the hotel.

"Tango, we've got a *huge* problem on our hands!" Fred yelled.

"Who are all these people and where did they come from?" he asked in dismay.

"They're a motorcycle gang called the Hell Avengers and they're two thousand of them. Joe just invited them to have a wild party here at the Lucky Jackpot Hotel. Tango, you've got to call the police before all hell breaks out!"

"We can probably handle this without the police," Tango stuttered out without taking his eyes away from the invasion that had taken over the hotel. "Besides, I don't want Mr. Redder to come back and find out the police has been here. He'll probably think I can't handle situations like this."

"You can't handle this, Tango!" Fred yelled. "It's too many of them. You've *got* to call the police."

Tango didn't say a word. He just stood in the doorway of his office staring wide-eyed at the ocean of black jackets of the Hell Avengers who had just taken over the hotel.

"Tango, you've got to call the police right now!" Fred kept imploring. "Did you hear me? Tango! *TANGO!*"

An hour later, the lobby of the hotel was so clogged with members of the Hell Avengers and the World Circus Association conventioneers packed together, that the place resembled a busy subway. All sorts of wild debauchery and revelry began to happen inside the hotel, and the poor clowns were the ones being taken advantage of by the Hell Avengers and used as guinea pigs for the butt of their jokes.

Clowns were being beat up, dangled and tossed around in the air like a game of hot potato by some of the bigger muscled-bound bikers. Bikers lit the seat of the clowns' pants on fire and hilariously watched clowns run and jump all around the lobby on fire.

Bikers also tied clowns together with rope and spun them around and around like a top. Bikers made clowns walk the high tightrope at gunpoint as they amusingly watched the clowns slip and fall off the tightrope. And worst of all, some clowns were forced to stand against a wall as a few drunken bikers tried to practice their skill at knife throwing.

At Chipper's Entertainment Booth, a large pack of rowdy, drunken bikers had crowded around Chipper's table. When they saw all of the amazing things that he could do with his left eye, they began to make all sorts of wild requests and demands for entertainment. And the drunker they got, the lewder and more risqué the requests and the demands became.

"Hey, bird, make Santa Claus come out of your eye riding on his sleigh doing something real freaky and naughty," one of the drunken bikers said with a hearty laugh as he took a swig from his beer bottle.

"I don't know, fellows," Chipper said hesitantly. "I don't really think I should do Santa Claus—"

"Ah, come on, bird. Do it."

"YEAH, DO IT, BIRD! DO IT! DO IT!" came the loud chant from the pack of rowdy bikers huddled around his table.

"Alright." Chipper turned his head to his two showgirl assistants standing behind his table. "Girls, sing *Jingle Bells*."

His two smiling showgirl assistants began to sing *Jingle Bells* as Chipper miraculously shot out of his left eye an image of Santa Claus riding across the sky on his sleigh with a hooker giving him a blowjob as he shouted, "HO! HO! HO! MERRY CHRISTMAS!"

The bikers rolled and guffawed with laughter.

"Hey, do something naughty with an astronaut out in space," another biker shouted.

Chipper suddenly shot a rocket out of his left eye. The rocket missed its intended target, the moon, and instead landed on a planet full of naked prostitutes as the astronaut quickly radioed Mission Control Center and said—HOUSTON, WE HAVE A PROBLEM!

The bikers once again roared with laughter.

"Hey, do something freaky with a policeman," another biker shouted.

"No, do something kinky with a sailor," another biker shouted.

"I want to see something wild and kinky with a priest," another biker shouted.

A big fight quickly broke out at the table among the bikers when they couldn't come to an agreement. As they tussled and fought, Fred suddenly weaved his way through the wild melee as he rushed over to the table to speak with Chipper.

"Hey, Tango wants you to go a couple more hours tonight because it's so many people in here and it's so wild and crazy," Fred yelled as the bikers around the table fought and slug one another. "He wants to try to keep things under control and prevent anything from happening."

"No way, dog!" Chipper yelled back. "This place is getting way out of hand and I need to go see my lady, Aquaflower."

"But Tango said—"

"Forget it, dog. I'm out of here." Chipper turned to the showgirls standing behind him. "Ladies, the show is over."

Chipper rose from the table and began to fly away.

"Hey wait! You can't leave!" Fred yelled as Chipper began to fly away. "Chipper, come back—*CHIPPER!*"

Mama Lulu woke up in the darkness of Tango's room and immediately called out for Benny to comfort her. After a couple of seconds of staring around the strange, foreign room and seeing there was no cuckoo clock anywhere on the wall, she finally realized that she wasn't in her bedroom.

Tired of sleeping, Mama Lulu slowly crawled out of the sleeping cot she was lying in. She looked over at the digital clock on the nightstand in the room and the time on the clock said it was three minutes after midnight.

Restless for something to do, Mama Lulu left out of Tango's room. She began to wander down the employee residential hallway when she suddenly ran into Joe as he came around the corner. Decked out in his Hell Avengers' black leather jacket and a red bandanna tied around his head, Joe was swigging from a bottle of rum. He immediately flashed his smile when he saw Mama Lulu as Mama Lulu instantly became riled.

"*You!*" She quickly balled up her fists as she glared at him. "Don't you smile at me. Put up your dukes. It's about time I put a couple of knots on that hairy head of yours, you stinking ape."

"Ah, mooly-mooly!" Joe said with a pompous smile. "What brings you out this late? Is there a mooly-mooly convention going on here at this hotel, too?"

"That's it you stinking, mangy ape!"

Mama Lulu went to swinging at the ornery orangutan, but Joe's fast, swift moves at evading her slow punches quickly made her look like a washed-up fighter.

"You can't catch me, mooly-mooly!" He laughed and taunted her as he danced all around her as she kept swinging one slow punch after another and missing. "*MOOLY-MOOLY!*" he kept saying and laughing. "*MOOLY-MOOLY! MOOLY-MOOLY!*"

A few seconds later, Mama Lulu was all punched out and breathing heavily. Standing in the middle of the employee residential hallway panting for air, she slowly raised her fist at him once again. She was determined to give him one good whack.

"You stand still so I can bop you good, you mangy, stinking ape!"

"Ah, mooly-mooly," Joe said as he took another swig from his rum and smiled. "Why are we always fighting? You know, we should be friends."

"I don't want to be friends," she said in a snarled voice. "I want to smash that hairy head of yours, you mangy ape!"

"Please, let me take this moment to most humbly and respectfully apologize to you, my dear lady, for my previous actions," Joe said as he suddenly gave Mama Lulu a gracious bow. "You are a queen that I will from now on worship the ground you walk on."

Mama Lulu slowly let her fists drop as she glared at the ornery orangutan. "Well, you just watch that mouth of yours, or I still might just bop you with a good one. You just make sure that you get that through that hairy head of yours, ape."

"Very well, my dear lady." Joe flashed his smile at her. "Come, mooly-mooly, let's play a game."

"What did you call me, you stinking ape?"

"Pardon me, my most gracious madam." He bowed again before her presence.

"That's better."

"Come on."

"Where we going?"

"To play a little game."

Joe took Mama Lulu into Chipper's room. The semi-dark room had colorful strobe lights flickering all around the room as the psychedelic paintings that hung on the wall glittered and gleamed. The room had no furniture; of course, the only piece of real furniture in the room was the lone five-foot red stool in the center of the room that had the large, empty picture frame welded to the seat of the stool.

"Why are all these lights flickering in this room?" Mama Lulu said in confusion as she scanned around the room. "And what's that empty picture frame doing on top of that red stool?"

"It's where Chipper goes to see the great Dr. Glittermoon," Joe said with a laugh.

"Doctor who?"

"Come, mooly-mooly, let's play a game."

"You watch that mouth, you dirty ape," Mama Lulu said as she once again balled up her fist. "I still might bop that hairy head of yours."

"Let's play the Big Indian Chief, Little Indian Chief game."

"What's that?"

Joe brought Mama Lulu over to Chipper's birdhouse that was attached to the wall.

"Let's see who can suck the most wind out of the pipe that's connected to this birdhouse," Joe said with a huge smile. "Whoever does, will be named Big Indian Chief."

"How do you do that?"

"Well, when I pull this chain that's connected to the birdhouse, I'll start sucking as much wind as I can from this pipe that's attached to the birdhouse. Watch me."

Joe pulled the chain that hung from the roof of the birdhouse as it ignited the kerweekee stored inside the house. He took a strong puff from the pipe as his eyes immediately started twirling round and round. He began bouncing off the walls like a madman as he fell on the floor laughing hysterically.

"Your turn, mooly-mooly!" He laughed as he lay on the floor.

"What did you call me, ape?" Mama Lulu said as she once again balled up her fists.

"Go, Little Indian Chief!" He laughed. "Suck up all the wind! Go!"

Mama Lulu hesitated as she stared at the pipe.

"You can't out do me, mooly-mooly." Joe laughed hysterically on the floor. "It looks like *I'm* the Big Indian Chief around here."

"Oh, yeah?" Mama Lulu suddenly glared down at Joe. "I'll show you who's the Big Indian Chief around here, ape!"

Mama Lulu pulled the chain connected to the birdhouse as she suddenly clamped her mouth around the pipe and took the biggest puff that she could. After her hit, she immediately began to stagger around the room as smoke flew out of both her mouth and ears like a teapot sounding off.

"That's it, mooly-mooly!" Joe laughed hysterically. "Blow it out!"

Mama Lulu finally stopped staggering around the room. She was so discombobulated and starry-eyed that she could've sworn that little birds were chirping and flying around her head.

"Who's the Big Indian Chief now?" Joe said with a laugh.

"I am," Mama Lulu said in a dazed voice as she wobbled back and forth.

"What's two plus two, mooly-mooly?"

"Three."

"What letter comes after B?"

"D."

"Who's the President of the United States?"

"*SpongeBob.*"

"Well, you've convinced me, mooly-mooly. I guess you're the Big Indian Chief around here."

"Damn right I am."

"Hey, let's go have some fun, mooly-mooly."

"That's Big Indian Chief to you, ape," she said as she continued to wobble back and forth.

Joe suddenly got up from the floor as he went over to Chipper's closet and opened the door. He grabbed the rest of the forty pounds of kerweekee from the closet that the Wonder Gang had brought to the hotel when they first arrived as he and Mama Lulu headed out of Chipper's room.

"Where we going, ape?" Mama Lulu asked in a dazed voice as she stumbled along as she followed Joe.

"To the hotel restaurant kitchen, mooly-mooly."

"Good, because all of a sudden I'm hungry."

When Joe and Mama Lulu entered the hotel restaurant kitchen, all of the kitchen workers had gone for the night and everything was shut down. Joe went over and turned on one of the stoves on high as he took all of the kerweekee he'd snatched from Chipper's closet and shoved it inside the oven.

Within seconds, kerweekee smoke began to drift out of the oven at an alarming rate as the entire kitchen became filled and congested with nothing but smoke. Soon the smoke drifted up into the air vents of the ceiling of the kitchen as it began to make its way throughout the entire hotel.

"Oh, ape," Mama Lulu said with her eyes squinted as she wobbled back and forth. "I'm *soooo* hungry, I could really go for a big juicy hamburger and fries right now."

Joe suddenly pounded his chest twice with his fist and snapped his finger. Poof! A cloud of purple smoke mushroomed in the air as a hamburger stand appeared in the middle of the kitchen as Joe was suddenly dressed in a purple fast food uniform with a cap on that said *Mooly-Mooly's Burger Joint*. Joe stood behind the hamburger stand flashing his beaming smile at the customer at his stand.

"Welcome to Mooly-Mooly's Burger Joint, ma'am," Joe said in a cheerful voice. "What can I get for you today?"

Mama Lulu squinted up at the glittering menu board of the hamburger stand.

"Let's see . . . I'll take two double Mooly-Mooly Burgers, a chili dog, extra large fries, an order of onion rings, and a large soda."

"Anything else, ma'am?" Joe said as he jotted her order down on a pad as he continued flashing his brilliant smile.

"And throw in a large chocolate milkshake, too."

"Coming right up."

Joe turned his back to her as he did his magical ritual. He quickly whipped back around with her piping hot order.

"Ma'am, here's your two double Mooly-Mooly Burgers, a chili dog, extra large fries, onion rings, a soda, and your large chocolate milkshake," he said in a courteous voice. "Enjoy your meal, ma'am, and have a nice day."

Mama Lulu took her order and like a famished person, she quickly ripped off the wrapper of one of her burgers and began to set out to eat it when Joe suddenly snapped his finger as everything disappeared.

"Sorry, madam," he said as he beamed his smile, "but *Mooly-Mooly's Burger Joint* has just closed."

"Why you stinking, mangy ape—*I'M HUNGRY!*"

With mad fury, Mama Lulu began to chase Joe all around the kitchen trying to whack him as Joe guffawed and laughed.

By one o'clock in the morning, the Lucky Jackpot Hotel had become even wilder and more hectic. The Hell Avengers were literally tearing up the place as glass and other assorted items were being shattered everywhere.

The two thousand members of the motorcycle gang had taken over the main showroom, the small showroom, and there were wild goings on in the casino, bar and lounge area, movie theater, and the restaurant. Not only that, several members of the Hell Avengers had even brought their Harley Davidson motorcycles inside the hotel and were riding up and down the lobby like they were out on a racetrack.

Fred was going insane trying to figure out what to do. He was the hotel greeter that had been charged with the task of making everyone feel welcomed to the hotel since the very first day Tango had assigned them all jobs and roles, but this was simply beyond his expertise. The Lucky Jackpot Hotel had turned into a madhouse that had been taken over by wild, drunken hooligans, and Fred and the rest of the staff almost needed the National Guard to come in and restore peace.

As the madness and insanity continued inside the hotel, Fred frantically weaved his way through the wild melee as he headed for the front entrance. He wanted to head outside to take a break from all the ruckus and commotion to get some fresh air. But as soon as Fred stepped outside, he quickly got a rude awakening.

Hundreds and hundreds of more Harley Davidson motorcycles came screaming into the parking lot of the hotel as literally an army of bikers, with black leather jackets on, suddenly came marching toward the entrance of the hotel.

"Oh, no," Fred said in dismay as he looked up at Cassie and Lonnie as they stood in their usual spots at the entrance of the hotel. "Please don't tell me more Hell Avengers are coming to the hotel."

"It certainly looks that way, Freddy," Cassie said in a somber voice.

"Yep," Lonnie quickly replied, "and they look meaner than the ones who are already inside the hotel."

The legion of rough looking bikers suddenly stopped at the entrance of the hotel as they quickly scanned the outside perimeter of the building.

"Is this the Lucky Jackpot Hotel?" one of the bikers asked Cassie and Lonnie in a hostile voice.

"Yes, it is," Cassie answered nervously.

"Please don't tell me y'all are more Hell Avengers?" Fred said to the biker in a dreaded voice. "We've already kind of got a handful of y'all already."

The army of rabid bikers all of a sudden looked at one another as if the name the Hell Avengers was blasphemous to their ears.

"Hell no!" the lead biker said as he glared down at Fred. "We're the Devil Guardians. We heard the Hell Avengers had come here. We just got through rumbling with the Hell Avengers out in the desert earlier today and we've come for some pay back. And this time we ain't leaving until we leave all those scumbags in there lying face down for good!"

The Devil Guardians stormed into the hotel like they were ready for war.

"Oh, my God," Fred said as his four legs literally buckled. "OH, MY GOD!"

Fred quickly shot into the hotel, weaving his way around all the mayhem as he dashed straight to Tango's office. But Fred quickly discovered that getting to Tango would require a great deal of work.

Tango's office was literally crammed with so many clowns it was like trying to maneuver around in a tight sardine can. Dozens of clowns had surrounded Tango's desk and were complaining, yelling, and bickering to him about the lack of service and for the total disruption of their convention. On top of that, Tango's phone on his desk constantly rung off the hook as dozens of other clowns and other circus personnel staff blasted him over the phone.

"This is a total disservice!" a clown yelled at Tango as the clown stood before his desk. "We paid good money to come here for our convention and this is the service we receive!"

"These hooligans have invaded our hotel rooms and are destroying our property!" another clown yelled. "We want a refund!"

"You have to do something with these thugs and hoodlums immediately or we're suing this dang blasted hotel!" another clown yelled.

The ring master of the circus suddenly pushed his way up to Tango's desk. "I just got word that these motorhead riffraffs have just broken into the elephant cages out back and have set all my elephants loose!" he said in a steamed voice. "Now my elephants are roaming around in the hotel! What are you going to do to get my elephants back?"

Tango was literally being twisted into a pretzel as he tried to accommodate and appease everyone as his phone kept constantly ringing off the hook. Fred finally maneuvered his way up to Tango's desk as he joined the pandemonium.

"Tango, you've got to call the police now!" Fred yelled over all the bickering, arguing, and commotion. "The Devil Guardians have just arrived and there's going to be *big trouble*!"

"Who are the Devil Guardians?" he yelled back at Fred as he tried to carry on a three way conversation as he held his office phone to his ear.

"They're the motorcycle gang that the Hell Avengers fought with in the desert, and now they've come here to finish the score!"

"Finish what score?" Tango said in a confused voice.

"Tango, you don't seem to understand that—"

Tango suddenly held up a finger to halt his good buddy as he addressed a complaint from a caller over the phone. Fred dropped his head in frustration as he sighed; doomsday had finally arrived.

When Fred finally looked up, he noticed smoke beginning to pipe out of the air ducts in the ceiling of Tango's office.

"What in the world is that?" he said to himself as all the arguing and bickering continued in the office.

Seconds later, the aroma from the smoke piping out of the air ducts was one Fred began to recognize immediately. No doubt about it, he knew the smell of Chipper's kerweekee anywhere.

"Oh, my goodness, I can't believe it," Fred said in dismay as he lowered his head once again in frustration. "It's piping out all over the hotel—now the party has *really* started!"

The party in the main showroom was loud and raunchy. A heavy metal rock band played on stage as a large number of the Hell Avengers acted like plum maniacs. Beer bottles were thrown and crashed on stage while bikers, on their Harley Davidson motorcycles, rode their bikes all around the main showroom as the band played.

Adding to the madness, kerweekee continued to seep out of the air ducts from the hotel ceiling as it inebriated everyone. It had been some time since any form of entertainment had existed inside the main showroom, but no one connected with the Lucky Jackpot Hotel could've predicted that the first form of entertainment to happen inside the main showroom in a long time would be presented by a wild, raunchy motorcycle gang like the Hell Avengers.

Joe and Mama Lulu were two of the participants inside the main showroom along with all the other wild ruffians and hooligans there, and the way they were dressed and carrying on, it would've been hard pressed for anyone to assume that they weren't a part of the Hell Avengers. Even Mama Lulu now had on a black leather jacket and a bandanna tied around her head, the same as Joe. All the wild revelry and mischief taking place inside the main showroom even seemed to stimulate her. Tonight, she wasn't a feeble minded eighty-year-old woman by any means. Tonight, she was a Hell Avenger; and she was raising as much hell as anyone.

Fred suddenly came dashing into the main showroom as the wild festivities took place. Dodging flying beer bottles, motorcycles skirting all around the place, and other miscellaneous items being lobbed and thrown, he scampered straight over to Joe and Mama Lulu. They were partying near the stage, right in the midst of all the madness and chaos.

"Joe, what the devil are you doing in here with Mama Lulu?" he yelled over the screeching, loud music. "You stupid moron, don't you know it's not safe for her to be in her with all of these wild hooligans. And why in the world is she dressed like that?"

"Hey, mooly-mooly wants to party, too," he said as he smoked on a cigar and beamed a grand smile. "A party is a party, and *everyone* is invited."

"I told you I'm Big Indian Chief!" Mama Lulu yelled as she rocked her head to the music. "And you better remember that, ape, or I still might bop that hairy head of yours."

"Alright, Big Indian Chief."

"And give me a cigar," she said as she rocked her head. "I want to smoke one, too."

Joe quickly reached into his black Hell Avengers' jacket, pulled out a cigar and handed it to Mama Lulu. Mama Lulu grabbed the cigar, shoved it into her mouth as Joe lit it.

"You crazy, stupid ape!" Fred yelled. "You can't give Mama Lulu no cigar!"

"Hey, if she can smoke Chipper's kerweekee," he said as his smile grew, "she can enjoy a fine cigar, too."

"What?" Fred screamed as his eyes went buck wide. "You gave her some of Chipper's kerweekee?"

"Not only her," Joe said with a hearty laugh as he blew out a smoke ring, "but everybody in this entire hotel."

"Oh, my goodness," Fred said as his head quickly dropped like a heavy medicine ball. "Mama Lulu, please . . ." He begged when he raised his head. "Please, I beg you. Let me walk you back down to Tango's room so you can rest yourself. It's not safe to be in here with all of this—"

"Dog, you can go take a flying leap!" She quickly interrupted him as she puffed on her cigar. "Tonight, I'm going to party till the bulls come home."

"You mean till the cows come home, mooly-mooly." Joe laughed.

"I told you I'm Big Indian Chief!"

Suddenly a large army of bikers came storming into the main showroom. The band on the stage immediately stopped playing as all the chaos and commotion around the main showroom came to a sudden halt.

The Devil Guardians came to the center of the main showroom as all of The Hell Avengers quickly formed together and met them. Face to face they stood glaring at one another in the center of the main showroom. Hundreds of black leather jackets faced hundreds of black leather jackets across from them. Michael Jackson's song *Beat It* seemed appropriate to play as the two biker gangs stood face to face, but at the moment, all was quiet and silent.

"What are y'all punks doing here?" the leader of the Hell Avengers said as he glared across at his counterpart.

"What does it look like?" the leader of the Devil Guardians said with a vicious snarl. "We've come to finish our little rumble."

"We already kicked your ass once," the leader of the Hell Avengers said in a cocky voice. "Y'all come all the way here for another butt kicking?"

"No, you ugly dirt bag," his counterpart said with a scowl. "Because this time, *we* will be kicking all of y'all asses."

"Oh, yeah?" the leader of the Hell Avengers said as he got nose to nose with his counterpart.

"Yeah, you heard right."

War was about to commence when Mama Lulu suddenly jumped in between the feuding opponents.

"Hey, we don't appreciate you ugly musket heads coming in here and disrupting our party!" Mama Lulu said to the leader of the Devil Guardians in a loud voice. "This is our turf. We've already kicked your ass once and we'll certainly do it again!"

"Tell him mooly-mooly," Joe said with a hearty laugh.

"MAMA LULU, WILL YOU GET OUT FROM BETWEEN THEM RIGHT NOW!" Fred screamed in a desperate voice.

"Who's the little, old lady?" the leader of the Devil Guardians said as he glared over at his counterpart. "Your dear, sweet mother?"

"I'm Big Indian Chief, that's who I am," Mama Lulu said as she bucked up against the stomach of the giant biker who towered over her. "And if you don't watch your mouth, Bubba, I'm personally going to kick *your* ass!"

Fred frantically maneuvered and squirmed his way through the large pack of bikers. He desperately worked his way to the center where the two gang leaders stood face to face, glaring at one another with Mama Lulu standing between them. With as much force as he could muster, he clamped onto the tail end of Mama Lulu's black leather jacket with his teeth, and with all of his might, he literally dragged her away from the two snarling bikers.

The two gang of bikers stood glaring at one another, just waiting for the other side to make the first move.

"Anytime y'all ready to go at it is fine with us," the leader of the Hell Avengers said as he glared over at his nemesis.

"We're just giving you dirt bags a second to pray before we send you all to the next life," the leader of the Devil Guardians said with his own vicious glare.

As an uneasy silence pervaded, Elvyra suddenly came over the hotel intercom system to give her promotional update.

"Good evening, everyone, and welcome to the Lucky Jackpot Hotel," she said in a sultry voice. "I see we have a lot of new visitors running around our fabulous hotel dressed in your cute black leather jackets and all. And how high spirited and rowdy you all are tonight. Well, as they say, boys will be boys," she said with a high giggle.

"Anyway, I want to let everyone know that our wonderful, fabulous casino and our bar and lounge area are still open," she said as she continued over the hotel intercom. "On top of that, our cozy movie theater across from the gift shop is showing a good movie tonight. The movie *Creed,* staring Michael B. Jordan, is showing right now. So, all you fight fans that love a good brawl—LET'S GET READY TO RUMBLE!" she yelled as she suddenly rang a bell over the intercom. "Well, everyone, tata!"

Like a fuse that ignited an explosion, Elvyra's little quip suddenly ignited Armageddon. At the sound of the bell, the Hell Avengers and the Devil Guardians went to brawling with one another like mad dogs out for blood.

"Elvyra—you silly, stupid cat! Look what you've started!" Fred yelled as he quickly dashed out of the main showroom to flee from all the violence and anarchy.

As all hell broke loose, Joe's wild jungle nature kicked in as he went around yelping, hollering, and climbing the walls in the main showroom. When he spotted a Harley Davidson motorcycle lying on the floor, he quickly hopped onto the motorcycle and took off as he skirted around all the brawling bikers like a mad devil.

Joe soon slammed his brakes on the Harley Davidson motorcycle near Mama Lulu when he spotted her standing off to the side. She was rooting on all of the violence, bloodshed, and mayhem like a spectator at a boxing match.

"Hop on, mooly-mooly!" he shouted over all of the noise as he smiled. "Let's ride!"

"I told you I'm Big Indian Chief, you mangy ape!"

"Sorry, Big Indian Chief," he yelled. "Hop on and let's ride."

Mama Lulu climbed onto the Harley Davidson motorcycle behind Joe as she held on to him tightly. "Ape, you better not be going fast—"

"Sorry, mooly-mooly," Joe quickly interrupted her, "but I can't hear you, my dumb dear!"

Joe, with a wild jungle yelp, suddenly burned rubber as he took off once again like a mad devil as Mama Lulu screamed for her life.

At top speed, Joe sped out of the main showroom as he flew up and down the lobby of the hotel, popping wheelies and jumping over barricades, barriers, and obstacles like a stunt man in an action movie. He eventually got onto the elevator with the Harley Davidson motorcycle as he went up to the second and third floors of the hotel. Like a speed demon in need of more power and speed, he flew up and down the hallways of the hotel at blazing speed as Mama Lulu hung on for dear life.

Fred was in a hurried frenzy. Knowing Tango was too busy at the moment trying to get the hotel under control to stop what he was doing, he rushed down to the employee residential hallway as fast as he could. He had to find someone to save Mama Lulu from all the mayhem and violence taking place upstairs before it was too late. Mama Lulu's life was literally in jeopardy, and every second that ticked by, was a second too late.

When Fred reached the Wonder Gang's employee residential room, once again he found the door closed and absolutely no one was around in the hallway to help him out. Fred could hear a lot of arguing and swearing going on inside the room, and he knew the boys were probably in a heated poker match with the Fletcher Boys.

The Fletcher Boys were also an entertainment troupe act of five dwarfs that the Wonder Gang had befriended and worked with on the road, and over the years, they'd had several run-ins with their counterparts. The Fletcher Boys were in Las Vegas for the weekend to perform at a function at another hotel, and the Wonder Gang had invited them over tonight for a hot game of poker. Fred knew whenever the Wonder Gang and the Fletcher Boys got together for one of their ritual poker game nights, all hell usually broke out.

"Hey, you stupid morons, open up!" Fred yelled toward the door as loud as he could. "I SAID OPEN UP IN THERE!"

One of the members of the Wonder Gang suddenly swung open the door and slung out one of the members of the Fletcher Boys without even noticing Fred standing at the door.

"You just stay out there for the rest of the night, you no good cheating varmint!" Eddie yelled as he slammed the door back.

"Why hello, Jimmy, long time no see," Fred said as he gazed down at one of the members of the Fletcher Boys who'd just been slung to the floor. "Got caught cheating again, huh?"

"No way, Fred. I wasn't cheating—I swear," the dwarf said as he lay pitifully on the floor, gawking up at Fred. "That card under my sleeve wasn't even mine—"

"Look, I don't want to hear it." Fred quickly interrupted him. "Just get your ass up and bang on the door. I got more important issues to deal with right now."

The member of the Fletcher Boys slowly got up from the floor and started banging on the door. A couple seconds later, Eddie once again swung open the door.

"I thought I told you, you lying cheating varmint to stay out here—"

"Eddie!" Fred yelled. "EDDIE!"

"Oh, it's you, Big Chief," he said in a stunned voice. "I didn't see you out here."

"Yeah, you don't see nothing," the member of the Fletcher Boys yelled. "I told you that card under my sleeve wasn't mine, you douche bag."

"Who are you calling a douche bag, you cheating piece of scum?"

"I wasn't cheating!"

"You were you lying piece of scum!"

"Alright, enough!" Fred shouted. "ENOUGH!"

Fred ignored the two squabbling dwarfs as he forced his way into the Wonder Gang's room.

It looked like war was about to commence. The Wonder Gang and the Fletcher Boys were arguing up a storm as all sorts of cash and poker chips were splayed all over the poker table. Not only that, the kerweekee smoke that hung in the air was so stifling that the whole entire room was virtually fogged over.

Suddenly one of the members of the Fletcher Boys threw a beer bottle across the poker table at one of the members of the Wonder Gang as all hell broke out. The room quickly erupted into Armageddon. Beer bottles, poker chips, and other assorted items were slung and flung across the room as the heated battle between the two warring parties got off to a torrid start. Fred walked over to the middle of the wild ruckus as he tried to get both parties' attention and quell the violent storm that had ignited.

"Hey, you morons!" Fred yelled as he suddenly ducked his head when a beer bottle came flying straight for him. "I SAID HEY!"

Freeze frame.

The action in the room suddenly froze. On the big screen over the main stage of the Magic Rainbow Hotel & Casino Theater, the audience suddenly saw scrolling on the big screen a message from the Magic Rainbow Hotel & Casino:

Kerweekee—a substance grown and cultivated in a field; been around for ages. Known to make one's mind go pop, zap, splat if too much is smoked!

When the words stopped scrolling on the big screen, Elvyra suddenly came strolling out onto the stage while the action was still frozen. Green smoke began to emit from her feline body as she suddenly transformed into a beautiful Latino woman dressed in a sexy, skimpy outfit with high heels on. She held a silver tray with all kind of snacks and goodies on it like a concession worker selling snacks to movie goers at the intermission of a movie.

"Folks, I got popcorn here, pizza, hot dogs, potato chips, Milk Duds, Raisinets, nachos, gummy bears, Twizzlers, Skittles, Junior Mints, and M&Ms for your munchies. And I *know* you must have the munchies with all of this kerweekee floating around here," she said with a playful giggle. "Well, enjoy the rest of the show, folks. I've got my own munchies waiting for me backstage," she said with a giggle. "Tata."

Elvyra strolled off the stage with her tray of snacks as the action resumed.

"Hey, you stupid imbeciles!" Fred yelled as he suddenly ducked his head when a beer bottle came flying straight for him. "*HEY!*"

The Wonder Gang and the Fletcher Boys all of a sudden stopped their fighting. They all looked at Fred as if shocked to see the big St. Bernard dog in the room.

"Big Chief, when did you get here?" Lou said. "I didn't see you come in here."

"Well, I guess not. You were too busy fighting World War III with the Fletcher Boys."

"That's because these lunkheads been cheating all night long," Lou yelled toward the direction of one of the Fletcher Boys. "We never should've invited their asses over for a game of poker."

"Hey, we weren't the ones who were doing the cheating," a member of the Fletcher Boys shouted back. "It was you thieves who were cheating us!"

"Are you calling us cheaters?"

"You durn right we are!"

"Why you—"

"ENOUGH OF THAT!" Fred yelled. "Now we've got a serious problem going on upstairs. Two motorcycle gangs have invaded the hotel and they're fighting each other right now. Mama Lulu is up there right now in the middle of it all, and I'm afraid if somebody doesn't go get her, she's going to get seriously hurt. Now I want all of you—and that includes all you Fletcher Boys—to go up there and rescue her and bring her back down here where she'll be safe."

"Who the hell is Mama Lulu?" asked one of the Fletcher Boys.

"Ah, come on, Big Chief." Lou complained with a gripe. "We got a good poker game going on here, if these *cheaters* over here would stop stealing cards from the deck."

"We ain't stole no cards from the deck, you lying pipsqueak!"

"Who you calling a pipsqueak, you ugly runt?"

"Why you—"

"Enough of that!" Fred yelled. "Now I want everyone in this room to hightail it out of here and go up there and get Mama Lulu and bring her down here to safety this instant!"

The Wonder Gang and the Fletcher Boys didn't move a muscle. They all stood staring at one another as if they wanted to resume their heated brawl.

"I SAID GO, NOW!"

The Wonder Gang and the Fletcher Boys quickly flew out of the room.

By three a.m., the Hell Avengers and the Devil Guardians had been in the longest biker brawl in recorded history. After nearly two hours, they were still going at it. They were all over the hotel brawling and fighting one another in a marathon for the ages.

Over four thousand bikers savagely fought one another in the main showroom, the small showroom, in the lobby of the hotel, the casino, inside the movie theater, the bar and lounge area, the restaurant, the gift shop, and even on the second and third floors of the hotel. No place around the Lucky Jackpot Hotel was without a skirmish of some kind. Total war had been declared and virtually everywhere was a battleground.

Joe and Mama Lulu had been riding all over the hotel on the Harley Davidson motorcycle they'd swiped in the main showroom for nearly an hour, popping wheelies and jumping over obstacles better than a professional stunt driver. As the bedlam continued inside the hotel, Joe and Mama Lulu were like two misfits out joyriding among all the mayhem and chaos. Bonnie and Clyde couldn't have had more fun than what these two unlikely rogues were having. They were the new lawless perpetrators that the world would soon know; Joe and Mama Lulu, the lawless wild coyotes.

As Joe and Mama Lulu skirted around the corner on the third floor of the hotel on their motorcycle for the umpteenth time, they suddenly spotted a huge elephant lying idly in the corner on the floor. Joe immediately hit the brakes on the Harley Davidson motorcycle as they came to a screeching stop.

"Why you stop for, ape?" Mama Lulu yelled from the backseat of the motorcycle as she held onto Joe. "Let's ride. I want to feel the wind blowing through my hair again."

"Hey, mooly-mooly," Joe said as he pointed at the elephant lying on the floor. "Let's ride him."

"What's that big beast?"

"He's a circus elephant. Let's ride him."

"Alright, ape. Yeah, let's ride that big boy," Mama Lulu said in a game voice. "Come on!"

They got off of the Harley Davidson motorcycle as Joe quickly hopped onto the elephant, but Mama Lulu's eighty-year-old legs wouldn't allow her to climb on.

"I can't climb on, ape," Mama Lulu said as she struggled to mount the huge elephant. "Help me up."

Joe suddenly pounded his chest twice with his fist and snapped his finger. Poof! A cloud of purple smoke mushroomed in the air as a small climbing ladder appeared as it extended from the elephant down to the floor.

"Climb aboard, my dumb, stupid dear," Joe said with a huge smile as he extended his hand to her.

"You better watch it," Mama said as she suddenly glared at him. "And I'm *still* going to bop that hairy head of yours, you mangy ape."

When Mama Lulu climbed aboard the elephant and held onto to Joe, the orangutan suddenly did his magical ritual again. After the purple smoke mushroomed in the air, Joe suddenly had on black cowboy boots with shiny spurs attached to them.

"You ready to ride, mooly-mooly?" Joe said with a smile as Mama Lulu held on to him.

"I told you, ape, my name is Big Indian Chief!"

"Oh, sorry, Big Indian Chief." Joe chuckled. "You ready to ride?"

"LET HER RIP!"

Joe gave the huge elephant a hard, swift kick with his spurs as the elephant quickly rose into the air on his hind legs, let out a great yelp, and took off running and rampaging down the hallway at full throttle. Dozens of bikers, who were fighting in the hallway, suddenly ran for their lives as the huge elephant began to smash into the walls and crash into the hotel rooms all along the third floor.

Demolishing and destroying the entire third floor at an astonishing rate, Joe suddenly pushed the elevator button when the elephant suddenly strode near the elevator doors. He guided the elephant into the elevator when the doors opened, but the weight of the elephant immediately made the elevator give way. Like a big plane falling out of the sky, the elevator came hurling straight down onto the lobby floor as it crashed with a loud, thunderous boom.

With the elevator all busted up and destroyed, Joe gave the huge elephant another hard, swift kick with his spurs as the elephant took off rampaging again. Hundreds of bikers, who were still fighting in the lobby of the hotel, fled for their lives as the huge beast came barreling their way.

The elephant smashed into everything. The movie theater, the restaurant, the gift shop, the bar and lounge area, and the casino were demolished and destroyed in a matter of seconds. The entire time that the mighty beast rampaged over everything in its path, Joe and Mama Lulu sat atop of the huge, green machine as they kept yelling and shouting for more.

Tango, Fred, the Wonder Gang, and the Fletcher Boys soon came running toward the elephant as they tried their best to calm the big, angry beast down. But the angry elephant wasn't about to be pacified. Several times he nearly squashed the scattering dwarfs like ants as they skirted back and forth and all around the big beast as they tried to get out of his way.

After several unsuccessful attempts, the army of rescuers finally began to calm the big, beast down. The big elephant, with a lot of persuasion and wooing, eventually stopped dead in his tracks as he came to a gentle rest on the floor.

Joe immediately hopped off the elephant, flashing his brilliant smile as if he'd just gotten off the best roller coaster ride ever. Tango and the Wonder Gang helped Mama Lulu slide off of the big beast as Fred immediately rushed over and started wolfing at Joe.

"You crazy, stupid ape—look what you've done to this hotel!" Fred yelled at the top of his lungs. He was more livid than he'd ever been in his life. "You've completely destroyed this hotel! And not only that, you've could've gotten Mama Lulu killed!"

"Ah, go somewhere and lick a bone, you no talent mutt," Joe said in a giddy voice. "Me and mooly-mooly had the time of our lives. Right mooly-mooly?" he turned and said to Mama Lulu as she wobbled back and forth on her feet. "Hey, mooly-mooly, let's go get some more kerweekee."

"Why you stupid ape!"

Tango quickly grabbed Fred and literally held him back with all of his might to prevent Fred from attacking Joe. Fred began to snap and growl at Joe like a mad dog with rabies.

"Lou, why don't you and the boys take Mama Lulu down to your room and let her sleep off all of this excitement," he said to Lou and the boys as he continued to hold Fred back with all of his might as Fred steadily snapped and growled at Joe. "I'll be down after a while to look in on her and see how she's doing."

"Sure." Lou nodded. "No problem. We'll take good care of her."

The Wonder Gang began to guide Mama Lulu down to their room as the Fletcher Boys followed along. Mama Lulu was a little wobbly from the wild elephant ride as she began to walk. Seeing that she was a little unsteady on her feet, the Wonder Gang began to hold on to her tightly.

As they held onto her tightly, the Wonder Gang quickly discovered that Mama Lulu was a little confused and delirious after the wild ride, too. The entire time as she strolled along with the Wonder Gang, she kept calling them Oompa Loompas and demanded that they take her to Willy Wonka's Chocolate Factory so she could get something sweet to munch on before she went to sleep.

With the red bandana still tied around her head and still cloaked in the black Hell Avengers leather jacket, Mama Lulu slowly began to wake up. She didn't know how long she'd been asleep. Her vision was all foggy and she was half coherent as she saw little stars. Suddenly, through her blurry vision, she began to see five little men with red and green party hats on sitting around her passing a whiskey bottle and smoking kerweekee. They were all laughing as they stared down at her.

Mama Lulu, dazed and confused, didn't know what to make of these little men with the party hats on as she lay in bed. They all looked like little Oompa-Loompa surgeons staring down at her as she lay on some operating table. In fact, she was so delirious she could hardly remember anything at all. The only thing that she did know was that she was hungry; hungrier than she'd ever been before.

"Benny?" she suddenly called out in a weak voice.

"Oh, I think she's beginning to wake up," she heard one of the little men say in a distant voice as they all smiled and laughed. "She's starting to call for Benny."

"Donuts, donuts, donuts, donuts . . . ."

"Y'all, I think she's got the munchies," another one of the little men said as they all laughed as they stared down at her.

"Come on, say mooly-mooly," she heard another one of the little men say as he smiled down at her.

"Ah, she ain't going to say it," she heard another little man say.

"I bet you ten dollars I can get her to say it," she heard another little man say.

"You're on, buddy," the little man replied.

"Come on, say mooly-mooly for me," the first little man said as he stared down at her smiling. "Come on—*MOOLY-MOOLY.*"

"Moo . . ." Mama Lulu said in a weak voice, then she began to cough.

"She almost said it," the first little man said.

"Almost ain't saying it," another little man said. "Pay up, Lou."

"Hold on, Sammy. I think this might do the trick here," the first little man said as he blew a puff of kerweekee smoke down to Mama Lulu's face. "That might get her to say it," he said with a laugh. "Come on, say it. Mooly-mooly. *MOOLY-MOOLY.*"

Mama Lulu began to twitch her nose when the smoke began to tickle her nostrils. Through her dazed confusion, she licked her lips and slowly opened her mouth.

"Moo . . . ."

"Come on, say it mama."

"Moo . . . ."

"She's almost there," he said in an excited voice. "Come on, you can do it."

"Moo . . . ." She twitched her nose and mouth again.

"Come on, don't let me down."

"Mooly . . . ."

"You can do it! Come on, you can do it!"

"Mooly-mooly."

"SHE DID IT!" the little man said as they all chuckled and laughed hysterically. "PAY UP, BABY!"

Mama Lulu twitched her nose and mouth once again as the little men laughed riotously. Finally, the little men in the red and green party hats began to fade away as she slowly drifted back to sleep.

By 5 a.m., the Lucky Jackpot Hotel had finally been corralled off by the law. Droves and droves of policemen were on the scene arresting both members of the Hell Avengers and the Devil Guardians. They were hauling them away in police cars, police vans, and police patty wagons as they took them away to jail.

News helicopters hovered overhead in the sky and ambulances were busy taking away all the ones who had been battered and beaten-up in the massive brawl. The Lucky Jackpot Hotel was like a cluttered battlefield after the white flag had been raised; the battle had ended, but the prisoners of war and the wounded still had to be tended to.

Tango did a thorough examination of the entire hotel when the white flag was raised, going up on the upper level floors and surveying the entire lobby of the hotel. He finally came to the conclusion that an earthquake, or even a tornado for that matter, couldn't have done the damage that those bikers and that circus elephant had accomplished doing. The destruction was massive. Tango knew it would take mega dollars to clear away all of the massive destruction and to rebuild. He knew that the Lucky Jackpot Hotel, in one single night, had been put into the grave with its casket closed shut.

After thoroughly surveying the ruins of the entire hotel, Tango finally strolled outside as he took in the fresh, early morning air. He quickly untied his necktie and yanked it off as he watched all the police car lights and police van lights flashing as the police continued to haul away all of the bikers and impound the countless motorcycles strewn all over the parking lot.

The sight of all the police lights flickering and flashing weren't even comforting to him after all the mayhem and violence that had taken place at the hotel. They just reminded him of one thing; he was unable to hold down the fort while the big boss and his wife were away.

As Tango stared out at the first sign of light as it slowly began to peek out from the darkened night, Fred suddenly strolled out of the hotel as he came and stood by Tango's side. They both remained silent for the longest as they stared out at all the police activity taking place.

"Well, look on the bright side," Fred said as he kept staring out as dawn ascended. "At least there were no reported murders or deaths, just a lot of battered, bruised up bikers."

"Yeah," Tango said in a dejected voice. "I guess you're right."

"Tango, you can't blame yourself for all of this," Fred said in a consoling voice as he glanced up at Tango. "If it's anybody's fault, it's that moron ape's fault. He caused all of this mess by bringing them rowdy bikers to this hotel in the first place."

"Where is Joe?"

"That idiot ape hopped on one of the Harley Davidson motorcycles about thirty minutes ago and just took off," he said in a hot voice. "He brings all hell here, and when it's all over, the jackass hops on a motorcycle and just leaves. I tell you, I hope some eighteen wheeler truck out on the road knocks that moron to smithereens."

"Well, as much of an imbecile Joe can be, I was the one left in charge," Tango said in a defeated voice. "I should've called the police a long time ago like you said, instead of trying to prove that I could handle the situation. Joe may be a jackass, but I'm the idiot for not calling the police sooner. Maybe all of this horrendous mess could've been avoided."

"What do you think Abner and Tutty are going to do when they get back?"

"What do you think they're going to do?" Tango said in a despondent voice. "We might as well start packing our bags right now and hitting the road, because not even Tutty can save us from this mess."

As Tango and Fred stared out into the distance as morning continued to ascend, the curtain slowly closed on the main stage as ACT II came to an end.

CLOSING MONOLOGUE

The house spotlight once again beamed directly on the massive, gleaming gold curtain on the main stage of the Magic Rainbow Hotel & Casino Theater as *The Fred Parker Show* emblem blazed on the curtain. The emcee, master of ceremonies, suddenly came over the theater's sound system as he once again addressed the sold-out crowd of four thousand.

"Everyone, let's give a warm welcome once again for the star of *The Fred Parker Show,*" the emcee said in a rich baritone voice. "Let's welcome back to the stage, Mr. Fred Parker."

The Magic Rainbow Hotel & Casino Orchestra began to play a lively musical number as the audience applauded. Fred suddenly came out from the gleaming, gold curtain escorted by two beautiful showgirls. He sat his backside on the floor in front of a three-foot microphone stand and gazed out into the audience.

"Well, folks, I hope everyone here inside the Magic Rainbow Hotel & Casino Theater enjoyed the first installment of *The Fred Parker Show,*" Fred said into the microphone when the musical intro number ended. The two beautiful showgirls, dressed in glittery, gold G-string bottoms, rhinestone-encrusted bras, and huge feathery headdresses, stood beside him and smiled. "We certainly had a marvelous time putting on this show," he said in an upbeat voice, "but folks, we have two more shows getting ready to come right at you."

"Oh, Freddy, I can't wait for the next production of this fabulous show," Cassie suddenly said with a smile. "I'm already getting goose bumps just thinking about *The Fred Parker Show II.*"

"So am I," Lonnie replied with a brilliant smile of her own.

"Oh, girls, I'm getting excited, too. It's going to be a blast putting on an entirely brand-new show," Fred said in a jubilant voice. "You know, girls, as I was telling you before, being a stand-up comedian and having my own show right here in Las Vegas sure beats the hell out of some of the crazy jobs that I've had to do along the way to making it to the big time."

"You've really had a lot of crazy experiences on some of these jobs, haven't you, Freddy?" Cassie said with a laugh.

"Oh, I sure have, Cassie. Take this one time when I was on the job working as a greeter at Wal-Mart. This rich lady, who was wearing this long, beautiful fur coat and had on lots of diamonds and pearls, suddenly came up to me and asked could she take me home."

"What did you say, Freddy?"

"Nothing. I looked at her and quit that job that very second."

"You did?"

"Yep. I knew I'd be *well* taken care of, even if I did have to hump that ugly, mule face bitch every night for my Keebles & Bits!"

The audience exploded with laughter as the stage spotlight circled out into the audience, then it settled back once again on Fred and the showgirls at center stage.

"You know, Lonnie, I achieved a great accomplishment a couple years ago," Fred said with pride. "In fact, I made history."

"You did?"

"Absolutely."

"What did you do to make history?"

"I became the first dog to compete in a long-distance marathon."

"But didn't you have an unfair advantage over all the other runners by having four legs?" Lonnie asked.

"The other runners?" Fred said in a confused voice. "No, this was a gin drinking contest to see how much we could drink in a day."

"A gin drinking contest?"

"Yeah. I came in fourth, a hobo came in third, and a wino came in second."

"Who came in first?"

"A public school teacher who just got off work!"

The audience suddenly roared with laughter as the Magic Rainbow Hotel & Casino Orchestra played a few quick musical notes then stopped.

"You know, Cassie, having these new incredible smartphones that they're coming out with these days is truly amazing," Fred said. "They can do just about anything. But one thing they can't do is make a dumb moron any smarter."

"What do you mean by that, Freddy?"

"Well, like one time I went into Burger King and got a whopper value meal that cost $7.49. I laid a hundred dollar bill on the counter. When the cashier was about to pick up the hundred dollar bill, he suddenly got a text message on his phone, so he grabbed his smartphone instead. Now while the cashier was distracted texting on his phone, I quickly took the hundred dollar bill from the counter and laid a dollar bill there instead."

"Oh, Freddy, that wasn't nice."

"Yeah, I know," Fred said with a grim voice. "You're right."

"What happened?"

"Well, when the cashier finished texting, he finally picked up the dollar bill, looked at it and said, 'I didn't know George Washington was on the new hundred dollar bill.' I said, 'Neither did I.'"

"What happened after that?"

"The guy proceeded to open his cash register and gave me back $92.51 in change. He then said thank you and please come back."

"What did you say?"

"I said, 'With this type of wonderful service, I most certainly will!'"

The audience laughed.

"Hey, Lonnie, you think he was dumb, one day I went into the bank to make a deposit when three men wearing masks came into the bank and held it up. When they robbed all the cash drawers and were about to make their getaway, money began to fall out of one of the money sacks and I suddenly yelled, 'Hey, your money is falling out!'"

"What happened then?"

"Well, the robbers were so fascinated with seeing a talking dog that they began to carry on a conversation with me. We ended up becoming so friendly and chummy with one another, when they were about to leave, I told them that I'd love to have a memory of our time together so I pulled out my smartphone."

"Did they take a picture with you?"

"Yep. They quickly yanked off their masks as they all smiled and posed for a selfie that I took. When they finally made their getaway, I forwarded the picture straight to the police. What a bunch of dumbasses!"

A gala of laughter thundered around the theater.

"You know, Cassie, Uber is starting to get some serious competition from other competitors," Fred said. "Last week I called for a ride from this company called the Kangaroo Express and a kangaroo actually came by and picked me up."

"You got to be kidding me." Cassie laughed.

"Nope, I'm not. When the kangaroo arrived, I just hopped into his sack and he whisked me away."

"Wow, that's unbelievable."

"Yep. But today I heard the Kangaroo Express may be going out of business."

"Why?"

"Well, the other day, this woman called for a ride from their company, and when the kangaroo arrived, the kangaroo looked at her and just took off. So now the woman is filing a lawsuit against the Kangaroo Express and I heard the company may be going out of business."

"Why didn't the kangaroo pick her up? Was the woman overweight?"

"No, this woman lived in a big ass shoe," Fred said. "That woman had twenty-five squabbling brats with her. That kangaroo took one look, said no way Jose, and took off!"

The audience laughed as a monkey dressed in a white tuxedo and a black top hat suddenly ran onto the stage and held up a sign to the audience that said: ATTENTION: THE KANGAROO EXPRESS HAS JUST GONE OUT OF BUSINESS. SO, IF YOU NEED A RIDE HOME FROM THE FRED PARKER SHOW, CALL AN UBER INSTEAD. After displaying the sign, the monkey in the white tuxedo and black top hat ran off the stage.

"You know, Lonnie, last night I was running from this dog catcher who was trying to take me to the kennel."

"That must've been a harrowing experience," Lonnie said in a concerned voice. "Did he finally catch you?"

"Yeah, he did," Fred said with a sigh. "When he caught me, he said I was being a nuisance to society by running around loose and he had to take me in."

"Oh, that must've been really terrible, Freddy."

"Yeah, it was. But he said he'd cut me a break and set me free if I could name who just recently won the distinguished Dog Catcher of the Year Award."

"What did you say?"

"I said, 'Sir, with your great tracking skills and ingenuity, no one could possibly be better than yourself. So, it's no question it had to be you."

"What did he say?"

"Nothing. He just looked at me, smiled, then took off."

"Oh, so I guess all your flattery and charm got you out of a tough jam," Lonnie said with a smile.

"No, it wasn't what I said. It was what I gave him."

"What did you give him?"

"I gave him permission to hump you two lovely ladies tonight."

"Why in the world did you tell him that?"

"Hey, the way he looked, I figured he'd humped enough dogs in the back of his truck!"

The crowd roared with laughter as two cops quickly ran onto the stage as they faced glaring at one another. All of a sudden, the cop on the right handed the cop on the left a box of Dunkin' Doughnuts, as the cop on the left handed the cop on the right a box of Krispy Kreme Doughnuts. They both suddenly smiled at one another, then they ran off the stage.

"You know, Cassie, the other night they had this big reunion party for the cast members of the show *Sesame Street* in honor of them being in show business for over fifty years."

"They did?"

"Oh, yeah," Fred said with admiration. "It was a huge affair. All the original cast members Big Bird, Elmo, Cookie Monster, Bert and Ernie, Oscar the Grouch, Grover, Kermit the Frog, and Count von Count were there."

"Oh, really," Cassie said with a grand smile. "Who else was there for their big reunion party?"

"They had a lot of A list movie stars there, athletes, pop stars, and even some famous mascots were there like Tony the Tiger, the Pillsbury Doughboy, Mr. Clean, the Keebler Elves, and the Geico Gecko. I mean it was a really festive happening."

"I bet it was."

"Even Snoop Dogg came and brought a little *something* along to help with the merriment of the party."

"Oh, he did, huh?" Cassie suddenly said with a hearty giggle.

"He sure did. In fact, as the night wore on, everybody got really hungry because of what Snoop Dogg had brought to the party, especially the Cookie Monster."

"What do you mean?"

"The Cookie Monster got so hungry that he finally slammed all the poor, little Keebler Elves up against a wall and angrily demanded that they hand over the keys to the Keebler factory so he could go raid all of their cookies!"

Laughter thundered all around the theater.

"Folks, thank you all for attending tonight's show," Fred yelled to the jubilant crowd. "We'll see you all in the next installment show, *The Fred Parker Show II*. Goodnight, everybody!"

Fred, and his two lovely showgirl escorts, turned and headed off the stage as the crowd cheered and applauded.

DOWNLOAD THE FRED PARKER SHOW II

Don't miss out!

Visit the website below and you can sign up to receive emails whenever Vincent Glen publishes a new book. There's no charge and no obligation.

https://books2read.com/r/B-A-JLCX-QWZFC

BOOKS 2 READ

Connecting independent readers to independent writers.

Don't miss out!

Visit the website below and you can sign up to receive emails whenever Vincent Glen publishes a new book. There's no charge and no obligation.

https://books2read.com/r/B-A-JLCX-QWZFC

BOOKS 2 READ

Connecting independent readers to independent writers.